A Game of Spies

Hearts in Hazard ~ Book 2

by

M. A. Lee

WRITERS INK BOOKS

A Game of Spies
Copyright © 2015 Emily R. Dunn
Doing Business as M. A. Lee & Writers' Ink

First electronic publishing rights: October 2015

NOTE FROM THE AUTHOR
This book is a work of fiction. The names, characters, places, and incidents are
products of the writer's imagination or have been used fictitiously and are not
to be construed as real. Any resemblance to persons, living or dead, actual
events, locale or organizations is entirely coincidental. The author does not
have any control over and does not assume any responsibility for third-party
websites or their content.

Published in the United States of America

Cover Illustration by Deranged Doctor Design

www.writersinkbooks.com
winkbooks@aol.com

Acknowledgements

My especial thanks to Diane and Steve, best first readers in the world.

And to **Deranged Doctor Design**, whose artistic designers
always create inspiring covers that keep me writing.

Novels by M.A. Lee

the Hearts in Hazard ~ 12-book series
A Game of Secrets
A Game of Spies
A Game of Hearts

The Dangers of Secrets
The Dangers for Spies
The Dangers to Hearts

The Key to Secrets
The Key for Spies
The Key with Hearts

The Hazard of Secrets
The Hazard for Spies
The Hazard with Hearts

Into Death ~ 3-book series
Digging into Death
Christmas with Death
Portrait with Death (coming soon)

Non-Fiction Works

Think like a Pro Writer series
Think like a Pro ~ 1
Think / Pro: A Planner for Writers ~ 2
Old Geeky Greeks: Write Stories with Ancient Techniques ~ 3
Discovering Your Novel ~ 4
Discovering Characters ~ 5
Discovering Your Plot ~ 6
Discovering Your Author Brand ~ 7
Discovering Sentence Craft ~ 8

*Just Start Writing ~ book 1, **Inspiration 4 Writers***

Table of Contents

Chapter 1 ~ Friday, November 15, 1811

Josette did not know if Lord Giles Hargreaves, younger son of the Marquess of Grasmere, would return to their salon tonight. He had absented himself for a fortnight.

She hoped he would appear.

She did not think he would.

She had one memory all her own of him, a memory she did not have to share with her widowed sister-in-law Celeste. They had partnered at whist, and early in the game he had looked up and smiled at her. Smiled because he had realized that together they outmatched their opponents. Smiled in a way that lit his green eyes and caused her heartbeat to speed up. When the rout was over and he had pocketed his winnings, he had bowed over her hand. "Would you partner with me again, Mademoiselle Sourantine, the next time I attend your salon?" When she agreed, he had again smiled then kissed the hand he still held. Then he had walked away.

Josette did not know how to gauge his interest. Had he only liked her card play? Then why had he exchanged such long glances with her? Why had he kissed her hand, when etiquette required only a simple bow? Yet he left without looking back, as if once he left the table she was far from his mind.

Two weeks and no appearance. She definitely was far from his mind.

Yet she could not forget the kiss that had graced her bare skin. She played gloveless, the better to shuffle and deal the cards. His kiss to her hand had sent tremors along every nerve ending. Once she had retired to her chamber, she touched the back of her hand to her cheek, like an infatuated girl instead of a young lady of four and twenty. Even now, a fortnight later, her skin still tingled. Even now, she still had to rebuke that inclination toward infatuation.

Lord Hargreaves would probably not appear tonight. Hadn't she heard at Monday's salon that he was gone from London?

Yet she dressed with care. She chose the brown moiré silk that turned her eyes toward the blue rather than grey. Reilly arranged her hair in curls tumbling from the crown of her head. She touched the silver cross her father had given her but chose to wear amber eardrops that glittered and danced when she turned her head. The maid pinned matching brilliants in her flaxen hair.

She hurried to join Celeste in their dual role of hostesses. She usually delayed going downstairs until the first guests were arriving. She hated the receiving line, but Celeste demanded it at the start of every salon. Unnerved by Celeste's tirade this morning, Josette only wanted to placate her sister-in-law. After all, she had caused the outburst.

The housekeeper Mrs. Bridgerton had brought the bills accumulating from the salons. Appalled at the amounts, Josette had approached Celeste. Instead of addressing the debts, her *belle-soeur* resorted to a rant about the additional costs since Josette and her brother had come to London. A half-hour later, she stormed out while Josette sank into a chair and stared at her shaking hands. No, she did not want another tirade from Celeste.

As she slipped into place at the top of the grand staircase, Celeste gave her a sparkling glance. "You have all the flags flying, is that not the expression?"

"It is." She curtsied to Lord Wynstane and greeted him warmly. When he passed on to the drawing room, she turned to her sister-in-law. "I come nowhere near your fireworks, Celeste. You look glorious tonight." Indeed, she did, in a bronzed red silk that echoed the flames in her hair.

"*Bien sur.* I am expected to be glorious. I did not think that *soie marron* would suit you. You show it to advantage."

Josette breathed easier. Celeste seemed to have forgiven her intrusion into the household management.

Several parties entered at once, and they had no further opportunity to talk. When the line thinned, Celeste stepped closer and spoke in an undertone. "You fly the flag tonight for a reason, *ma chere*? Is it that you expect to bring Monsieur Kennit or Lord Musgrove 'up to scratch'? They are your usual partners."

Josette had lost the trail of the conversation and had to think quickly. "Don't be silly, Celeste. They are only enamored of my card play—unlike the members of your court. Have any new swains declared themselves this week?"

"Charles Bray."

"Mr. Bray? I do not know him."

"His father is a minister of Parliament, newly elected. They attended the salon on Monday."

"And the son fell in love with you immediately?"

"*Enfin*, the evening begins. We have a crowd tonight. I shall watch, *ma belle-soeur*, to see the man you catch with your finery. *Va-tu, maintenant.* The tables will be filling up."

Josette withdrew to the enfilade that became the card room during the salons. All the doors between the *petite salon* that overlooked the garden and the front room that had been her father's study stood open. The enfilade matched the *grande salon* in length. That formal room, with its tall mirrors and music dais, was reserved for dancing.

She strolled through the enfilade. The card room with its score of tables was her appointed hostess' duty for the twice-weekly salons. She greeted the people she had missed earlier and spoke a warmer welcome to the newcomers. At the back of the *petite salon*, next to the terrace door, three men waited at her usual table. Her usual opponents, Lord Musgrove and Mr. Kennit, had already paired up. She hid her chagrin that she must again partner Lord Costell.

The two peers stood at her approach. Musgrove assisted her with her chair. Josette cast a brilliant smile around the table as she drew off her silk gloves. "Dare I ask if you wish a game other than whist?"

Musgrove, almost seated, checked. Kennit laughed. "Never fear, Miss Sourantine."

"Unless our fair goddess favors another game tonight?"

"But I came for whist," Costell protested. "I had a good game at Waite's this week—."

"By a good one, you mean they didn't fleece you?" Kennit, older than Costell by a decade, looked ready to laugh at the cub. "How many rubbers did you win? One or two?"

"Three," Costell retorted.

Josette intervened before Kennit pointed out the errors of thinking a win at a gambling den translated into competency. "Shall we play, gentlemen? Lord Musgrove, will you keep the tally tonight? I would rather not."

"I am here to serve our goddess of fortune."

She laughed at his extravagance and picked up the cards. "Usual stakes, gentlemen?"

As the next hour progressed, she noticed everyone who came in, but Lord Hargreaves did not appear. She had felt so certain that he would attend tonight. So much for certainty. She laughed at herself.

"Good hand, Miss Sourantine?"

Tobias Kennit eyed her over his cards.

She shook her head, as much to banish her foolish hopes as to answer his question. "A stray thought, Mr. Kennit. Lord Costell, it is your play."

The young man threw the queen trump to match her play on Kennit's knave heart. *Boy*, she amended her thought, not man. *He is as old as my brother Albert and yet half his age. Will he never learn to think about more than his own hand in the game?*

Lord Musgrove slid the card back. "You must play a heart, Costell.

I know you still have hearts."

Face reddened, he threw out the ace, taking the hand she had already won with the trump.

Josette hid a sigh as he led with the club queen, a suit that had not yet been played. Kennit topped him. She played her only club, a nine. Musgrove finished the hand with a club trey then slid the trick to his partner. Kennit played the club eight, she trumped low, Musgrove played club seven, and Costell played the club king to win the hand she had already won.

Josette sighed again and studied her hand, wondering how deeply in arrears she would fall before her partner decided he'd played enough cards and returned to Celeste's court.

.~.~.~.

Lieutenant Colonel Giles Hargreaves, son of the Marquess of Grasmere, formerly of His Majesty's 57th Regiment, arrived more than fashionably late to the Sourantines' Friday salon. The crush in the wide entrance had dispersed. Having left off his vivid red regimentals, few people noticed his slow climb up the grand staircase to the reception area centering the first floor. One young man did. Tall and lean, he lifted a hand in a salute that drew Giles to a halt.

"Hargreaves!" Michael Armitage extricated himself from his friends and crossed the diagonal tiles patterned in cream and black. "When did you return?"

"Two days ago."

"All go well?" Like Giles, he worked for Sir Roger Nazenby, tracking French spies and English traitors. Unlike Giles, he hadn't spent over a decade in the military. Armitage felt completely at ease in London's whirl.

"Partly. Our bird escaped the cage. She's to be left loose a while longer. Sir Roger wants to discover who teaches her the songs she loves to sing."

He spoke obliquely for any listeners, yet Armitage understood. "We'll find plenty of singers here. These salons draw from all levels of society. That's partly the attraction. A society doyenne like the dowager Eaton can rub elbows with a rum cove like Robert LeBrun."

"Has Sir Roger arrived?"

He nodded toward the drawing room that their French hostess called the *grande salon*. "Asked for you, half-hour ago."

Giles grimaced then turned obediently toward the large room. On the threshold he paused, watching dancers turn through a set as intricate as a battlefield maneuver.

A world of difference drove his reason for attending tonight's salon. O the last occasion he had passed the evening in idle conversation with a wide range of London's ton. He had enjoyed matching wits with Josette Sourantine over a game of whist. And he had relished his light flirtation with the young widow Celeste Sourantine.

Tonight the widowed beauty danced with a young man who looked like one of London's golden peers. His gaze sharpened as she flirted with her partner. This time he viewed her with a jaded eye. This time he knew she spied for France and that the traitor who supplied her with information must do so at these salons.

"The beauty is in great form tonight."

Giles turned to the man who had appeared at his elbow. Sir Roger Nazenby, affecting shades of grey in his attire, did not take his gaze from the dancers. Giles looked back and let himself appreciate the Titian beauty of their hostess. "Who is her partner?"

"Westover's son. Lord Westover, you remember, is attached to the War Office. One of the chosen few who reviews the despatches to be sent to Wellington. Keep an eye on how lightly he steps." The spycatcher's quiet manner hid a razor-sharp mind, and his conversation veiled much more than it said.

"Too obvious. Too easy," he said in code. Too obvious that Westover's heir was the spy's source. Too easy in that his mission was over before it began. As the couple interacted, Giles judged that Westover did not look as enthralled as many of the beautiful spy's court were.

"The father enjoys his ministry speeches." Then, at a tangent, he asked, "And you, Hargreaves, do you enjoy being out of your regimentals?"

In truth he felt lost, as if he no longer knew his home's location. A red coat with gold braids and brass buttons had defined him for so many years that he had seen the uniform before he saw. Tonight, after he dismissed his valet, he stared in the mirror at a stranger in dark clothes and white shirt and ascot. His decommissioning papers and Nazenby's order of transfer had arrived while he was on the coast. He had read them twice while the earth quaked

He should have predicted the decommissioning, especially since his slow-to-heal wound had kept him desk-bound in England longer than he liked. The regiment needed able-bodied officers. In the last month, however, his stamina had returned, and he began to consider a return to Spain. For the last two months he had worked for the spycatcher, creating a network of men to discover the spies who supplied Napoleon with information about Lord Wellington's campaign in Spain and Portugal. Through a fellow veteran he had found both spy and her transport to France.

Yet that hadn't been enough. Now Nazenby wanted the spy's source for the War Office memoranda. And he wanted Giles Hargreaves to continue working for him. Giles had refused a roundabout request from the older man. He hadn't anticipated that the spycatcher would move the mountainous War Office to have Giles in his full command.

As if Giles had answered, Nazenby added, "You will find it difficult to distinguish yourself with Madame Sourantine. Her admirers press close. It is the French flavor, don't you think?"

"Part of her attraction, undoubtedly, but not the greatest."

The older man's eyes narrowed as he watched the French spy dance around her partner. "You are not as handsome without your regimentals."

"Or as heroic. Merely handicapped." He leaned heavily on the cane he didn't need. His leg worked fine unless he forced it a long distance or into the required turns of a dance. "Doubly so, for I am unable to partner her in a dance. Yet I have it on good authority that our hostess is actively pursuing the son of a marquess. Behold, her wish."

Nazenby's mouth quirked. "Ah, still useful, then." His conversation took another lightning turn that illuminated his advance planning. "Your father the marquess, has he settled for the winter at Grasmere?"

"Yes. He is requesting my presence for the holidays."

"We shall see. I would not hesitate to use Grasmere, Hargreaves."

"I understand, sir." His father would not like it. His mother would be disappointed.

Grasmere had been an ill fit, too. Not once during his July visit to his former home had he felt settled. The estate was his parents' home; it would be his brother's—although Dominic was rarely in evidence.

The rooms he'd taken once he left hospital, they were another ill fit. A place for his possessions, a place for his head and weary body to rest. Not home. Definitely not home.

"Does your father want his younger son to select a lovely butterfly like our hostess?"

"That is more my mother's wish, sir. She understands, however, that I must pursue before I can net. London has many lovely butterflies. When I select one, she will be welcomed to Grasmere." There, he had answered Nazenby's unspoken question. He would disappoint his parents if he introduced them to a lovely butterfly. Expecting a bride, they would be appalled to discover he only pursued a spy.

London's dreaded spycatcher, however, was pleased. "So we progress. We must not discount the other young men in the hunt. Lady Eaton reminded me of that just this afternoon. This late in the year, society is very thin. We cannot depend solely on these twice-weekly salons. We need a daily presence. Only a close association will help us find the source. Come, Lady Eaton expects me to meet her in the card room. You play cards, I think? You can find more than one game in the card room." On that broad hint he led the way from the *grande salon* and its lovely hostess.

Nazenby had obviously changed the original plan of his pursuit of this French spy. What did he plan now?

They progressed along the reception hall. Sir Roger stopped occasionally and presented Giles to a few people. He could not decide if the introductions were casual or pointed, but he'd been out of England for so long that he was grateful to have faces connected to names he had only heard or read about.

They entered the quieter enfilade. Fewer candles created a more intimate scene than the countless candelabra and reflecting mirrors in the drawing room. Nazenby strolled about, occasionally stopping to view the play of cards. After a quarter-hour they entered the *petite salon* and stopped near Lady Eaton's table by the fireplace. The fashionable dowager was gowned in purple silk and wore a striped turban with feathers. She noted their entrance with a smile but continued her game. Giles took the opportunity to scan the room. He glanced over the people talking and laughing and intent on their various games. Who did the spycatcher think could give him a constant entrance to the Sourantine household?

And then he saw her, the woman Nazenby must want him to pursue. *No*, he thought, *not her. Not Josette Sourantine.* She was pretty, a pale candle flame against the night-dark windows, a faded flame if he matched her to Celeste's vivid beauty and vivacity. She was more intelligent than most men could tolerate. And doomed by her height. Only inches shorter than he was, he remembered, and he overlooked most men. Inexplicably, he didn't want to hurt her.

He didn't know her well enough—only two hours across a whist table, that was all.

And he hunted for a spy and a traitor to England, people who passed vital information to France, information that would get soldiers like himself shot to pieces.

Why, then, this reluctance to involve her?

He turned to the spycatcher, who always had an answer. "What do you know of her, Sir Roger? An *émigré* like her sister-in-law?"

"Daughter of one. Father came over several years before the Revolution. Married a wealthy mill-owner's daughter. His family we don't know. Possibly a *chevalier* of his own making. The Terror was convenient to a number of *émigrés* with more pretensions than blood."

"An adventurer?"

"Perhaps. Vincent Nemours had no qualms marrying his daughter into the Sourantine family, and Nemours is a known *chevalier d'honneur*."

Josette Sourantine laughed at something Tobias Kennit said. The candlelight sparkled all around her. Why had he ever thought her pale? With a shake of her head, she played a card, and Lord Musgrove leaned forward to take the trick. A youth just a hair past university partnered her, and he looked to be losing.

Giles had enjoyed their game of whist. They had trounced the opposing Tobias Kennit and Edward Garland. He had no liking for either man, known rakes the both of them. He had relished their defeat. Josette Sourantine's flashes of wit and her brilliant card play were to be prized. When she smiled, the whole world had sparkled. Yes, he had looked forward to another partnership with her.

Nazenby had more in mind than a game of cards. The older man played to catch spies, and he played to win. If Giles refused to court her in order to gain entrance to the house, who would be sent in his place? A man who would not care if she were hurt?

He dropped his gaze from Josette. Lady Eaton's game had ended. She greeted them then introduced her tablemates, her young friend Mrs. Davenport and the men partnered against them, Rafe Lockhart and Robert LeBrun. As they chatted, Giles had to will his gaze not to lift to Josette Sourantine.

The game resumed. Nazenby leaned on his Malacca cane. Giles allowed himself another look at the table near the terrace doors, closed against the mid-November chill.

Lord Musgrove spoke to Josette, but she only smiled and shook her head. Kennit dealt. She gathered up her cards and spread them, reading them with the practiced glance of a gamester. And like a gamester she didn't organize them, not wanting her opponents to guess her hand. A mistake her partner fell into as he diligently sorted his suits. She gave a little shake of her head and lifted her lashes to scan the room.

And saw him.

Giles saw her stiffen. Then she smiled, just a touch wider, and inclined her head. He bowed. She played her next card as if she'd never been distracted.

Musgrove had noticed. He looked to see who had caught her attention. When he saw Giles watching them, he frowned. That frown caused Kennit to glance around. The black-haired rake gave him a level look then called for more wine.

Josette Sourantine played like a gamester. The daughter of a suspected adventurer, she must have learned all the tricks that helped a rogue survive. She chose as her usual table partners a rake and a peer not known for his discrimination. Together, they fleeced a youth just out of university. Josette Sourantine was not an innocent who would be hurt by a simple deception. She could be as deeply involved in the spying as the Frenchwoman was. If that were the case, then Giles need have no scruples. *Why, then, do I hesitate?*

Sir Roger stepped closer. "Well?"

"You are right. We have a suitable butterfly in here. You will excuse me?" He walked away to begin his hunt.

Chapter 2 ~ Friday, November 15

Josette hadn't expected her heart to flutter when she saw Lord Hargreaves.

Why did he affect her so? He had attended exactly four of Celeste's salons. In his regimentals he had stood out from the other men. Gossip named him a war hero; his limp certainly fueled the report's danger. Ever observant, Josette had watched him but could not divine what drew him to their salons. He had had the occasional *tete-a-tete* with Celeste, but a two-week absence did not denote a serious flirtation. Partnered with Josette against Tobias Kennit and Sir Edward Garland, he had played a fast game both brilliantly and ruthlessly. Yet he was no gamester, for he had walked away, pocketing his winnings without a backward look.

Now he had returned, as striking in a dark suit as in his regimentals. He had come in with Sir Roger Nazenby. The older man conversed with Lady Eaton, and Lord Hargreaves looked about the room. A half-smile lightened the stern cast of his lean face.

Kennit jarred the table, bringing her attention back to the game.

"Your play, fair goddess," Musgrove prompted.

She flashed a glance around the table. Kennit scowled at her. Harder to read, Musgrove had half-lidded his eyes, never a good sign, although his tone had remained pleasant. Busily recounting the tricks stacked at each player's elbow, Costell had noticed nothing.

Josette inhaled deeply, willing her concentration back to the game. She did not want to land in the suds, a real danger with Costell's wild play. Yet as the next round of cards started, she again lifted her gaze to Lord Hargreaves. He was nearer, slowly moving among the tables to watch the course of play. He reached their table as the last card was played. He stood and watched Kennit take the last trick.

Like the child he still was, James Costell pushed out his lower lip while Kennit and Musgrove tallied their winnings. Then he looked across at her. "Another round?"

He asked it with such hopeful brightness that she could not deny him—although another such round would find her owing money. She did not want to be in Kennit's or Musgrove's debt. She liked them as whist partners, but Kennit was a libertine and Musgrove—. She eyed the peer's ready smile and gilded hair and the exquisite fall of his cravat. Musgrove she still had not managed to define.

With Hargreaves at hand, she doubted she could play with the ruthless skill needed to win back what she'd lost. "Only if we play penny stakes."

"Only if we switch partners," Kennit interjected, "and I'll not take you tonight. Costell."

"I cannot help the fall of cards," he defended.

"You cannot take such risks with your declarations, Costell."

"Nothing risked, nothing won. You yourself told me that, Mr. Kennit."

"Takes a little savvy as well," he drawled. "You haven't shown much of that."

"Mr. Kennit!" Belatedly, Josette realized that people beyond their table were listening. "Lord Costell, I shall gladly partner you at cards. Whenever you wish."

"Play with more attention and less distraction," Musgrove murmured. Josette blushed, for the distraction was her fault. "Miss Sourantine may seem an omniscient goddess when she can predict our hands, but she is not omnipotent."

"No, Lord Musgrove, I leave that to you and Mr. Kennit."

Costell pushed back from the table and stood. "You are right, of course. My mind is on something else."

Kennit grinned. "Madame Sourantine's red hair and perfect form?"

Josette frowned at him, not wanting to increase the young man's fascination with her *belle-soeur*. Celeste was a decade older than the youth.

Costell flushed. He bowed stiffly and stalked away.

And Lord Hargreaves placed his hand on the abandoned chair. "May I play as fourth?"

Musgrove assented. Josette smiled a welcome.

"Mademoiselle Sourantine, we partnered so well before, will you accept me again?"

"You will not," Kennit snapped. "I'll not be trounced again. Musgrove, take Costell's seat." He gathered up the cards and shuffled.

As the men exchanged chairs, Josette leaned forward. "Lord Musgrove, I am a little distracted tonight. I hope I do not cast *you* in the suds as I did Lord Costell."

His affable expression reminded her of the marbled Greek Apollo in the museum. "You, divine Miss Sourantine? I am not worried. I know my new partner will not over-declare."

"I am well acquainted with Lord Hargreaves' style of play, sir. You were not here when last he honored us, but—."

"I told him," Kennit interrupted. He flipped out the cards. "I told him I was saddled with Garland that night." He gave her a hard look from his glittering blue eyes. "And there should be no more distractions."

Chastened, Josette gathered up her cards. When she looked up from fanning them, she found Hargreaves' gaze on her. Such a waiting look was not unusual in play, but his eyes seemed to flicker over her. As if he catalogued her every feature, as if never before had he marked her appearance or behavior or conversation.

She looked away and resolved to concentrate.

With three months' experience, she knew Musgrove had a similar gaming approach to hers. They counted the cards in their heads and worked out their opponents' hands with the turn of each trick. Years of play helped them anticipate what a skilled opponent would play and when. He always declared conservatively, depending on Kennit to play at the edge of his declaration. The two men were well partnered: Musgrove coolly rational while Kennit capitalized on flashes of risky brilliance.

A sole evening as Hargreaves' partner had revealed that he was as bold and brilliant as Kennit. With ruthless efficiency, he seized on any weakness and knocked down his opponent's plans with each following turn of card. Josette squared her shoulders. She would not be the weak one.

She played the first card, a diamond six, deliberate bait, and learned much of the opposing hands as each man topped her card.

Kennit always spoke little and then only of the cards. On his mettle, Musgrove chose not to speak at all. For the first four tricks, Hargreaves played silently. Then he startled her when he snapped a card down and asked if she had enjoyed their first partnership.

"Oh! Indeed I did, Lord Hargreaves. You were a great surprise to me."

"How so?" Hargreaves asked.

She watched Kennit play under Musgrove then glanced at her hand. *What is Kennit doing? He should have taken this trick.* "I expected the usual evening. You quickly changed my mind."

Musgrove gathered up the cards and played an eight club to lure out a high card.

"I suppose my presence is never a challenge," Kennit interposed.

"You are always a challenge, sir." She batted her eyelashes at him. He laughed and played the king. He laughed again when she trumped him.

Hargreaves played the expected low card, giving Josette the trick. "Do you often play throughout these salons, *M'selle* Sourantine?"

"I play more than I should. My *belle-soeur*, however, asked that I serve as hostess here until the supper." She gathered up the cards and added them neatly athwart the stack at her elbow. Then she set out her last good card. "Then Celeste would have me dance and talk and dance some more."

"You do not like dancing?"

"I do like it, but I am often eclipsed."

"I'll dance with you." Kennit took the trick then turned up a trump as his last card.

Josette played a useless heart, her hand exhausted. "You, sir, never leave this card room. You are perfectly content here. As is Lord Musgrove."

"You are here, lovely goddess," her partner claimed. "We are content to bask in your glory."

"But you are not content here, are you, *M'selle* Sourantine?" Hargreaves' soft voice implied intimate knowledge of her preferences.

"Not when Costell's her partner," Kennit drawled and grinned at her brightened color.

They finished. The men passed the cards to her waiting hand. Musgrove kept the tally. As she shuffled and dealt, her heightened senses knew Lord Hargreaves watched her. Her expertise might label her as much a gamester as Tobias Kennit. *Is that how he judges me? Is that how he judged me a fortnight ago?*

When she quickly fanned her cards, he said, "You have played for a long time."

"From infancy." She covered Kennit's diamond and took the hand, an unexpected win. Musgrove murmured satisfaction. She flipped out a useless club and turned to Hargreaves. "Papa said this was a better talent than playing the harpsichord. My elder brother Edmund had no head for it, and Albert has no patience. Papa taught me everything he knew."

"Which is a far range," Kennit drawled. "I wish I had met your father."

"He would have trounced you, sir."

"An adventurer, *M'selle*?" Hargreaves asked, as softly as before.

She flashed a glance at him. A soft voice for hard questions. Did he think to milk information from her? Did he expect to lure her into secret revelations? She had no secrets. And what if she did? What he learned did not matter. A marquess's son, he was far above her level. Celeste had aspirations of a title, but Celeste always had aspirations.

The little spurt of anger dissipated. Josette even managed a guileless smile as she played an innocuous club to lure out a higher card. "My grandfather called him an adventurer. He was not pleased when Mama eloped with my papa. But Papa did not fulfill his 'worst fears', as Grandpapa said."

As she wanted, he played the club knave. "Your grandfather is——."

Musgrove quietly played the winning queen.

"William Newland of York. He owns several spinning mills, sir." She enjoyed Kennit's scowl as he had to play under Musgrove's lady. She enjoyed Hargreaves' scowl even more. Her partner took the trick and returned her smile then opened with a mid-range trump.

Hargreaves took that trick and shifted suits before returning to his questions. "You mentioned an elder brother Edmund."

Sadness dimmed her artificial smile. "My *belle-soeur's* late husband. He died four years ago, in a riding accident."

"And your brother Albert?"

"My younger brother. You will find him in the *grande salon*. Flirting. I have an even younger brother and a sister, sir. They are with Grandpapa in Yorkshire. Do you wish to know their names?" She smiled sweetly as she asked the facetious question. And took the trick with one card higher than Hargreaves'.

"Enough conversation about family," Kennit growled. "Talk about horses. Or the theatre. Or Brummel and fashion. Or even Bonaparte. Just get your mind on the cards."

"I apologize." He topped her opening card. "Happy now, Kennit?"

"Not until Musgrove goes down."

Musgrove went down. Kennit's brow cleared as he played a low card and let his partner take the hand. They finished the game in virtual silence, but Musgrove and Josette had managed to best the other two.

Sir Roger Nazenby came to watch their play. Celeste had scored a coup with his returned attendance at their salons, another coup with Lady Eaton's first attendance at their salons. Having seen him enter with Lord Hargreaves, Josette studied the elegant man standing behind her partner. She knew him by reputation only, one of the old families. At some long ago point, she had heard something more, but she could recall neither the words nor the person who told her. Was it a warning? The memory didn't ring like one. She puzzled over it until Kennit took a trick she had expected to win.

Nazenby moved behind Hargreaves. After a few more tricks, he moved behind her.

And that flustered her. Nazenby could see her hand, could watch her select. Other people had never disturbed her game, no matter where they stood, but he did. She felt a child, with Papa watching her cards, judging her game. She stiffened her back and tried to ignore him.

Costell's reappearance helped. "I'm back," he announced unnecessarily.

"Did you dance with Madame Sourantine?" Kennit asked.

"Her card is full. Even after supper."

Watching him pout, Josette decided that disappointment might help him overcome his infatuation. He did not need to be one of Celeste's flock of paramours. On a whim she blew hot and cold with them, and the men appeared to relish the game. Josette had never understood that, but she remembered Edmund's fascination in the months before their marriage. At times he had seemed in heaven; at others, in the dark woods of despair.

"How long has she had you on her leash? A month?" Kennit asked.

Musgrove put in, "Over a month."

"I'm not on a leash."

"You run panting when she offers a treat," the rake countered.

"You never stray far from her," Musgrove put in.

"When she does give you dance or a stroll around the room, you come back, tail wagging. Very like a dog, don't you think, Musgrove?"

"A Corgi?"

"A Spaniel. See that silky hair. Definitely a Spaniel. Definitely a lap dog."

Costell spied a seat opening at another table and hurried to take it.

"I thought," Josette said tightly, "that we were to concentrate on the game. Please do not tease him so. You will make his obsession worse."

"You think?" Kennit snapped out a card.

"Protecting him won't help him get over her," Musgrove added. "Did you know he plans to stay in town over Christmas?"

"I have tried to depress that plan," she murmured. Then she realized that Hargreaves watched her, something lightening his eyes.

They fell back into silence.

Musgrove took three tricks in a row. Josette beamed at him, for they were seriously down in this round. Then Hargreaves returned with a trump. She sighed and studied her cards and re-plotted her strategy.

At the end of the fourth game, they were even. That pleased Kennit, who remembered his trouncing. Musgrove cared only that he had gone neither down nor up. Josette could not decide how Lord Hargreaves felt. He seemed an enigma. Over two hours in his company a fortnight ago, another two hours tonight, and still she had no reading of him. What would he say when this night was over? *Thank you for an interesting evening. I hope we play again.* Would he again leave without looking back?

Two weeks ago, after the maid finished undressing her and had retired, Josette had stared at her mirrored image and realized she had not impressed him at all.

Would tonight be any different?

Chapter 3 ~ Friday, November 15

Kennit gathered up the cards to shuffle them. Sir Roger watched patiently behind her. Musgrove drummed his fingers on the table. Lord Hargreaves drained his wineglass.

And Josette tired of cards.

She would end the evening with fewer coins than she'd started with, but she was often down and up over a series of evenings. Her only concern was never to be in arrears. Only then did she step up her game.

Before she re-thought her decision, she stood.

Musgrove leaped up. Hargreaves stood more slowly. Kennit lounged in his seat. An ironical gleam lit his glittering blue eyes. "Had enough?"

He saw too much. "I have neglected our other guests too long, gentlemen. I must circulate. I thank you for the games."

When Kennit laughed, she wanted to box his ears.

Then Lord Hargreaves picked up his cane. "I grow tired of playing as well. May I escort you, *M'selle* Sourantine?"

"My lord, we will leave our table void of two players. I am not certain—."

"May I assume your place?" Sir Roger interrupted. "Lord Musgrove will find that I am an adequate partner, although not one as pretty as you are." He bowed with a courtly grace.

She smiled at his rescue. "Sir Roger, you shall have me blushing."

"That would need more than a compliment," Kennit drawled. "A kiss would do it. A kiss under the stars."

"How should anyone see me blush in that darkness?" Josette retorted. "Thank you," she said to Musgrove, who draped her shawl over her shoulders.

"Still one short," Kennit complained. "Certain you want to leave, Hargreaves?"

"Lady Eaton will join us," Nazenby offered. "Lord Musgrove, would you be so kind as to invite her—."

Affable as ever, Gordon Musgrove bowed, but he turned first to Josette. "May I secure the first dance after supper, divine Miss Sourantine?"

"Another dance, sir? You already have the first quadrille." She twinkled at him and was rewarded with his half-smile.

"I would take a third and a fourth, if you were willing."

"I thank you, but we shall stay at two dances only. I do not want Celeste to rebuke me for being too forward."

"And I," Kennit drawled, "I'll have a dance, too. After all, if you partner us in the card room, it's only fair we should partner you for the dances."

She wrinkled her nose at his graceless invitation and picked up her reticule from the table. "I shall be charmed, thank you. Good evening."

Before she stepped away, Sir Roger said, "But, *M'selle* Sourantine, you do not collect your winnings."

"I'll hold them for her," Kennit said and reached for her three little stacks.

Lord Hargreaves propelled her away, moving rapidly for a man with an injured leg. Josette glanced back to meet Kennit's scowl as he dropped her coins into his coat pocket.

Hargreaves spoke in her ear. "Do you worry that Sir Roger and Lady Eaton will not match Kennit's play? You need not. They have overset his sort since he was in nappies."

"Mr. Kennit has a sharp tongue when he's displeased."

"They are not puppies like James Costell. Yes, I know the comparison displeases you. Kind of you, but foolish. Costell must learn not to play whist with the big dogs."

"Better here than elsewhere," she retorted. "We will not fleece him here. He is my brother's friend."

The wide hall with its angled square tiles was empty save for a footman. Seeing the whirling crush in the *grande salon*, Hargreaves steered her past the stairs climbing to the second story and toward the terrace. Tall candlesticks beside the doors lit the way for those willing to brave a mid-November night to gain privacy.

"You do not fleece him here? Yet I saw him drop several hundred pounds a fortnight ago, and he did not win tonight. Costell can ill afford to lose steadily, especially that much."

Josette disengaged her arm, refusing to go any further with a man who snapped at her, let alone a man she barely knew, no matter how much he attracted her. "I worked very hard to help him recover those losses, my lord. He is down only tonight's few coins."

"Recover it? How could he possibly do that? How did you help him to recover it?"

She crossed her arms. "I have my ways. Do be assured: he won it back, a little at a time, over the last four salons. Had you been here, you would have seen it—though I doubt you would have marked it."

His green eyes searched hers. She saw his unasked questions—she could almost hear them—but she volunteered nothing more.

His next comment surprised her, echoing as it did both Kennit and Musgrove. "So now he thinks he can win at gaming. You should not encourage him."

"I do not. Besides, he is not lured to our salons by the card play. He is not a gamester."

"No, not yet. He comes for Madame Sourantine's blue eyes and cupid smile. You just let him think he can win at cards."

"I would rather he played here than somewhere else, like Waite's," she repeated.

"What do you know of Waite's? Do you go there yourself?"

She felt scalded. "I have *heard*. Lord Costell mentioned this very evening that he had gone there. They will indeed fleece him there. He is safer here."

"Where you can temper his losses? You amaze me. His mother should know how far off the leash her son has run."

"We will not argue over that, Lord Hargreaves. Yet it is not my office to inform the Lady Costell. Yours, perhaps?"

"You truly helped him recover his money?"

Josette was nearly as tall as he, putting their eyes almost on the same level. She turned fully toward him and opened her clear eyes very wide, wanting Lord Giles Hargreaves to believe her. "I always partner him, my lord. He wants to play whist. I try to improve his game. And thus I can help him regain what he lost."

"You are a better card player than I credited. No fluke then, when we controlled the table against Kennit and Sir Edward Garland?"

"Garland is a predictable opponent."

"All this learned from your father."

She bowed her head in acknowledgment. The twinkle returned to her cornflower-pale eyes. "I was Papa's prize pupil."

"Kennit and Musgrove, they are complicit in this?"

His choice of words dimmed her sparkle. "They understand the challenge and accept it. We do not cheat here, Lord Hargreaves." She used the courtesy title to distance him.

His brow constricted fractionally. "I had not thought that, *M'selle* Sourantine."

Josette glanced at the moonlit terrace, no longer an enticing option. She glanced back and saw the dancers whirling in the drawing room, other people watching, talking. She caught a flash of red, a daring color that only someone like her sister-in-law could carry off.

The reminder of Celeste further dimmed her hopes. She walked to the settee tucked behind the stairwell. Arranging her skirts over the green cushions, she looked up and gave Hargreaves a very deliberate smile. He had questioned and censured her. The turn of conversation should now come to her deal. "And you, my lord, what brings you back to our salons after a fortnight's absence? You do not court Celeste. You do not gossip or talk politics. And you are no gamester."

He leaned both hands on his cane. She thought his smile reflected her heightened tension. "Must I do all these to an extreme to have an evening's entertainment?"

"It would be easier if you did one to an extreme."

"Which should I elect? Gossip? Politics? Cards? Flirtation?"

"You must choose, my lord."

He straightened, lifted one eyebrow, then joined her on the settee. His shoulder brushed hers as he leaned back against the cushion. "I choose flirtation."

Her cheeks heated under his steady regard. More calmly than her fluttering pulse, she reminded, "Celeste is in the *grande salon*, sir."

"Is she the only woman suitable for a dalliance?"

She remembered his questions, his censure. He had an odd method of flirtation. "My *belle-soeur* has claimed you. '*Mon marquis*,' she says. Your defection will disappoint her."

Shifting position, he propped an elbow on the settee's back and stretched out the leg he favored. "Did you mark my absence, fair M'selle Sourantine?"

"I did."

He rewarded her candor with a genuine smile. Josette tried not to heed that open smile. She glanced down at her hands, linked in her lap. "How long did you serve in the military, sir?"

"Fourteen years. I served in India and Turkey, Portugal and the edge of Spain."

"And you were wounded where?"

"Albuera, this past May. I was not released from the hospital until July. I find that I am slow to heal. Thus you see me, stripped of my commission."

"You must have enlisted at a young age. Did you not wish to attend university?"

"The university was for my brother the heir. I chose the military to distinguish myself."

"But you missed so much, the reading, the colloquy with great minds."

"Do not think that my life on campaign was devoid of scholarship, *M'selle*. I read Voltaire and Rousseau, Locke and Adam Smith. I am not quite illiterate."

"I did not intend to suggest you were uneducated, Lord Hargreaves. Perhaps not as widely read as a university scholar—."

His smile turned ironical. "My brother Dominic read very little at university. But I interrupted you. Do proceed."

"I was just—you may lack a university degree, but in world experience I am certain you must excel."

"Flattery now, *M'selle* Sourantine?"

"Do I swing from one to the other, sir? I do not intend to, I assure you."

"And what is your reading, since a university education was also denied you?"

"Defoe, my lord. Pope. Thomas Grey. Wordsworth."

"Ah, satire and poetry. No novels? No Richardson? A virtuous woman rewarded for her virtue? An example for every lady. You have an interesting arrangement with Mr. Kennit, letting him hold your winnings. Or do you merely return the coins he fronted you for the evening? I did not realize you were such intimate friends."

Josette blinked at that conversational turn. Had he just questioned her virtue? Or was that hard tone evidence of his aim to turn the conversation away from personal questions about his life? He was difficult to understand. Now that he was decommissioned, the years he had invested in the military must seem wasted. Not wanting to believe he had a cruel bent, she decided the latter choice drove his hardened tone. Yet she could not lift her eyes to search his. What if she saw spite in them?

She fiddled with her reticule. "Mr. Kennit does not front me money, sir. He merely holds my winnings from salon to salon. It is only a convenience. No one objects."

"Gordon Musgrove would not; they're old mates. Puppies like James Costell wouldn't dare. A libertine like Edward Garland wouldn't care about a woman's reputation."

The hardness had left his voice, but his assessment earned a frown. He stated facts without censure—yet the scene he painted could appear very ugly with only a few more brushstrokes. She had to lift a hand to smooth her brow before she looked up.

His green eyes merely watched her. They lacked the ice she had feared she would discover. With forced lightness, she countered, "I play whist with more people than those four, sir. Certainly you have seen that in your few times here."

"I have. You have an easy familiarity with Kennit. He was not pleased that I walked away with you tonight."

"He was not pleased that a challenge walked away from the table," she retorted with a real laugh. "We are friends, nothing more."

"He is a rake."

"Are you warning me, sir? I know what Tobias Kennit is. He is *no* more than a friend."

"A friend who holds your winnings."

Josette leaned closer and lowered her voice. "I will tell you a secret, Lord Hargreaves. I am a curiosity. I do not like to gamble. I do love to play whist. I love the challenge. But I do not like this exchange of money. I cannot convince you Londoners to play for pebbles. That is what my father used. Yet here, should I suggest such stakes, I would be ridiculed. So I conform. And since I play cards so often with Mr. Kennit, he keeps my winnings from salon to salon. It affords him no other privileges."

"Not even first to secure your hand for a dance?"

"Not even first. That honor is Lord Musgrove's, who will have two dances after supper."

"Were Gordon Musgrove your husband, you would lead him a merry dance. Kennit would hate him for it. I would like to see those two have it out."

"I am not angling after Mr. Kennit or Lord Musgrove for a husband."

His hand shifted. Hypersensitive to him, she felt him fingering the brown silk ruffle that adorned her gown's neckline.

"Are you not? That will disappoint Musgrove. I believe he has set upon you as the perfect ornament for his house."

"His Palladium?" Josette gave a mock shudder. "Cold as Lord Elgin's marbles. I thank you, sir. You think me no more than a cold statue for sale. Galatea perhaps?"

"Waiting for a lover's kiss to bring you to life?"

Her cheeks heated, embarrassing her with that evidence of innocence. The ton didn't celebrate innocence. How many times had Celeste preached that society's opinion was sacrosanct? She saw Lord Hargreaves smile, and her embarrassment grew. Josette did not want him to think her a casual flirt any more than she wanted him to think her a country miss.

"I do not think you a cold Greek statue," he continued. "Musgrove does. And he does not think you Galatea. No less than a goddess."

"Aphrodite?" she parried, struggling to regain the lightness. "That is my *belle-soeur*."

"Oh, for Musgrove, no goddess so vibrant. Pure Athena? Or Hera to his Zeus?" He tugged her ruffle. "He does not understand your living heat at all."

Josette smothered a laugh at the image of Musgrove as curly-bearded Zeus. "No, he must not. I am no goddess. You have misread him, sir. He is not courting me."

"Ah, have you not heeded his compliments, *M'selle*? You are his 'divine Miss Sourantine.' 'How statuesque.' 'Lovely goddess.' 'Above this world.'" Hargreaves' deep voice recited tonight's compliments drolly, deflating their weight.

She giggled. "It is because I am tall!"

"And look like golden ice."

"No?" She giggled again. "I am flattered. And to think I have not listened to him. He is extravagant, yes, but it will be good practice for him. Lord Musgrove is too reticent. Please do not make the mistake of thinking that I lure him toward the altar. His family would never countenance his attachment to anyone lower than a peer."

"Though he desires two dances after supper?"

"Yes. Of course."

"How much lower are you, *M'selle* Sourantine?"

She could not believe he was again antagonizing her. Papa had taught her never to withdraw from a game until the last card was played. Only then would the winner be revealed. Maybe Hargreaves tested her mettle. Maybe he enjoyed tempting her to anger. She didn't understand him. But she would not walk off in a huff. Let Hargreaves call the conversation over, not her.

Yet the words hurt. They again dashed her hopes. Foolish little hopes.

"Don't you remember, my lord? I am an adventurer's daughter. And I am *Miss* Sourantine, please, not *mademoiselle*. My father anglicized our name at my grandfather Newland's request."

"Your sister-in-law styles it as French."

"Oh, Celeste, she is herself an *émigré*. Her family fled here during the Terror. You *do* ask a multitude of questions disguised as conversation."

"You intrigue me, *M'selle*—Miss Sourantine. I have never met anyone quite like you. I want to understand you." His hand, so hot, covered her shoulder, three of his fingers on the bare skin revealed by her wide neckline. "

His touch ricocheted through her. Her breath wanted to shatter. But her mind still controlled her emotions. "Come, sir, you can surely be honest with me. You need not dangle such lines. I am well past my first season. I will not take their bait."

His green eyes searched hers. "Is it possible you do not know comely you are?"

She shifted her shoulder, but his hand remained heavily in place. His fingers contracted gently. She tried more words to restore the distance between them. "Celeste is the beauty in this house, Lord Hargreaves."

"The obvious beauty, which never lasts beyond youth. Lasting beauty is a fire that does not burn too brightly, a fire that does not flash over the wood without consuming it. Lasting beauty builds a strong, steady heat."

Her face flamed again. She did not know how to reply.

Celeste's appearance ironically saved her, announced by the clicking of her heels.

Hargreaves lifted his hand from her shoulder but did not otherwise change his position. Her *belle-soeur* came past the staircase. When she saw them sitting together, she stopped and placed her hands on her hips. Her cupid's bow mouth pursed. She advanced with a pronounced sway of her dress.

"*Voila*, I find you, Josette! The supper approaches. La, it is Lord Hargreaves. I did not recognize you, *mon seigneur*, in such drab attire. You do not wear your regimentals?"

He stood. When she proffered her hand and gave the smile that had won countless beaux, he bowed formally. "Madame, you will not again see me in the colors. I am decommissioned."

Josette had stood when he did. She stepped away to gain physical distance from him. Hearing restraint in his voice, she studied him anew. His mouth had tightened. His eyes had constricted slightly. Only someone who had seen him relaxed, as she had marked flashes of it in the past half-hour, could see his tension.

"The uniform I will miss, *mon seigneur*. In the colors you are a dashing figure."

"I am not dashing without the uniform?"

"Just another man in my court, is it not so? Why is it that you are decommissioned?"

"My wound refuses to heal strongly, *Mdm.* Sourantine. After much discussion, the War Office decided that I should not retain my field commission. Regiments need field officers, not desk-bound cripples."

"*Alors*, you come to my salon in dark attire and skulk in a corner. This you cannot do."

He reached toward Josette, but she maintained her distance. His hand fell to his side. "Miss Sourantine and I were enjoying a few quiet moments after our card game."

"*Je n'ai rien à voir avec cette*. It is that we must go down to supper. Josette, you are to be escorted by Lord Costell, yes? Will you see to him?"

Celeste was dismissing her. Josette pulled her shawl onto her shoulders, cold since Hargreaves had removed his hand. "Of course, Celeste. I believe he is in the *petite salon*."

As she started past him, Hargreaves stepped forward, delaying her with a touch to her arm. "I enjoyed our conversation, Miss Sourantine."

She did not glance at her sister-in-law. She did not want to see

Celeste's narrowed eyes or tightened mouth. She met his smile with a level and clear look. "I enjoyed it as well, Lord Hargreaves. I hope we may continue it after supper."

His touch slid down her arm to take her hand. "Not tonight. I must soon leave. And I will not be in town for the coming week. Duty calls me to Grasmere."

"That is your home, isn't it? Then I wish you safe journey, sir."

"Do you attend the Davenports' soiree Saturday week?"

"We do plan to attend, yes."

"Then I will see you there." He bowed, lifting her hand briefly to his lips. "Good evening, Miss Sourantine."

Josette's hand retained his warmth when he released it. "Good evening, Lord Hargreaves." She tried not to float on air as she walked away.

Chapter 4 ~ Friday, November 15

Giles paced Sir Roger's study as he waited for his superior's arrival.

This evening's work pleased him. Josette Sourantine was more than aware of his interest; he could not mistake the signs of her attraction to him. And he had to admit his own attraction. He admired the way she had fended his questions. He had also admired the curve of her cheek and her long slender neck, the creaminess of her skin and the softness he had finally had to touch.

Yet her explanation of her relationship with Tobias Kennit gave him no satisfaction. Even though her light answers seemed open, he sensed a deliberate blurring of clear truth. And he sensed she could be obstinate. He must be careful not to mismanage her.

He must also be careful of her intellect. Twice tonight she had stepped close to his mission. On the first occasion Giles had turned the conversation rather than let her pursue her questions. On the second time, startled by how easily she drew information from him, he had taken the attack to her. And attack it was, questioning her association with Tobias Kennit.

Remembering how easily she had discomposed him, Giles drug his fingers through his dark hair. He had stood calm under cannon fire and musket shot. He had held his men steady while an enemy column advanced, keeping them in check until a volley would have effect. Josette Souratine had unsettled him in ways the French army never had. *God, help me with her.*

Giles took another turn around the room. He was not the only one discomposed tonight. Celeste Sourantine was obviously disgruntled by the transfer of his affections. She had not been pleased to find him alone with Josette, even though the settee between the stairwell and the terrace door was available for anyone to view. She had not been pleased that he had concerned himself with Josette's attendance to the Davenports' soirée. She had most definitely not been pleased when he said his 'good evening' and left rather than lead her down to supper.

Celeste Sourantine would spend this next week undermining every advance he'd made with her sister-in-law.

His father's request to come up to Grasmere had arrived inconveniently for his mission. Sir Roger would not be pleased that family duties called him away.

A commotion in the hall announced Nazenby's return. He heard the spycatcher's butler speak; he couldn't hear a reply. Giles squared his shoulders and waited before the fire.

Sir Roger came in, still elegant in shades of grey. Giles started to speak, but the older man lifted a finger for silence. He crossed to the crystal decanter and splashed cognac into two snifters. Bringing back the glasses, he indicated the leather chairs angled before the fire. Giles lowered himself slowly as the spycatcher took his first sip then leaned back and closed his eyes.

"Lady Eaton safely bestowed, sir?"

"Safe and snug."

Giles stared at the dark liquid. He did not want to plunge boldly into his errand. "How does she judge this evening?"

He wanted to know, although he had not planned to ask. Lady Eaton was much more than a social doyenne. She had the ears and the heart of the master spycatcher. When Giles had proposed his plan to discover the spy's source—to court Celeste and gain constant entrée to her home—Sir Roger had turned to the society doyenne for advice. Sharpened by observation and experience, Sally Eaton's intelligence foreshadowed that Josette Sourantine might become the same kind of social leader. If only Josette's loyalty to England were as assured as Lady Eaton's.

"She stayed on the periphery." Sir Roger swirled his cognac, releasing its aroma. "She saw what any casual observer would. She did manage a small chat with *M'selle* Sourantine. A very small chat only, after the supper, to discover what the woman thought of you."

"And?"

"*M'selle* Sourantine spoke only the most noncommittal words, but Sally said she blushed and smiled. She thinks you have opened the door, just as you intended."

He rewarded himself with a first sip of cognac. "Then we progress. I court Josette Sourantine to gain full entrée to the household."

"You did not come to me for Sally Eaton's assessment, though, did you?"

Sir Roger's prescience no longer surprised Giles. He looked into the crystal snifter. "I am called to Grasmere. I leave in the morning. I hope to return by the week's end."

Nazenby scowled. "This is most untimely. Your pursuit has just begun. Several days away from *M'selle* Sourantine may cool her attraction to you, especially with Lord Musgrove and Mr. Kennit in pursuit." He stretched out his legs and appeared to reflect on his silver shoe buckles. "I do not like this at all, Hargreaves."

"This visit may serve a purpose, Sir Roger. It may remind both of the Sourantine women that I am a marquess' son and a good catch."

"There is that. And I have heard that the younger Sourantine is here in London for the express purpose of finding a husband. Your title, even though it be a courtesy one, should have any young woman eager for your attention. Perhaps that will keep her attraction strong. Yes, it should, especially if you throw out a lure to visit Grasmere."

"I cannot guarantee an invitation from my mother, sir."

"If you hint that a certain young lady has caught your eye, your parents will extend an invitation. They may also think twice about calling upon you to visit them, if they think one son is finally looking to settle into married life. Yes, Grasmere can be useful. We shall hope that *M'selle* Sourantine considers an alliance with an illustrious family in a stately home as much as an attraction as you yourself. Then she will not be annoyed at this week-long defection."

"My parents would not call me back, sir, if it were not urgent."

"No doubt, when you return, you shall find it no more than that the steward has run off with the quarterly payments. You should also tell your parents that you are now decommissioned. I am certain your mother will welcome that news."

"And I will mention nothing of my work for you, Sir Roger," Giles added drily.

"Good, good. We cannot have a long wait to discover who provides *Mdm.* Sourantine with the war despatches. Anthony Farraday is certain that she is our spy?"

"She admitted it to his fiancée."

"We shall take that as fact, then. When is their wedding? I suppose they do not wait."

"Only upon the reading of the banns, sir."

"If necessary, we can use that to our advantage. Many fingers in the pie, Hargreaves, then we can pull out a plum when and where we need one." He sipped the cognac then resumed swirling the snifter. "While you are gone, devise some information for another engineered despatch about Wellington's plans in Spain and Portugal."

"Another forgery, sir?"

"Something that reeks of vital importance, something the source will immediately recognize as valuable. We must catch spy *and* source, Hargreaves. A faked despatch in the spy's hands gives us only her. She might lie through her teeth to protect her source and her spymaster. We must have the source."

Giles shifted uncomfortably. Tony Farraday had complained of plans that changed, of agendas that were incomplete, and of arrests that were delayed. The smugglers that Celeste Sourantine had used as her couriers had nearly murdered his friend. With their captain dead, Sir

Roger had decided to wait upon arresting the others. The identity of the traitorous source was of vital importance. Was it not also vital to find the man who controlled all the French spies in England? "You do not seek her spymaster?"

"I have my suspicions, but I want the man only when I can wrest his other operatives from him. For now, *Mdm*. Sourantine's source for the War Office memoranda will suffice. That person we must discover. For the nonce we will ignore the petty reports of conversations overheard at parties."

"You've never shared who you think the source could be."

As if uncomfortable with providing any information, the spycatcher shifted in the leather chair. "Someone who can steal the information from the despatch box when it is provided for a convenient review. The only man who seems not to keep close watch on it is Lord Westover. For a man who's so intelligent in some ways, he has a blind eye for security, although we've warned him several times."

"So Westover's house it is. You don't suspect his servants?"

"No. We've been through those. The source has to be a visitor to the house, someone who comes and goes with regularity, someone who has the run of the place while there. The son runs in a pack: James Costell, Clarence Wilton, Richard Malbury, the youngest Armitage, and Albert Sourantine."

"The spy's brother-in-law?"

"The very same. Albert Sourantine could steal the information when he visits Westover's house. The whole Sourantine family could be involved. They could be hosting the salons to hide more than one nefarious deed."

"I am informed by Miss Sourantine that their gaming is above board."

"Indeed? Tonight's conversation must have had some interesting turns. How do you judge her, Hargreaves? Could she be involved in this spying?"

Giles shrugged. "I cannot say, not from one night's *tete-a-tete*."

"It's not too late to resume your pursuit of the *Mdm*. Sourantine?"

The suggestion repelled him—although only a few hours earlier he had not cared. Yesterday he and Sir Roger had discussed this mission. At some point the spycatcher had decided to shift his focus to Josette Sourantine, for by the time Giles entered the house, the older man had decided to re-direct his pursuit, abandoning the widow for the girl. Like a good soldier, Giles followed the changed orders. He hadn't cared which Sourantine woman he courted. Yet somehow, in the few hours for a game of whist and a simple conversation, the difference in the two women had built a strong wall he no longer wanted to cross.

He marshaled his arguments as he set his snifter on the occasional table. "By the time I left, sir, that path was blocked. *Mdm.* Sourantine was not pleased when she saw me without the regimentals. She told me that I was unrecognizable. And she was not happy about my *tete-a-tete* with her sister-in-law. I must continue what I have begun, Sir Roger. You told me to pursue Josette, and so I will. She will be flattered by my attentions, and I have only to push the flirtation a little more rapidly than I would with Celeste. Our French spy might be suspicious if I pressed her; the overlooked Josette will be even more flattered. If she is like most women, she will relish stealing one of Celeste's admirers."

"Sally is of the same opinion."

"I hear a doubt."

Nazenby's light eyes were sharp and unwavering. "I have talked with *M'selle* Sourantine on a few occasions. During your absence, I partnered with her against Tobias Kennit and Gordon Musgrove."

Giles suspected Sir Roger played a deep game that far outpaced what he himself was anticipating. He could not fathom how deep the game would run. *Many fingers in the pie.* He almost laughed. What more did the spycatcher hold hidden in his hand? "You aimed me for her," he reminded.

"I did. *M'selle* Sourantine appears to have a good heart. You are right; she is not as experienced in London society as her sister-in-law. But she is not slow-witted. You cannot push her too quickly. As for your start with her this evening, your questions pressed her too hard. Twice I thought she would walk away from the table."

"Only twice? I had the number at three. But she did answer every question, sir. She is remarkably open."

"If she were a spy, that would be her wisest conduct. Secrets draw attention. Lady Eaton also remarked on the woman's frankness. She is as curious as I am about your conversation on the terrace. Or did you talk at all?"

"Josette would not go outside."

"Ah, protective of her reputation. With Kennit keeping her coins, I didn't expect that. Where did you go? *Mdm.* Sourantine was not pleased that her sister-in-law had left the card room and even less pleased to learn you escorted her."

"Yet all she said was that I looked drab without my regimentals. Who told her that Josette and I were together?"

"Kennit." Sir Roger grinned. His eyes widened, revealing their pale blue, usually half-lidded to hide his emotions. "The one good moment he had after you left. He quite enjoyed telling Madame where you were and who you were with. She was most displeased, and he enjoyed that even more. He scowled the rest of the evening. The next time you attend a Sourantine salon, you may not so easily pry *M'selle* Sourantine away from Kennit. They have some kind of relationship."

"She admits he is a friend, no more. Gordon Musgrove as well."

"Strange friends for a young lady to have. I know you left before the supper. Where do you stand with *M'selle* Sourantine?"

"I look to see her at the Davenport soirée. Do you want to know anything more of her background?"

"I shared the little we know earlier. The father came over in the '80s, eloped with the mother. We have no information from France about him. The mother's family is wealthy but definitely not blue-blooded. Find out what she knows of the Nemours, her sister-in-law's family. Vincent Nemours lectures at Cambridge: Voltaire and Rousseau, Montaigne. Your friend Farraday predicted that our spy was an *émigré* hoping the family holdings will be restored by Napoleon. Keep that in mind. Now, off with you. My greetings to your mother."

"I begin to suspect, Sir Roger, that you were a rake in your heyday."

"Never a rake, Hargreaves, but I did set a few hearts to fluttering."

. ~ . ~ . ~ .

Before he left on Saturday, Giles gave orders that flowers were to be sent to Miss Josette Sourantine of Portman Square. He hoped she noted that he used the English address, not the French *mademoiselle*.

His leg stiffened on long rides. Forced into the boredom of the carriage, he whiled away the hours describing his new mission in a letter to Tony Farraday. Then he created a good draft of the proposed despatch. One of Sir Roger's lackeys would ensure that Giles' fake plans for attack did not actually coincide with Wellington's while another lackey could insert reduced troop numbers and circuitous routes of supply. Only a spy familiar with the Spanish-Portuguese border would spot the faked information. He did not think Celeste Sourantine or her source was that familiar with ground operations.

His parents emerged from the house to greet him when he arrived at Grasmere. His mother peppered him with questions about who was still in town and which parties he had attended. His father wanted to know who he had met at Gentleman Jackson's and at the club and if he had won any good stakes. Giles hid his weariness and pain from the jolting of the carriage. He did not like to admit it, but the War Office had been correct to decommission him.

Twice on Sunday he considered writing to Josette Sourantine. He sat beside his mother at chapel and watched a golden shaft of sunlight shine on the altar. Motes danced in the air and accompanied the swirl of his thoughts. A letter suggested familiarity. He knew her for only— what? Four, five hours. Five hours spread over two evenings, with much of that time focused on the game of whist. But a whole week away—it was much too long, as Sir Roger had suggested. He had promised to meet her at the Davenports on Saturday. On such short acquaintance, social rules dictated nothing more. Perhaps more flowers.

On Monday he rode over the family estate with his father. The places of his childhood seemed strange to his adult self. The land, the people had not greatly changed. He had radically altered. He had always loved Grasmere. As a boy he had yearned for it, dreamed of being its steward once he comprehended his brother Dominic would inherit. He joined the army to flee that dream. In the hot alien Indian lands and the harsh rocks of Portugal he had dreamed of the greenness. Now the estate was home yet not home. At the end of the day he ached in more than his body. And he had seen the steward and knew the man hadn't absconded with the rents.

On Tuesday, the earl and countess of Dombley arrived with their two daughters, the Misses Peverell, Phyllida and Roberta. "Quite suitable young ladies," his mother emphasized.

On Wednesday he discovered that the Peverells, parents and daughters, were staying through next Monday. By then he could admit that the Misses Peverell were attractive—yet neither had spun gold hair or clear eyes that seemed to hold no artifice. Neither young lady had more than the wit God had given her. They had never heard of Defoe or Pope and saw no reason to become acquainted with dead writers. They certainly did not understand whist and giggled when they played the wrong card. They were, however, quite proficient on the pianoforte.

Thus, on Thursday, Giles informed his mother that her hopes for the Peverell daughters would be dashed—unless Dominic wanted to be in the running. Dominic, with his sharp good looks unmarred by a hotter sun, would have the girls vying for his attention. Lord Peverell would prefer the title for one of his daughters. And the countess would approve of Dominic's preference for country living. The marchioness of Grasmere looked downcast at her son's assessment of their guests. She brightened considerably when Giles hinted at an intriguing young lady he had met at a London salon.

At Friday's breakfast he informed his parents that he would leave for London immediately. When his father became obdurate after Giles' lack of explanation, his mother quietly said, "Giles may return to London when he wishes."

His father glanced at his wife and then to his son. "I trust your pressing business will have consequences beneficial to this family's posterity."

Giles assured him that it did. Should Napoleon win and Bonapartists control Britain, a Hargreaves would not remain marquess of Grasmere. He refused to consider any other consequence beneficial to his family's posterity.

Not with Sir Roger wondering if all the Sourantines were involved in spying.

He drove back to London that day, in the rain.

Chapter 5 ~ Saturday, November 23

Giles did only one thing right on the evening of the Davenports' soirée. He arrived fashionably late, as was his wont, well after the hosts abandoned their receiving line.

The carriage dropped him at the entrance. From the people crowded behind the windows that glowed with light, he expected the Davenports would term the evening a success. The butler bowed and took his cape, informing him woodenly that his hosts would be in the drawing room. It took Giles several minutes to negotiate the crush and find his hostess and say all the polite words. Then he stepped back, letting others take his place, letting the crowd flow around him and push him toward the wall. From there he scanned the room for the Sourantine party. He didn't see them.

The musicians finished re-tuning and started the next dance. The sets quickly formed. Giles shifted to position closer to the door and kept looking for his quarry.

"Becoming a wallflower, Hargreaves?"

Nazenby had arrived. Tonight he affected a gold waistcoat with a bronze cutaway.

"What news, Sir Roger?"

"That the Peverell daughters and not the steward called you back to Grasmere."

Giles' head jerked around. "You heard that?"

"The countess Dombley wrote her sister, and her sister wrote Silly Wilton, and thus all London knows. Your *mademoiselle* will have heard."

"Does Lady Eaton have a suggestion?"

"Flowers."

"Ah, I am ahead of her. I sent two posies, one this very morning."

"Word of that has not entered the ton's flood of gossip."

Giles frowned, but his response was forestalled by a commotion at the room's entrance. He saw a flash of vivid blue, heard a spate of rapid French, then the crowd parted enough for him to see Celeste Sourantine on the arm of a man he vaguely recalled. The man was older than her usual swains. He glimpsed pale gold hair over the man's shoulder. Then the crowd shifted again, and he saw no more.

"Duty calls," Sir Roger murmured and sidled away.

When he reached the French spy, following in the wake of three of her admirers, she was speaking rapidly to Amelia Davenport. "La, so many people, *Madame*! You must be delighted with your success."

Her escort still blocked Giles' view. He shifted to see who stood beyond them.

Mrs. Davenport was introducing her companion. "Mrs. Lockhart, this is Mdm. Sourantine. Madame, this soirée is in Mrs. Lockhart's honor. She is newly married."

"*Bon soir, Madame*, but did you not attend our salon last week? With your new husband, *oui*? Ah, I thought I remembered. You talked to Sir Edward Garland, *oui*? But I monopolize you, and we came to dance. *Bon soir, Mesdames*." She steered her escort away.

Giles finally saw Josette, making a curtsey to her hostess. Dressed in pale pink. And carrying no flowers. Her brother served as her escort. They turned away and followed the French spy. He followed, trailing after the three determined admirers.

As Celeste was surrounded, her escort stepped back, obviously used to his role. The widowed beauty laughed gaily. Beside her vivid colors, Josette looked pale—and paler still when she looked around and spied him.

Celeste rapped one man's sleeve with her fan. "Is it not that we have just arrived? You do not wish me to catch my breath? Very well," and she bestowed her hand on one swain while she smiled and promised the next dances to her eager court.

Giles bowed to Josette. "Miss Sourantine, I have anticipated seeing you this evening."

Her lashes flickered. She pasted on a smile that lacked last week's sparkle. "Lord Hargreaves." She glanced around, but her brother had disappeared. Celeste's escort stepped forward. "May I present Robert LeBrun?" She gave his name a French pronunciation. "*M'sieur*, this is Giles Hargreaves, recently with our army in the Peninsula. He is the son of the marquess of Grasmere."

"The *marquis* of Celeste?" LeBrun bowed.

Traces of silver glistened in the man's hair. He had dressed in blue brocade, with Sir Roger in following the last century's affectation. LeBrun's smile was polite; his voice cultured. But Giles did not like the man, primarily because he had defined Giles as Celeste's property. He glanced to see how Josette had taken LeBrun's question. She was looking away; he could not see her eyes. The color had not returned to her cheeks. So he looked back at LeBrun and stiffly returned the man's address. As he straightened, he said, "I am hardly that, sir. My father is still hale, and my brother is the elder."

"I have seen you at the salons, is it not so? You were in uniform."

"I am recently cashed out, sir."

"And what was your rank? You were a colonel?"

"Lieutenant Colonel," he corrected. "Before a wound sent me to the rear. Of late I have ordered around the papers on my desk at the War Office."

"Ah, a man who plans the campaign for Wellington. Do you prepare for his next attack?"

The question sounded innocuous, but Giles' ears, pricked for spies, heard ominous overtones. "Never that, *M.* LeBrun, nothing so grand."

"Do you think that Wellington will hold his position in Spain through this winter?"

Even Josette looked around for his response. Her curiosity for that answer did not bode well for her innocence in the spying.

"Wellington makes his own plans, sir. He will not share them with a desk officer in rainy London. And that *was* my work. I am decommissioned now."

"Ah, you said you cashed out. Did you tire of the war?"

Josette caught a breath and glanced away. Giles leaned more obviously on his cane.

LeBrun's aplomb carried him past the awkwardness. "I see. A pity. When you are at the salons, you spend most of your time in the card room. As Josette does."

His familiar use of her name labeled him closer than an acquaintance and more than a mere swain of Celeste's. Giles glanced at her, but she watched the dancers, refusing to participate in the conversation. "My evenings, *M'sieur*, would be flat if I did not play a few games of whist. The ladies find me a poor partner for dancing."

"And as Celeste said, we came tonight for the dancing. Excuse me, my lord, Josette."

She looked around then. Her brow constricted faintly as LeBrun faded away. Celeste's disappointed admirers had also drifted away.

Giles did not care why LeBrun had suddenly abandoned their conversation. He shifted to stand beside Josette. Remembering his past week and the silence-laden conversations he had endured, he was eager to talk with her. Josette did not seem so eager. Her blue eyes looked dim when they lifted to his. She tapped a toe in time to the music. Too tall for most men to partner, she must never dance to her heart's content. And he could not remedy that. He had to continue the pretense of a slowly healing wound.

"Would you like to retire to the card room?"

"No, my lord. I came to enjoy the evening."

"I thought you enjoyed whist—if not the gambling."

"I do not spend my every waking hour at cards, my lord." Her voice had a bite.

He knew, then, that she had heard the gossip about the country party at Grasmere. She did not know how glad he'd been to escape. He could not baldly say that. Their acquaintance was still too new for him even to hint at the declaration that would attach him to the Sourantine household.

Giles mentally backed up and started again. "Tell me about Robert LeBrun."

"What is there to tell, my lord? Celeste chose him for our escort this evening. She often prefers him as an escort."

He heard the weight she gave the words. He remembered LeBrun's question: 'Celeste's *marquis*?' What had happened to turn Josette so cold? "How does she know him?"

She sighed. "He is an old friend of my father's. They came to England together."

"He dangled you on his knee when you were an infant?"

"No. I did not meet him until I came to live with Celeste. *M.* LeBrun and my father parted ways after they arrived in Dover. My brother Edmund met him at a horse fair. They fell into conversation and realized the connection. Celeste likes him. He often comes to dine."

"Do you like him?"

Josette shrugged. "He is Robert LeBrun."

Giles realized he would get no more from her on the man—but he had another line of inquiry for Sir Roger. His task now must be to break through the ice that had frozen her. "How did you amuse yourself this week?"

Those clouded eyes flashed to him and away. Her bosom rose and fell a little faster. "In the usual way, my lord. I partnered with Lord Costell against Mr. Kennit and Lord Musgrove. Did you expect me to do otherwise?"

"Did you not just tell me that you do not spend your every waking hour at cards?"

Josette compressed her lips than gave a little shake of her head. "I went riding with my brother Albert. I met his friends Lucas and Michael Armitage. They said they knew you. I went with Celeste on a round of visits, and we received visits on Thursday. I shopped. I wrote to my grandfather Newland and sent presents to William and Antonia."

"And who are they?"

She looked startled then regained her composure. "My younger brother and sister. William is thirteen; Antonia is eight. They want to come to London. They think it a great adventure. I tell them that they have more fun in Little Houghton."

"That is your home, Little Houghton? Do you miss it?"

"Sometimes. It is not the same since Papa died." She took a deep breath and faced him. "Did you enjoy your time at Grasmere, my lord?"

Only a gamester, he thought, would attack when her cards were weak. A bluff, to hide what she really held. But he set himself to answer her question, for it introduced the gossip he could not directly mention. "I enjoyed the day I rode the estate. That was Monday. My father loves Grasmere, and he likes nothing better than to talk about his plans for it. He is glad that I have cashed out."

"You have an older brother, do you not?"

"Yes, Dominic, but he does not love Grasmere."

"And you do?"

"I always have. I joined the regiment partly because the estate would not be mine." Would she pursue that evidence of a past unhappiness, or was she still ice?

"Is your brother married?"

"No. But he knows his duty. I do not look to inherit."

"Yet you love it—."

"I can love it without coveting it. I'll have a property of my own one day, not as grand as Grasmere, but I do not think I would enjoy life on the grand scale. I had forgotten that part of living at home. This week reminded me: the long walk down the gallery to reach my chamber, a dozen footmen to ensure I never open a door myself, dining nightly at a long table with an Indian silver epergne depicting elephants attacking tigers and poor humans getting in the way. That tends to kill conversation."

Josette glanced down, listening to him more than distracting herself with the dancers. The ice had cracked. He admired the creamy bend of her neck, the soft curls of her golden hair escaping from the braid that wrapped her crown.

Then she asked, "And the rest of your week, my lord?"

She used his courtesy title, Giles knew, when she tried to block the familiarity growing between them. She would misconstrue any hesitation to her question, so he plunged in. "My matchmaking mother had invited guests. They arrived Tuesday. The earl and countess Dombley and their daughters." And he waited.

After several seconds, Josette looked up. Her cornflower eyes searched his. "I hear the Peverell sisters are quite pretty."

"Attractive, yes. The title and their portions elevate that. They didn't need the epergne to kill conversation; they have no conversation. And no poetry. Certainly no heads for whist. But they are accomplished musicians, quite accomplished on the harpsichord. I left as soon as duty permitted."

Her mouth curved. He was winning, reminding her that he had

forgotten nothing she had said to him a week ago. Perhaps he should have written to her.

Giles pushed further, stepping over propriety to see what she had thought of his gifts. "I had hoped to see you carry my flowers tonight."

Her smile faded. "Your flowers, my lord?" Josette interposed his title again, but for the first time she looked straight at him, her gaze open and steady. "I received no flowers."

"A posy last Saturday, another this morning."

Color flooded her cheeks. "Posies did arrive. For Celeste."

"I sent them to *Miss* Sourantine. I wrote the cards myself."

"The flowers came with no card, sir."

Now he understood her ice. Josette thought that he had forgotten her, and she had guarded her heart. Sir Roger had warned him. Giles needed no evidence to know who had intercepted the cards. He chose not to pursue it.

The set had ended; another was forming. They had stood here long enough.

He offered his arm. "Shall we take a turn around the room, Miss Sourantine? I may be incapable of a dance, but my leg will hold for sedate walking."

As she placed her hand on his arm, she said, "I do not think it wise to allow you two dances, my lord, even though we do not take the floor. My *belle-soeur* would not approve."

"I could care less what Mdm. Sourantine approves or disapproves. Besides, we have merely stood and talked. I do not call that claiming you for a dance. This," and he covered her hand and drew her closer, "this I call claiming you for a dance."

Her color heightened again. Her lashes lowered, but not before he saw the sparkle in her eyes. The ice was rapidly melting. "I am almost glad you do not dance, Lord Hargreaves. Were you in regimentals, I fear I would swoon. A wounded hero, the son of a marquess, handsome enough to turn even Celeste's head. I am quite honored."

Ah, here was the wit he'd missed. "Do you mock me, Miss Sourantine?"

"Did your brother never tease you, sir?"

"Dominic was above teasing his beastly little brother."

"Where does he live? Does he come to London?"

"Never to London, thank God, or I should have to distract him from my own goal. He is quite content on his Yorkshire estate. My father warns me that I am the future of Grasmere, and my mother subjects me to matchmaking."

"Your brother may surprise you all. Yorkshire lasses can turn any man's head."

"Aren't you a Yorkshire lass, Miss Sourantine?" Her deepened blush pleased him. "Now, my years in the Army have limited my London acquaintances. Tell me the dancers."

Josette obliged, with the occasional droll description that kept him smiling.

At the end of the set, the supper dance was announced. Giles had intended to claim that as well—but he faced a wilier opponent than he had anticipated.

Celeste appeared, Robert LeBrun at her shoulder. She planted herself in their path and fluttered her fan dramatically. "La, I am *fatigué*. Who would think it possible? Lord Hargreaves, you must take me from this so hot room. I must breathe the cooler air."

"I would oblige, Madame, but Miss Sourantine promised me the supper dance." Josette inhaled sharply at his lie.

Celeste, however, did not care. She confiscated his other arm. "You cannot so monopolize my *belle-soeur*. It will cause gossip, and she needs no more gossip about her. Be the gallant, my lord, and rescue her and me. Josette for the ton, and me for the cooler air. Robert, do you dance with my *belle-soeur*, *s'il vous plait*. She never dances enough. *Voila*! We are well disposed."

One evening's conversation with Josette was not enough to consider a match claimed, not when he'd had several such *tete-a-tetes* with Celeste. And he wanted no scandal to touch Josette. What had the woman said? *No more gossip about her*. The words warned him not to cause a scene. Eyes were already on them, drawn by the French beauty and the loudly spoken word 'gossip'. Another refusal would attract even more attention.

So he let himself be tugged away. He saw Sir Roger frowning at him. He looked back and saw Josette allowing Robert LeBrun to lead her into the set. She smiled at the man, giving freely the pleasure that Giles had had to win back. No, one evening's conversation was not nearly enough to claim a match. He'd have to impress her more strongly next time.

Celeste would have towed him farther along the hall. At a *Directoire* table with a side chair Giles dug in his heels. Josette's comment that he had turned even Celeste's head echoed. He may have done so. In pursuit of his mission he could manage a flirtation with this woman he was learning to despise—but she would keep him dangling with her other beaux: sometimes accepted, sometimes excluded. He needed her source for the War Office despatches.

Only through Josette did he gain the necessary access to the household. His mission needed her, not the beauty.

Celeste's *tete-a-tete* would undermine all the ground he had won back. So he dug in his heels and maneuvered her into the chair in the hall before she towed him into a private room.

Chapter 6 ~ Saturday, November 23

Robert LeBrun led Josette past the forming set to the far corner of the grand drawing room where they could speak more privately. He stationed himself beside her, enabling him to overlook the room. Then quietly and in French he said, "You worry me, *enfant*."

She raised her eyebrows and replied in English. "I beg your pardon?"

"You understand me, *enfant*," he retorted and returned stubbornly to French, "You are as fluent as I am, as Celeste is. Do not pretend that you do not comprehend the reason for this our conversation."

"I am too much in the company of Lord Hargreaves," she hazarded.

"*Exactement*. Celeste warned you. The lord Hargreaves has spent this week past choosing between the Peverell sisters, yet tonight you decide to resume your flirtation."

"We were hardly flirting, M. LeBrun."

"Is it that you want a broken heart?"

"Is he planning to break it?"

He snorted inelegantly. "Tobias Kennit could tell you better than I."

"M. Kennit is not here tonight. You shall have to tell me."

LeBrun managed to look pained. "Do one favor, *enfant*, a favor for the man who called your father his friend. Do not accept any more advances from Lord Hargreaves tonight. You need not be rude, but do not be so welcoming."

His avuncular advice did not match well to the man her father had long ago described as a compatriot but not a friend. Over the past several weeks she had gradually comprehended that his relationship with Celeste was more than that of an older swain. He often seemed her *belle-soeur's seigneur*, but she had not realized LeBrun not only gave Celeste orders but also obeyed. Celeste warned Josette off Giles Hargreaves; now LeBrun attempted the same.

She glanced at the couples performing the cotillion. She had hoped to dance, yet here she was in another conversation.

"Josette?"

"I am obliged, *M.* LeBrun, for your concern. May I ask why you believe I am to be warned about Lord Hargreaves?"

"Remember, his flirtation began with Celeste. When she did not fall for his bait, he threw his line to you. Why would he do so?"

She shivered and drew her shawl over her shoulders. "Perhaps he is a man who sees more than shallow appearances."

"Celeste is an acknowledged beauty. He should not so easily set her aside."

His argument sounded like Celeste's superficiality, and his use of it angered her. "I prefer to believe," she retorted, "that he chose me once he recognized what she is like. You are over two years in the company of my sister-in-law. Have you not recognized her primary flaw?"

"Do not put on blinders, *enfant*."

"I am not an *enfant*, *M'sieur*. And I am well acquainted with my *belle-soeur's* dishonesty. Shall I give you an example? Last Saturday and this, two posies arrived at our house. I was not at home. When I returned, Celeste informed me that she had received each of them from an undisclosed admirer. I accepted both lies, *M'sieur*. After all, I have no serious suitor who would favor me with flowers. Yet tonight Lord Hargreaves asked why I had not carried his flowers and tells me, unprompted, that he also sent a posy last Saturday."

"Is that what he told you? And you believed him? You are a *naïf*."

"How else would he know of the flowers, *M'sieur*? Has he not been absent from London for a week? Courting the Peverell sisters, did you not say?"

"You imply that she destroyed the cards and kept the bouquets for herself? You imply that she is jealous of you?"

"Is he not 'the son of a marquess' of whom she has been boasting?" LeBrun scowled at the question. Josette played her trump card. "And I can ask our butler Reynolds. He will know if flowers came with a card and to whom they were sent."

She had defeated his argument, but he just returned to his first point. "All this is mere distraction, Josette. You should not harbor hopes of a suit from Hargreaves. He will disappoint you. *Perhaps* he did send the flowers to you. That does not whiten his designs on you. At best, he is merely playing with your heart. At worst, he will soil your virtue."

"You describe a more practiced rake than Tobias Kennit."

"*Oui*, he has learned well, during his years in Europe, how to toy with a woman."

"As you did?"

He answered her riposte with a courtly bow.

"I know you obey Celeste's dictates in this, *M*. LeBrun."

"That is so. But, tonight, grant me this one favor. Test this Lord Hargreaves. See if he again switches his attentions. The rake he is will want an easy catch, I assure you. He will not care for your neglect. Refuse him the rest of this evening. Tomorrow he will be gone."

Josette wished to say, *And if I do not want him gone? If I enjoy his attentions, rake though he may be?* She merely asked, "One rake undermining another?"

"Will you do it?"

"I do not believe you. I believe only that Celeste is miffed that one of her beaux abandons her."

"She does have your interests in her heart, Josette."

"She is jealous."

"*Peut-etre.* Yet she is wiser to this world than you are. Admit that, *enfant.*"

Josette played with the fringe on her shawl. Reluctantly she said. "I will admit that."

"It will need only this night."

The music ended. The people dispersed, paired to go down to supper—and still she didn't acquiesce to his request. He prompted her by again asking. She did not want to refuse Lord Giles Hargreaves; she enjoyed his conversation, his attentions. But she sensed that LeBrun would not lead her after the others until he had her agreement. "I will do it. If he is the rake you describe, then I want nothing to do with him."

He offered his brocaded arm and led her from the drawing room, among the last couples crowded at the door. He nodded and spoke to those waiting with them to leave. And Josette examined her reluctance.

When Sylvia Wilton had shared news of the country party at Grasmere, her heart had ached. It began to beat steadily again only when Giles Hargreaves gave his own description of the Peverell sisters, a description that echoed their conversation a week before. In those words he had proved that he had not forgotten her.

She prayed that LeBrun was wrong, that Hargreaves was too honorable to pursue her with only a deceitful design in mind.

. ~ . ~ . ~ .

"Here?" Celeste gasped as Giles propelled her into the chair. "But a private chamber for the two of us, that would be very much the better."

"Only to be banished from your sight for a week after? No, thank you, *Mdm.* Sourantine," Giles said sturdily. "I have finished with those days. No more."

"*Tiens*, you flirt with *ma belle-soeur*. You have a *tete-a-tete*. You send her bouquets—."

"Ah, my flowers *did* arrive. And you claimed them for yourself. Jealous, Madame?"

"It is that which is your intent? *Pour moi etre jaloux de Josette?*"

"No. Josette is ten times the woman you are. She is not always desperate for flattery," he added, knowing she would rise to the bait.

Her flashing eyes rewarded him.

"As I am? Josette is no beauty. She—she is too pale, too tall."

"The right height for kissing," he retorted. As he said the words, he realized that he wanted to test that claim.

"You flirt with her. Ah, but she is little more than *une innocente*."

"You, Madame, said she needed no more gossip about her."

Those blue eyes rounded. Celeste played the innocent very well. "*Moi*? Did I say that? It is that I malign *ma belle-soeur*? Not I, *M'sieur*, not I."

"You did." Giles crossed his arms and looked down at her. For years he had dressed down subalterns with little more than a cold stare and a few cutting words. He didn't think the same technique would work on a French spy, but he would test it first. "Do not try to wiggle out of it, Madame. You said that I should not monopolize her, that she needed no more gossip about her. What did you mean? What gossip?"

"There was talk when you and Josette were so long absent during the salon a week ago."

"There is always talk. There will be talk about this conversation. You said 'gossip'. That is much more than talk."

Celeste pursed her lips, as if reluctant to explain. A quick dissembler, she was a good choice for a spy. Yet he thought he knew a few ways to fluster her, to throw her off her game and take control himself.

She glanced down, stretching out her pretended hesitation. Then she spoke slowly, softly, as if fearing her words would carry. To any idle passer-by, their conversation would appear intimate. "You do know that she plays cards during every salon with *M.* Kennit? Do you also know that he fronts her coins for each evening's play?"

What Giles knew was how little Celeste Sourantine knew of her own sister-in-law's evenings at whist.

She leaned forward, increasing the appearance that she shared a great secret. And giving him a better view of her *décolletage*. "They are always in company at my salons. Not every man, especially a man like *M.* Kennit, would so willingly part with his coins for a woman's gaming. Josette is special to him."

Yes, he had to admit that Josette and Kennit had some sort of relationship, one that she had not explained to his satisfaction, one that he could not work out on his own. A relationship he had to understand before he continued his pursuit of Josette, no matter what Sir Roger said. "And Lord Musgrove?" he prompted, wanting to hear what the French spy had decided about Kennit's friend.

"He waits for *M.* Kennit to tire of her. Is it not obvious?"

Giles glanced along the hall. Only footmen near the door might hear. He knew the servants would gossip. Most of Nazenby's leads came from servants' gossip. "Lower your voice," he urged.

"We should have gone to the private chamber."

"And you should have more of a care for Josette's reputation," he snapped.

Celeste clenched her hands in her lap. Her eyes narrowed. Her lips twisted. For a brief moment the society mask dropped and he saw a classical harpy. Then she regained her composure. "I wish only to protect *ma belle-soeur*. I ask you—I plead with you, *mon seigneur*: do not amuse yourself with her."

"I do not, Madame. Josette herself attracts me. She has interesting things to say. I am never bored in her company."

"As I saw you with her tonight? You laughed often. Your conversation, it was very intent." She gave him a sly look from the corners of her eyes. "*Mais, peut-etre* you are not the only one she so favors. You are only the latest."

She was back to her earlier stance, the one intended to drive him away from Josette. Giles relaxed. "Yes, I know. Tobias Kennit and Gordon Musgrove, her gaming partners."

"Oh, they are much more than that. Certainly *M.* Kennit is. Especially after you left her for a week. Josette was much ... saddened when Silly Wilton informed us that the Peverell sisters visited your home at the express invitation of the *marquis* your father."

He tensed but had relaxed again by the time she leaned back, well satisfied with her words chosen to devastate any feelings he had for Josette. "Too late, Madame. I explained my mother's matchmaking to her. As I explained about the flowers I sent to her—which you claimed as your own."

Her shrug was very French. "Is it that you think she will believe your claim about the bouquets? And about this conversation?"

"I have only ever spoken the truth to Josette." Oh, yes, he told her the truth, even as he committed a great deceit. Giles smiled tightly and delivered the retort that won the game for him. "How many times have you lied to her, Madame?"

Not expecting a rude truth from him, she looked flummoxed.

"Come, Madame," he advanced his position while he had the advantage, "you must straighten out your arguments. You would have me believe a contradiction. First Josette is an innocent, too pure for my attentions. Then you claim she is a rake's plaything. Which is the lie, Madame?"

But she recovered, and Giles began to understand how she was successful as a spy. "I tell you the gossip, *mon seigneur*," she huffed. "Josette *is* an innocent. She is so innocent that she believes close association with a rake like Tobias Kennit will not harm her."

"Your insinuations come too late, Madame. Josette has explained to me her associations with Kennit and Musgrove." Even as he countered her, he winced inwardly. His lingering reservations pricked him.

And her instincts sensed his disquiet. "She has explained to your satisfaction?" A tightening around his eyes betrayed him. "Ah, I see. You wonder why a rake like Kennit associates with her, is it not so? You wonder how much more it is than card play, yes?"

Again she had fastened on the questions still haunting him. Josette's answers to his probing had been deliberately light. Did she hide something from him?

Whatever his doubts, he did not want Celeste Sourantine, a French spy, to have confirmation of them. Giles shifted his stance, leaning to one side with the cane as his prop, withdrawing intensity. "Madame, you said you were informing me of the gossip. Surely it is more than this. Josette's participation in your salons goes back some months, doesn't it? That would be old gossip. Is there nothing new?"

"Oh, *oui, mon seigneur*, but perhaps it is that you have not heard it. You have been gone to Grasmere this week. So you did not hear the words that flew, swift as birds, about your long *tete-a-tete* with Josette. You were gone so long."

"We stayed in the hall, Madame. With footmen well within earshot. You yourself are witness to that. You could easily have scotched those rumors. You purpose to be the protector of her reputation. Is there evidence that you have been?"

Again he flustered her. For a practiced spy, she had not prepared herself well for his interview—but she had had only two dances to plan. Perhaps she had thought to enamor him and win him back into her court. That would explain her bustling intent to reach a private room, a plan miscarried when he refused to leave the hall. Perhaps she had thought intercepting the posies would be enough to crush Josette's attraction to him. There she had nearly succeeded.

"I may state my wishes to Josette, to have a care for her reputation, but I cannot dictate to her," Celeste defended herself. "Only M. Newland, her *grandpère*, may do so."

"She is in your house, under your care."

"Josette is above one-and-twenty. If she chooses to ruin her reputation with *M.* Kennit or with you, *mon seigneur*, then she may do so."

"As you choose to do so with your many beaux."

Giles had hoped to anger her. When Celeste's blue eyes widened and her mouth dropped into an O, he knew his shot had failed.

"*Tiens*! *Tu est jaloux*!" She clapped her gloved hands together and stood. "And you have fastened upon *ma belle-soeur* to attract my attention, to have me to be jealous, only to discover she is not the innocent you thought her. *Pauvre* Giles." Quickly she stepped forward and pressed her hand to his arm. "Perhaps it is that you are well rid of the Sourantine women."

With that parting shot, she whirled and left, her heels clicking on the floor.

He watched her, shaking his head at her self-absorption. Only when she had sashayed into the drawing room did he recognize the thread in her last words that was common to the insinuations she kept arguing.

A prepared speech, with prepared actions, and carefully selected last words, all to send him away, far away. She had waited to deliver it until he spoke the words she needed. And considering him dismissed, she had left the field.

Giles grinned. He might be dismissed, but he wouldn't retreat. Celeste Sourantine would not be pleased when he presented himself at their door with another posy for Josette.

As paired couples left the drawing room to attend the supper, he attached himself to Lady Eaton and Sir Roger. Josette, he saw, went down on the arm of Robert LeBrun. Celeste had called upon one of her eager suitors for her escort.

The spy was a wilier opponent than he had reckoned. He counted that neither of them had won tonight's verbal battle; he did not think she would consider it a draw. Yet he wouldn't overrate her. While she could think quickly, she had prepared only a basic argument. An argument she had built on a mistaken reading of him. Everything she had said revolved around that one point. Too bad she had selected the wrong one.

Wide of the mark as she had been, however, the spy managed to pinpoint the two facts that haunted him. Her instincts were good. He would have to be a little wilier.

After supper, he delayed seeking out Josette. Claude Terry partnered her for the first dance while Giles sat with his hostess Mrs. Davenport. For the second, he obligingly walked about with the honoree Mrs. Lockhart. Josette was led out by one of Celeste's beaux.

Lady Eaton claimed his attention when the third dance began. When he scowled at the unknown man dancing with Josette, the dowager gave him a shrewd smile. "My son Jasper. Recently elected to Parliament. His wife is somewhere—ah, there she is, farther down the line, in the blue gown with silver netting." She gave Giles an arch look. "I knew Miss Sourantine would not give you another dance, after two before supper."

"How do you know this?"

"I heard Robert LeBrun command her not to give you any considerations at all. He spoke French, foolish man, as if no one in England has ever learned it. There is no easier way to attract the attention of the gossips than to try to speak privately in a public room."

Giles watched Josette smile at her partner. When the movements of the dance allowed, they chattered easily. She even giggled at one of Eaton's sallies. "And Miss Sourantine, was she amenable to LeBrun's command?"

"Not amenable at all. She did eventually acquiesce."

"And you sent your son to dance with her?"

"Of course. She should not depend solely on her sister-in-law's cast-offs. John Davenport will ask her for the next dance. And we shall join Sir Roger in the card room. I hope Miss Sourantine may oblige us with an appearance there."

"She won't. She intends only to dance this evening."

"All the better." She steered him out of the drawing room before he could see the fourth man that Josette would dance with. When they reached the wide hall, she said, "Now, Lord Hargreaves, tell me what trick the Sourantine beauty tried, and we shall plot your next move."

Chapter 7 ~ Sunday, November 24

Not wanting another day's delay, Giles called on Sunday at the Sourantine house. As proof of his pursuit, he had located pale pink roses. He held them gingerly. An elderly butler opened the door and gave him a dour look. Nor did he step aside to admit Giles.

"Please inform Miss Sourantine that Lord Hargreaves calls upon her."

The man did not blink. "*Mdm.* Sourantine chooses not to receive visitors today, my lord."

"I did not come to see the madame. I want—I wish to see Miss Sourantine."

"Miss Sourantine attends church with her brother, my lord."

"The service should soon be over. I will wait for her, if I may."

The man continued to block the entrance. "Miss Sourantine often walks with her brother on Sunday afternoons. Do you wish to leave the flowers, my lord?"

Giles glanced at the roses. After his previous luck with the posies, he did not want one tender petal crushed. "No, I would prefer to deliver them myself. I do not want my admirations misdirected again."

The butler remained expressionless. "I cannot say when they will return, my lord."

Had they refused him the house? "I will leave a note on my card then. I can call upon her tomorrow."

"You may, my lord, but I must inform you that the family accepts no visitors on the days of salons."

"No callers tomorrow? Then I will see Miss Sourantine tomorrow night. Unfortunately, these blooms may not last until then. What is your name? I will mention to her that entrusted my message to you."

That shot went home. The man's eyes flared. His mouth primed. Had he known about the misdirected posies? "I am Reynolds, my lord." He confirmed Giles' guess by adding, "Should you wish to leave the bouquet, my lord, I will ensure it reaches only Miss Sourantine."

Ah, the man had finally opened up. Giles quickly stepped into the breach with a seemingly innocuous question. "Have you served the family long?"

"I came with the house, my lord, when Mr. Newland purchased it for his daughter and her new husband. I was footman then, serving the Viscount Everett until he sold up."

"My father knew Everett. Flooded the Thames with debt, didn't he? That was in—'82?"

"Yes, my lord. Mr. William Newland purchased the home in '83."

"And you've served them since. A comedown, wasn't it, serving a commoner after a viscount?"

Reynolds took the offensive question without a change of expression. "Mr. Newland is a little rough, sir, but his daughter Miss Amelia and his grandchildren are better than most quality-born. My lord."

That was a definite shot at him, cannily oblique. Reynolds was better at delivering a set-down than his own man. "What of Amelia Newland's husband? A Frenchman, wasn't he?"

"Mr. Henry Sourantine had manners to please a duke, sir."

"When did the present Madame Sourantine take charge of the house?"

"Mr. Newland allowed the late Master Edmund the place when he married Madame, Celeste Nemours that was."

However bland the statement seemed, it revealed that the staff didn't consider *Celeste Nemours that was* as part of the Sourantine family. The butler carved fine distinctions. Did the man know she was spying for the French? His first loyalty had to be the family, but if the servants didn't view Celeste as family—would this man Reynolds give evidence against her? What evidence could he have?

Giles tried to conceal his rapid thoughts. "I understand that Madame Celeste is quality-born. I believe her family fled France only a few months before King Louis and his family were imprisoned."

"I could not say, my lord. I know little of the French."

Giles drew out a visiting card and tried another bid to gain entrance. "If I might write a message to Miss Sourantine—."

"I will have writing tools brought, my lord."

Even for a message, the butler would not admit him. Orders from Mdm. Sourantine or his own obdurance? If he ran the household this strictly, any new servant would stay below stairs for weeks, if not months. No wonder Sir Roger had leaped at Giles' suggestion of a mock courtship. "My good man," he tried again, "I do not believe I can manage to write standing up."

Reynolds unbent enough from his inherent notions of propriety to say, "My orders from Madame are to admit no one this afternoon. I will take your card up to Madame as you wish—."

"*Not* Mdm. Sourantine, Reynolds. *Miss* Sourantine. Miss Josette Sourantine. Mr. Newland's granddaughter. She is the only one who needs receive my card."

Ah, was that a flicker in the man's glance? Gone now, betraying very little.

"As you wish, my lord."

Giles handed over the visiting card without a message and took his leave. That butler had a wealth of information about the Sourantine household—if only they could unlock it! The man must know all of Celeste's comings and goings as well as her visitors and her letters. Yet a good servant—and Reynolds seemed the embodiment of one—kept a closed mouth. Giles did not want his own people chatting to visitors. The longer he pursued Josette, the more familiar to him the butler would become—and that increased his chances of unlocking Reynold's tight jaw.

He walked back to his curricle. In the cold air his horses had become restive, and the Sourantine groom had walked them to the corner. As he waited for the man to return, he glanced in the other direction and saw a couple turn onto the street.

Josette and her brother.

Her cheeks were flecked with cold, her blue eyes sparkling. Her brother met his salute with grinning good humor. She smiled as well—then she schooled her features into a blank mask. How much had her sister-in-law said after last night's soirée? He had gained back the steps he lost from his week away, but the French spy had obviously said enough to set his pursuit back several more paces. As for the butler's deliberate misunderstandings—had he been ordered into them? Had Celeste ordered the man to refuse admittance to everyone who visited or only Lord Hargreaves? Or was the order Josette's? Even if he managed to gain entrance, would he encounter constant interruptions when he needed her whole concentration?

The groom arrived with the curricle just as Josette and her brother reached him. Giles tossed the boy a coin and greeted the Sourantines.

The brother Albert ran an assessing gaze over the equipage. "Fine pair you have, Lord Hargreaves." Josette, perforce, stopped beside him. She caught Giles' steady gaze and looked away, pretending to study the matched greys as her brother tolled off their points. "Did you buy them here in London?"

"From my brother Dominic. He breeds horses up in Yorkshire. Your groom has taken good care they did not stand in the cold too long. Your butler refused me admittance."

At the final statement Josette glanced around. Albert nodded. "Yes, Celeste ordered him most fiercely not to admit anyone. She's claiming some sort of upset from last night's party."

"A pity. I quite enjoyed myself at the Davenports. Especially before the supper dance."

Her lashes flickered, but her gaze remained steadfastly on the horses. Her brother apparently knew nothing of last evening's maneuvering. "As did I. Josette would only say the evening was 'nice'." Albert snorted. "Say, have you had this turn-out long? Westover's talking about a new coachmaker in Mount Street."

Giles answered his rapid questions with good humor, but he watched Josette. When he caught her glancing for a third time at the roses, he knew he had an opening. He waited, however, until her brother finished his questions. When Albert stepped down to look more closely at the horses, Giles closed the distance between them. "I brought you another bouquet, Miss Sourantine."

She took a deep breath, then her pale eyes lifted to give him the direct look he had sought. "Roses this late in the year, my lord? They must have been dear."

"You deserve the best. I did not leave them with your butler for fear they would again be misdirected."

Again her lashes flickered, but those blue eyes continued to hold his. "I spoke to Reynolds last evening. He confirmed your claim about the other flowers."

Ah, she knew her sister-in-law had lied and that he had spoken the truth. Why, then, did she remain so distant? What had the spy told her? Had she repeated her insinuations about Kennit, maintaining they came from him? He had to know. Just as he opened his mouth to ask, the greys suddenly backed. The groom held grimly onto the harness as Albert Sourantine retreated. The near-side gelding snorted and tossed its head.

"I cannot leave my horses standing much longer, Miss Sourantine, but I do wish to speak with you. Will you come for a ride?"

"I cannot. Celeste expects me to return."

"Oh, Josette," her brother exclaimed, "she's just kicking the traces because you argued with her last night."

"If you will come, Albert—."

"Can't," he denied her request cheerfully. "I've an appointment with Westover. That's the reason we came back so soon. There's no reason you shouldn't go. It's an open carriage."

"You have nothing pressing, I hope?" Giles put in.

"Be just the thing," Albert added, unknowingly aiding Giles' pursuit. "You've moped all morning. This will get your spirits up. And keep Celeste from pealing another tirade over you."

Josette narrowed her eyes, as if expecting a trick rather than a flirtation. She was still young enough to have romantic dreams. What had dashed them?

Her brother handed her up. Giles set the bouquet in her hands then sprang up to sit beside her. The advantage of a curricle, he quickly found, was how close the occupants sat. Concerned that she might take a chill, he settled a rug over her knees. After a nod for the groom to step back, he snapped the reins. The matched greys walked forward.

When he had the curricle moving at a steady clip, he glanced at Josette. She looked stubbornly away, watching the passing garden in the square, dormant as winter approached. "Your butler," he said and marked her slight jump, "should join our diplomatic corps. He maintains a position better than some of our ambassadors. He was of no help to me."

"Reynolds has been with us a long time."

"Since your parents' marriage, he told me. I don't think he approved of me. My title impressed him not at all." Rather than respond, she buried her nose in the rose blooms. "If he's like my man, he knows everything that goes on in the house."

A definite jerk from her.

"Conversations in the breakfast room, arguments in the upstairs hall."

"You think we argue in front of the servants?"

"I think your sister-in-law would not care who heard her say anything. She has that arrogant disregard of those she considers inferior."

Again she refused to respond. He would have to ask.

"What did she say to you, after she and I talked in the hall?"

A long pause, long enough to think he would have to speak again, then she asked, "Why do you think she said anything?"

"Because you will hardly look at me. Because you said last evening was only 'nice', and I know you enjoyed the dancing. Because the butler who watched you grow up was very obstructive. Protecting you, as family servants are wont to do for those they like." He paused, but she did not choose any of those reasons. "Come, what did Madame say? That I flirted with her?" He dared not hope it was only that.

"I'm cold. I wish to go home."

"I didn't flirt with her."

"I am cold, my lord."

"I'll take you back." He turned the horses down the next road, intending to work a box back to their square, but he didn't turn from his point. "I offended your *belle-soeur* because I said, very clearly said, that I was not interested in her." He glanced at Josette. The horses pulled against his hold, and he had to give them his attention. He wished they were walking. He could stop and look at her, look and gauge her reaction. When the greys had dropped back to a slow walk, Giles continued his point. "Your sister-in-law didn't want to hear that I no longer admired her. What did she say to you?"

He began to think she would not answer, then she exhaled audibly. "You are like a dog with a bone, my lord. Celeste said—and *M.* LeBrun agreed—that you used me to make her jealous. He said that I should ignore you for the rest of the evening. He said a rake would not be pleased at my indifference to his pursuit and would look elsewhere."

"Ah. I scotched that view, I trust, by retiring to the card room."

"Did you know?"

"How could I, Josette?"

She shifted. She touched the rose petals. "I have not given you leave to address me so familiarly, my lord."

He refused to apologize. He took the horses around another corner, choosing a longer path back to their house. "And what did your sister-in-law say? She must have had much more to say after you returned home."

"She said—one of the things she said was that you led her to a private room, that you kissed and caressed her."

Giles' bark of laughter startled the horses. He pulled them to a halt and gave Josette his full attention. "The opposite is the truth. I gave her a seat in the hall, in view of the footmen at the entrance. I had to tell her repeatedly to keep her voice down." He snapped the reins and let the horses go forward again.

"Celeste didn't say that."

"I have no witness you can easily question this time. Mrs. Davenport would think it odd indeed if I drove you to her house so you could question her servants. Did *Mdm.* Sourantine," and his mordant tone made mockery of that formal title, "did she mention the gossip that she so eagerly told me? The nasty insinuations she shared about you and Tobias Kennit?"

His answer was in her stiffened back. He had no doubt what Celeste had said—and they had reached the turning for her street. He didn't think Josette would agree to a private meeting tomorrow. He would not be able to see her until the evening's salon—while her *belle-soeur* would have hours to pour out more venom. He had to say something that would linger through those poisonous hours. Something true. Something that even a practiced liar like the French spy could be startled into admitting as true.

The curricle straightened out from the turn. The groom saw their approach. He ran to the street to hold the horses again.

And Giles said, "I know what your sister-in-law would have failed to mention. Something that she would not want you to know. I told her that I wanted to kiss you. I do. I have since that first card game, when I realized you were so close to my height."

"Lord Hargreaves—."

"Did she tell you that?" And on the question he drew the horses up. The groom took their heads. Giles did not move to assist her to alight. He reached to remove the rug but left his arm before her, blocking her in.

Josette leaned back against the seat. "My lord—."

"We must talk," he interposed. "I do have questions I must ask you, for my own peace of mind. Questions about Kennit, other questions. Should you choose to answer them—well, that will determine if I go forward." *Be clever*, Giles thought, *be careful*. He walked a sword's edge. God forbid she divine the deceit that drove his pursuit of her. "Your sister-in-law said more, much more, that you should hear, for your own reputation's sake. I cannot conduct a conversation while I manage these horses. And I would swear that we will be interrupted if I attempt to speak with you inside."

"My lord—. I can ensure that we will not be interrupted."

He doubted it, but he followed her in.

Reynolds met them, his expression wooden. "Miss Sourantine, Lord Hargreaves left this card for you, but he refused to leave a message."

Giles grinned at her, as if no ill ease existed between them. "I couldn't possibly manage quill and ink on the doorstep. Besides, a simple message would be inadequate when we have so much to say."

Josette smiled slightly. "We can talk in the library."

"Madame," the butler intervened, "has asked repeatedly for you, Miss."

"I will go up in a moment, Reynolds."

"She is most insistent, Miss. She ordered that you come up immediately upon your return. She says she has taken ill."

Josette hesitated. Giles leaned toward her. "Our first interruption. Should I wait?"

"If she thinks herself ill, I may be hours. Celeste can be very— demanding."

He had given her the truth. He had proposed another conversation and named its difficulty. He had constructed several blocks to build a wall against her sister-in-law. He needed to step back now and let her realize that other blocks already existed. Giles took her gloved hand and bowed over it. "Then I will see you tomorrow evening. You will remember everything I've said? Every time you look at the roses, you will remember?"

"Yes, my lord."

"Miss, it would be best if Madame waited no longer. She was most adamant."

"Tell her I am coming, Reynolds. Until tomorrow night, Lord

Hargreaves."

Her use of the courtesy title no longer seemed to be used to create distance. He watched her climb the stairs, listening to the murmured comments of the butler. A maid appeared, and Josette gave the roses over to the woman with a soft comment. She glanced over the banister to see him still below, watching. He bowed slightly. She smiled, then her mouth tightened, and she turned back to Reynolds.

As the liveried footman ushered him out, Giles prayed that he'd laid sufficient groundwork. Last evening he'd burned all bridges to Celeste. If Josette turned against him, then he had also burned any chance to watch the household and determine who stole the information for the French spy.

.~.~.~.

Josette cautiously entered Celeste's bedroom, glad to notice that the maid had left it darkened. The blue-and-gold decorations that her sister-in-law had chosen offended her eyes.

Celeste propped against the headboard, trying to look fragile even though her cheeks were flushed with health. "La," she said weakly, "you come. At last. *Allez-vous-en*, Reilly."

Josette drew a chair closer to the bed. "Reynolds said you felt ill."

"He told to me that you had gone driving with Lord Hargreaves. You entertain yourself while I have this malaise. You care nothing for your *pauvre belle-soeur*."

"Did your illness come before or after he told you that?"

"Pah! You know that I did not feel well this morning. It is the reason for my refusal to attend the church with you and Albert."

"You often refuse to attend church, Celeste."

Her pretty lips pouted. "You are not being very kind to me."

"Shall I fetch you some broth and a tisane?"

She rolled her head and plucked at the covers. "I should have gone with you. Then I could have forestalled your foolish drive with Lord Hargreaves."

"We did not drive long. It was too cold."

"But you listened to his pretty words, is it not so? You smiled at him and giggled at his little flatteries, yes?"

"Not quite, Celeste. He does not really pay me the empty compliments that so many of your beaux think will win your heart."

She pushed her hands through her tousled red hair. "I told you about him, *ma petite enfant*. I told you. I told you that he is using you. I said—."

"He said that you were the one who claimed I was involved with Mr. Kennit."

"He twists my words! He lies to you, *ma belle-soeur*."

Josette stood. She walked over to the window and looked out over the November garden, barren and cold. "Lord Hargreaves did not lie about the posies, Celeste; you did. As you have lied on other occasions."

"This—I do not lie about this. He has persuaded you that in you he is *très intéressent. Il est un libertin. Robert dit—*."

Whenever Celeste stayed in French, Josette knew she was very agitated. Arms folded, she turned away from the window. "*M.* LeBrun said what you ordered him to say. He also said that, if I were unavailable for the rest of the evening, Lord Hargreaves would lose interest, that I would never see him again. I acquiesced to your command, Celeste. I danced with LeBrun and Claude Thierry and a half-dozen of your swains. I tested your theory. Yet today, here he is."

"Robert misjudged him. He is still a rake and an inappropriate partner for you."

She laughed. "But I can partner Tobias Kennit for weeks on end? Perhaps you should have heard what my other partners for last evening thought of him. Mr. Eaton approves, as does Mr. Davenport our host. And several others. *Rake* is not Lord Hargreaves' reputation."

"Not in London, no."

"Have you information about his behavior on the continent? *M.* LeBrun hinted that Hargreaves learned to flatter women when he served in Portugal, but he had no evidence that he would share with me. Have you, Celeste?"

"How would I have evidence from the continent? France closed its doors to the Nemours. But, *moi, je suis un homma pour ses actes*. See you how he is with us two. He flirts with me, then he changes his interest to you. For what cause? For what reason?"

Josette would have repeated her argument to LeBrun, but she refused to. Celeste's narrowed eyes and drawn mouth, her clawed fingers clutching the bed linens, all revealed her temper. She could not believe that her sister-in-law was so angered by a beau's rejection, even one so highly placed as Giles Hargreaves. He wasn't wealthy like Rafe Lockhart. His title was courtesy only; his brother would inherit title and estate. She had other suitors more highly ranked than Giles. Something else had to be driving Celeste; she seemed almost to hate him.

"Why are you so against him, Celeste?"

"I do not trust him."

"Why not?"

"How can I say? I know, I just know." She threw back the covers and slid from the bed. "I will not have you hurt, *ma belle-soeur*. I told this to Hargreaves, I told him last evening, you are in my care. I must watch over you and guard your reputation. I warned him off. And he laughed at me. At me!"

"Did he say that he wanted to kiss me?"

"*Oui*, he said that! *À moi!* And he dares to come today—." She faltered and stole a look at her sister-in-law.

And Josette did not realize she made the wrong play when she kept her face devoid of expression. "He came today to discover what lies you told to me. As you lied about the flowers he sent." Tempting Celeste's anger, she added, "He brought me roses today."

"*Imbecile!*" She stamped her foot. "I warn you about him, and you jump into a curricle with him. He will ruin you."

"As you told him that Tobias Kennit already had."

Celeste launched into rapid French. Josette endured the tirade, refusing to respond either to her snapped questions or her detestable accusations. At last her sister-in-law stopped and drew a deep breath. She hoped Celeste was gauging the effect of her angry outburst. Then the blue eyes that had won hearts closed. Celeste dropped into a chair. She covered her face. "*Allez-vous-en. Tu est imbecile. Je suis agacant. Allez-vous-en!*"

Josette quietly rang for the maid then left.

When Reilly appeared, she said, "Mulled wine, I think. And take her that bolt of yellow silk I found at the drapers last Tuesday. Say the drapers sent it over, that they thought of her when they saw it. That may distract her. Do not mention me."

Later, much later, she saw Reilly hand notes to the footman for delivery. She called the maid to her. "Has Madame calmed?"

"Yes, Miss."

"She has written a letter?"

"Two letters, Miss. Mr. LeBrun will receive one of them. I do not know the other man, Miss. I must return to Madame."

"Of course, Reilly."

She closed her book and continued upstairs to her room. Who was the other man to whom Celeste had written? Was he an *émigré* as LeBrun was? Surely LeBrun and the other man were not that close to her? Josette understood why her sister-in-law would refuse to speak any further with her. Yet why did she not reach out to her own family when she was so upset?

Was Celeste still upset by the housekeeper Mrs. Bridgerton's insistence that she deal with the various bills that had been re-presented on Saturday? And Josette had not helped matters, questioning where her sister-in-law was getting the money to fund the salons.

"The management of this house is my business," she had snapped.

Josette had tried to speak calmly and reasonably. She wanted to support Mrs. Bridgerton, not undermine her efforts to settle the bills.

"Yes, I know."

"You agreed, when you and Albert arrived, that you would not interfere with my management. You agreed that you would not question my decisions about the house."

"Yes, I did agree, Celeste, but the money for the salons ... ."

"I do not see you refusing to participate in the salons."

She did not mention that she had never liked the salons. That would start a different argument, and she had to convince Celeste to deal with this matter of the bills. "You need not have two salons a week. And there are other means to economize."

"Do not interfere, Josette."

She bit her lip and intended to drop the matter. Yet she could easily envision Grandfather Newland's wrath when the collectors bypassed Celeste and presented him with exorbitant bills. She remembered an earlier tirade of his, exploded over the head of one of his mill managers when the man had been skimming from the employees. Grandpapa had no special love for his granddaughter-in-law. He had been glad when she left the house a few months after Edmund's death. When she wrote asking that the London house be re-opened for her residence, he had groused, but he had allowed her to reside there, with the caveat that she remember it belonged to him. He had predicted that she would soon run into debt.

In four years Celeste had managed to keep her debts at a reasonable level, and Grandpapa had paid a few minor bills with only a little grumbling to his grandchildren. His grumbling over these bills would not be minor. The salons, begun the Spring before last, were generating such debt that Josette—used to the management of the York house and the country estate—had never seen such numbers.

Perhaps her sister-in-law did not understand how angry Grandpapa would be at such waste. She tried another warning. "Grandpapa will not be pleased with your expenditures, Celeste. These are—well, they are extraordinary. I have never seen such numbers."

"What is that to me?"

"He might threaten to cut off your allowance. You are Edmund's widow only; you have no child he must provide for. He might feel that your parents should resume your support."

"Your grandpapa will not be called to pay these bills. I have the funds to cover them."

"You do? From your widow's portion? Celeste, these debts would decimate that fund. I know it is not that large. Unless you have another source? Do you have another income?"

"You dare to question my finances!"

"I just want to know how you are going to pay for these bills."

"That is none of your business," she had cried. She began to rant about all the slights she had received from the Sourantine family, both when Edmund was alive and after his death. "I came back to London, here where I am alone, with no one who cares for me, no one to help me, because *M.* Newland does not want me in his house. He blames me—me!—for Edmund's death. I know it!"

Josette stood quietly during the tirade. When her sister-in-law finally flounced from the room, she felt drained of all energy. Eventually she had gathered up the bills that Celeste had thrown to the floor and returned them to the housekeeper.

"What am I to do with these, Miss?"

"My sister-in-law says that she will cover these debts, Mrs. Bridgerton. She reminds me that she is in possession of this house and that my brother and myself are mere visitors."

The housekeeper took the bills with a frown. She primmed her mouth as she placed them on her desk. "Madame has not paid anything on these bills in three months, Miss. She may order all the supplies she wishes, but the purveyors will refuse to provide them if something is not paid."

"You must tell her that. At her behest I must have nothing to do with the management of the house."

"You are Mr. Newland's granddaughter, not she."

"I do not think it would be wise to use that point with her, Mrs. Bridgerton. If the bills are not paid before Christmas, you must write to my grandfather."

"He won't be pleased, Miss."

"Yes, I informed her of that. She says that she will pay the bills from a personal fund."

"Very well, Miss."

Josette had returned above stairs to dress for the salon.

That was over ten days ago. Mrs. Bridgerton had relayed yesterday that the bills remained unpaid, but Madame had promised to pay them soon. And Josette continued to wonder where Celeste would find the money to cover such astounding debts.

Chapter 8 ~ Monday, November 25

"Good evening, Reynolds."

"My lord Hargreaves." The butler motioned to a footman to take Giles' cloak.

"I see that I am not forbidden the house."

"We have an open door for the salons, my lord."

"Or Mdm. Sourantine would have closed it to me?"

"Miss Sourantine would not allow that."

The words revealed Reynolds' loyalty. Would the other servants follow, or were some of them more loyal to the French spy than to the Sourantine family?

Squaring his broad shoulders, he entered the drawing room. His greater height enabled him to find his hostess, surrounded by her admirers. Social rules dictated his first courtesy be to her. As Giles worked through the crowd, he reckoned he would stand on the edge of her court a long while before she deigned to notice him.

On the outer fringe of the cluster of eager swains stood Lucas Armitage. He lifted a quizzical brow at the young man. "Joining the court?"

"Not I," he denied with a wide grin. "Waiting for my friends to get bored. The beauty awards only an occasional notice. Costell's already given it up."

"Is he bound for the card room?"

"Yes. He hopes to partner Miss Sourantine. He says he's lucky with her."

Giles grinned at Armitage's words, for they supported Josette's claim that she had not fleeced the young lord. "And your hopes for the evening?"

"To cut Malbury out with the lovely Miss Lockhart." He nodded to the formed set.

By dent of a previous introduction, Giles knew Richard Malbury. The young gentleman turned the lovely Miss Lockhart through their part of the quadrille. Her wide smile and dark eyes revealed her joy in the evening. As she waited for their next steps, she stood on tiptoe and waved at someone across the room. Then she resumed the dance without missing a step.

"An ingénue."

"Refreshing, ain't it?" Lucas said.

"And who is this lovely Miss Lockhart?"

"Daughter of Rafe Lockhart. Financier or something like. Newly married. The Davenports' party last Saturday was given in the new Mrs. Lockhart's honor."

"I remember. Is the charming step-mother here?"

"Card room, I think. No, there she is, suffering through Silly Wilton's conversation. Are we on for tomorrow? Michael has a new set of pistols, but he won't let me try them. Says the master should go first."

"I am flattered that he thinks so highly of my skills."

"Lord Hargreaves!"

Celeste had deigned to notice him. Giles turned inward to the court. The spy had extended her hand in welcome. Obediently he stepped forward and bowed over it. "Mdm. Sourantine, I see you are blooming after yesterday's illness."

Her eyes glinted. Most men would have called that light a sparkle, but he knew the venom that the spy could pour out. "I am grateful that you attend my salons twice in a row. Does no message again call you to Grasmere?"

"No message, Madame. I am free to follow my own choosing."

"Your parents are well?" She languidly plied her fan. "And their guests? The earl of Dombley and his family? Especially his two daughters?"

"I left them all well. I would not miss another salon. I enjoy the card play too much."

Her fan snapped shut. Those beautiful eyes narrowed. "You enjoy the cards because you are not capable of the dancing?" she sniped.

Ah, he had truly angered her. As an accomplished flirt, she knew better than to let her swains see any malice. Rather than risk increasing her anger, Giles merely lifted his cane as a response. He started to retreat, but again she spoke directly to him.

"We are thin of company tonight, my lord. I often think I should leave off this Monday reception." Her admirers chimed out a chorus of protests. He did not join in. And she marked it. Her color heightened. Her eyes glittered. Her thin smile, however, did not change.

Giles returned that smile, matching it in lack of friendliness. The more on edge she was, the greater the chance that she would reveal something incriminating, something he or the Armitage brothers or Sir Roger or even Lady Eaton might hear, something that might guide them to her White Hall informant. So he let Clarence Wilton give the speech that her twice-weekly salons were *de rigueur*. He let the other pups crowd in to protest that they never missed a salon. Soon he was back on the fringes, even though he hadn't taken a step, and he considered his duty to his hostess performed.

He recognized a few people as he maneuvered back to the door. Years on the Peninsula had limited his friendships to the military, but he stopped to talk briefly with John Davenport, standing with Jasper Eaton. He saw Edward Garland lead out Mrs. Lockhart. Beside them in the set, Lucas Armitage joined hands with the blushing Miss Lockhart.

Sir Roger accosted him before he reached his goal. The spycatcher wore red with a blue waistcoat. With the white dinner breeches, he looked a version of the Union Jack. "I saw you conversing with our charming hostess. She seemed pleased with your attention, all smiles and the press of your hand. Haven't been distracted, have you?"

Giles grinned. "Not I. You witnessed a performance fit for the Drury Lane boards. Had you been closer, you would have seen the daggers in her eyes. I'm certain she would rather have me chained in a dungeon than admitted to the house."

"A falling out?"

"That's a rather mild expression for our heated argument at the Davenports', sir. That bridge is well burned, in case you might ever assume it could be re-crossed."

Sir Roger compressed his straight mouth. He gave Giles a curt nod then led him out of the drawing room and to the reception hall. There he stopped. Keeping his voice low, he admitted, "I should have expected it, when two sisters are courted by the same man. You *do* still have an entrée through the sister-in-law?"

"She is cautious."

"That surprises me. Most gamesters aren't."

"She's no gamester, but I feel like one. You should wish me luck, sir. I have a difficult *tete-a-tete* with her tonight."

"Difficult how?"

Giles shrugged. "Thank our hostess. On Saturday she raised certain insinuations about her *belle-soeur* that I must have answered—if you wish me to continue the pursuit."

"We need you in that house. What is it? Gossip about her and Kennit? Can you not ignore it?"

He didn't tell Sir Roger that, in the last twenty-four hours, he had discovered it imperative to learn the truth. Nor had he examined why. He only admitted to himself that he didn't want to play with the fire of their attraction if he didn't know the truth. "Do you want this to appear a serious courtship?"

"That would be best."

"Then I shouldn't ignore the gossip. Wish me luck, sir."

"Luck has nothing to do with a well-played hand."

"Ah, but I'm not certain of my cards, Sir Roger."

He tugged on his yellow waistcoat, gripped his cane, and walked to the card room, ready to begin a difficult maneuver over rough ground.

He would never make a spy who built a life on lies.

But he hoped to catch one—even if he burned a few fingers.

Lady Eaton had claimed the table closest to the door and was engrossed in play with Claude Terry and a couple he had not yet met.

Derwent Wilton waved to him, indicating the empty seat at his table. As Giles threaded across, he looked toward Josette's usual table near the terrace door. Tonight she was gowned in pale green silk. She partnered with Costell against Kennit and an older man. Musgrove lounged nearby, talking desultorily with Robert LeBrun.

"Lord Hargreaves," Wilton said a little loudly, "well met. You know my wife? And your partner is Oliver Stanbrough."

He bowed to Sylvia Wilton then looked across to the man who would be his partner. Pouches under the man's eyes revealed he was a heavy drinker. A flame-haired footman stepped forward to refill his glass; the others had only sipped at their wine.

Giles didn't need a long game to divine the limits of his tablemates' skills. Within a handful of tricks, he knew he could play with only a corner of his mind. The rest he devoted to watching Josette and her tablemates.

She had boasted that she kept Costell from losing great sums. She had claimed that she didn't cheat. He watched their game through three rubbers, unable to see the turn of cards and determine how she managed the game. The coins before Costell went up and down then recovered. Surely Josette could not control the fall of the cards without help. Kennit? Would the rake allow a young woman to manipulate him into losing? The elderly stranger? Her glances, her smiles, all were open. She gave the three men equal attention, hiding nothing except her cards and her thoughts.

"Distracted, Hargreaves?" Wilton asked as he gathered up the trick.

"Who is the older gentleman who partners with Kennit against Miss Sourantine and Lord Costell? He looks familiar."

"Lord Wynstane," Mrs. Wilton answered.

Derry Wilton did not hide his smug smile. "Musgrove wasn't pleased to find his seat taken. Arrived late. Unusual for him. He's a man who lives by the tick of the clock."

Giles ignored the bid for a conversation about Gordon Musgrove. "Lord Wynstane? Of Chalmsford? Ah, I thought I recognized him. I met him long ago, before I bought my commission. He had a good stable then. Has he kept it up? I'm in need of a hunter."

"He closed his stable about ten years ago. Had to," Wilton added. "Money ran close."

"A shame. Perhaps he can direct me to a good horse dealer. I must ask him."

Josette's gaze lifted from her cards. She looked directly at him. She didn't smile. Her gaze didn't waver as Lord Wynstane sorted through his cards. Only when he finally played did her gaze drop. That gaze was the only one she allowed herself. She had schooled herself well. What did that single look mean? Had she designed it to lure him, or had she returned to ambivalence?

He had to speak with her, privately. And their *tete-a-tete* must happen before supper. After that, Josette must join forces with her sister-in-law in the drawing room. The hour for supper rapidly approached. Giles reckoned her table was halfway through a rubber. He sped up his table's game, prodding Stanbrough to make quicker decisions. The Wiltons easily fell in with his pace. He won the last hand. He pushed back his cards while he thanked them all for the game. As he rose from the table, he swept up the coins he'd won. At the corner table Lord Wynstane gathered up the last trick. Giles reached their table as Kennit finished the tally.

"Have you won again, Miss Sourantine?"

She looked at Kennit. "Did we?" He nodded and began stacking the cards.

"The last trick but one, that won it for us. When I played the knave," Costell boasted. "Glad I played the nine earlier and saved the game."

"Brilliant strategy," Kennit drawled. He shoved over several guineas.

Lord Wynstane had drawn out his purse and counted out a handful of guineas. "I shall have to send the remainder to you on the morrow, Miss Sourantine."

"My lord, there is no need."

The elderly man looked pained. "It is a debt of honor, Miss Sourantine. You may depend on me. And you, Lord Costell, what is your direction?" Receiving it, he rose from the table. With obvious effort he straightened his spine. "I believe I shall find it safer with the dowagers. Good evening, Miss Sourantine, gentlemen."

"My lord, I shall expect a dance after the supper."

His polite smile did not displace his furrowed brow. "I shall be pleased to oblige you, dear lady." He bowed. Musgrove slipped into the empty seat before Giles could claim it.

Before Wynstane had left the room, Costell spoke. "He shouldn't play if his pockets aren't deep enough."

Josette shot him a dagger-glance. "You should not have raised the bets, especially after we had declared."

"Makes it more interesting," the cub said.

She compressed her lips. Lifting her hand, she smoothed away her frown.

Kennit leaned back and played with the tally sheet. "You can't have it all your way, Josette. Either Wynstane wins or Costell, not both. Those who play must be prepared to pay."

"You know he——." She bit back the rest of it.

Costell reached across and shifted the deck of cards from Kennit to her. "Your deal."

"No, gentlemen, you must excuse me. I fear I am quite played out." She picked up the gloves across her lap. Her gaze lifted to Giles for only the second time. "Here is Lord Hargreaves. I am certain he wishes to play."

"Not tonight, forgive me," and he bowed to remove any perceived snub. "I am here to convince Miss Sourantine to take a stroll with me— since I cannot partner her for any of the dances after supper."

Josette paused in the midst of drawing on her gloves. "Perhaps *M. LeBrun?*" She twisted around, offering a strained smile with her appeal. "Will you take my place, sir?"

He hesitated. Giles guessed that Celeste had ordered the man to intervene should any contact between Josette and Giles loom. Civility, however, had caught him, just as it had Josette. He bowed stiffly.

The table newly arranged, Josette stood. Giles stepped forward. After a brief hesitation, she took his proffered arm and let him lead her from the card room.

He guided her away from the crowded salons. Her willingness to turn away revealed her reluctance to let her sister-in-law see them once more in close conversation. "The terrace?" he suggested.

"Too cold."

The settee still resided in its hidden place behind the stairwell. He stood while she sat, her gaze pinned to the reticule she clutched. A mere two feet, the distance between them felt like an ocean.

Bracing both hands on his cane, he leaned forward. "You puzzle me, Miss Sourantine. I feel my painting of you has pieces missing, and I am determined to find them all."

"I puzzle you?" She inhaled deeply. Her light blue eyes lifted. "What do you expect of me, Lord Hargreaves? I would have that clear between us."

"What do you think I expect?"

"I will not have an *affaire* with you."

Ah, her sister-in-law's insinuations still rankled. In the hours since their brief drive, the spy must have added more slanderous innuendoes. Or had a repetition of her previous insinuations been enough? "As you had an *affaire*, according to your dearest *belle-soeur*," he uttered the French appellation with heavy sarcasm, "with Kennit. And Musgrove. Has she repeated that gossip to you?"

"Gossip? You call it that?"

"What would you call it? I say *gossip* because I do not believe it is true. I do not believe that of you. Nor am I pursuing you for a brief *affaire*. Have our conversations not conveyed that? You interest me, Miss Sourantine. I want to know you, the mind of you, the heart of you. I am here, at this salon, for no other reason except you." The practiced speech came out as smoothly as he had hoped.

Josette sat upright, her spine not touching the settee. She twisted the little straps of her embroidered reticule. "A pretty speech, Lord Hargreaves. You flatter me with both your attention and words. You should be careful with such compliments. They might be construed as a declaration. They can go to a naïve girl's head."

In the drawing room the music resumed.

With easy sincerity Giles vowed, "I would rather my words went to her heart."

Her laugh sounded brittle. "You are flying rather close to the mark. Anyone who overheard us will not believe this is only our fifth meeting, my lord. I can scarcely believe it."

Giles had to smile at her refusal to be flattered, yet he wondered at her pragmatism. Who had set her romantic dreams to full flight? He joined her on the settee, sitting so closely that his shoulder brushed hers.

She tried to look away, but the darkness beyond the glass defeated her. She retreated back to twisting the velvet strings of her reticule. Then, as if drawn by a magnet, her cornflower eyes lifted to meet his intent gaze.

Softly, his lowered voice increasing the semblance of intimacy, he asked, "Have you ever before met someone with whom you had an instant connection, Miss Sourantine? I discovered that, with you, at our first meeting. We are well-matched for card-playing, are we not? I am certain that we could play other games just as well."

She trembled. Her lashes dropped. Her cheeks flushed. He watched the rise and fall of her creamy skin as she tried to control her erratic breath. He noted each sign of her flustered state, signs which did not add up to the response an experienced flirt would give to his provocative remark.

Then Josette's lashes lifted, revealing the sea-change of her eyes, now more grey than blue. Her cheeks were still pinked, but she managed a mournful tone that carried an ironic edge. "I would not best you for some time at any game, my lord. I believe we should continue only with whist."

The music and voices in the salons seemed far from their secluded seat. "It is more exciting, more dangerous to explore new things."

"Not if I will lose."

"Where is your spirit of adventure, Miss Sourantine? Aren't you your father's daughter? You like to win. Who does not? Yet you also enjoy adding a bit of risk when you play. With Costell as partner, you are certainly not playing to win."

"I explained that. Lord Costell is my brother's friend."

"Or is the reason you partner with him that he is one of Celeste's beaux?"

He felt her stiffen. In a blink her yielding vanished. She shifted to lean away from him, pressing against the settee's upholstered arm. "Celeste does not need me to protect her admirers." Her voice hardened. "I do not lie to you, Lord Hargreaves. I have never lied to you."

Chapter 9 ~ Monday, November 25

Giles believed her. He didn't know why. He didn't know how Josette would answer the harder questions still to come. He didn't even know the direction this conversation would travel after that—if at all. He simply had to follow the path he had marked out, had to pursue it until her answers satisfied him. The music, the talk and laughter, everything in the salons, everything they represented was unimportant. This conversation, this single moment was extremely important.

"Do you consider yourself well-matched to Kennit and Musgrove? You are always in their company. I never see you with women."

"You see me only in the *petite salon*, my lord, and women of my age are rarely addicted to card play. And you never remain after the supper. The Davenports' was the first time I have seen you in a room where people are dancing. Do you miss it so much?"

Shot at him so quickly, the question pierced his guard. He had to take a deep breath before he could respond, and even then he avoided answering it. Instead, he returned to his marked-out path. "Have you no women friends? Or do you view them, as your sister-in-law does, as competition?"

"I do have," she retorted, "but I am hampered here in London. The women here who are of my age are married and think only of their babies. My greatest friend is Melinda Ratcliffe. Her father is the vicar in Little Houghton."

Giles had no immediate response. He continued to watch her, until she shifted uncomfortably. "I cannot figure you out," he repeated.

"I do not understand why you are so puzzled."

He propped an elbow on the settee's back. "The night we met, you played with such *éclat* that I deemed you a Captain Sharp." He ignored her gasp of outrage. "But Kennit wouldn't play if you cheated—unless he gambled for more than money. His keeping of your coins seemed to confirm that assumption. Yet how then do I explain Musgrove? He is courting you assiduously, and he would not take Kennit's leavings."

"Sir, I am neither a cheat nor a light muslin!"

"Then you declare you helped that cub Costell win back most of his losses. He's an obvious duffer, yet he wins when partnered with you. I cannot determine how you do it, Miss Sourantine. No one can be so brilliant a player."

"Thus, my lord, I am again a Captain Sharp."

"How can you be while Kennit continues to play? Unless—."

"It is an endless whorl," she said with a bitter edge, "that only circles upon itself."

He grinned. She blinked, for his wide smile was not how most would have countered her controlled indignation. "You see my dilemma. I begin to think you have somehow enlisted Kennit or Musgrove or both to help you manipulate the game."

"My lord," she admonished, "we play against each other. It would be dishonest to assist each other against our own partners."

"I know this. My dilemma only increases. Rake that he is, Kennit still would not involve himself in dishonorable play. You have assured me that the play here is honorable. And what is the point? Is it some campaign to ensnare Costell? Yet why would you ensnare Costell?"

"For his beautiful eyes?"

"Won't do, Miss Sourantine. He's not your admirer. You treat him like a little brother, not a potential suitor. And how would you enlist Kennit and Musgrove?"

"With *my* beautiful eyes? Am I again a light muslin?"

He stretched out his aching leg. He looked up again with a wide grin. "A jade."

She inhaled sharply. Her voice hardened. "Ah, your riddle is solved, my lord."

A woman's rippling laugh resounded along the tiled hall. The intruding sound reminded Giles how fragile their intimacy was. It could be so easily broken, by other guests, by his probing questions.

Josette leaned forward as if to leave. He caught her arm. She glanced at his hand then looked up, her changing eyes narrowed. She said nothing, just waited for him to release her.

He didn't. Not wanting to bruise her, he relaxed his grip, but he dared not release her. He had barely started his questions—all of them necessary. He had to be interested in her, clearly interested, if his mission were to succeed. A mock courtship this might be, yet he could not play his intended role with society's gossip unanswered.

He softened his voice to counter the hardness of hers. "My riddle is far from solved, Miss Sourantine. I would have solved it Saturday or Sunday, but your gracious *belle-soeur* interrupted us."

"You think I am a puzzle, a light muslin, a Captain Sharp, and a—a jade!" Her words rang, evidence of how he had hurt her with them. "I do not know which is worse. And I am amazed, my lord, that you seek me out again tonight. Or does my sullied character attract you?"

"Haven't you confessed to me that you tell no lies? I find myself believing you, believing everything you tell me."

"Against your will, I am certain."

"No," he countered, "I am no young cub to be gulled by an attractive flirt. I am no starry-eyed youth. I've been about the world, Miss Sourantine. I've seen tricksters and frauds, liars and *demi-mondes*. You are not one of these. Not a light muslin or a Captain Sharp or a jade. But definitely a mystery." Her lips parted. She sank against the upholstered back. Giles slipped his hand down her arm and possessed her hand, covered in dark green silk. He threaded his fingers between her long tapered ones. "I remain very interested in you."

She looked at their clasped hands. When her pale eyes lifted, tears had drowned their slaty blue. Yet her mouth tightened. "Whose jade am I, my lord? Surely you need an answer to that question. Am I Kennit's or Musgrove's? Or both?"

Giles shifted, closing the distance. "Musgrove is territorial."

She tugged her hand, but he didn't release it. Harshly she reminded, "He won't take Kennit's leavings."

"He doesn't like the way you coddle Costell. I saw that the other evening, muttering his displeasure. That's more emotion than he usually displays."

"Unfair, sir."

Giles ignored her interjection. "Now, Kennit is a rake. If you're his, the whole world would know. He'd announce it himself—but he soon tires of his light muslins."

"Perhaps he has already tired of me."

"Then he wouldn't offer to leave the card room and dance with you."

She leaned away. A flush burned her cheeks. "Which is it, my lord? His jade or not?"

Releasing her hand, he shifted abruptly. He crossed his good leg over his weakened one, blocking her in with his booted calf. He draped an arm along the settee behind her. Josette sat utterly still. Only her flickering lashes and flushed cheeks betrayed that she was not a cold statue. Still angry, he judged. Not so angry that she would slap his face or stalk away. Angry enough to tell him the truth, to be eager to prove him wrong.

He pitched his voice lower, for her only. The noise flooding into the hall drowned everything else. Only his words came clearly. "I watched you tonight. You played a third kind of game, not the direct skill you exhibited to me that first night, not the brilliance that protected Costell the other night. I think tonight I saw your usual game."

"Did you? From so far across the room? How do you judge me now?"

"You are not what I expected."

"Oh." She feigned regret. "I am back to being a puzzle. Jade was more exciting."

He laughed. Her tears had vanished. Her pale eyes now glittered dangerously. "Ah, Miss Sourantine, you said you did not like to explore dangerous territory."

"Is being a jade dangerous?"

For answer, he lifted her gloved hand to his mouth. He kissed her palm through the green silk. Her eyes changed, brightened, a clearer blue than he'd ever seen. "Very dangerous, Josette, more dangerous than you know."

"Am I to become your jade, Lord Hargreaves?"

Whatever his answer, she was still angry enough to take the opposite course. He placed her hand over his heart. "What is your relationship to Kennit? Celeste claims you are his jade."

"We are only friends," she snapped. Then her eyes narrowed, her pretty mouth twisted, and Giles knew she had realized too late that she should have lied.

"You cannot be friends with a rake like Kennit."

He expected her to spin out some lie. A spy would. Her hand jerked in his. She pushed it against his chest, as if to hold him off. Then Josette surprised him anew. Tears again pooled in her blue eyes.

"I do not understand you. You question me until I am angry, but you do not seem angry with me. You say you know these—these insinuations are only gossip, but I cannot tell—. Then you touch—and kiss my hand as if—. I do not understand you." A tear slipped onto her cheek.

Giles released her hand and caught the teardrop with his thumb. He cupped her cheek. "I don't quite understand myself, Josette Sourantine."

"We should—should return to the salon."

"We should," he agreed. His thumb grazed over her soft skin. Her hand pressed against his yellow waistcoat, as if she tried to capture his heartbeat. Her remarkable eyes searched his. Her breath was again erratic. Giles leaned toward her, and her lashes fluttered down.

A loud voice, clearer than any other, broke the illusion of intimacy.

He released her. He leaned back, uncrossed his leg so he no longer blocked her. Josette caught her breath, gave herself a shake, then surged to her feet. She tugged at her dress, at the shawl slipping down her arms, at her gloves, as if she tried to settle her world as she straightened the fabrics. The hand he'd kissed she pressed to her midriff. She stumbled a few steps then stopped and looked back.

"I am no great mystery, Lord Hargreaves. I am not ... those other things either."

He stood and bowed. "I do believe you, Miss Sourantine."

She walked away, her slippers soft on the tiles. The staircase quickly hid her.

Giles chose not to follow and resumed his seat. He had his answers, not in direct words but in her eyes, in her tears. The kind of answer that Sir Roger would not accept. But he did.

And he began to wonder at the spycatcher's plan, ordering Giles to cast aside a budding flirtation with the French spy to focus on her sister-in-law. The older man had anticipated no difficulties with such switched affections. He had only anticipated a woman's glee at winning a march over Celeste. Sir Roger didn't understand Josette at all. Celeste now, he had her pegged neatly to his board.

What had he expected Josette to be? A flirt like her sister-in-law? A gamester?

The signs were there, Giles admitted, but Josette defied those easy classifications.

Footsteps on the angled square tiles heralded someone's approach. Expecting the spy, Giles again stood and leaned on his cane, assuming his most nonchalant guise. The butler's appearance shocked him.

"My lord, will you be leaving now?"

"Hurrying me off, Reynolds?"

The man's wooden mask revealed nothing. "Mdm. Sourantine remains in the *grande salon*, sir."

"I have no desire to seek her out, not even to make my farewells. Did Miss Sourantine return to the card room?"

"No, my lord. She has withdrawn briefly. She informs me that she will join Madame in the *grande salon*, should you care to converse with her."

"I've had my private conversation with Miss Sourantine."

"I am aware of that, sir. If you have finished here—."

If Reynolds were younger or a man of higher rank, his obvious dismissal might have angered Giles. However obliquely the butler expressed his displeasure, Giles felt himself confronting Josette's defender. The man had seen her perturbation and correctly gauged the reason for her retreat upstairs.

"I upset her, didn't I, Reynolds? I didn't intend that—but she has me twisted around."

"Mdm. Sourantine, my lord?"

At the renewed deliberate misunderstanding, Giles scowled. The man needed a dressing down. "No, not madame," he corrected curtly. "*Miss* Sourantine. Miss Josette Sourantine. I should have kissed her."

"I beg your pardon?"

"I wish I had, then we'd both know where we stand. Have my

coach brought round, Reynolds. It's best that I encounter no more temptations from Miss Sourantine tonight."

As Giles left, the butler unbent enough to wish him "good evening". Somehow he had won some points with the man.

The wish to kiss Josette stayed with him the rest of the night.

. ~ . ~ . ~ .

After supper and an obligatory number of dances, including a stately minuet especially requested by Lord Wynstane, Josette retreated to the cooler air. Halfway along the hall she chose a chair and stared at the opposite wall. Brow furrowed, she considered her hour with Lord Giles Hargreaves.

He thinks I *am the mystery*? How could he flirt with her then interrogate her, insult her then hold her hand and kiss it? Her fingers curled into her palm. She could still feel his heated breath through the silk of her glove.

She tried to be angry. *He called me a Captain Sharp! A jade! How dare he!*

Yet they had nearly kissed. Her contrary heart ignored the insults and yearned for him.

"Ah, Miss Sourantine. Snatching a respite?" Lady Eaton, emerging from the card room, had seen her and turned her way rather than continuing to the *grande salon*. "Quite alone?"

Josette stood and curtsied. "Have you enjoyed your evening with us, ma'am?"

The dowager rattled on about her card play, about her desire to partner with Josette against Sir Roger and Lord Hargreaves, about the dancing, about the new Mrs. Lockhart. Josette hardly listened. She finally realized that Lady Eaton was staring at her and sharpened her focus.

"You are distracted, Miss Sourantine. I see your hour with Giles Hargreaves had a definite effect."

"My lady? What do you mean?"

"Lord Hargreaves is a considerable threat to any girl's heart. In my youth I had many a thrilling evening, flirting with my admirers. Now Sir Roger is my only constant swain."

"Lord Hargreaves is not—he and I are not—. He did not flirt with me, ma'am."

"I am an old busybody. Do forgive me. Yet I saw him escort you from the card room. Your *tete-a-tete* lasted almost to supper. Did he not fill your ear with sweet compliments?"

To Josette's horror, tears welled up and spilled over. The dowager looked aghast. Then she reached down and grasped the younger woman's hand. For a second she hesitated then propelled her past the staircase. *Not the settee!* she nearly cried out. Lady Eaton, however, sought complete privacy. She continued past the settee and opened the door to the terrace. Cold air rushed in, but she didn't hesitate. With Josette in tow, she plunged into the night air.

"It is freezing out here." She offered a dainty lace handkerchief. Josette refused it and mopped up with her seriously dampened one.

"I apologize, Lady Eaton. I do not cry generally, I promise."

The dowager glanced into the house then tugged her shawl closer. "If you cried at the least thing, Tobias Kennit would refuse to play cards with you. Do not apologize, my dear. I take it that Giles Hargreaves did not fill your ears with sweet compliments?"

She blushed. "He did do that, but—. He took me to task for—. He called me a jade!"

"Ah. He is normally not so rude. I have found that a man often says the wrong thing when something confuses him. You must have seriously overset his heart."

"His heart? He insulted me!"

"Yes. Men become fools when their heart is troubled. I hazard that Lord Hargreaves was questioning your relationship with Mr. Kennit? I confess, I have often wondered myself. There *seems* nothing untoward in your interactions, but you and he have an easy familiarity. And he does front your coins every time you play cards. And you always play cards together."

"He keeps my winnings each evening, that is all. He does not give me any money."

"Yes," the dowager said mildly, "that is a husband's office."

Viewed through Lady Eaton's eyes, Josette could see the reason society frowned on her convenient use of Kennit's pockets. "If Lord Hargreaves thought I was ... involved with Mr. Kennit, why did he even approach me?"

"Ah, now that speaks to the power of attraction. I trust you had sufficient evidence of his attraction during your hour with him?" She examined Josette's downbent face with an approving eye. "Any kisses?"

Her fingers curled into her palms. "No."

"These young men—the beaux of my day knew how to steal a kiss. Where did he take you? Somewhere private. Surely not out here? It's nearly December."

"We sat in the hallway, underneath the stair. There." She pointed at the settee clearly seen through the window although hidden from the reception area by the stairs.

"Right there? Tsk. Have young men no foresight? You can be interrupted there."

She remembered how close they had been to a kiss. She could still feel the heat emanating from his body, his breath on her lips. A noise *had* interrupted them, and she had escaped, unkissed.

"What else did he take you to task for?"

Josette shivered, beginning to feel the coldness. "He does not like Lord Musgrove."

"That man needs a hoyden to shake up his settled world. What else?"

"He thinks I encourage Lord Costell to gamble."

"So you do. You help him to win."

"Lady Eaton—."

"He should lose in the company of friends, not enemies. He will not always be lured to these salons by his fascination for your sister-in-law."

Josette twisted her damp handkerchief. "I did not consider that."

"I am twice your age and three times your experience in our sad, corrupt world. It offers few sanctuaries for innocents and children."

"Lord Costell will not be happy with the change in his level of play."

"He will learn. And Lord Costell's happiness is not your concern. Perhaps Lord Hargreaves' happiness is?" Lady Eaton patted her arm. "What else did Hargreaves chide you with? The men who cluster around your sister-in-law? The bad *ton* she admits to her salons?"

"Bad *ton*? Who do you mean, ma'am?"

"Robert LeBrun, for one."

"He was an acquaintance of my father's."

"Your father I knew and liked." That information startled Josette. "Robert LeBrun is not your father. In my younger days he was well known as a libertine. He killed a man in a duel and wounded several others. He finally set up with a merry widow and faded from London society. Now he returns. And no one truly forgets, my dear."

"I did not know, Lady Eaton."

"My dear, of course you would not. Your father had no reason to tell you of those scandals. I would not, except that LeBrun has made himself a great companion of *Mdm.* Sourantine. Since his return to society, he is an accepted fixture in this house. He is perhaps another reason that Lord Hargreaves wonders about your relationship with Tobias Kennit."

"Celeste and *M'sieur* LeBrun are not intimates, ma'am!"

"Then he has a different reason to pursue their acquaintance." The dowager did not pat her arm again, but she felt as if the older woman had. "You are a bright child. Be observant; you may discover the reason." Embroidered silk rustled as she linked her arm through

Josette's and guided her back into the house. "Now, I really must leave."

Josette tried to smile. "I should thank you, Lady Eaton."

"I said no more than a few reassuring words, my dear."

"I believe you helped my—my confusion."

"I trust Lord Hargreaves received enough from you to banish his jealousy?"

"Jealousy?"

"My dear, what else but that? Now, it is the time I appointed myself to leave." She surveyed Josette critically. "Much better, I think. And no more crying. Your sister-in-law will take advantage of that. Now, we shall chatter about fashion as you escort me downstairs, and no one shall guess we had to retreat to that cold terrace." She suited words to action and propelled the younger woman toward the grand staircase.

Josette wanted to apologize for her embarrassing tears. She wanted to ask Lady Eaton when she had taken such a close reading of Celeste. The dowager had a pragmatism that saw the world clearly. In a few minutes she had given Josette much food for thought. And the greatest dish she had served was Giles Hargreaves' evident jealousy.

Chapter 10 ~ Tuesday, November 26

Josette rose late, the autumn light flooding into her bedchamber and Lady Eaton's last words about Giles Hargreaves flooding into her mind. She greeted Reilly with more cheer than she usually did after a salon.

Apparently lying in wait for her, the butler appeared as she descended and opened the door to the center room of the enfilade, restored once more to the breakfast parlor. "Good morning, Miss Josette."

"Indeed it's a good morning, Reynolds. Is that not wonderful sunshine? Am I the first this morning, or has Albert beaten me to the eggs and toast?"

"Your brother has not yet left his chamber, Miss. Madame remains in her chamber. Master Albert did wish me to convey to you that he would like a private word this morning."

"Good Heavens, he need not make an appointment. How late did he come in? I know he left with his friends before the salon concluded."

"He returned only a couple of hours after that." He held the square-backed chair for her then crossed to the sideboard to pour hot water into the teapot.

Josette sorted through the letters stacked beside her plate but saw none from Little Houghton. Her grandpapa timed his weekly letter to arrive early in the week. Her friend Melinda, who had the primary care of her little brother and sister while her mother tended her ailing aunt, wrote only in reply. She would barely have received Josette's last missive. Sighing, Josette broke the seal on the top note. Several pound notes fluttered out. "What's this?" She retrieved the ones she could reach then looked for the letter's author. "Oh, that man."

Reynolds placed the banknotes that had fallen to the floor beside her plate.

"These are from Lord Wynstane, to cover the money he lost last evening."

"Does not he often refuse to play cards, Miss?"

"He does. He can afford only the lowest stakes. I did not intend the stakes to increase while he was at table. I thought I had assured him that he need not pay me."

"Lord Wynstane would consider it a debt of honor, Miss Josette."

She scowled at the old-fashioned phrases that closed Lord Wynstane's debt to her. Obviously the letter had not been easy for him to write. "Yes, he would. He follows that gentleman's code to the letter."

"If I may be so bold, may I know who raised the table stakes?"

"Lord Costell."

The butler did not respond. Josette looked up to see his lips pursed, his expression bland. He was most wooden when he was most disapproving.

Jane the kitchenmaid appeared with fresh eggs and toast. Reynolds turned stiffly on his heel and brought back the tea, pouring it into a fragile cup. He placed the marmalade before her then straightened, hands behind his back.

Josette scowled at Lord Wynstane's letter. She liked the elderly man with his courtly manners. His bows were always performed with a flourish. He paid her extravagant compliments. He flirted with the older dowagers. He had only an independence, no great wealth. Last night's losses would pinch his purse for the rest of the quarter. And at Christmas!

As tears welled, the butler cleared his throat. "Shall I have the money returned, Miss?"

"Yes—. Yes, but I must write a note. A carefully worded note. I do not want that dear man's honor hurt. I should have paid more attention to the course of the play last night."

"I have noticed you are not often distracted, Miss. Was there a problem last night that I should be made aware of? A difficulty with the service, perhaps?"

Her tears cleared. She glanced at Reynolds' expressionless face. She dared not share that anticipation had distracted her, that her expectation of another *tete-a-tete* with Giles Hargreaves had had her thoughts flying in all directions. "I should have paid more attention," she repeated. "Mr. Kennit was partnered with my lord Wynstane. I expected them to win."

"Are you not often the winner, Miss?"

"I did not intend to be, not last night, not against Wynstane. But Lord Costell played well, for once. He took the last hand and thus the rubber. I don't suppose I can write to Costell to tell him he must return his winnings? Wynstane will have sent him a similar note, I am sure."

The butler did not deign to answer that foolish question. "I have been in Mr. Newland's employ for over two decades—."

"Are you going to read me a scold, Reynolds?"

"I beg your pardon, Miss."

"No. Say it. God would not have prompted you to say it if I did not need to hear it."

He drew himself taller. "I do not make mock of the good Lord, Miss."

"Nor do I. Say it, Reynolds. I am in a fix with Lord Wynstane, and you must see the sin that caused it. Tell me."

"Only this, Miss Josette, that Mr. Newland would not approve of the house he bought for his daughter, your own mother, Miss, being turned into a gambling den."

"We do not run a gambling den. A simple salon, with good conversation and dancing and a few card games. We do not keep a betting book."

"No, Miss."

"Grandfather knows about the salons."

"Yes, Miss."

"He sent me here, expressly to be part of them, to mix with London society, all in the hopes that I'll *take* this time."

"Yes, Miss."

She tried to outstare him, but Reynolds had mastered the technique years ago. Josette dropped her gaze to her cooling eggs. After several moments, she admitted in a small voice, "We do have gambling."

"Yes, Miss. Shall I have Angus ready to return Lord Wynstane's money this afternoon?"

"Reynolds, you have a sharp distinction of right and wrong."

"Yes, Miss."

"Oh, off with you."

He bowed. She glimpsed his mouth curve into a satisfied smile. He closed the door quietly behind him. At least Reynolds had offered a reason that she could use to return the money to Lord Wynstane. Josette ate her cold eggs as part of her punishment.

She was on a sixth draft of her letter to Lord Wynstane when Albert found her in the library on the ground floor.

"Egad, you are busy. Who are all these notes to?"

"It's an apology. I cannot quite find the words." She laid down her quill and turned to give him her full attention. He sprawled on the daybed, long limbs stretched out, making him appear lankier than he was. He finally had stopped growing only last Spring. "Albert, how would you convince someone to give back the money they've won at cards?"

"Can't be done."

"It's in a good cause."

"Don't even try." He looked at her sharply. "Don't tell me you've been losing."

"I don't lose."

"No, you don't. You choose to let the other gent win."

"Albert—."

"I ain't saying you cheat. Lord, Josette, don't you know I had a reason not to play cards with you or Papa? I ain't in your league."

She recalled Reynolds' words and her own boast to Giles Hargreaves and his comments last evening. He had thought she cheated. He had thought she had enlisted Kennit and Musgrove in her shady play. A Captain Sharp he had called her. And a jade. She had only ever thought it was skill at deciphering her opponents and their hands. Uncanny omniscience, Kennit had once said early in their acquaintance while Musgrove declared she must be the goddess Fortune herself. She had laughed at what she thought was mere compliments. Was it more? Had she honed her skill so much that an observer would think she must cheat to predict the fall of cards so well?

"Albert, do you think it's wrong to gamble?"

"I don't gamble. I only bet on a sure thing."

"Like your horses?"

He laughed, acknowledging the hit. "Stick to Kennit and his sort, Josette, and leave the small fry to grow. They'll get eaten up some time you're not there to protect them from the bigger fish."

She spread her hand over her letter to Lord Wynstane. "You are not the first person to tell me that."

"See, I *can* talk good sense."

She smiled. "My little brother is growing up."

"I am grown up." He sat up and propped his elbows on his knees. "That's why I want to talk to you. I am grown up, Josette. A man. And a man ought to do things, especially when he knows it's something he can do."

"Indeed yes." She laughed. Which young lady had he decided upon? How would he take the suggestion to wait a year? "You have grown into a fine young man."

"You know, Josette, better than anyone, how much I want to do something to stop Napoleon. I can barely tolerate Celeste when she crows about another of his victories. I've decided something." His mouth tightened. Briefly he looked at his clasped hands. Then he glanced up, his gaze steady, his face set. "I've decided to join the Hussars."

Shocked, she glanced down at the half-written letter. She pushed it back and turned fully toward her little brother. "Is that the newest rage?" she asked lightly. "A fortnight ago you wanted a naval command."

He didn't respond. His eyes, so like Papa's, stared back at her.

"Why the Hussars?" This time her tone matched his seriousness.

"I know horses," he said simply. "I can ride better than you play cards. I can shoot."

"And nothing less will content you?"

"I plan to write Grandpapa this week. Will you add your support? He listens to you."

"The Hussars, Albert—. The cavalry, even the light cavalry, is more than an elaborate uniform and parade ground maneuvers."

"I know that!"

She listened to his reasons, agreeing with some, worried over the ones that sounded like an eager schoolboy's. Five years younger than she, still her little brother, but she had to admit he was becoming a man.

When he wound down, she asked, "And your friends? Will they also join the Hussars?"

"No, they're not interested. I decided this for myself, Josette."

That denial struck her. To choose this when his friends did not— Albert must truly want it. "Not Westover? Or Costell? Or Clarence Wilton?"

"Wilton and Costell are only interested in catching Celeste's eye. Westover is trying to convince his father to turn over one of the lesser estates to his management; he has marriage in mind. The younger Wilton girl."

"She's not out yet, is she?"

"He's willing to wait."

Josette looked back at her letter. Her struggles to find the right words to soothe Lord Wynstane's honor seemed hours old. "How do you think Grandpapa will take this, Albert? He still grieves for Edmund."

"I'm not his only male heir. We're not one of the great families to worry about a title to be passed on. I don't even carry his name."

She had often worried that his association with the titled nobility tainted his sense of worth. Or was it Celeste's influence that belittled their family's worth? Albert had watched daily as their sister-in-law weighed her flock of admirers, as she ignored men worthy for themselves alone while she courted the titled and the landed gentry. Old names or illustrious names or moneyed names, only those kept her attention.

"Will you support me with Grandpapa, Josette?"

She hesitated. What could she do to help him realize the sacrifice of his life that he might have to make? Then she remembered Giles Hargreaves. Lady Eaton claimed he was jealous. His attentions bespoke some feeling for her—even though he had thrice insulted her. If he used her only, for some purpose she could not divine—well, she would use him. "I will write to Grandpapa—."

He sprang up and pumped a fist into the air. "Yes!"

"Let me finish, Albert. Please sit down. I will write to Grandpapa, on three conditions."

From *alt* he sank to a dark valley. "Impossible conditions."

"They should not be impossible, Albert. I think they are very reasonable. I will want to meet the commander of this Hussar regiment. I want you to speak with Lord Hargreaves. He was in a line regiment, I believe. I want you to listen to what he says about the realities of war."

"Those are easy. The third?"

"You must visit an army hospital, daily for a week, no less than two hours each time. You must interact with the injured soldiers. Talk with them. Read to them. Write letters for them."

"You are trying to frighten me away from the military."

"Indeed I am. I do not want you to die in war, Albert. You are my little brother. When we are very old and you have white whiskers and gout, I want to look at you and say, 'You are still my little brother'." His hunched shoulders and down-bent head struck her heart, but she could not relent. "Two conversations and seven days of your time. Are these too much to ask? When you have done these three things, we will talk again. If you still wish to join the Hussars, I will support you with Grandpapa Newland. Will you do these?"

He looked up, Papa's eyes very bright in his young face. "I'll do them. When you really want something, no obstacle can stand in your way." The clock on the mantle chimed. He glanced at it then stood. "I must leave now. Westover wants me to visit the Wiltons with him."

"What is the name of the older daughter?" How simple life would be if he had expressed an interest in marriage instead of the military.

"Christina. And no, I am not interested in her. Couldn't live with her laugh. Josette—thanks for listening, for—for taking what I want seriously." He pressed her hands then strode away, already seeing beyond the house, seeing far beyond England's limits.

Josette turned back to her half-written letter. The words blurred. She searched out her handkerchief and wiped her eyes. Her little brother would soon be gone, whether she was ready for him to grow up or not. She certainly was not ready for him to face the terrors of war.

Giles Hargreaves still suffered the lingering effects of his wound. What would he think when Albert approached him to fulfill her request? What if he were not amenable to discussing his experiences? What would she do if he refused? She must tell him first, to ask his help, as a favor. And what favor would he demand in return? A favor that would be the equivalent of re-opening memories he might want to consign to oblivion.

As Josette handed her letter to Angus for delivery to Lord

Wynstane, Celeste descended the grand staircase. She yawned prettily, patting her mouth with her fairy hand. "Your brother is certainly busy this morning. Up and down the stairs three times. He quite woke me up when I needed hours more of sleep."

"Albert wants to join the Hussars."

"*Vraiment*? What a dashing figure he will cut. Ah, but you refused your support with Grandpapa, did you not?" She followed Josette back to the library. "Are you determined that he shall have no fun? You will not let him purchase a racing curricle. You criticize his attendance at the Newmarket Fair and the races. You tell him he will not have your support if he asks his grandpapa for a boat."

"That was a wise refusal." She managed a genuine laugh. *Do I really refuse Albert so much*? "He was seasick when he went out with Richard Malbury."

"You do not wish him to have any fun, Josette. He is a boy. Let him have fun."

"Going to war is not having fun, Celeste. And I do not chain Albert in his room. I try very hard not to play Mother Hen. Only—well, I do not want him to make the same mistakes that Edmund did."

"When he married me?" Tears filled her eyes.

"Oh, dear. I did not mean you, Celeste. I meant when he bought that hunter he could not handle. I have never said—. He was happy with you."

She dabbed her tears with a lacy wisp of cloth. "You blame me, I know you do. I encouraged him to buy that hunter, and it killed him."

"You are not to blame for that. You know I do not blame you. No one does. Edmund knew the risks. He bought that horse, knowing its reputation. He knew the horse was acting up that very morning. The grooms warned him. Grandpapa warned him, often enough, of buying too much horse. He ignored us all. Edmund's death was on his own shoulders, not yours. Have we not told you that often enough?"

The tears magically dried up. Josette watched, fascinated as always, as Celeste tucked away her handkerchief and looked up with eyes unreddened by the tears. Had her crying been real?

No, Josette scolded herself, *that's uncharitable*. Did she not have pricks of conscience enough this morning, with Lord Wynstane and Albert? And also for her too-strong enjoyment of Giles Hargreaves' company? Part of her enjoyed his attentions for her own sake. The petty part of her relished receiving attentions from the man who had abandoned Celeste's court. *There, I am admitting*—but the glee outlasted the stinging guilt.

Celeste sat down in the chair pulled to the writing desk and picked up one of her twisted attempts at a letter. "La, what a number of papers.

Have you been writing to your grandpapa? Do you warn him of the plans of Albert?"

"No, I was not writing to Grandpapa."

"Oh? To whom do you write? I saw you give to Angus the letter. You have had this letter delivered by hand, yes?"

Josette assented but did not share the letter's recipient or its contents. She would not make Lord Wynstane an opportunity for gossip. She collected the twists of paper and dropped them into a basket. Then she held the basket for Celeste, who was untwisting the note. The action gave her sister-in-law pause. She started to resume her investigation, but Josette continued to hold out the basket. With a little shrug, Celeste dropped in the paper unread, and Josette carried the basket to the fireplace.

She had foiled Celeste's reading of the notes, but she knew that would not stop Celeste from speculating about both recipient and contents. Celeste dearly loved to gossip. She had made an art of it, doling out information, holding the best back until it could be spent to her advantage. In the months since Josette's arrival, she had watched her sister-in-law trade gossip, withholding tidbits until they would reap a benefit. She could spin out the tiniest snippet so that it seemed much more than it was. And she could couch the most innocent of information with such insinuation that a swirl of speculation would arise—which she could then sit back and enjoy.

Had that been Celeste's ploy with Lord Hargreaves? Had she planted suspicions in his mind with carefully worded facts? If she still wanted 'the son of a marquis', if she were incensed at his switched attentions ... . Yes, Josette realized, even about her own sister-in-law, Celeste would be capable of shading the truth.

Until the last couple of weeks Josette had admired her *belle-soeur*. What had changed her opinion? She didn't know. Perhaps she had seen too much of Celeste's efficiency that came across as callousness. She abandoned anything and anyone that might prevent her goal of another wealthy husband. How long would Grandfather Newland support her lavish life here in London?

Is this the life that Grandpapa wants me to emulate? He did send me to find a husband. Thus far, only Tobias Kennit and Gordon Musgrove could be construed as prospects. But Kennit was too much the rake and Musgrove too controlled.

And Giles Hargreaves was too puzzling. She almost laughed. He claimed not to understand her. If nothing else, they had confusion in common. Lady Eaton's counsel had given her hopes last night. She had awakened with those hopes, but as the bright day progressed, her hopes seemed more and more incredible.

"You will not tell to me to whom you write? Perhaps it is that I can guess. You write to Lord Hargreaves, yes?"

"No."

"I can always ask Angus."

"Do that." She would first have Reynolds order Angus not to speak about her affaires. She seated herself calmly in a slipper chair next to a window and picked up her embroidery.

"You did have another *tete-a-tete* with Lord Hargreaves last evening, did you not? This becomes quite common, yes? You must greatly enjoy your time with him."

Celeste's voice dripped sugar. Josette had not enjoyed his insults, but she would not share that with her so-sweet *belle-soeur*. "He is an interesting man to talk with. Were you surprised that he did not join your entourage?" she countered. "After all, did you not claim him as '*mon marquis*'?"

"La, last evening so many were pressing about me that I did not know who attended the salon. I only learned of his presence when *M'sieur* Kennit told to me where you had vanished during the supper dance."

She lied, Josette knew, but she didn't pursue it.

"And he was never *mon marquis*. Did he not disappear for nearly a month? All without a word. A beau never vanishes for so long, never."

"You were gone yourself part of that time. To the seaside."

"*Oui, je me souviens*. It is no matter. I knew he did not seriously court me. He is very often rude, do you not find? How long did you talk alone together?"

"Hardly alone. We were in the hall."

"The hall? Yet again the hall?" Her tittering laugh grated on Josette's temper. "Did you tell him your entire life story? That would not take long, would it? I am surprised it took three evenings."

"Only half my life story," she allowed smoothly.

As if she had too much energy to sit still for very long, Celeste jumped up. She walked over to Josette. "You do not need to tell Lord Hargreaves everything. You should not tell any man everything. A little mystery is very alluring." With her French accent drawing out the R's, the words had a cattish purr. "Did you not tell him enough on the first evening? Did you tell him of Grandpapa Newland? Did you tell him of my family?"

"We do not *only* speak of family, Celeste." Her laugh sounded light, thank Heaven. She calmly pulled the needle through and set the next stitch. "But yes, I did speak of Grandpapa and of my father Henri and of your family."

"What did he wish to know?"

"When they came to England. It is natural, in this time of war—."

"*Tiens*! You are a *naïf*. The least thing, the *ton* will turn to scandal. You should not speak of us to Lord Hargreaves."

She nearly laughed at the irony: Celeste the gossip worried about scandal! She continued to work the daisy stitch on the light linen. "The *ton* cannot be worse gossips than the people in Little Houghton. They quickly accepted my papa. And how can your family's arrival during the Reign of Terror become scandalous? If Lord Hargreaves does ask something that is not intrusive, I will answer, Celeste. I have nothing to hide."

"Do you suggest that I have?"

"No, no, no. I suggest nothing." Guilt pricked her. She should have followed her previous behavior, sitting quietly while her sister-in-law had her say.

She felt miserable for hours after, as Celeste's undermining words thrust home. Was there no middle ground?

Reynolds came in, a note on the salver. He bowed. "A letter for you, Miss Sourantine."

Josette set aside her embroidery and took the letter. She could spy nothing in his wooden face. Nor could Celeste. Her sister-in-law laughed harshly as Josette broke the seal. "A reply to your letter, *ma belle-soeur*?"

"Angus has not yet returned, Madame," he droned then quietly removed himself. On the heels of his departure the kitchen maid Jane came in with a coal hod to refresh the fire. She fed the twisted notes into the flames then began to add the coal.

Josette skimmed the closely written lines. "It is from Melinda."

"Who?"

"My friend Melinda Ratcliffe, from Little Houghton. You should remember her, Celeste. The vicar's daughter. She is in London. She is staying with her aunt and uncle. Oh, I have missed talking with her."

Celeste dropped into a wing chair and yawned.

Jane gave a quick curtsey and left.

Josette excused herself. She found Reynolds in the hall. His eyebrows lifted when she asked him to tell Angus not to share any of her business with Mdm. Sourantine, including the letter he delivered this morning. He gave no other sign of surprise.

"Of course, Miss Josette. Does that include the delivery of any flowers?"

"Have any come?"

"No, Miss."

It was stupid to feel deflated. "Yes, I think we should include the delivery of flowers. Thank you, Reynolds."

"Of course, Miss."

Josette climbed the stairs. Her heart lifted with each step. Her friend was here. Level-headed, far-seeing, so sane Melinda. She would tell her about Giles Hargreaves. She would tell her Lady Eaton's counsel. Maybe Melly could help dismiss the niggling doubt that Hargreaves seemed not quite open in his pursuit of her.

Chapter 11 ~ Tuesday, November 26

"He can't possibly hit that," Lucas Armitage declared.

"Wrong, little brother. Didn't Hargreaves' convince you with his first shots?"

"Can't be done," Lucas insisted. "Look at it." The target, a watch suspended on its chain from a tree limb, slowly spun. The sun flashed on its brass back. "It's too far and too small. It's moving too much."

Giles lowered the pistol. "Your confidence inspires me," he said drily.

Michael Armitage laughed. "Shut up for ten seconds, Lucas. He'll prove you wrong.

Giles sighted along the barrel of the dueling pistol. He took a steadying breath, eased the tautness of his arm, slowly squeezed—.

When the powder flash and smoke dissipated, only a chain glinted in the sunlight. Lucas whooped and ran to the target.

"Fine shooting," said a voice behind them.

The men turned. Sir Roger Nazenby stood behind the board covered with the wide variety of pistols they had been testing. He leaned on his swordstick cane, flicked an imaginary speck from his bottle green coat, and smiled as sunnily as the blue sky.

Michael greeted him. "Sir, we did not expect you. Have you stopped at the house?"

"Only to discover your location, although I could have followed the noise. Hargreaves mentioned that you often shoot on Tuesday, but I expected a brace of pheasants, not shattered metal."

Michael grinned. "Would you care to try your hand, sir?"

As Nazenby refused, Giles wondered what the spycatcher wanted. He was far afield from his usual London haunts. Did he want an update on Giles' progress with Josette Sourantine? Or did he have more information about the French spy? Working to keep his expression from revealing those inner questions, he handed the dueling pistol to Michael. "A fine weapon, Armitage. Where did you acquire the pair?"

"Hawkins. You know him? These are from Italy."

Lucas returned with the target. "I confess to curiosity," Sir Roger said. "What remains?"

The younger Armitage dangled the chain. Only the casing at the watch stem and the fob clip remained. "The rest is in bits, sir."

"Admit he's the better shot, little brother. Admit you should have listened to me."

"I do admit it. I'm glad we didn't bet on the outcome."

"Big brother knows best," Michael advised. He turned to Nazenby. "Do you stay long?"

"Unfortunately, no. I have business to discuss with Hargreaves, then I must return."

"I will have Father's study opened for you, sir. He rode back to the manor this morning. He's not expected to return for a seven-night. Would you want some coffee?"

"Ah, coffee and a brief visit with your charming mother, certainly. As for the offer of your father's study, I must refuse. I am an aging man, and long drives stiffen my old bones. Hargreaves and I will walk over the hill to your garden, if that is acceptable."

Though sunny, this late in November the day was cold, but Giles had not felt the chill until he turned away to walk with Sir Roger. They climbed the hill in silence and paused to overlook the long green lawn and the road winding toward the great house. A few late trees displayed their autumn colors. Beneath the clear blue sky and the brilliant sun, the house in its setting looked like the tranquil Avalon of its name.

The spycatcher sighed. "A lovely prospect. You would not expect to see such so near to London."

"It is peaceful," Giles agreed. He waited, letting the spycatcher choose his own time and his own means to explain the reason for his half-hour's drive from London. He did not have to wait long. After a few desultory comments about Lord and Lady Armitage and his drive here, Sir Roger turned fully toward him and began his interrogation.

"How does the courtship progress?"

"It's not a courtship, sir, not yet. We're still getting acquainted."

"We do not have time for a slow courtship, my man."

"I will not rush her, sir. Remember, we had to negotiate my switched affections from Celeste to her. Given those limitations, we have progressed well."

"Limitations? Who limits you? Is our spy kicking up?"

"My own limitations, sir. If our plan is to work, then this mock courtship must have the semblance of reality. I cannot just declare myself and expect Josette Sourantine to believe me—or anyone else to believe me. Nor can I appear blind and deaf to the gossip that swirls around her. I have had only three meetings with her. And I find it difficult to woo a woman when I cannot dance with her and when she can spot empty flattery."

"Ah, the agonies of a first courtship. Are you enjoying hitting every mark, Hargreaves?" The spymaster's irony delivered the rebuke more strongly than a lecture would have. "

"Forgive my tardiness, sir. I am new to London's strict rules that govern a man's interactions with a lady. I spent my courtship years in India and Portugal."

Sir Roger hesitated. When he spoke, his words removed the previous rebuke. "Be grateful you missed those agonies. Although I do have some bittersweet memories."

"Of Lady Eaton?"

He smiled but did not speak of the past. "You must visit Sally Eaton. She wishes to give you some pointers for your courtship. Quite her idea alone, but you would appear to agree that you need some guidance. She will tell you what any callow youth would like to know when he is embarking upon his first courtship. And second. And third."

"I will visit her tomorrow, sir. Did you come all this way for that alone?"

"I coupled other business with this one. You are my last visit."

"Nothing more?" Nazenby had to have more birds for the single stone of this circuit into the countryside. A request to see Lady Eaton was not important enough to draw the spymaster from his constant finger on London's pulse.

"Ah … . Well, there is Robert LeBrun. You mentioned him earlier. He is known to us. Nothing ever proved. He came over with Henri Sourantine, years before the Revolution, but they parted ways within a year. He has no means of income, but he never runs up debt. He's rusticated with a merry widow until four years ago. He's been in Celeste Sourantine's pocket for the last three years."

"Is he her spymaster?"

"Don't think so. Could be a spy himself, but I don't think that either."

"Any news of him in France?"

"None, but we had to rebuild our chain of sources. It's only now producing good information again. LeBrun is much like the elder Sourantine; came out of nowhere. Probably both of them are adventurers. Ran one game too many and jumped the Channel when France became too hot beneath their feet."

"Sourantine was a Captain Sharp."

"According to his daughter?"

"He taught her everything she knows. Watching her run a game, I can believe he sharped many a mark before he found a wealthy heiress to pay his way. Miss Sourantine vows that she doesn't cheat, but I don't see how she can control a game and not cheat."

"If you asked her that, you do need Sally's pointers on courtship."

"We covered rough ground last evening," Giles admitted. "I called her a Captain Sharp and a jade. I questioned her relationship with

Kennit. I told her the insinuations her own sister-in-law had made. I wanted her to know that I had reasons to hesitate in my pursuit of her, and that if she could bury my misgivings with honest answers, then she had me well nigh captured. I considered that we ended the evening with her having no doubts of my attraction."

"Sally said you insulted the girl."

"Told you, did she? And how does she know? Our conversation was private."

"She caught the girl crying later that evening. She tried to smooth the path you had made rough, my man. She doesn't know if she succeeded. And where are you? Here, miles away, unconcerned that you may have destroyed your entrée to the house."

"They don't accept visitors the day after a salon. I will visit tomorrow."

"And did you send flowers?"

"I'll be taking them."

"Better send some as well."

"As you wish, Sir Roger."

"Damned fool."

"Your coffee will be ready, Sir Roger."

"Trying to get me off your back?"

"I know what I did. I know the reason I did it. I'm not a fool, sir." He didn't share his personal reasons. He clasped his hands behind his back and spoke slowly, as if his interrogation of Josette had been well considered. "If Josette Sourantine can jump that hurdle, then I've snared her, sir. I have complete entrée to the house. We can spring our trap."

"You didn't forewarn me."

"You would have ordered me not to do it." As Giles had nearly ordered himself. He had expected to cross rough ground. He had tried to get over it as lightly as possible. He had thought himself successful, but since Lady Eaton had caught Josette crying—. He gave his own justifications to Nazenby. "We needed this courtship to progress rapidly. Trust me, sir. I know how this woman thinks. I've played cards with her and against her. She's intelligent. Last evening we covered the doubts she herself would have raised about my courtship. Now that those questions are laid to rest, we can only go forward, not backwards."

Sir Roger didn't respond for several seconds. When he did speak, it was only to say, "I'll have that coffee now." He strode down the hillside.

Giles followed, slowly. Maybe he should have sent a bouquet this morning.

.~.~.~.

Wednesday, November 27

Melinda's younger siblings sprang up from the floor where they'd been playing spillikins with their cousins. "Josette, Josette!"

She managed to keep her footing as young Matthew embraced her. After her hug, Miranda kept an arm entwined with her and poured out a description of their long journey from Yorkshire and their arrival in London. Melinda left her needlepoint by the window and came to perform the introductions to her aunt and uncle. The Bradleys smiled and nodded and asked where Josette lived and if she had taken a hackney or come in her own coach and finally deplored the clouds that had covered over yesterday's sun. After she answered everything politely, Josette extended an invitation to Friday's salon.

"Oh, my." The offer clearly flustered Aunt Bradley. "We shall meet the *ton*, won't we, Mr. Bradley? However so obliging, Miss Sourantine. Oh, we shall have to have new gowns, Melinda. I doubt they shall be ready in time. Will it be a grand reception?"

"Nothing grand, Mrs. Bradley. You will not meet royalty, I assure you. I remember my own excitement at my first salon. My gown would certainly have been too flamboyant if my sister-in-law had not taken me in hand."

"Have you been long in London, Miss Sourantine?"

"Only a few months."

"Ages," young Miranda put in, leaning on the arm of Josette's chair. "You have been gone ages and ages. You missed the harvest ball!"

"I did indeed. Were my sister and little brother there? Did young Will cause any calamities? I find that I miss them more each day. Tell me about the ball."

"Will was very well behaved," Melinda said. "Your grandfather had him reined in with some promise he refused to share with me."

"A new shotgun," Matthew said, obviously impressed with the promised gift. "He'll be able to go shooting with Mr. Newland on Sir Charles Audley's land."

"Sir Charles Audley? What is this? Has he deigned to visit his manor in Little Houghton?"

"He came after you left. His arrival was so exciting. He rode through the village on a great black horse. And he had two carriages, one for his luggage and one for his books. Books!"

"Miranda!"

"That's what Lyddie said."

"Sir Charles Audley was outfitting his manor, Miranda," her sister reproved. "Do not make it sound as if he did not impress you. You were as wide-eyed as Matthew when he described his travels the night that he came to dinner."

"What kind of man is he?" Mrs. Bradley asked. "Is he young?"

"I think he is above thirty, Aunt. He is recently returned from the Palatine in Germany, where he was posted by our government. Father said he lost his wife there."

"A widower is he? Oh, poor man. How comes he to Little Houghton?"

"A family connection, I believe. I am not certain what it is."

Miranda bounced on her tiptoes. "His old uncle left him the manor, Melly. He's a lord on his daddy's side, but the property was on his mummy's side. Ridings belongs to his mummy's brother. That's what Lyddie said. Mr. Cable told Mr. Watkins, and Mr. Watkins told Mrs. Watkins, and she told Mrs. Montague. And Mrs. Montague told Mrs. Harte, and Lyddie overheard them, and she told me."

They all laughed. "Such a chain of information!" Josette exclaimed. "We must believe it is true."

Aunt Bradley continued her questions. "And what did you think of him, Melinda dear?"

"He is well spoken and quick-witted. Certainly well read in the classics and the Bible. Father was impressed. He does not put himself forward."

"He likes music," Miranda added. "He turned the pages for Melly to play several songs."

"Have you won another admirer, Melinda?" Josette asked with a twinkle.

"He is everything that is courteous and kind, but no, I do not think I attracted him. He spent the rest of that evening talking with Mr. Newland."

"They spend hours talking," Miranda claimed. "Hours and hours. He rides over to your house almost every day, Josette. He and Mr. Newland talk and walk about the garden and go shooting at the manor. But I was going to tell you about the harvest dance. I danced eight dances, two with Father and one with Mr. Newland." A younger version of her sister, her dark curls and violet eyes had already broken a few local hearts. Were the sisters ever launched into society, they would be the diamonds of their respective seasons. Yet the Ratcliffes were not worldly. Neither girl anticipated a London debut.

Josette turned to their little brother. "Did you dance, Matthew?"

He turned beet-red. "I'm too young for that."

"Never too young to learn, my boy," Mr. Bradley interjected. "Knowing how to dance will stand you in good stead a few years from now." They laughed at Matthew's appalled face. Then Miranda launched into the events at the ball.

The excitement of Josette's arrival finally wore off. Matthew was the first to return to his cousins, then a few minutes after, Miranda defected. Aunt Bradley returned to her sewing; Mr. Bradley, to his newspaper. Melinda drew Josette to her quieter bench in the window embrasure.

"What brings you to London, Melly?"

"Aunt Frieda is not well. Doctor Coldwell does not think her illness is contagious, but he thought a quiet house would be best, for her recovery will be slow. And Miranda and Matthew are anything but quiet."

"How long are you to stay away?"

"Two weeks at the least, perhaps longer. We may be here until after Christmas." She glanced at her siblings, engaged in a minor dispute over whose turn came next. "I do not mind having Christmas without Mother and Father, but it will be difficult for them."

"We shall pray for your great-aunt's speedy recovery. I always liked her. She is so funny, with her yards and yards of tatting. And if you cannot return for Christmas and are still here in London, I will do my utmost to make a happy Christmas for Miranda and Matthew."

"You are a treasure, Jos. Now, tell me all the news since your last letter."

She had planned to mention Giles Hargreaves, but the words that came out were, "Albert wants to join the Hussars."

"Surely not!"

"He wants to support England against France. He wants adventure. And London can be sadly flat for a young man full of energy."

"But the army—! How far away he will be! Months on campaign. And the battles!"

"You have my own reaction to his news. I am certain," she added drily, "that Albert only sees the opportunities for heroism. A few weeks ago he wanted a yacht. I am hoping the delay of another few weeks will have him pursuing a different adventure."

"How will you delay him?" As she outlined her plan, Melinda nodded agreement. "I think those are good conditions, Jos. The regiment commander may only be fueling this dream of his. Talking with a returned veteran and seeing the wounded in hospital should give him a strong dose of reality. Will your grandfather approve of Albert's plan?"

"I cannot foretell what Grandpapa will do. He has lost one grandson already. Will he countenance losing another? But he is as patriotic as Albert; they have that in common. Before we came to London, Grandpapa often lectured Albert on doing something purposeful with his life. My brother has no head for business or the law and no heart for the clergy. Soldiering may be the one road for him."

"It could be the making of Albert."

"I think he may have grown up, Melly, and I did not realize it. When he spoke to me this morning, he was so reasoned, so serious. He did not sound like a little brother but like a man. But I must confess: I do not want him going into danger."

"This Lord Hargreaves that you wish Albert to speak with, who is he?"

"He is recently decommissioned from his regiment. Infantry, not cavalry. He was wounded in Portugal, at Albuera, I believe."

"Does he come to the salons?"

"Yes. We have—played cards together, several times." Here was the opportunity to speak of Giles Hargreaves' pursuit of her. No one would overhear them. Didn't she want Melinda's perspective, a counter to Lady Eaton's? Why, then, would the words not come?

"I shall pray," Melinda continued, "that Albert finds the road God wants for him. And I shall write my parents, too. They will keep this news quite quiet. They are great prayer warriors." She smiled, looking even more beautiful with tears misting her violet eyes. "Which is why Father is content in Little Houghton. The powers and principalities ignore the small parishes, so no one accuses him of preaching one of those radical new sects. But I will grow homesick if we talk of them. I have a question, Jos. You referred to it earlier, when you spoke of your grandfather telling Albert to find his purpose in life. I remember you said he gave you much the same speech. Have you found that purpose here in London?"

"I must say no, unless my purpose is to play whist. I grow tired of card games, Melly."

Her friend laughed. "But you play so well. Nothing more? No secret admirer?"

Giles' image appeared. She wanted to share—but where did she begin? Certainly not with Monday evening's conversation—castigation—. What name should she give to the way he'd taken her to task as a jade, as a Captain Sharp?

As she hesitated, Melly smiled. She leaned close. In a conspirator's whisper, she asked, "Tell me of Tobias Kennit and Lord Musgrove. Have they managed to leave the card room at any point during the salons? Do they enjoy dancing?"

.~.~.~.

Giles watched the French spy flirt with two of her admirers. Where was Josette?

In advance of his visit, he had sent a mixed bouquet tied with the palest blue ribbon the flower seller had had. Armed with Lady Eaton's pointers, he arrived at the Sourantine house with plans to leave her in no doubt of his interest. The butler Reynolds had thwarted him by announcing that Miss Sourantine was not at home.

"I cannot say when she will return, sir. She left only a half-hour ago."

"That disappoints me." He started to turn away, but laughter echoed down from the first floor. At the top of the grand staircase, Robert LeBrun conversed with a young man who looked familiar. What had Nazenby said about the man? Not the woman's spymaster, but he could be a spy. LeBrun had no means of income, yet he was never in debt. Giles decided to see how LeBrun interacted with the French spy.

"Mdm. Sourantine is entertaining guests?"

"It is her receiving day, my lord. Several people are here."

Remembering the lingering wound he had to affect, Giles climbed the wide stairs slowly.

The doors to the large drawing room were closed. Voices came from the *petite salon*, the largest room in the enfilade that turned into the card room for the salons. As he paused for the red-haired footman to open the door, he glanced to his right, past the second staircase. The settee was tucked behind the stairwell, out of sight. Maybe he should have kissed Josette instead of interrogating her and trusted that the power of their attraction would overcome any of her doubts.

Covered by clouds, the late November sun needed additional candles to light the room. Settees and chairs were pulled out from the walls and arranged into three conversational areas.

Celeste had chosen the middle circle. She sat on a gilded divan as if it were a throne. The yellow of her gown cast its own brilliant rays. Her court had claimed the available seats, and three of them had to stand in a cluster behind their hostess.

The French spy did not let Giles' entrance go unremarked. "*Mon seigneur* Hargreaves, you honor us."

He stopped just outside the circle and bowed. When he straightened, he nodded to the gentlemen he knew as he addressed his hostess. "Madame, I see you have no lack of visitors."

Did her tittering laugh have an edge only to his ear? "I am demanded, *mon seigneur*—demanded!—to choose among them. They wish me to decide who will be honored to drive me in the park tomorrow afternoon. I would not hurt any of them. How can I choose?"

If she intended his offer to be her decision, he frustrated her by ignoring her lead. "I am certain, Madame, that you will divine a solution." He bowed again and retreated a few steps, enough so that Clarence Wilton could resume importuning her.

Giles strolled away, making a mental note of the callers who found it necessary to visit the Sourantines. Wilton's sisters were present, the younger one talking animatedly to Alex Westover as they sat together on a settee before the fire. The other sister hovered on the edge of Celeste's circle, occasionally bending to speak to her brother. Richard Malbury spoke quietly to the young lady that Lucas Armitage had pointed out the other evening. They had drawn their chairs close to the window, giving themselves the illusion of privacy. In the circle nearest the fire were three women he did not know, although he had seen them at the salons. He knew he had played cards with one of them some weeks before, but her name escaped him. He bowed politely. They smiled and nodded and continued their exchange.

His quarry LeBrun had moved past Celeste's court. He had joined the third circle, nearest the window overlooking the elevated terrace. On the settee were Mrs. Davenport and her friend Mrs. Lockhart, chatting easily while LeBrun talked quietly with Claude Terry. Giles joined them, and the men broke off their private conversation. LeBrun turned to Mrs. Lockhart and asked about her home in Angelshold. Terry rose and returned to Celeste's court. He gingerly took the abandoned gilt chair.

Mrs. Davenport's eyes twinkled, as if she guessed his worry about the chair's fragility. "You do not join the admirers surrounding our hostess, sir?"

Here was new ground for his plan of attack. London gossip could be turned to his favor. "No, ma'am. I came to visit Miss Sourantine."

"I understand she is visiting a friend newly arrived in London."

Would it help his deception to pretend a little jealousy? He decided it would. "Are you acquainted with this friend?"

"I have not had that privilege, sir. Mr. LeBrun." She broke into the other conversation. "Do you know, sir, the name of Miss Sourantine's friend, the one she has gone to visit?"

"A Melinda Ratcliffe, *Mdm.* Davenport."

Now how did LeBrun know that? An old friend of her father's, Josette had described him, someone who often comes to dine. Someone Celeste likes. Was he only a friend, a family intimate? "Is this Miss Ratcliffe also from Little Houghton?" he asked, to keep the man in the conversation.

"I believe her father is vicar there. You know of Josette's home?"

Giles smiled deliberately. "We have spoken of her home and her family many times. I look forward to meeting her grandfather. I believe he is the head of the family. He seems a redoubtable man, starting his own mill and expanding it through the years."

From there the conversation delved back to the ordinary through

Mrs. Lockhart's comment that the wool from her sheep went to the Newcastle mills. LeBrun added an amusing story about an altercation between his curricle and a flock of sheep, which the sheep won.

When the clock chimed the quarter hour and LeBrun hadn't budged from his chair, Giles decided he would learn nothing useful today. He leaned forward. "I must cut short our enjoyable talk, ladies, Mr. LeBrun. I have a pressing appointment. I came only in the hopes of seeing Miss Sourantine, even if only for a few minutes."

The two women exchanged pleased glances.

Giles returned to his hostess, who yawned prettily as the young men debated Napoleon's plans for Russia now that it had sent another ambassador to London. He bowed politely as he took his leave. Celeste frowned but chose not to remark on the brevity of his visit.

Reynolds came forward, the perfect butler. After he donned his coat, Giles asked, "Did Miss Sourantine receive my flowers?"

"She did, my lord, this morning. I took them up myself. The delivery was quite early."

"I intended it to be." He pressed a coin into the man's hand and left, satisfied that he had accomplished one goal. His interest in Josette Sourantine would quickly become common knowledge. Neither Sir Roger nor Lady Eaton could fault him for today's step in his courtship.

He had barely gained the street when a voice called behind him. "Lord Hargreaves, a word, *s'il vous plait*." He looked back and saw LeBrun. Leaning heavily on his walking stick, he offered the French *émigré* a pleasant smile.

Still tugging on his gloves, LeBrun managed to alter his hawk-like features into a concerned expression. "I fear you have somehow offended our hostess."

"I am not concerned with Mdm. Sourantine."

"Ah, yes, you are interested in Josette. Do you not realize that Celeste can throw stones in your path with her?"

"As she has already done? Miss Sourantine and I have spoken of her sister-in-law's interference. Madame is miffed to have lost one of her court to her *belle-soeur*, that is all."

"*Peut-etre*. Impossible to say if that is true. *Mais*, if it is that you think Josette is not concerned with the displeasure of Celeste, then you must think again."

"You are offering me advice?"

"A word only. I would see neither lady hurt."

One will be, he thought then amended it, *the other may be, before this is over.* He prayed that Josette was not too hurt by his deceit. Giles gestured with his cane. "Shall we walk?"

"You are not too much incapacitated by your wound?"

"Exercise improves it." They turned down the street together. Giles started with a casual question asked in a carefully casual voice. "Have you known the Sourantine family long?" He already knew the answer, but he wanted to hear what LeBrun would admit to.

"Many years ago I was acquainted with the father Henri Sourantine. We lost the connection over the years. He settled in Yorkshire with his wife; I stayed in London."

"The flood of *émigrés* during the Terror would certainly have widened your acquaintance. Is that how you met the Nemours?"

"Celeste's family? No, I did not meet her until I met her husband Edmund. At a horse fair. I recognized the name of my old compatriot. He introduced me to his bride. Such a tragedy, his loss, to die so young. I tried to provide some distractions for her when she returned to London after his death."

"I gather that you did not know Miss Sourantine or her brother Albert until this year?"

"We met in August of this year. And you, Lord Hargreaves, how did you come to know the Sourantines?"

"Through the salons. I escorted a friend on my first visit. Lady Eaton."

"Ah, the lovely Lady Eaton. Sally Wallace she was. Even as a young debutante, she had an air of—it is the French '*je ne sais quoi*', yes? I did not wish to deny any of her requests."

"She still has that air. I dared not refuse her command for an escort, even though I was only a couple of months out of hospital. I am glad that I did not, for I met two beautiful ladies."

"You include Josette; that is a good thing. Not many appreciate her pale beauty; Celeste's is so vivid. Josette can be very aloof when she wishes. But not to you, I think."

"My good fortune."

"Yet—do pardon me, *mon seigneur*—you are the son, are you not, of the *Marquis* of Grasmere? I do know that Celeste was infatuated with the son of a *marquis*."

"Ah, but then Mdm. Sourantine decided I am too drab, I abandon her too much. Thus, I am not worthy of her attentions."

"After this, you turn to Josette? This is not wise, *mon ami*. A woman does not wish to be second choice."

"Forgive me, I did not speak clearly enough. I spoke only of Mdm. Sourantine's decision about me. I ceased to admire her long before then. And in looking closely at the two ladies, I discovered in Miss Sourantine a greater heart, a livelier intellect. She is not my second choice, LeBrun; she is first choice."

"Wise of you to realize that. Ah, do you not continue this way,

Lord Hargreaves? *Non*? Then it is hoped that we shall converse again. At Friday's salon I hope? Good day, sir."

Giles watched the man saunter away. He hadn't learned much, but he sensed hidden depths. Could Sir Roger be wrong about LeBrun? The man must know many of the *émigrés* scattered around England, those who had entered London society with scarcely a misstep as well as those driven down to the working class by the tragic Reign of Terror. LeBrun bore watching. His contacts needed to be named and assessed. Among them, Giles was certain, was the French spymaster. How else would the newly widowed Celeste Sourantine have turned to spying?

Chapter 12 ~ Thursday, November 28

As Giles approached the Sourantine house, he saw Robert LeBrun handing Celeste into his curricle. They did not see him; the horses were pointed in the opposite direction. He paused, watching the man take up the reins, and reviewed again his visit of yesterday. Clarence Wilton and the other young swains had lost their bid to drive Celeste to the park. Why had the spy chosen LeBrun? Spy and spymaster? Or fellow spies who betrayed the country that had welcomed them?

The butler's eyebrows arched when he opened the door and discovered Giles on the step. "Lord Hargreaves!" Then he resumed his wooden mask. "Mdm. Sourantine has just gone out."

"I come, yet again, to see *Miss* Sourantine. Is she in and accepting visitors?"

"A moment, my lord, while I inquire." Instead of climbing to the first floor, he went through the archway on the grand staircase's left. Rather than wait, Giles followed the man's unhurried walk down a long passage. At the end of the hall was an exterior door; he could see a garden topiary through the glass. Reynolds reached a door before that and entered after he knocked. The butler's announcement came clearly. "Lord Hargreaves to see you, Miss."

"Oh, Reynolds, I did not expect to see anyone."

"He came expressly to see you, Miss, today and yesterday."

"Celeste did not say that. She said that she enjoyed their hour's private conversation."

"Lord Hargreaves stayed not a quarter-hour, Miss, and left with Mr. LeBrun. Quite a number of people were present, the Wiltons and Mr. Malbury, Lord Westover's son, Mrs. Davenport and her friend. I informed you of them when you returned from Miss Ratcliffe's."

An old family servant, Giles thought, who took liberties to speak what newer employees would not. He began to think that Reynolds— for all his deliberate obtuseness about whom Giles came to visit—was on his side.

Josette broke the lengthening silence with a question. "You say he came expressly to see me?" And Giles wondered if Monday's *tete-a-tete* had stretched beyond her tolerance?

"Tuesday and yesterday and now today, Miss," the butler reiterated. "He did tell me, before he left Monday evening, that your private conversation had quite overset him."

"Reynolds, invention does not suit you."

"I am not given to flights of fancy, Miss Josette."

The butler reappeared. He seemed unsurprised that Giles had already reached the door.

He entered a library, its colors subdued yellows and browns. The burnished gold curtains were cast back to admit the November light. Josette stood in the pouring sunshine, her hand gripping the back of the chair that stood before a writing table. A ledger stood open, scraps of paper spindled and cast to one side, his flowers in a vase on the corner. She held an embroidered cloth. Twists of thread covered a little table close at hand. She had obviously abandoned the accounts for the meditative needlework, a sign that revealed inner agitation. That reassured him while her carefully blank expression did not. She gestured toward the comfortable daybed.

He did not want to be a few feet from her. Proximity, Lady Eaton had lectured, shatters the first wall in a woman's defense. He had known that and used it in their conversations. He would use it now.

As she retook her seat, he took a chair from the library table and set it on an angle to hers. That put his back to the sunshine and gave him her full face. He needed that advantage, for cardplayer that she was, she could mask thoughts and emotions.

Josette had looked startled when he lifted the chair with one hand. When he set it close to her, she flushed. Her eyes dropped to her needlework. She began to fold around the hoop.

"Show me," Giles said. "My mother enjoys embroidery. As a boy, I was fascinated by the pictures she created with needle and thread."

Those cornflower eyes lifted and searched his. He met her gaze unwaveringly. He had given her a glimpse into his childhood, another of Lady Eaton's lessons.

She unfolded the cloth to reveal a garden gate, the design far from finished. Pencil marks created an outline to guide her. With his forefinger he traced the sketch of a tree with its overarching branches.

"Your design? You still have much to do. What flowers will you have?"

"Bluebells and clove pinks. Yellow flags here." Her slender finger touched more places. "Bracken under this silver birch. And a wild rose climbing the gateway."

"Ambitious." His finger followed the frame of the arch over the gate. "And you do not hesitate. Did you learn as a child—when you would not learn the pianoforte?"

Her eyes lifted at that reminder of their earliest conversation. He won a smile. "My mother taught me, and then Mrs. Ratcliffe. She helped after—."

He did not want this conversation to dwell on sadness. He bent again to the cloth spread over her lap. "You need a cage in the tree."

"A bird cage?"

"A cage for a heart."

Her eyes narrowed. "So the lover won't lose his heart again, my lord?"

He laughed but disagreed, wanting to create a story that would aid his courtship. "See, it is a pretty garden, a place of color and life. It is designed to tempt a beauty."

"And she will see the heart in the cage and free the captured lover."

"She will see the wild heart in the cage and tame it with her love."

Josette shook her head at his story's plot. "And who has this wild heart?"

"A man who has never known love."

"No. No, I do not like this story, sir. I think it is a captured lover who must be set free."

"Who imprisons him?"

"False love. False desires. False needs. It is a caged lover who must be set free from the deceit that ensnares him."

Did her intuition warn her? Did some deep heart of her naturally apprehend that his courtship was deceit? "While only a true love can free him from the cage?" He hoped he had successfully masked his surprise.

"Is that not the story of many fairy tales, my lord? The hero falls for a deceitful beauty who wants to feast on his soul, and only the pure love of an innocent maiden can save him."

"I would rather be the wild hero tamed by love."

She laughed. "Better to be wild than to be stupid."

"Not stupid. Foolish. Blinded. Gullible, even."

"But not stupid?"

"Definitely not," and they exchanged a smile.

She would have folded the cloth then, but he dared to touch her and stayed her hand. "My mother should see this, now and when it is finished. She would appreciate your skill."

"Do your parents come to London? No? Then that day shall be far in the future, if ever."

"You could go to her at Grasmere." A quick inhalation revealed her shock at the indirect invitation. "My mother would like you," Giles added quickly, before she could reject the words.

Her eyes closed briefly. She shook her head. "My lord Hargreaves—." She stopped, not knowing what to add.

Josette had used his courtesy title again, an attempt to create a wall of formality between them. He had to break down that wall before she built it firmly. "Too soon?"

"Yes," she whispered.

But he proceeded with his assault. "I knew the first night, after we played cards together. Similar minds, similar thoughts. Do not tell me that you were not as attracted as I was."

"One night, a scant two hours." Her voice was faint. She again shook her head. Her voice rallied to an ironic tone. "We said little to each other that night, my lord, and nothing of importance. And then you disappeared for a fortnight."

"Family business."

"More eligible daughters to meet?"

The wry question startled a laugh from him. "No, not that time."

"Lord Hargreaves—."

"Hush," he said. He covered her hands, still holding the embroidery hoop, and leaned toward her. The deceit that had started this courtship had long since vanished, burned away by this truth between them. "It's a wild heart that needs taming, Josette." He leaned closer, intent on the kiss denied him the other night.

The door opened, and they sprang apart.

"Albert," Josette said. She folded the cloth over the hoop. "I did not expect you home until evening." She sounded remarkably calm, only her heightened color betraying her emotions.

"Westover is in a meeting with his father and their solicitor."

"The expected estate? Good. But were not Mr. Malbury and Mr. Wilton also part of your group?"

"Good day, Lord Hargreaves." Albert dropped onto the daybed and directed his answer to Josette. "They were going, but they changed their minds this morning. They decided nothing better would suit them than a sedate ride through the park."

Giles remembered yesterday's conversation when he had visited the house. "Still pursuing your sister-in-law, are they?"

Albert grinned and leaned back, crossing one leg over the other. "Exactly, sir. So I came to tell you I'm off to see Major Fellars. I'll likely stay a couple of nights with the regiment."

"Major Fellars? Oh, the commander you want me to meet? Lord Hargreaves, Albert wishes to join a Hussar regiment."

"Ah, the Hussars," he said with thrilling tones, while his mind raced to tally this information into the spy equation. Sir Roger would be very intrigued by a Sourantine wanting to enlist in the military. A lot of information flew around a posted regiment, not the least its strength and missions. Did the youth intend to open a new line of spying for his sister-in-law? "A new pursuit of yours?"

"Yes and no. I want to do something to help the war, sir. To fight against Napoleon. I've wanted to do that for—well, for years."

"A worthy ambition. Nelson has had more success against Bonaparte on the seas."

"Yes, but he'll have to be defeated on land, sir. I want to be part of that campaign."

"Why the Hussars?"

"Josette asked that same question. I'm a good horseman, sir. No one better; at least, not in my acquaintance. And I can shoot. Grandpapa says I have a natural eye for it. Those are two skills that a cavalryman needs."

"When do you join the regiment?"

"Not yet," Josette hurriedly put in. "Our grandfather must be informed first."

"To buy the commission?" he asked cannily. When the youth agreed, Giles credited him for not shying away from the truth.

Albert turned to his sister. "When shall I tell Major Fellars to visit?"

"At his convenience, any day except Sunday."

"Good." He put his hands on his knees and stood. "I've packed, so I'll take my leave now. A pleasure to see you again, sir."

The Sourantines walked into the hall. Giles listened to the murmur of their lowered voices. Albert Sourantine's eagerness to help Wellington was commendable—but Sir Roger could twist that eagerness into a spy's need for frontline information. He himself knew how many opportunities abounded near the front line for a spy to meet privately with the enemy.

Josette returned, but she did not resume her chair. She stood before the fireplace, a hand on the coolness of the white marble, the other pressed to her brow.

"Worried about him?"

"He is my little brother. I would have him safe at all times." She turned to him. Her hands wrung together. "I—I have not asked you much about your time on the Peninsula."

"He'll be in a cavalry regiment. I commanded soldiers."

"Yes, I understand there is a great difference. Were you—were you often in battle?"

"Not every day. Sometimes I was bored out of my mind."

"But you were in battles." Her twisting hands revealed her agitation. "You were wounded in battle."

"Yes." What was it that she wanted to know? "Your brother is eager for adventure. He'll find more than he wants on the front lines."

"You commanded men?"

Ah, he thought he knew what she hesitated to ask. "I went with them into battle. I gave the orders that sent them to their deaths. I was an officer. That was my duty, and I did it."

She made an abrupt gesture. "What is—what is battle like?"

He had thought the coming question would be easy to answer. It wasn't, not seated like a gentleman at leisure, a gentleman in the comforts of green England. Giles stood. After a second's pause, he walked to the sunny window and looked out. November had stripped the garden bare. His soul felt like that, when he opened a window to the worst days.

"Not—." He cleared his throat. "Not as bloody as you would expect. Loud. Very loud. All sorts of noises. The drums that beat out the advance. Gunfire. Cannonfire. The blasts that shake the ground you're crossing. Men yelling and crying and screaming. Everything confused. The god of war must be a god of chaos. You get orders, and you try to execute them, and somewhere in the trying the orders change. You have to change them, or the commanders change them. And all you can do is keep your men together and your shot aimed at the enemy. And you've never felt so alive. Men are dying all around you, and you feel so alive. Insane, isn't it? Death makes living so— clear. Every breath afterward is like a gift."

Giles hadn't heard her cross to him. She was just suddenly there, her eyes wide and searching, her skin young and fresh. He felt so old, as if he had lived a hundred years longer.

She touched his arm. "If I may, Lord Hargreaves, if I may, I would beg a favor of you."

He guessed it. How could he not, knowing her concern for her brother and her questions of him? He turned fully to her. She removed her hand and pressed it to her stomach, as if she hesitated to ask the question that he did not want to hear. Chaos was laughing at him, laughing that he hadn't escaped, laughing that the question came from this woman who so attracted him. And Nazenby's mission had him on cleft stick. If he retreated from the question, what bar would drop between them? If he accepted the question, what healed memories must he now rip open?

Even Josette hesitated to ask it. "I fear it will be a great intrusion," she temporized.

"Nothing you ask can be too great an intrusion," he lied.

"I fear this will be. I fear—. I ask only because I fear for my brother. Please understand that, sir. I wish—I wish for Albert to speak with you, about your experiences."

He did not know what to answer. His mission and his lie trapped him.

"I do comprehend what a great favor I ask. You need not tell Albert everything. He has—he has such visions of grandeur. I want him to understand the realities of war. He wishes my support when he approaches our grandfather. I have set him three conditions: I wish to speak with his commander. He should visit one of the military hospitals daily and interact with the patients. And the third—it is for Albert to speak with you about your experiences." As he continued mute, Josette pushed her fingers on her forehead. "You need not personally grant this favor, my lord. I would not want to bestir what you would rather forget. You could recommend someone. A fellow veteran. Or another officer, temporarily returned from the Peninsula."

He turned to the window and the barren landscape, and Josette was wise enough to let him have the moments of silence for his decision. She had offered a way out, but he found himself reluctant to take it. "Have I not sworn to help you?" He managed lightness far above his feelings. "What is your chief worry about your brother?"

"I fear his wish to gain a commission is more to impress the young ladies with his regimentals than to defend England."

"The way I impressed your sister-in-law?"

She flinched but answered honestly. "Exactly that, sir. And see how she ignored you when you were decommissioned. What was it she said? That you were too drab for her court?"

Lady Eaton had warned him of this treacherous bridge, explaining why he had crossed from Celeste to her. Robert LeBrun had warned him. Even the butler, with his purposeful confusion of names, had warned him. Giles had deliberated how to cross it long before the formidable dowager's coaching.

He found it easier to head straight for the bridge than answer her request. "I did not care," he said softly, "that she ignored me. Had I not spent two whole evenings in your company, talking with you alone, before she declared me dashing only in my uniform? Your sister-in-law did not lure me back to your salons. Pale blue eyes, sparkling at me over a hand of cards, they enticed me back."

"I find it difficult—." She stopped, not able to finish the easy retort.

"You find it difficult," he said for her, "to accept that I prefer you to her? She is lovely, yes, but there is no substance behind the glitter. I have been at war, Josette. I do not want artifice. I want truth."

He broke society's rules by using her Christian name, a second time this very day. He intended to break more rules than that one.

Those clear eyes watched him, judged his words, but she couldn't or wouldn't step onto the bridge he needed her to cross. He desperately needed her to believe him—a desperation that had nothing to do with Sir Roger's mission to trap a spy.

He couldn't agree to her question, not yet, but he could offer something. "Your brother Albert will change in many ways when he goes to war. This way is one of them. He will have a low tolerance for the shallow lies and subterfuge that many in society thrive upon."

"In what other ways did you change?" she whispered, her gaze fixed upon him. In her yearning for his help, her body leaned toward him, a slender tree seeking support.

Giles told her the easy things. "Do you like chess? I never did. Never had the patience for it. War teaches patience. Either you're fighting for your life or fighting boredom. You find inner reserves, or you get drunk. You learn what matters most. I missed home. I missed my parents more than I can ever express. I even missed my brother. I yearned for England's green, for bird songs and children's laughter and the quiet murmur of voices instead of cannon and gunfire and men screaming with rage and pain."

Sympathetic tears welled in her eyes. Her hands unconsciously sought his, offering the comfort of human touch. "You said you were decommissioned because of your wound. If you had not been wounded, would you have stayed with your regiment?"

He didn't hesitate. "Yes. Until Napoleon is defeated. A dictator who oppresses people, who squanders their lives for his own expediency—that dictator cannot continue his tyranny."

"Do you not feel your purpose ripped from you by your wound?"

Giles returned the clasp of her hands. "I have discovered other ways to serve my country." He had strayed onto the verges of his mission. He backtracked. "I will speak to your brother. I may not say what you want me to say, Josette, but I will grant your favor." A mischievous impulse prompted him to add, "And you can grant me one favor in return. I must consider what. Something scandalous, I assure you."

Her pale skin flamed. She tugged away her hands. He wanted to laugh out loud. Josette was not the ice queen Musgrove and LeBrun believed.

The clock chimed the passing hour. He should leave now, before Celeste returned and watched their interaction with a jaundiced eye.

Giles did more than bow over her hand. He pressed a kiss to her soft skin. Her blush fired his imagination. Lady Eaton would be proud of his progress. He was proud of it. He had taken great strides in one hour. His conscience would rest as well, for he hadn't lied to her.

And in the conversation he had somehow achieved a conscious peace with the injury that had sidelined him. Never before had he expressed what he had so missed while in Portugal, facing French battalions intent on his blood.

Chapter 13 ~ Friday, November 29

The music ended. Laughing, Josette curtsied to her partner. He stepped forward and offered his arm. "Shall we take the next set as well, Miss Sourantine?"

"Thank you, but no, Mr. Rampley. What I would most like, if you would be so kind, is a glass of punch."

He bowed. "Your servant."

She fanned herself. Melinda squeezed to her side. "Where is Mr. Rampley?"

"He is braving the crush to bring me some punch."

"Punch! He has been so attentive since he arrived, and you sent him off for punch?"

"Of course. He wanted to do a service for me, don't you think? And I am thirsty."

"I think he enjoyed watching you dance more than he wanted to do you a service. You certainly laughed at his conversation."

"How does one not laugh? His descriptions are so droll, and he has the funniest way of relating the ordinary details of life. I enjoyed our talk."

"I would think the poor man had captivated you did I not know you better. Who is he?"

"A budding MP. He came with Jasper Eaton. Did you enjoy your dance with Mr. Stephenson?"

"I did."

"And did he ask for another?"

"He did, but I sent him off for punch."

"Melly!"

They dissolved into giggles, not quite restored when their respective suitors returned. They toasted with the punch then proceeded to fend off offers for tomorrow: driving in the country or walking in the park or meeting for tea at Mrs. Abbot's.

"The museum," Melinda said firmly. "I am to go to the museum tomorrow. My uncle Bradley has planned the day. There are bones to see." The men laughed. She pouted. "I promise you it is so."

"Which museum?" Mr. Stephenson asked.

"I don't know. I didn't ask. But I have promised to go with my sister and brother and cousins, and so I shall."

"Do you go, Miss Sourantine?"

"Yes," she said promptly, although she had had no such plan three minutes before. "I am also promised for the day, Mr. Rampley. Perhaps we can dance again later?"

"It shall be my delight, Miss Sourantine."

Celeste appeared at her elbow. "Planning more dances, Josette? You may indulge yourself after the supper. Perhaps. For now, I believe those in the card room miss their hostess."

"Celeste, my friend is not—."

"Josette, you have a duty to our guests. Is it not so?" She sailed away.

Josette stared at her unfinished punch. Then she pasted on a smile. "I am sorry, gentlemen. Perhaps after supper, as my *belle-soeur* suggests." They bowed and faded away. She turned to her friend. "Melinda—."

"Don't apologize. You know what I think of Celeste's exiling you to the card room."

"I am required there. Where is your Aunt Bradley? I won't leave you standing here."

"Sitting somewhere. And I won't be standing here. I would like to go with you."

"You don't like gambling."

"Nor do you. But you enjoy the challenge of the game. And you have written of Lord Musgrove and Mr. Kennit. I would like to meet them, Jos. I would like to match my imagination to the reality. I cannot do that unless I venture into the card room. Did you not tell me that they rarely venture from it?"

They greeted Mrs. Lockhart as they passed through the doorway. She seemed distracted and gave them a nod and a belated social smile.

As they crossed the black and cream tiles, Josette tried another warning. "Your aunt may not approve, Melly. Your father certainly will not."

"I do not plan to gamble."

Beyond the upper stair they surprised Richard Malbury and Connie Lockhart tucked behind one of the arched pillars. The couple fell silent. Only when the two friends were several feet away did they resume their murmured conversation.

"Planning an assignation?" Melinda whispered.

Josette remembered her *tete-a-tetes* with Giles Hargreaves, conducted behind the shelter of the upper stairwell. "Perhaps it is the only place for a private conversation."

They entered the *petite salon*, converted into one of the three card rooms. She glanced over the scattered tables. Giles Hargreaves hadn't appeared yet this evening. After he had come so close to a declaration yesterday, had her request on Albert's behalf driven him away?

Kennit and Musgrove had their usual table. From the stacks of coins before them, she knew they were trouncing James Costell and his friend Clarence Wilton. She didn't like seeing that. Melinda would judge them harshly.

Hoping that their game would soon end, she guided Melly in the opposite direction, stopping occasionally in her role as hostess and introducing her friend. She was relieved to see other women dotted through the enfilade, although the number was not large when she counted.

Robert LeBrun partnered Didier Vernon against Sir Roger Nazenby and Lady Eaton. Vernon was a younger *émigré*. When Josette introduced Melinda to them, he seemed immediately enthralled. *How could he not be enthralled?* Josette thought as she oversaw their brief chatter. Melinda's friendly smile and violet eyes only enhanced her pleasing countenance, all of it crowned with tumbling dark curls that owed nothing to artifice. Her height was the only average thing about her. Vernon tried to engage her in conversation as he continued to play. When he botched a trick, LeBrun said, "I have money in this game, Vernon. Keep your attention on the cards, not on the so lovely Miss Ratcliffe."

Laughing, Josette led Melly away. They stopped at several other tables. She timed their arrival at her usual table as Costell and Wilton left. The neat stack of coins before one set of partners only made obvious what could be read from Costell's protruding lip and Kennit's gleaming eyes. The two young men barely avoided the young women as they barreled away.

When they arrived at the table, only Musgrove rose, having better manners than his friend. Josette glanced to see how Melly would take Kennit's slight. She only looked amused.

"Good evening, gentlemen," she murmured in her throaty voice. "Josette has written much about you in her letters to me."

Kennit looked up. Seeing the beauty at his elbow, he surged to his feet. "Join us?"

Her smile was like a cat's when offered cream. She slanted a look from her violet eyes, a look practiced on the pitiable swains of Little Houghton, and her look reaped the harvest of Tobias Kennit. "I am not a gamester, sir.

Josette hid inner laughter, especially when Kennit offered, "No stakes." Musgrove barked a protest as Melinda acquiesced to a game. Kennit only heard the beauty.

She watched Kennit seat her friend, watched him collect a wineglass for her, watched him watching Melinda as if he dared not look away. His reaction proved that she needed nothing but her plain gown and no jewelry to impress London's most discerning eyes.

He continued to stare. Melinda opened her eyes wide. "Is something wrong, sir?"

"Stop staring, Tobias," Musgrove said drily.

Kennit cleared his throat. Dropping his gaze, he collected the cards and gave them more attention than usual as he shuffled. Then he presented the deck to Melinda to cut. "What will you play, Miss Ratcliffe?"

She named a nursery game. He frowned; she chuckled. "I have anticipated your reaction to that ever since Josette wrote that she had discovered two masters of cards. I am proficient at whist, sir. We can play that. You did promise no stakes." She glanced at Musgrove for confirmation.

When the peer hesitated, Josette said, "I can front you some money, Melinda."

"From what Mr. Kennit keeps for you? See how much I remember from your letters? But no, I think not."

"We can play no stakes," Musgrove agreed, grudgingly.

Her friend said "good" before the offer could be rescinded and picked up the cards Kennit had dealt.

Having taught Melinda the game, Josette had no fear that the men would trample them. And her friend had a devious streak that no man affected by her beauty would ever expect. She sorted cards to confuse her opponent, having learned from Josette that a canny competitor would watch her selection to guess the cards she still held. She had a half-dozen such ploys that she would use without hesitation.

Josette settled down to enjoy this game. She altered her own play slightly to give her partner a chance to see the men work together. She gave up an easy take; she threw out a lure and saw their dissatisfaction at being reeled in on the next trick; she won another that Kennit expected to take and laughed at his grumble. All the while Melly watched Musgrove: the lift of an eyebrow, the purse of his lips, the slight smile of satisfaction. Kennit was harder to read, Josette had written. Only after several hours of play had she deciphered his hidden signs: the negligent lean in his chair when he was ready to pounce, the narrowing of his eyes when Musgrove did not play the card he wanted, their glistening when the trick would fall to him. And watchful Melinda saw everything.

After the first rubber, with the men slightly ahead, Melinda asked for a second game. Third trick in, she asked Kennit why he played a king on Josette's lowly trey and Musgrove's feeble eight. "Do you not hold the knave?"

The rake's eyes widened. Then they narrowed. "Are you another of Mr. Sourantine's prize pupils?"

"No. Jos taught me. I would have played the ten to lure out the queen, but I am not certain you have her."

He looked at her, looked into her violet eyes, looked and realized how closely she had watched his play. With a devilish glitter of his blue eyes, he picked up the king and laid down the ten. When she smiled at him, he smiled back.

And Melinda played the queen.

"Here now," Musgrove complained.

"Shut up and play," Kennit growled.

Melinda collected the round then played the nine. Musgrove slapped down a five, Josette played the four, and Kennit claimed the hand with the knave. He led off with the trump king, certain of it since Musgrove had earlier played the ace.

As he took the sixth trick with the maligned king, he asked, "Rector's daughter?"

"Vicar's."

"On his strict orders to avoid the sins of London?"

"Which sins are particular to London?"

His eyes widened at her retort. Silently Josette applauded her friend. She had captured Tobias Kennit's attention in ways he would never have anticipated.

He acknowledged her truth with a nod. "I'll amend that. Does your father want you to avoid the sin of gambling?"

Melinda coolly sipped her wine. He waited, holding up the play until she answered, as if it mattered to him.

"He taught me that gambling is sin, yes, but this is my decision as well. Is not the fall of cards random? Why waste the money that God has given you?"

"I don't waste my money. I win."

"At some point early on you must have lost."

"Yes. And determined that wouldn't happen again."

"But why gamble on something so uncertain as the random turn of cards?"

Kennit's mouth tightened. Musgrove coughed. "That's the gamble, Miss Ratcliffe."

"You could as easily bet on a coin landing heads up or down. Or when a fish will take the bait. Or if your eyes will open in the morning."

"There's been mornings when I would have bet my eyes wouldn't open, but they did."

"More of your London sins, Mr. Kennit?"

He gave a lop-sided smile then shrugged and played his card, the eight of hearts. Melinda laid the diamond eight next to his. "Is it the randomness that makes the game?"

Musgrove slapped down the heart knave. "Save philosophy for the lecture hall."

But Kennit had looked at Melinda. A frown between his black eyebrows, he obviously was giving her question serious thought. Josette held up the game and stopped Musgrove's irritated protest with a touch to his hand.

Tobias Kennit looked at his cards, studying them as if he'd never before seen such an array. Then his blue eyes returned to her. "No, the random fall is not the attraction. It's the skill in dealing with that random fall. The competition in dealing with it better than your opponent."

"It can't be a true competition," Josette interjected, "unless I am equally matched in skill with my competitor." Deliberately she played the heart queen. "If we are not equally matched, I have to find something else to provide the rush of competition. If I play far over their skill, I am only taking advantage of the weaker player." And she opened the next trick with the heart ace.

Kennit mouthed, "Costell."

Even as she nodded, Musgrove objected. "That may be the point for some, to defeat the weaker opponent."

"Not a good point, not a worthy one, not an honorable one," Josette countered, willing to have the criticism coming from her rather than her friend. Kennit was already scowling at his cards. "And that's not a worthy reason to gamble."

"You're taking the fun out of whist, out of any game," Musgrove protested.

"What is the point of the game? To show who is the better player by trouncing the weaker one? To take someone's money? Or to enjoy matching wits? To surprise and trick someone? I know I am speaking heresy to you," Melinda concluded, "but it is only whist."

Kennit leaned back. "Did you two plan this conversation?"

"We did not. It is one way, however," she batted her lashes at him, "to pry you two gentlemen from the card table and into the *grande salon* for the dancing."

He laughed. "May I claim a dance with both of you, after the supper? Two sets, if I am lucky in the turn of the dance." They laughed and assented. He then played his heart king and, as the hand continued, he prodded Musgrove to return to his even disposition.

After supper, Josette watched like a happy mama as Melinda and Kennit danced. Her friend's eyes sparkled; Kennit's tense features had relaxed into smiles. How long since the man had thought about what he did instead of blindly continuing old habits?

Hargreaves found her there, smiling as she sipped wine, unpartnered for the moment. "Mdm. Sourantine no longer requires your presence in the card room?"

A thousand candles lit her smile. "I have completed my duty tonight, thank you, sir."

"How did you manage to pry Kennit from the table? And Musgrove as well?" He nodded toward the peer turning in the steps as he partnered Constance Lockhart.

"Feminine wiles. But I believe Lord Musgrove will soon retreat. Alas, I disappointed him when I refused a third dance."

"No awakened desire to be Hera?"

"No. Have you been here long, my lord? I did not see you earlier."

"Long enough to count your four partners. Who was the young man after Kennit's first dance?"

"That was Didier Vernon. He wanted to dance with my friend Melinda Ratcliffe but had to wait a dance. I became his second choice."

"An *émigré*? You seem surrounded by them."

"M. LeBrun brought the Vernons to our salon tonight. And yes, he is an *émigré*. He was just a child when his parents fled France. He has little memory of his home."

"His family is here tonight?"

"The older *M. Vernon* is by the palms, talking with Mrs. Wilton. I do not see his mother, but she is here."

"I thought their name was Vernon." He said it without the French accent.

"They have Anglicized it, yes."

"But you give it the French pronunciation. You also do this with LeBrun. Most people do not. Has that something to do with your father, when he Anglicized his name?"

His perception startled her. "Why, yes, I think it must. He always introduced himself as *Henri Sourantine*, even though my grandfather and many others gave his name the English sound. He said once—oh, many years ago, after Mama died—that he missed hearing his name as it was his name. She always called him *Henri*. He said that *Henri* was a touch of home. And for the refuge *émigrés*, it is a touch of home that does not have to be lost to them."

He looked around the room and spotted another *émigré* with an Anglicized name. "Thus, Mrs. Clara Arnold is ... ."

"*Mdm. Claire Arnaux* from Nimes."

"Mr. Theodore Gerard ... ."

"*M. Théodore Giraud.*"

"And Miss Josette Sourantine?"

She laughed. "I am still Josette Sourantine, sir. England *is* my home."

He saluted her claim then put his goblet on a side table. "Shall we take a tour of the room for this next set, Miss Josette Sourantine?"

She gladly slipped her hand into the crook of his elbow. She wished he would lead her somewhere quiet and kiss her, as he had so nearly done yesterday and Monday evening. Instead, she chattered and smiled and walked about with him and prayed he wouldn't see into her heart.

. ~ . ~ . ~ .

Saturday, November 30

"Your best conquest," Josette confided to her friend as they reviewed last evening, "was Tobias Kennit."

"Do you truly think so?" Melly handed over the teacup then joined her friend on the cushioned bench. She looked outside, but the rain-soaked window blurred any view. The dreary day, however, did not depress her spirits, for she smiled. "I hope so. I like him. He has such a dry wit, such an intriguing view of the world."

She would not be a good friend if she didn't warn her. "He is jaded, Melly. A notorious gamester and a rake. Your father would not deem him a suitable match for his daughter."

"I considered that several times last evening."

"And yet you continued? I think Mr. Kennit also made a conquest."

Melinda smiled and sipped her tea. "Should I have brought up the gambling question?"

"Yes."

"What if he dislikes me for it when he considers all my question entails?"

"You caused him to think, Melly. He needs to realize what gambling does." Ironically, she remembered, Reynolds had reminded her of that same lesson only Tuesday morning.

"I think his friend did not care for that conversation."

"No, Lord Musgrove did not. He enjoys winning. Did you not hear him? 'The point, for some, to defeat the weaker opponent.' "

"And to save my philosophy for the lecture hall. I definitely did not please him, did I?"

"He is wealthy. He has never had to consider the cost of losing." As she said it, Josette realized that she had been glad for more than one reason last evening that she had never been attracted to the privileged Lord Musgrove. How terrible to be married to a man who claimed a worthiness but was revealed to have a littleness of character.

"He is very wealthy," Melinda said. "Mr. Stephenson told me so when Musgrove claimed a second dance with you. And he paid you a flattering number of compliments. Are you interested in him?"

"He is only a close acquaintance."

"You play cards with him at every salon and willingly dance with him, but he is only an acquaintance. You called Mr. Kennit a friend."

"And so he is."

"You should not let Lord Musgrove have false hopes, Jos. It is neither wise nor kind."

She deflected the advice. "Celeste would have me keep several suitors on a string. Who would I have, do you think, after my time here in London? Lord Musgrove. Mr. Rampley." She forbore to mention Giles Hargreaves, hoping Melinda had not seen them tour the *grande salon* and the two sets they devoted to conversation in a corner of the room. He had not offered her an intimate *tete-a-tete* last evening. The depth of her disappointment had first embarrassed her and then worried her. An attraction to Giles Hargreaves she would willingly admit to; was she also falling for him?

"Do you model yourself on Celeste now?"

She didn't answer. She was too aware of listening ears.

"Are you interested in anyone?" Her blush answered for her. Melinda clapped her hands. "Oh, this is wonderful. Your grandfather will be pleased. Who is it?"

Josette scolded herself, *Tell it now to Melly. Now.* She should tell it all, from the confusing way Giles treated her to their undeniable attraction. Yet she couldn't; still she couldn't. "I shan't say. Not until I am more certain."

"Was he at last evening's salon? Tall and dark, I think, and with a cane. I won't tease you. He must have dangled on Celeste's string."

"Melinda!"

"I'll say nothing more. Except that you are blooming. And if he is worth having, then naturally he must prefer you over Celeste's flighty dash. Now, I'm done. Will you introduce me to him?"

Josette gave her friend an arch smile. "Of course, even if I risk losing another of my few suitors to you. Ah, my turn to tease you! You need have *no* fears that I was ever attracted to Tobias Kennit, or he to me." Then she deliberately turned the conversation down other avenues, determinedly keeping it off suitors and whist.

Only as Melinda was leaving did her friend return to her chief worry. "Oh, Josette, what if I did offend Mr. Kennit?"

"You didn't. You didn't dictate. You only questioned. I delivered the sermon."

"He must think I am a crusading vicar's daughter."

"Aren't you?"

She laughed. "Yes. Yes, I am."

"Then he should know that from the beginning."

"He does now." She laughed again, and Josette envied her bubbling happiness and the simple path her attraction was following. The rumble of carriage wheels sounded on the paving stones. Melly glanced around as Coleman rolled the Sourantine carriage to a stop then pressed Josette's hand. "You are so sweet to offer your carriage for Nellie and me. The hackney we hired to come here leaked dreadfully. I'm so grateful, and Aunt Bradley will be terribly impressed. Nellie will feel quite above herself. And I'm glad, Jos, so glad I came to London. I am glad that we convinced Aunt Bradley to come to the salon."

"She did not need much convincing."

"She did after you left. She was very worried that our dresses would be too plain and that it was a gambling den."

"And this morning?"

"She was pleased with the evening and approved of my attendance at another salon. She even told Uncle Bradley that he should attend."

"So you will come Monday evening?"

"I would not miss it."

"But not to be with your old friend. No," she laughed in her turn as Melinda would have protested at her teasing, "not *just* to be with your old friend. You have several new ones as well. Look, the rain is letting up."

It thundered. The carriage horses jolted forward then settled as Coleman reined them in. Melinda looked up at the purpled sky. "Only a brief reprieve. I must go. Will you join us at church tomorrow? And afterwards? Aunt Bradley wanted me to ask."

"Then I shall come. I know Celeste has no plans to attend, and Albert has yet to return from visiting the Hussar regiment he wants to join."

She watched Melly dash to the carriage where her maid already waited. She waved. Coleman snapped the reins, and the coach jolted forward.

Lightning streaked. Thunder boomed. And the rain poured down. Josette watched until it obscured the coach. Then she shivered, drew her shawl closer, and stepped inside so Angus could shut the door.

Chapter 14 ~ Sunday, December 1

As he waited in the hall, Giles congratulated himself on passing Reynolds without the butler's usual obstructions. Hearing footsteps on the stairs, he looked up. Josette came around the curving stair and descended to him. She wore pale yellow silk that reminded him of the earliest days in summer. She came forward to offer her hand without hesitation. Even as her eyes asked questions about his early visit, her bright smile warmed him.

"I am early, I know, but I have family business later."

"Business on Sunday, sir? You refuse a chair and wait upon me in our hall. Indeed it must be pressing. Does your family recall you to Grasmere?"

He did not answer her question, choosing instead to throw out another bit of Lady Eaton's advice, hoping Josette would snap up the lure of his eagerness for her. "I wanted to see you, and I did not want to wait until Monday evening. I hoped you would come for a drive in the park. The sun is blazing, and my curricle is equipped to keep you warm. I would have come yesterday, but the rain ... ."

Her glow dimmed. "A drive with you sounds wonderful, but I am committed already this morning, to attend an Advent service with a friend."

He hadn't anticipated another rival for her attention.

"Would you care to join us?" she added. As he hesitated, the light left her eyes. "I will understand if you cannot."

Her friend could not be Tobias Kennit, not going to a church service. Gordon Musgrove perhaps? Or one of the other men who had danced with her after supper? He decided not to commit. "May I drive you to the service?"

Her eyes flashed with joy. "That would be nice. Please, give me only a few minutes." She turned to the butler, telling him that she would not need the coach and reminding him that she would not return until early evening. Her whole day was planned then. She hurried up to her room.

When she joined him the second time, she had donned a green velvet coat and matching hat. A single black feather curled down, grazing her cheek, reminding him of the softness of her skin. Giles complimented the dashing hat as he handed her into the curricle.

Josette laughed. "A foolish buy, but I could not resist."

He covered her with a fur, for clear cold had replaced yesterday's rain. "Where must I take you?"

"St. Clement Church. I understand it is in Eastcheap, near the river. Do we have enough time, or shall we be late?"

He snapped the reins. The horses started smoothly. "We have enough time. Who is this friend you are joining?"

"Melly. Melinda Ratcliffe, I should say. She arrived in town last Tuesday. She is staying with her aunt and uncle, the Thomas Bradleys. I think you met her at Friday's salon."

"Is she the young lady who tempted Kennit from the card room?"

"The very same. She is a great beauty."

No, he thought, *I will not fall into the trap of comparison.* "I would define her as a siren, to have tempted Tobias Kennit onto the dance floor. He hovered around her most of the evening. How did she manage that?"

"I am not quite certain. They had a philosophical difference over gambling."

"Which she must have won." Josette gurgled a laugh in agreement. Giles whistled. "Impressive enough that she lured Kennit from a game. To have kept his attention after they disagreed—amazing. No wonder Gordon Musgrove looked out of sorts. Who is this Miss Ratcliffe, besides your friend?"

"My oldest friend. I am perhaps wrong to feel such glee at her success. I want it to last. It may not when society discovers she has no connections and only a small stipend. She is a vicar's daughter."

"And a beauty," he reminded. "A beauty who caught Kennit's roving eyes. That will keep her at the vanguard of attention. I shall be curious to see how long he remains interested. They will be betting on it at the clubs."

"Betting on how long she keeps his attention? Surely not."

He shrugged and turned onto another street, starting to bustle even though it was Sunday. Giles steered around the frozen puddles. "Kennit is known for his dalliances. If your friend wants to snare him, she'll have to intrigue him. He's had all the usual lures thrown at him."

"My lord, you would appear to believe that Melinda's purpose—any woman's purpose—is only to snare a husband."

He glanced over at her, her cheeks and nose reddened by the cold, the feather blown away from her cheek by the speed of their travel. "You have a few other purposes as well," he said expressively. He didn't elaborate. From the way her eyelashes fluttered down, he knew she wouldn't pursue his comment.

He smiled inwardly. He would enjoy teaching her the delights of marriage. The thought startled him. Much about Josette Sourantine he admired. He had never hesitated to acknowledge their mutual attraction. But he had never planned beyond the original goal of arresting the French spy Celeste Sourantine, her source for the War Office despatches, and any other spies caught in the net. With that between him and Josette, what future was possible?

Did he want to think of marriage to Josette? Was he prepared for marriage? His life this year had already had two major disruptions, from his wound and his decommissioning. Last New Year he had planned to stay with the campaign until Wellington defeated Bonaparte. Returning to England had not crossed his mind. He certainly had not considered a leg-shackle. Would marriage to Josette be a burden?

He shifted the conversation back. "A vicar's daughter doesn't sound like a good match for a rake."

She willingly followed his change, as if she had also stepped too close to a commitment she was not ready to contemplate seriously. "I warned Melinda that her father would not approve. She herself knows that. She is a sensible young lady."

"But she will continue to throw lures his way?"

"Yes, even if you must put it in such a hateful way."

"Leopards don't change their spots, Miss Sourantine."

"I know that. So does Melinda. But—." She shook her head and buried her nose in the fur. After a moment she emerged from the soft beaver. She didn't continue to contradict him, choosing instead to describe the people he would soon meet.

Seated beside her during the service, Giles remembered that conversation. At his club yesterday, he discovered his pursuit of Josette Sourantine had also entered the betting book. He had intended for the information to enter society; that had been his goal when he visited the Sourantine house on Wednesday. Yet what would happen to her when the arrests occurred? She would know his deceit then; that would be painful enough. Coupled with that, however, would be society's avid nose, sniffing out her pain at being trifled with. Everyone would understand his motives; of course, they would. The nation had to be protected from spies. His reputation would not suffer. Hers would.

Giles had never considered that before.

Seated beside her, standing when she did, sharing the same Prayer Book, watching the lighting of the Candle of Hope for the first Advent Sunday, he could foresee her bleak future in London society. She shouldn't have to face that. But what could he do? Nazenby wouldn't let him withdraw, not when he had an easy entrée into the Sourantine house. Withdrawing now would not rescue Josette from society's speculation and censure.

He was trapped between his duty to country and an emotion he had never expected, an emotion he wouldn't name, couldn't name, God help him.

.~.~.~.

They dined *en famille*, around a table that barely accommodated them all. Giles sat elbow to elbow between the Bradley boys, a new experience for him. Along with the young Ratcliffe boy, they peppered him with questions about the war. Once they discovered he had been wounded, only Mrs. Bradley's intervention kept the gory details unasked.

After the luncheon, the boys disappeared, but Mr. Bradley took up the banner, wanting to discuss the war, eventually extending to Napoleon's intentions toward Russia. "They broke their compact with Bonaparte by resuming trade with us. Do you think he will attack them?"

"It's a massive country for an invasion."

"But their army has nothing but illiterate peasants for soldiers and aristocratic officers for leaders. Napoleon can easily defeat such a rabble."

"Their army is much the same as our own."

"A good point. 'Twill be bleak days for us if Boney brings Russia back under his heel."

"He doesn't hold the continent yet, sir. And we have the seas. Since he cannot challenge us on the seas, his blockade against us must fall apart soon."

The women bustled in. Giles stood, watching Josette's affectionate interaction with her friend and Mrs. Bradley and the younger girl. She held her own sister-in-law at arm's length. Could she know about Celeste's spying? Did she hold her brother's death against Celeste?

Then he took himself to task. Her relationship with her *belle-soeur* did not matter. He used Josette to get information and for no other reason. His own feelings didn't matter at all. And if she were arrested with the spy, so be it.

Buttoned into the green coat, the black feather of her hat brushing her cheek, Josette looked across to him. "I hope I have not delayed you too much, my lord. You did say that you had business this afternoon."

He had to harden his heart to her. He had to remember his mission. For his mission he had put his crack team and curricle in the hands of an unknown hostelry. For his mission he had endured the boys' questions and the uncle's worries about Napoleon. For his mission he had risen early on Sunday and attended an Advent service at a church not his own. He did much for his mission. Nazenby would owe him dearly. "We have time."

Giles bowed to the ladies and shook Mr. Bradley's hand. The boys jostled for the best position on the steps. He handed Josette up and saw her properly covered with the fur rug. She waved and turned in her seat, still waving, as he drove off. Then she settled back with a happy sigh and tucked the furs close.

He cleared his throat and settled to Nazenby's business. "Mr. Bradley asked how long you have been in London. I did not know."

"Since late summer."

"Not your first time in London, I believe you said once."

"It's the second. My debut was five years ago."

"Did you have no suitors at all?"

"None," she admitted. "I hardly had time. I was scarce a month here when word came of my grandmother's death."

"You waited a long time to return."

"Five years might seem a long time, but I had more important concerns than an endless round of parties to attend. I had the chief responsibility of my younger brother and sister. William was eight then, and Antonia, barely three. And then our father died two years later. Both parents gone and only one grandparent remaining, that is very difficult for young children. But I have returned," she added with forced cheerfulness. Grandpapa says I must stay in London—and not buried in Little Houghton—until I lure a suitor into my trap. See, I admit you are right. I use your words."

He checked the horses so a wagon could rumble past. They started again with a jolt. "You did not come to London to visit your sister-in-law?"

"Celeste was devastated, poor thing, when Edmund died. They had only been married a couple of years. I was of no help, grieving for my father and devoting myself to my sister and brothers. And Grandpapa would keep saying that he knew it was only a matter of time, with the wild hunters that Edmund would buy. After a few months of our gloom and his doom, Celeste fled. First to her parents, but she stayed with them no more than a month, I think. Then she came to London. She re-opened our house. I do not think that I even considered joining her here until Grandpapa suggested it this past Spring. She wrote that she would be at the seashore or visiting her parents and advised that we wait. And so we came in August."

"Where do her parents live?" he asked as if he didn't know the answer from Sir Roger.

"In Cambridge. Her father Vincent Nemours lectures at the university. Did I not tell you this earlier? In the *ancien regime* he was of the *noblesse de robe*. At least, that was my father's opinion. I do know that Celeste's mother wishes to return to France, but I don't think *M*. Nemours would, not even under Napoleon's new order."

Josette had not noticed his start at her question. He had received information from so many sources that he could not remember from where all his facts about Celeste Sourantine had come. She had continued talking, giving him time to compose himself after his slip. "Would your father have returned to France? When did he come to England?"

"Did I not tell you? I thought I had. I do remember telling you that he came over with his friend Robert LeBrun. That was in '85. And I have told you he was an adventurer."

"Yes, I remember that. He taught you to play cards. With pebbles."

She smiled at what he chose to remember. "Papa knew too much of gambling, on the cards, on the horses. I compare him to Tobias Kennit. Gamester that he is, he is still *haut ton*. My father never was."

"He fell for a Yorkshire lass. And it seems Kennit may have fallen for your Miss Ratcliffe. I do remember your telling me that Yorkshire lasses can steal a man's heart."

"Isn't Melly the sweetest girl?"

He let her chatter on, not wanting this drive back to seem too much like an interrogation. They neared the square too quickly. He thought of driving around a bit, but he had started the day with the lie about a later appointment.

Giles drew up the horses at the house. A footman started forward, but he signaled for the man to wait. She glanced at the servant then to him and leaned back, expecting the question.

"Your father, did he never return home?"

"Never. He never spoke of his family. He might have sprung from the ocean's foam. I did ask him once. He didn't answer. He looked sad."

"And tender heart that you are, you never asked again. Have you decided? Was he an adventurer?"

Josette's eyes widened, looking very blue. "Oh, an honorable *chevalier d'epee* or a dishonorable *chevalier d'industrie*?" She wrinkled her nose. "I have never decided. Grandpapa claimed that Papa lived by his wits, that my mother was a lucky chance he seized upon. He had the grace to treat her kindly—or the wit to know Grandfather Newland wouldn't tolerate anything else. And now I must go. Celeste will quiz me." She signaled the footman and thrust away the fur.

"Miss Sourantine—." She looked round at him, her eyes wide and trusting, unaware of his great deception. He must continue to deceive her—although the line between truth and deceit was getting blurred. The truth kept pouring out of him, unplanned and without any cunning couched with it. The only lie seemed to be the mission that had begun his pursuit of this woman. Looking into her clear eyes, he gave her the truth again. "I enjoyed our day together."

Her smile widened. "As I did, sir."

"Lady Eaton plans a party this week. I shall see that your family receives an invitation."

"Lady Eaton? Celeste will view an invitation from her as a real coup. Thank you, sir. I trust you are not too late for your business."

"It will wait. Good day, Miss Sourantine."

He could have driven off, but he wanted to see if she would turn for a last look. She did. Giles touched his hat then let the horses start.

. ~ . ~ . ~ .

Celeste pounced as soon as Josette was within doors. "I see that you spent your day with Lord Hargreaves."

"He kindly offered to drive me to Eastcheap. I attended church with my friend Miss Ratcliffe. We stayed to dine with the Bradleys. The boys were quite taken with Lord Hargreaves' stories about the war." She gave her outdoor things to the waiting Angus then walked upstairs to the *petite salon*, set up for receiving. She did not want to hear Celeste's critique of her day while the servants listened.

Her sister-in-law did not care who heard. She had a word for every step up the stairs. "Lord Hargreaves in Eastcheap! Did he dine *en famille* with the *bourgeoisie*? I never would have expected him to lower himself so."

"Lord Hargreaves is not an arrogant aristocrat, Celeste. He is not shallow. He understands what is most important in life." She shut the door firmly. Thank Heavens the fire was lit and burning cheerily. The servants would not overhear every word of the tirade that she would apparently have to endure. What bee had buzzed into Celeste's bonnet?

"*Oui*, a church service in Eastcheap is important. Dining with schoolboys is important. And sitting with you in a carriage on our very doorstep, that is very important. What were you talking about?"

Ah, they had come to the reason. "He asked about my background, about my family."

Her sister-in-law flounced onto the blue-cushioned divan. "You have no right to tell him anything about me!"

"My family, Celeste, not yours." Josette felt a twinge of guilt at the lie. A few questions *had* addressed Celeste. She walked to the mantel and held her frozen hands to the fire's heat. "Lord Hargreaves wanted to know about my father."

The woman's deep blue eyes narrowed. Her face twisted with a malice never before unveiled. "That—that *chevalier d'industrie*! That Captain Sharp!"

The insults left her unruffled, as if Giles Hargreaves' comments about them had inured her. "Yes, I think my father was that." She dropped into French, hoping Celeste's native language would have a soothing effect. She still could not divine what had set her off. It must be much more than Giles' courtship. "Why are you so upset, *ma belle-soeur*?"

"If Lord Hargreaves wants to know about *me*, he should ask *me*."

"I told you: he asked about my family, about my father. He asked when Papa came over from France and how he met my mother and what Grandpapa Newland thought of their match. What is wrong, Celeste? You have been on edge since you returned from the seashore. Is it about your debts?"

"*Tiens*, you continue to harass me about those debts. Did you tell Hargreaves that I was in debt? Did you tell him that I have been 'on edge' since I returned from the seashore? You have no right to talk about me."

"Celeste, we did not discuss you." She ignored the guilt at her continued lie. She patiently offered what she hoped would be a balm. "Hargreaves mentioned that Lady Eaton will host a party this week. We can expect an invitation. You should wear your new gown. You look lovely in that midnight blue studded with brilliants."

Her sister-in-law snapped up the bait. "That would be perfect! With my new fan and—but no. No! I refuse to attend the party of that harridan."

"Harridan? Lady Eaton? She has shown us nothing but kindness."

"*Tu es une imbecile!*" Celeste threw up her hands. "You know nothing!" She jumped up and sped to the door. "I cannot speak to you anymore. I want to see not one of you." She slammed the door as she left.

Reynolds had no cause for Celeste's distress. "She has received neither visitor nor letter today, Miss. She seems to await someone."

"Where is she now?"

"In the Blue Room, Miss. She has been there much of the day. She either stands at the window overlooking the street or she paces the floor. She complained the room was cold, but then she snapped at Angus when he went in to light the fire. I did not ready the Blue Room this morning, Miss, it is so rarely used on Sunday."

"She did not go to her chamber? You are right; she must be waiting for someone. But why is she so upset? Did she receive a message last evening, Reynolds? Or a late visitor? I did not speak with her this morning before I left, but—."

"No, Miss, no message or visitor, this morning or last evening."

On the heels of the butler's denial the footman announced Robert LeBrun.

The Frenchman entered, dressed in the height of fashion as always, a complacent smile on his handsome face. He thumped his cane on the floor as he bowed. "Miss Josette, a delight to see you. I understand you were away most of the day."

The butler's eyebrows shot up at LeBrun's knowledge of events of the house. By no blink of an eye did Josette reveal her own surprise. Celeste must have sent a message that Reynolds knew nothing about. How had that been possible? Reynolds kept a finger everywhere.

"M. LeBrun, you look well this cold day. Bring tea, please, Reynolds. I am still chilled through by my drive with Lord Hargreaves." She gestured toward a chair and waited until the surprising visitor had seated himself. "Yes, I was away for several hours, calling upon my friend Miss Ratcliffe. I believe you met her Friday evening."

"A most charming young lady."

"And I attended an Advent service before noon."

"Advent already? Noël will soon be upon us."

"Are you aware that Lady Eaton will host a party this week?"

"No, I was not, but—."

"We are invited, but Celeste now claims she will not attend. I returned not an hour ago to find she is greatly distressed. No one can tell me the cause. She is not like herself, *M.* LeBrun. I do not know how to calm her."

"She is distressed?"

"Very distressed. She seems almost unbalanced. She will not listen to reason." Josette had an inspiration. "I appeal to you, sir, as one of her oldest friends."

"*À moi*? What can I do?"

"After a visit with you, Celeste is always smiling. What secret power do you wield, sir? Flattery? Whatever it is, you must work your magic again." She gave him no option if he were to maintain his role of close family friend. Josette rose and held out her hand. "Come, I will take you to her."

LeBrun hesitated, but she continued to hold out her hand. Perforce he rose and allowed her to lead him to the front room decorated in blues.

When the door opened, Celeste snapped, "I do not wish to be disturbed!"

"*M.* LeBrun is here," Josette said reasonably. "You always enjoy his visits, Celeste. To refuse to see him would be rude."

"You cannot force me!"

"No, of course not, but you are so cheerful when he leaves. Please, talk with him a little. I will leave you two alone."

"He is not the one—." She pressed her lips together. In French she said, "I will see you and only you, Robert."

Josette closed the door and retreated. Reynolds had brought the tea. As she seated herself by the fire and took up the steaming teacup, she asked, "Did you discover how she received or sent a message?"

"You have much faith in me, Miss Josette."

"I am well acquainted with your skills, Reynolds. Tell me what you've learned."

His wooden face could not quite hide his smirk of success. "Reilly, Miss, handed a letter to Coleman last evening and again this morning. Madame has awaited a reply all day. She has inquired repeatedly of Reilly but still has not received one."

Josette hesitated to inquire further, for she would be prying into Celeste's private affaires. She appeased that biting self-reproach with a simple remembrance of her sister-in-law's agitation. "To whom did she send this letter?"

"Reilly could not say, Miss. The only direction was a curious symbol."

"A symbol?"

"A fleur de lis, Miss."

"The French flower? And Coleman needed only to see this symbol to know who was to receive this letter?

"That is what Reilly conveyed to me."

Was this mysterious message tied to Celeste's visits to the seashore? Hargreaves had once questioned who Celeste went to see. Had her *belle-soeur* been conducting a secret *affaire de coeur*? Were all her other beaux merely shields to mask her true feelings? And only Coleman knew the recipient of the message. That would fit, for only he accompanied Celeste to the seashore. Why, then, had she suddenly become so distraught? Had she seen her beloved with another woman? Was that it?

And now, after a day's waiting, Robert LeBrun unexpectedly appeared, with knowledge of the morning's events. Had he come in response to Celeste's secretive missive? He was French. The *fleur de lis* could be his sign. Josette remembered how her sister-in-law had greeted LeBrun. How grudging Celeste had been. Surely if she had awaited him, she would have been eager to speak with him. No, LeBrun must not be the mysterious recipient. Yet he knew the events of the house. The recipient must have sent LeBrun in his place. Yes, that seemed probable.

"What do you make of it, Reynolds? A secret letter addressed with a symbol sent to an unknown person?"

"I could not say, Miss. Shall I have Reilly or Coleman speak to you?"

"No, Reynolds, do not. Please see that Reilly does not convey to Coleman that we have questioned her about this message. And I would like to know if my sister-in-law receives a reply." That would be definite evidence that LeBrun was not the intended recipient.

"Very well, Miss Josette."

"When M. LeBrun finishes his conversation with Madame, I would like to speak with him, to thank him."

He bowed and left. She sipped her tea, relishing its heat but puzzling over the mysterious letter. She had divined no answer when LeBrun returned. He carried himself with his usual aplomb; only the narrowing of his eyes revealed a concealed tension. If she hadn't spent several weeks in his company, Josette would not have realized his earlier insouciance had evaporated.

He seated himself and leaned back, seemingly at home. "She is your Celeste again. The harpy has vanished."

"I am greatly in your debt, M'sieur. Did she speak of what had so disturbed her?"

"*Non.* You must repay me, Josette. I was—what is your phrase?—ah, at my wit's end at the beginning."

"But she is calmer now?"

"She is calm now, yes. *Triste* but calm."

"What do you think so upset her? Do you have any idea?"

"You spend most of the day with one of her former beaux and ask that? Ah, you blush. This *affaire* must truly be one of the heart." He rose. "You will not forget my little favor, yes?"

Josette stood as well. "What could I possibly offer you, *M'sieur* LeBrun?"

"A winning hand against M. Kennit, perhaps? *Non,* I jest. I will inform you later. Do you remember, Josette. A little favor only."

Chapter 15 ~ Monday, December 2

As promised, the invitation from Lady Eaton's reception arrived in the next mail. After the first excitement ebbed, Celeste remembered her refusal. "You may go," she said grandly, "but I shall not." She kept to that stance as she and Josette watched the Eaton party ascend the staircase to attend Monday's salon.

The Jasper Eatons followed the dowager. Then came the Davenports and the Lockharts. Trailing behind Miss Lockhart were Alex Westover and Richard Malbury.

"La," Celeste exclaimed, "again it is that you arrive together. You must purchase an enormous carriage, yes, with many horses to pull it. Then you may talk together as you drive through London." Her tittering laugh carried down to the Wiltons just beginning their ascent. She seized upon John Davenport's sleeve to engage him with something that to Josette's ears sounded like nonsense.

Lady Eaton glanced at her hostess then turned with a wide smile to Josette. "You sister-in-law appears very excited this evening."

"No more than usual," she lied. She did not know why Celeste chattered so loudly. With her heightened color and glittering eyes she looked feverish. The start of a salon, however, was not the time to inquire after her *belle-soeur*'s health. She dropped a quick curtsey. "I thank you, my lady, for the invitation to your reception."

"It will be a delight to have you attend, Miss Sourantine. Will you all come, your brother and your sister-in-law?"

Josette flushed, hoping the second lie did not reveal itself on her face. "We hope to, although my *belle-soeur* has mentioned a previous engagement that evening. My brother Albert is expected to return tomorrow. I received a note from him this morning."

"Then I shall see you there. I expect quite a crush. I am surprised at the number of people who remain in London."

"This is my first December in London. I would have thought that most people would return to their homes for Christmas."

"More and more of them reside permanently in London, as your sister-in-law does. Your family is lucky to have this house, with its private grounds. I expect, as more estates are developed into terraces, that London will soon be quite crowded at Christmastime. The city is becoming the destination."

"For some, perhaps. I wish I were packing for York. I have never spent Christmas away from home. I have a little brother and sister, you see. I will miss them." She blinked rapidly to banish the threatening tears.

"Ah, family. If all goes well, we shall be rolling toward Eaton Place in a fortnight." She patted Josette's gloved hand. "I shall hope this holiday will not be the first one that you are apart from your family." She inclined her turbaned head then walked on to the *grande salon*, trailed by their extended party.

Celeste had moved on to the Vernons and Claire Arnaux, but when the larger group moved away, she shooed them off. "*Allez-vous-en*," she laughed. "Go risk your purse, eh, Didier?" She fluttered her fan. In an aside to Josette she added, "He does not need to pursue that Constance Lockhart. Richard Malbury almost has her in his pocket."

"I think he just likes to flirt. My friend Melinda caught his fancy last week."

"Ah, the one who stole your *M*. Kennit."

"He wasn't mine to have stolen, Celeste."

Her sister-in-law ignored her. She glanced over the people lingering in the reception area then snapped her fan shut. "I am surprised that Lord Musgrove has not yet arrived. Is he not usually early? I do not see him. Where is he, Josette?" Her voice carried across the tiled floor and dropped to the entrance hall.

She shrugged. "Perhaps he has found another amusement."

"What is this? Does he pursue something besides you and cards?"

"I am not privy to his pursuits, Celeste."

"Is he not one of your beaux?"

Heads swiveled around. The other conversations stopped.

Hoping to prevent any gossip, Josette lowered her voice. "He is only an acquaintance, Celeste, nothing more. He partners Mr. Kennit when we play whist."

"But you often dance with him. Twice each salon. I have counted. I thought he was a beau. Such marked attention from a man usually means courtship, is it not so? You should number him among your beaux, yes? They are so small in number that you may easily keep track of them. Especially now that you have lost *M*. Kennit to your friend."

The loiterers would love this dispute. In an hour virtually every person at the salon would have heard of it and speculated about it. Hoping to keep the gossip in the realm of accuracy, Josette matched her voice to *belle-soeur's*. "Oh, Celeste, don't tell me that you counted Mr. Kennit as one of my beau? You know him not at all."

"Then who is to be counted your beaux, *ma belle-soeur*? Lord Hargreaves?"

Celeste's sweet tone was always a sign of her pettiness. Trying to smooth down her own ruffled feathers, Josette chuckled. "I do not have to write down their names. My court is small enough that I can easily remember them." Providence brought an elderly man up the stairs to rescue her. "And chief among them is Lord Wynstane." As she said the name, Josette glided forward to greet the elderly peer. She held out her hands. He obligingly took them after his courtly bow. "My lord, you come at last. We have missed you."

He beamed and with a flourish kissed both her hands. "I would come more often if you greeted me so fairly, lovely Miss Sourantine."

She slipped her hand onto his proffered arm, sleeved in a brocade long out of fashion, and guided him away from the stairs. Her serene façade hid the gleeful imp celebrating her triple victory, evading Celeste's questions then trumping the gossip she tried to start and finishing by escaping the reception line.

"Lord Wynstane." She squeezed his arm. "I know you plan to adjourn to the *grande salon* to flirt with your dowagers, but may I beg of you one game of whist?"

"I did not come prepared for a card game, Miss Sourantine."

"Do you only angle for a third wife, my lord? You seek those ladies' company more than my poor card play."

"It is not their charms but my pockets," he admitted. "I like my purse plump with coin. In the card room my purse will lighten more than I like."

His comments echoed Melinda's critique and Reynolds' reminder and Costell's nearly constant fate. Pricked by her conscience, she wheedled, "Will you play with me, we two alone and with only markers?"

He acquiesced, and she settled them at her usual table. Angus brought the markers. Soon they were deep into a friendly game, one that needed not an *nth* of her wit, one that held more conversation than competition and brought up her spirits after Celeste's sniping.

Kennit came in and started across. When he saw her sole partner and the markers, he veered away. Costell came in and likewise chose different partners. Yet after they had completed a second rubber, Sir Edward Garland slid into the vacant chair. He signed for a partner, and Claude Thierry joined them. Josette scowled her disappointment, but she dared not aim for a fourth victory. Celeste would come out the winner if she refused the men the table. They were guests in the house. Her parents and her grandparents had drilled in her that courtesy came before her own selfish wants.

She did the only thing she could. "We play only a simple game," she warned them.

"So I see," Garland said. "Time for a deeper game worthy of your talents, Miss Sourantine." He called for wine and had the bottle left on the table. Then he cast aside the markers and named a high stake.

Panic flooded Lord Wynstane's dim eyes. Josette tried to lower the stakes, but Thierry agreed with his partner. The elder peer could not, in honor, refuse, but his lowered brow bespoke his disquiet. Unhappily, Josette also had to acquiesce. She could not abandon him to Garland and Thierry; she could only hope to protect him.

Without Kennit to restore her coinage, she had to rely on Wynstane's pockets. That shamed her. And the shame doubled her anger. The imp that had hold of her this evening demanded vengeance for this intrusion on their friendly game and for alarming Wynstane.

Garland dealt. She had one hesitation, when Wynstane tried to be conservative, but her imp decided to double the number for their expected tricks. The old peer looked apprehensive. Josette wanted to reassure him. She tried with a smile, but he only looked at his hand, sorting and resorting his cards, his eyes blinking again and again. Fate helped, for chance dealt her a handful of the trump cards. Yet she could not win with those alone. She stepped up her game, taking tricks early with three daring uses of her mid-range cards. They won by a whisker, and she could breathe again.

Honor served, Lord Wynstane refused a re-match. "I am plumper in pocket than when I started, but I should not spend another hour at table. 'Tis past time that I went to flirt with my dowagers."

"You played a good game," Sir Edward allowed.

"I thank you for the compliment, but I tell you fairly that God never favored me as a gambler, not even in my salad days. Miss Sourantine, forgive my retreat."

"Dear Lord Wynstane, there is nothing to forgive. I regret that our easy game was ended. You will allow me to restore the coins you fronted? I have sufficient left to continue my play."

He took them with good grace and another courtly bow. "I will leave you now. Good evening, Miss Sourantine, gentlemen."

Josette watched him cross to the door, his silvered head held high.

Sir Edward did not wait for the elderly man to exit the room. "Why did you ever let that old fellow use markers? No game in that."

His voice, backed by privilege and wealth, carried. From her seat facing the card room, Josette saw people look toward them and away. She could not be certain if Lord Wynstane heard his fellow peer. The old man was a little deaf. Thankfully deaf, she hoped. She saw no check in his walk. Then she turned her head and scowled at Garland.

A Corinthian, handsome and wealthy, admired by countless women. She despised him.

"We were quite content with our game, sir. You did not have to join us."

He laughed. "Felt duty bound. You're past the nursery, Miss Sourantine, although Wynstane might be approaching it again."

Josette narrowed her eyes and planned another revenge.

Kennit's hand dropped onto the vacant seat. "May I partner you, Miss Sourantine?"

She eyed him. Yes, he would help her. She saw a glint in his eyes. He had no liking for Garland; he never had, though he tolerated him as a player and sometimes partner. Kennit would help her now.

She smiled. He blinked at its brilliance. "I am quite looking forward to you as a partner, Mr. Kennit," she purred. "We so often play as opponents. Please do join us. Unless you object, Sir Edward? *M. Thierry?*" They did not object, more fools they. "You have my winnings from Friday, Mr. Kennit?"

He produced the coins. Josette stacked them with her first winnings while Kennit shuffled and dealt. Thierry named the same high stakes.

"Oh, let's double them," she said and pushed forward all the coins she had won in the last match. Only Kennit raised his eyebrows. The other two men didn't hesitate.

They played fast, moving rapidly from one trick to the next so that the rubber ended in half the time. She and Kennit won by only one trick.

"That low trump," Sir Edward begrudged. "I didn't expect it. Thought you still had hearts."

"Oh, I was quite heart-less," Josette said and giggled at her pun. Kennit laughed with her. "I only had one heart the whole game. A woman does well to have only one heart, don't you think, sir?"

"Won't do her to have two," Garland agreed and began picking up his cards.

She watched him sort his hand into suits then spied Kennit watching her. A glance revealed Thierry also involved with his hand. She gave Kennit a tight smile. His eyes narrowed, but he nodded. "Same stakes, gentlemen?" he asked. "Or shall we double them again? Make it a real risk? Thierry?"

The Frenchmen studied his cards. "If Sir Edward agrees."

The peer turned from ordering another wine bottle. "Yes, yes. Go ahead and bid, man."

They settled into the game. No one spoke much during this rubber. Garland grunted satisfaction as he took two tricks with the ace and queen of diamonds, but Josette ensured those were the last tricks he won. As the game continued, Kennit leaned back, seemingly at ease, but she knew that signaled his sharpest wits, acutely dangerous to unwary opponents. Garland was blind, either from egoism or the wine or both. Thierry was a different fish. He grew more and more silent, his gaze shifting from her to Kennit and thence to his partner. Garland continued to drink down the second bottle of wine and did not seem to realize how close the game was until he again lost by one trick, this time taken by Kennit.

Sir Edward complained of the fall of the cards, complained that the gods did not favor him tonight, complained that he was unused to his partner.

"Try me for a partner," Kennit offered. "Or Miss Sourantine? Lady Luck might favor you if you partnered a woman. *M.* Thierry, are you willing to change?"

Josette looked up from shuffling. She had not realized Kennit knew Thierry was French; not many did. She had known from her first days in London. Celeste had let it slip. She had also quickly realized that Thierry hid his Gallic background. Yet Kennit knew.

Although that should not have surprised her. Kennit was wise to many a trick.

Then, as if struck, she wondered if a man who hid his French birth would accept a letter addressed with only a *fleur de lis*?

Thierry glanced at his partner. Garland frowned but acquiesced. "I'll take Kennit for partner. We'll see who Lady Luck favors."

"Very well," Josette began the deal. "I warn you, Sir Edward; I feel well favored tonight. The goddess of fortune might favor you if you partnered a lady."

"I'll take Kennit," he said stubbornly. He downed the wine and picked up the bottle, but it was also empty. He signaled to Angus for another. The footman looked at her. Josette nodded. If Garland thought to drink himself to success, he had much to learn about card play.

On her right, Kennit grinned at her. His eyes glittered with deviltry. He knew what she was about, and he was willing to empty his pockets if she desired it. She had to smile at him.

Kennit pushed in his coins. "Same stakes."

Sir Edward played the first card. Josette took the trick. His luck did not change. He took not one trick even though his partner took his expected share. Game over, the unfortunate man stared at the coins he'd lost.

"Shall we go another?" Josette offered. "I did warn you that the goddess of fortune favors me tonight."

Garland had manners enough not to swear. He drained off his glass then stood.

"Not retreating to the dowagers, are you?" Kennit gibed. Josette wanted to hug her friend for that.

Rather than respond, the peer uttered a brusque "good evening" and left the table.

Kennit had more grace than Garland had had, for he waited until the man was well away from the table. "Happy with what you won back, Thierry?" When the Frenchman agreed, he cocked an eyebrow at Josette. "Miss Ratcliffe should have witnessed this. She would have another unworthy reason to play cards: to punish someone. Still angry?"

She stopped arranging her winnings in neat stacks of ten. Tobias Kennit knew her well, too well. "I do not like the person I just revealed myself to be."

He grinned, his black eyes still glittering. "Punished his pockets since you couldn't punish him? I've been there. What set you off?" Josette pursed her lips, but he knew the answer. "Insulted old Wynstane, didn't he?''

"Mr. Kennit—."

"Enough said. I know. Ready to play and not murder my pockets?"

She had to laugh.

Without looking around, he lifted a hand. Gordon Musgrove came forward from where he had leaned on the wall to watch their game.

Surprised and gladdened to see her usual table partner, Josette beamed at him. "Lord Musgrove, I did not know you had arrived." Then Celeste's earlier comments about her beaux echoed. Her smile dimmed, and she wished she had not appeared so pleased.

"More evidence of how vengeful you were," Kennit murmured. "Thierry, will you continue to partner our fair goddess of fortune? She seems to rule the table tonight. Musgrove and I will try not to anger her."

The Frenchman looked a little shocked by Kennit's remarks, but he managed his usual suave smile. "I will. After the past few games, I think she is my best bet. But how did you manage it, Miss Sourantine? I have frequented all sorts of gaming houses, and I know many tricks myself, but I did not see you fluff any cards."

"I do not cheat, M. Thierry."

"Lord, no, never suggest that," Kennit drawled. "Never even think it. Miss Sourantine has a mind for cards, that's all. Takes a lot of the gamble out of it. Takes all of the gamble out of it when she's angry."

"Then I wonder, gentlemen, that you often seek her table for your play."

"Keeps my skills sharp," Kennit said.

"And she's the loveliest opponent in the room," Musgrove added. "Do you not agree, M. Thierry? As her partner, your purse is now safer."

"I shall endeavor to keep my wits also sharp."

"So you should, *M'sieur*," Josette warned him. "Our opponents also have the minds for cards. It is the reason we play each other so often. Our skill levels match."

"I hope to be worthy of my opponents and not disappoint you, Miss Sourantine."

"You could not disappoint me, *M'sieur*."

Kennit grinned. "And here I thought you had slipped your *belle-soeur*'s bonds."

"I beg your pardon, Mr. Kennit?"

"Be nice to the guests," Musgrove clarified.

Josette's guilt over the punishment she had meted out increased. Thierry's sharp gaze narrowed on her. She dropped her eyes and picked at a slub in the linen cloth.

"Usual stakes?" Musgrove asked calmly and dealt.

The play began. Kennit and Musgrove bantered about the cards that went down, the tricks taken, and gradually Josette's jangling nerves stilled. She glanced around the room, watching the mood at the other tables, motioning to Angus when he should re-supply the wine. The match ended, a second started. She looked up after taking the third trick to see Lord Hargreaves crossing to her table. She could not prevent a brilliant smile, and her reward came when he signaled to Angus to place a chair beside hers.

On the seventh trick, Reynolds approached and spoke quietly to Kennit. He closed his fanned cards. "Hargreaves, will you take my place?"

"If you like."

"I don't like," Musgrove snapped. "Where are you off to?"

Kennit didn't answer, just vacated his seat and strode away. The peer slapped a card down, and Thierry played under. With scarcely a glance at Kennit's cards, Hargreaves took the trick. He shared a smile with Josette. "I think Kennit has taken the bait."

"What do you mean?" his partner demanded.

Josette bounced in her seat. "Miss Ratcliffe must have arrived. I think she's snared Mr. Kennit."

"I didn't expect that," Musgrove said. "I would have bet he was wedded to the table."

"Need to change your bet at the club?"

The peer eyed Hargreaves over his cards. "I may have to. Seems bells are in the air for more than one couple."

When she saw him look at her, Josette blushed and devoted herself to her cards. "Your play, *M. Thierry*."

The awkward moment passed. After a few tricks more, the game ended. Thierry thanked them politely but excused himself from another game.

In a lowered voice, Giles said, "I did not realize he was French."

"He has been over here for many years," Josette advised, also in a lowered voice. "I believe he came some years after the Revolution. I do not know the exact year."

"Doesn't make a point of being an *émigré*," Musgrove added, "not like some."

"He has no accent."

"A great compliment to his efforts," she said. "My father struggled for years to make his accent not so strong, but he was definitely a Frenchman to his dying day."

"As are *Robert LeBrun* and *Théodore Giraud*."

"Yes, somewhat Anglicized but still French." She remembered their earlier conversation.

"*Claude Thierry* works very hard to be simply Claude Terry." Musgrove picked up the cards and prepared to shuffle. "Are we for another game?"

"Not again, my lord Musgrove," Josette said, as calmly as she could manage. His earlier comment still embarrassed her. He seemed to have transitioned from complimenting her to accepting Hargreaves's suit with decent grace. "I think, sir, that I have burned through all the good fortune I will have tonight. My wits are quite in ashes."

"I can believe that. You should have seen those games, Hargreaves. Garland slighted her friend Lord Wynstane, and she proceeded to empty the man's pockets."

"I discover a vengeful spirit inhabits me," Josette said plaintively. She stacked her coins.

"I'll keep those for you," Musgrove offered.

"No, thank you, my lord. I'll find Mr. Kennit and just drop them in his pocket."

"I can keep them as well as he."

She studied the peer. Everything that Lady Eaton had said and Melinda had seconded echoed. Hargreaves' insults also echoed: Captain Sharp. Jade. After she ran through Garland's pockets she deserved such insults. Hargreaves sat beside her, he had pressed his pursuit of her, but he did not offer to keep her coinage. 'A husband's office,' Lady Eaton had advised.

"I thank you, my lord, but no. I should keep them myself. I should never have started my arrangement with Mr. Kennit. What began as a simple convenience has raised eyebrows, you know. I will not burden you with it." She poured the coins into her embroidered reticule.

"It's no burden, not for our goddess of fortune."

Josette shook her head and pulled the strings tight. She stood. Both men also rose.

She did not take Giles' arm, but he walked with her from the card room. In the hall he murmured, "A very unhappy man back there. First Kennit abandons him, and now you."

"Perhaps he will be unhappy enough to decide I would not make a convenient wife. Then we may both avoid that embarrassment." He drew her toward the settee behind the stair, and she was content to follow.

"Why did you choose Kennit to keep your coins and not Lord Musgrove? He doesn't have a reputation as a rake."

"Kennit was never interested in *me*. He only tolerated me until he discovered how well I played whist. Our friendship, if you can call it that, is based on cards. I hope Melinda redeems him."

"No man can be redeemed unless he desires to be. But I do agree that one of London's rakes has fallen hard. I hope he does not break your friend's heart, either this year or in the future if they marry."

"Lord Hargreaves, have you not heard that reformed rakes are the best husbands?"

He grinned at her. "I have heard they make overly protective fathers." He took her hand and held it on his knee. "Has Lady Eaton's invitation arrived?"

"Yes, this very morning. You were kind to secure our invitation to such an exclusive party. Albert and I shall be in danger of arriving too early and thus exhibiting our eagerness."

Giles stiffened. "Your sister-in-law will not attend?"

"At this moment, no. She may change her mind. She likes to be contrary. This weekend she has been distraught, snapping at us for not reason and sending off mysterious messages."

"Mysterious messages?"

"Notes addressed only with a flower, a lack of address which is no hindrance for her coachman, who is the only one she will allow to deliver these secret messages. She wrote two notes, one Saturday evening and one early Sunday morning, and has had no reply as yet, according to Reynolds. I did notice Saturday afternoon that she seemed very distracted. She became even more distraught when I arrived home yesterday."

"After we spent the day together?"

"I explained our visit with the Bradleys, to no avail. Only *M.* LeBrun calmed her."

"Jealous." He sounded smug. "Don't worry. As long as she doesn't refuse me the house, I'm not concerned with how she feels."

"I am not reassured, sir. You do not have to live with her when she is disgruntled or distraught. She has not been herself since her last trip to the seashore, but it did not unhinge her." The description she had used to LeBrun still seemed accurate, so Josette repeated it. "Celeste was almost unbalanced yesterday evening."

"Mysterious notes. Secretive trips to the seashore, especially during early November. Could it be an affair gone wrong? A paramour?"

"Who would she need to meet away from London? It is not a regular meeting. She does not go often, and she never stays longer than a fortnight. She is usually happy when she returns. Were she indeed meeting a paramour, would she not be a little *triste* at parting from her love?"

"She wasn't happy on her return this last time?"

"She was—I think the best word would be 'angry'. Albert and I avoided her for days. And she must have left in the small hours. Her coachman grumbled about lack of sleep for days. Something happened; it must have. Since then, Celeste has been distracted and on edge."

"Will you ask her what the problem is?"

"Most definitely not! I do not want the sharp edge of her tongue."

His clasp tightened. "I did not come here this evening to talk of your sister-in-law." Giles shifted on the settee and asked her opinion of Rafe Lockhart's new wife. "I have heard she is the widow of Ivor Symonds. Did you ever meet them? You would likely have been only a girl when she was a debutante."

Their conversation had changed paths three or four times when Celeste came around the staircase and spied them. Josette was very glad she had not obsessed over her sister-in-law's behavior on Sunday.

"*Mon seigneur* Hargreaves, I find you hiding here rather than coming into my salon."

He stood politely when she approached. "You weren't paying attention to your guests then, for I stayed there a half-hour before continuing to the card room—." He reached a hand to Josette, and she obeyed the unspoken request, lifting her own and clasping his. "—To join Miss Sourantine. I wonder you did not see me, even without my regimentals to make me a dashing figure. I spoke with M. LeBrun and talked almost a full set with Mrs. Eaton and Mrs. Arnold."

"Ah, you conversed only. I had forgotten. *C'est impossible* for you to dance. Your wound. I must find someone else for dancing." She turned away.

Appalled, Josette stood up. She stepped to his side, their hands still joined. "Celeste—." Her sister-in-law ignored her call and tottered away, her old-fashioned heels clicking on the tiled floor. She turned to Giles. "My lord, allow me to apologize for—."

"Hush." He used his other hand to enclose hers in a warm grip. "She spoke the truth. I would like nothing better than to dance with you. I cannot. That is not cruelty, only reality."

"You are too considerate. Perhaps someday we can dance? When your leg is stronger?"

"Yes." Giles leaned close and brushed a kiss on her cheek. "Someday we shall dance together. For now, I would like nothing more than to take you down to supper."

Chapter 16 ~ Tuesday, December 3

As the smoke cleared, Giles lowered the rifle.

Lucas Armitage whistled. "Dead on, Hargreaves."

"Better than the musket," his brother Michael judged.

He hefted the rifle, looking at the serviceable weapon he had bought a few weeks ago. The musket Armitage held had its silver plates chased with intricate scrollwork. In comparison, the rifle's ugliness hid its deadly accuracy. "I knew some riflemen on the Peninsula. A rough lot, but deadly accurate and faster on the reload."

"Lucas has never fired a rifle."

"I hunt with a shotgun," the younger man explained.

"Then let today be your first test." Giles handed over the rifle and oversaw the loading. He explained the sights then stepped back to let the younger Armitage come to his own understanding of the weapon.

Lucas sighted, lowered the rifle then lifted it again, settled it comfortably, then sighted again. The rifle cracked.

"Expecting a battle?" Sir Roger had again approached without their noticing. He swept off his fashionable tall hat as the three men turned and greeted him.

"You surprise us again, sir." Michael Armitage gestured to the array of long-barreled weapons. "Prudent to be ready, would you not say?"

"Training young Lucas for the riflemen, Hargreaves?"

The younger brother spoke for himself. "I'm more interested in the Hussars, Sir Roger."

Giles glanced up. "You are not the only young man who has recently expressed such an interest. Do you know Albert Sourantine?"

Lucas nodded. "He has me considering it, yes. He came back last night, full of his past few days with the regiment. He brought one of the officers with him. Major Fellars."

"Will your parents want a conversation with him as his sister Miss Sourantine does?"

"Sourantine told me about his sister's conditions. Are you going to speak with him, sir?"

Giles recalled Josette's request. "I have said I would."

"To dissuade him with the horrors of war?"

"That was not going to be my subject."

"His sister wants to scare him off the plan."

"Would not the women of your family want you to be scared off?"

"If a woman's worries had any effect on a man, then he should not enlist," the young Armitage said sturdily.

"A worthy statement," Sir Roger said, "but I've seen men claim bravery only to run at the first sign of a French advance. A word, Hargreaves."

Giles left his cane on the table with the rifles and walked back up the hill with the spycatcher. At the crest Nazenby stationed himself to overlook the distant house; Giles looked back at the Armitage brothers, focused on reloading the muskets and rifle.

Nazenby cleared his throat. "I did not quite expect a report after last night's salon."

"But you wanted one, or you would not be here now."

"Matters proceed. I need to know your progress."

"The lady continues to accept my attentions. I lie my way into her home and heart. Is that all you want to know?"

"Not quite in smooth trim today, Hargreaves? This courtship was partly your idea."

"I find it has repercussions I didn't anticipate, sir."

"Such as?" The spycatcher's voice sounded as smooth as butter.

"Such as hurting innocents." He turned to face the older man. Beyond him far down the hill, the drive wound to the manor, and on that road a coach waited, facing away from the Armitage home. Nazenby did not intend a long meeting, then. He would give short shrift to any of Giles' arguments defending Josette.

That sudden insight was proved when Nazenby growled, "Do you truly believe anyone in that Sourantine household is innocent? Think again, Hargreaves. We know Mdm. Sourantine is not. We know a regular visitor to the house is Robert LeBrun, who crossed the line years ago and still walks its edge."

"We have no evidence against Josette or her brother Albert."

"The brother could be stealing the despatches. Isn't he a friend of Westover's cub?"

"Several young men who visit the Sourantines also run freely in Westover's house. Costell. Malbury. Wilton. They are all anxious for our spy's attention. Malbury and Wilton run short of money. And Lucas Armitage, he frequents both houses. I could name a dozen more, Sir Roger."

"And of those, none have a better link to our spy than her own brother-in-law."

"You heard Armitage: Albert Sourantine wants to join the Hussars."

"He may be mad for the Hussars this month. By January he'll be on to something else, something that will distract attention from what he really does."

"Or not. Just because he has a French father does not mean he is a Bonapartist. He could be as honest as you, Sir Roger, while our blue-blooded sons of England could be supplying the information to Mdm. Sourantine and her spymaster. Any of the young men she has enthralled would go to great lengths to win her attention."

"You argue a good point, Hargreaves. We shall know our source soon enough." The older man swiped his cane at a sturdy weed still surviving into December's cold, then he leaned on it, his gaze fixed on the waiting carriage. "Your defense of the Sourantines surprises me. I thought you too wise to be deluded by her, especially when she names LeBrun and Kennit as friends, and she flirts with Edward Garland and James Costell."

"She's no light muslin. I called her a jade, and it hurt her."

"So Lady Eaton informs me. I remind you that she's an excellent card player who spent her Monday evening emptying Garland's pockets. Josette Sourantine is no innocent."

"Are any of us?" he retorted. "I know what happened. I had it from Gordon Musgrove at my club this morning. Perhaps you should ask him."

"Another of her swains?"

Giles shrugged. "Think what you will. We've strayed from the point. I am convinced that Josette Sourantine is not involved in the spying. She is too open with me. I can find no hesitation or subterfuge in her answers."

"Spies are masters of using the truth to lie."

"I know this, sir. It's not in her. I think she's more in the dark about her sister-in-law's spying that we are."

An icy breeze swept across the hill, freezing them. Neither man moved to shelter from the cold, their conversation too important to stop for mere wind.

Nazenby's narrowed eyes didn't blink. "You blind yourself, Hargreaves."

Giles shoved his hands into his pockets. "Do I, sir? I think not. Josette tells me anything I ask. She tells me that our spy has been out of sorts since she returned from the coast. We know why: the muck-up at the inn and the death of her master smuggler. She nearly lost her transport to France. Now Josette tells me that over the weekend Mdm. Sourantine sent out two letters, both addressed with only a flower. These letters were delivered by her coachman, the only person who goes with her to the coast. If Josette were part of this spying game, would she point me to their transport? Would she inform on her sister-in-law's secret messages?"

The spycatcher didn't answer, pursuing instead the information Giles had just given him. "Two letters? Addressed with only a flower? This *is* news. What kind of flower?"

"Josette didn't say. Her concern was with her *belle-soeur*'s behavior. She said Celeste had not yet received a reply and seemed nearly unbalanced. Only LeBrun could calm her."

"Were the letters addressed to him?"

"Why would they be? He frequents the house. He often escorts her. She would not need to secretly contact him. No, Sir Roger, I think we have discovered how she contacts her spymaster. We have a means to identify the man. A man who moves freely around London. Perhaps a man who hides his true background. A man like *Claude Thierry*. I discovered only last evening, from Josette herself, that he is French."

"*Claude Thierry*? Not Terry?" Those clear eyes looked inward as Nazenby searched the vast banks of information in his mind. "That is a name I have not heard. I'll put people on it as soon as I return to London. But this does not solve our chief problem, Hargreaves. We still need Sourantine's source for the War Office despatches."

"We may soon have him as well, sir. I think our spy knows, somehow, that some important information is out, information she must acquire to help her cause. Why else would she become so distraught this weekend? LeBrun would have Josette think that she is jealous. I think that would have been Celeste's reaction two weeks ago. Could it be, sir, that our French spy has heard hints about Wellington's Spring campaign? Her reward for that information would be great. If Wellington is stopped this Spring, his whole military operation will be in shambles. He'll have to retreat. And Napoleon can push us right off the continent."

"That's the groundwork I laid," Nazenby said smugly. "My people started those whispers. Last week we prepared the despatch you drafted. Cavanaugh has it now. Tomorrow it goes to Westover's."

"A warning that the despatch was out would have helped, sir."

"I'm warning you now. I would have done so last night. You chose not to report after the salon."

"You're not worried that the despatch will be taken before it reaches Westover's?"

"No one at Cavanaugh's or the Regent's has close ties with Mdm. Sourantine, and we've watched closely for any contact outside the norm. They've stayed to routine, as she has. If our little spy follows her normal pattern, then only after the box reaches Westover will she leave London and head for her smugglers and France."

"You're certain the source is connected to Westover?"

"We tracked every possible contact. Only at Westover's do we have several connections to our Madame. We've even checked all the servants, down to Cavanaugh's coachman. He drinks at the same pub as the Sourantine coachman. We've got a man there, watching to see if they connect. I'll get a question to that man about letters addressed only with a flower. And we'll get a man onto the Sourantine coachman. He obviously knows more than I had reckoned."

"His name is Coleman. You'll be spread thin, assigning people here and yon."

"Not too thin. That was good information, Hargreaves, about the letters and about Claude Thierry. After a dry couple of weeks, we finally have something to take action on. Although your young lady could be distracting us."

No wonder the spycatcher had had success for so many years; he was like a dog with a bone. "Not she," Giles said firmly. He'd given his arguments. He would let Sir Roger mull them over. And he'd gather further arguments for their next meeting.

Nazenby's mouth twisted. "I trust you are not disillusioned. A woman's betrayal ruined one of my best spies. And consider yourself warned, Hargreaves: the despatch is out. By Thursday afternoon we should know if it was touched at Westover's."

"You want to put your watchers on the Sourantine house as well. Celeste Sourantine may not attend Lady Eaton's reception tomorrow night."

"Will she not? That I didn't expect. Another bit of information from your Miss Sourantine?" He didn't await an answer. Another breeze chilled them. Nazenby tugged his coat closer and settled his tall hat on his head. "I will see you tomorrow evening then. And I'll expect another report after the soirée is ended."

"As you wish, sir."

"As I demand." The words reminded Giles that he was the servant in this business for the Realm, and the spycatcher was the master. Nazenby touched the brim of his hat then strode down the hill toward the pond.

Giles watched until the carriage rolled away. Sir Roger would not be easily convinced that Josette was innocent. The man wanted the spies in a neat bundle; he would not be willing to unfasten any part of it.

In the next few days things would move rapidly. He had to keep his wits sharp. The smallest comment, the smallest gesture could hide information. The faked despatch gave the best chance to round up the spies before the year was out and Wellington geared up for his Spring campaign.

He returned to the Armitage brothers. The older Michael was one of Sir Roger's men, off the leash while he awaited new orders. Lucas was privy to his brother's secret, having been enlisted a time or two. Giles enjoyed his Tuesdays with them, finding it a relief not to have to guard his tongue, not having to explain any of his cryptic comments. Without preamble he asked, "What more can you tell me about Albert Sourantine? Does he gamble?"

Lucas laughed. "Not he, not even on horse races. And he dearly loves the horse races."

"But the Sourantines have gambling at their salons."

"Any party that sets out card tables will have gambling," Michael retorted.

"Compared to the dens Malbury and Westover drag us into, their games are tame."

"They have to drag you, little brother?"

The younger man reddened. "Let's say I find Covent Garden more alluring than a deck of cards or a roll of the dice. Lots of pretty chorus girls. Albert Sourantine's of my point of view."

"And the Sourantine ladies, what do you think of them?"

The brothers exchanged a glance. "Did you not go over this with Sir Roger a month past?" Michael asked.

"I want your opinions. Honest opinions."

Again they looked at each other. Michael shrugged, so Lucas spoke up. "The widow enjoys her court. I can see what draws them; she is a beauty. I don't see what keeps them."

"And his sister, Miss Sourantine?"

"I know she gambles. Costell likes her."

"Does Costell's word weigh with you?"

"Not much."

Michael asked shrewdly, "Sir Roger has focused on all three Sourantines?"

"The spycatcher?"

"Not so loud, little brother. And not a word to anyone, as usual." He looked back at Giles. "I knew he had the widow down as his spy. I'm guessing he thinks the brother steals the information for her. What role for the sister?"

"Any role that will fit. He's looking for the last link in a long chain."

"Ah, the red despatch box he's had me deliver from door to door. And he's maneuvered you into the bosom of the family. Things become very clear. How many in this last link?"

"The source."

"Luke, could Sourantine take anything from the despatch box at

Westover's without anyone knowing?"

"With a bit of trouble, yes. I could. Anyone could. Don't think he did. Don't think he would. He's got an English heart, not a French one."

"But if the Sourantines spied for money?" Michael asked, playing advocate for Sir Roger. "The French would pay well for any information about Wellington, from his Spring plans to his boot polish. Those salons must consume their ready cash. Does the merry widow have debts?"

"Not that we've heard," Giles said. Edward Garland's fleecing took on a sinister intent. He could only pray the source was proved to be someone else, not Albert Sourantine. He could only pray Josette escaped any taint of blame.

Nazenby's comment rang, louder than a death knell: Spies were masters at using the truth to lie. Josette had warned him, several times, that she was an adventurer's daughter.

His reason, his instincts, his heart—all three told him Josette wasn't involved with the spying. He had to believe she wasn't. His throbbing leg, however, reminded him daily that he could trust one time too many. He had trusted a scout and led his men up a road into disaster. Would his heart remind him for the rest of his life that he had trusted the wrong woman?

He should have kissed her last night. He might never have another chance.

Chapter 17 ~ Tuesday, December 3

Giles drove to the Sourantine house, though the day had advanced far past the accepted time for callers. He had not intended to see Josette until Wednesday at Lady Eaton's. As his replacement he had sent another posy. After Nazenby's dour information, though, he needed to see her, just as he had been driven to confirm she was neither gamester nor jade. *As if seeing Josette can cure my doubts*, he chided himself.

The visit, though, might serve a purpose. Sir Roger would approve: having to see her every day would build the façade that he was lovelorn and desperate, ensuring his welcome in the house just as the despatch reached Lord Westover's. Following last week's romantic difficulties, smoothing the path this week was vital.

The red-haired footman admitted him, and he came in as Claude Thierry prepared to leave, receiving his hat and gloves from the butler.

Josette, standing on the lower step of the grand staircase, sparkled when she saw him. "Lord Hargreaves, I did not expect to see you today."

See, he told himself, *I am serving my mission*. "I was passing and thought nothing could improve the day more than a half-hour with you."

She blushed. "Sir, I have never received a better compliment. *M. Thierry* also chose a late visit with us, but he is now leaving."

Thierry extended his hand. "Good day, my lord."

He would have released his grip quickly, but Giles retained it a second to delay him. After last night's conversation, he was not quite ready to let the man escape so easily. "I had not realized you were French. It's *Thierry*, isn't it? Not Terry."

"Yes. Of course. An *émigré* among other *émigrés*." His narrowed eyes and slight frown belied his suave tone. "Mdm. Sourantine and her late husband, they were great friends. She is kind enough to continue our acquaintance. And now, if you please, I am expected elsewhere."

Reynolds opened the door and waited beside it.

As Thierry bowed over Josette's hand, Giles asked, "An early dinner, Thierry? Who are your companions?"

"M. LeBrun joins me. I think he brings some younger friends. We plan an evening of whist. After watching your performance last evening, sweet lady, I must improve my skills."

"I would not call it a performance."

"*Non*, that is perhaps not the best word. Massacre, I think? And now," he touched the brim of his fashionable hat and gave another little bow.

The butler shut the door firmly behind him.

Following Josette down the long passage to the library, Giles enjoyed the sway of her skirts. Thierry's explanation, however, had set his mind to ticking. The man should not have found it necessary to explain his acquaintance with Celeste Sourantine. Coupled with the new information that he was French, it only increased Giles' speculations. A need for explanation and the hidden secret of his home country, together they smacked of guilt.

The library seemed almost dreary without the sunshine. Only the crackling fire and a candelabrum on the table fought against the clouds that had crowded across the December sky. Josette walked over to the fireplace and held her hands to its warmth.

Giles leaned his cane on the chair squared up beside the fireplace then rested a hand on the upholstered wing. "Does Thierry come often to see your sister-in-law?"

"Not very often. He attends the salons only once or twice a month. He wanted to see Celeste today; they have been closeted together for nearly an hour."

"How did your brother and sister-in-law meet him?"

"I do not know. Perhaps with Robert LeBrun at the horse market."

"Did he come over before the Terror or after?"

"During, I think. He has never spoken of his reason for leaving France. Unlike the Nemours and the Girauds, who fled for their lives."

"Musgrove said Thierry doesn't make a point of his being French."

"That is what he said," she confirmed. She still did not lift her gaze to him. Her tone sounded flat.

Giles took the warning. He wanted to ask if she thought Thierry deliberately tried to hide his Gallic background. He wanted to ask if she knew his other friends in London. If he continued the questions, however, how quickly would they seem like an interrogation? Would they reveal his worry that she might know about the spying?

Could he trust her? Dared he put that question into words?

His attention should be on Josette. Was that not his mission?

The silence had lengthened dangerously. He took a step toward her. "Have you forgotten I am here? I shall suspect you of taking me in disfavor since I no longer wear the uniform." His teasing earned a smile—but it did not reach her cornflower eyes.

"I am not as superficial as that, Lord Hargreaves. I am not Celeste."

"For which I am very grateful. I was quite mistaken in her."

"Blinded by her beauty?"

The smile still did not light her eyes. "I quickly discovered my mistake, please grant me that. One evening of whist was all I needed to appreciate you over her."

She rubbed her arms to warm them. "We do not know very much of each other, do we?" Giles thought at first that she spoke of their relationship, but as she continued, he realized she critiqued society. "We talk to people at parties. We meet them at salons and soirées and dance with them and sup with them, but we do not truly know them. Only time can tell us if the person is good and honorable."

He went to her, bracing an arm on the mantel. "You are serious today. Have you become a philosopher?"

She glanced up. Her eyes searched his. "Do we truly know anyone? Do we ever truly know the people we see every day, the people we call friends, the ones we share a house with?"

"Our family we know," he said slowly, seriously, "from their daily lives, their smallness and their greatness, to the heart of them. And a few friends we are fortunate to discover in needful times."

"Your friend Mr. Farraday?"

"Yes. He guarded my back many a time. He pulled my troop out of the ambush that got me this," and he indicated his wounded leg.

"Then time and war and tragedy can teach us a person's heart. Is there no other means?"

"Surely there are. All the conversations we humans indulge in must teach us something about each other."

"Unless we are clever at the art of deception."

His ears rang with Nazenby's words: Spies are masters of using the truth to tell lies. Leaning closer, he lowered his voice to an intimate level. "Do you practice to deceive, Josette? Are you spinning a web to ensnare me?"

Her blue eyes looked lucent. "Not I."

"Do you think I practice to deceive?" The question sharpened on the knife edge he walked with her. He did not know if his heightened tension was for Nazenby's mission or his own heart.

Her gaze dropped. "You ask a lot of questions, Lord Hargreaves." Her voice was stiffly formal. "Questions about Claude Thierry. About Celeste."

"Did she warn you against me again?"

Josette shook her head.

He inhaled sharply. He had anticipated this. Hadn't he stopped questioning her earlier? But obviously not early enough. She was quick-witted. She used her mind to calculate the ploys her opponents used. And she had now applied her card-playing skills to their relationship.

Why hadn't he applied his own tactics to their relationship? No matter what he'd said to Sir Roger, had he been building his own romantic dream?

Giles took her hand, rubbing his thumb across her knuckles. "Ah, my failed conversational skills. I spent years in the Army, Josette, telling men what to do, asking people for information. I don't know the *on-dits* that drive society. I don't know ninety percent of the people I see at parties. I don't know the latest novels or plays or games. I can't talk politics without getting angry. The shouting matches I've had with my father since my return ... . It is perhaps better that I stay in town than at Grasmere. If my questions sound like an interrogation, blame those hard years in the military. Not deceit, Josette, never deceit."

Her lifted face looked like a halo of light burnished by the fire-glow. He hoped the truth of what he said, the truth of what he felt for her in this moment, hid the deceit of his mission. "I believe you."

"At last." He sighed. He touched her chin, keeping her face uplifted, and bent his head to her. "Say my name, Josette."

"Giles. I believe you, Giles."

He kissed her, a tentative kiss, a chaste kiss at first, the kiss he had wanted but had never intended to take. When Sir Roger had directed him to focus on the other woman in the Sourantine household, he had expected only a brief and shallow dalliance. Then Josette had revealed her true self to him, a woman of a different ilk than the French spy they needed to trap. Rather than build a wall, he drove his mission to serve his growing desire.

He hadn't intended to kiss her, not for the mission, not to advance his deceit. He had stopped himself the other night, after his jealous interrogation; the sounds of the party had stopped him. The desire hadn't stopped.

He wanted to kiss her. He wanted to hold her. And when she accepted his kiss with a sigh, he stepped against her. He slipped an arm around her slender waist. He tilted her chin to accommodate another kiss, a sweeter kiss. And she kissed him back.

The awareness that she accepted, that she wanted his kiss raced through him like a missile. He broke the kiss before it deepened more than she was ready for. "Josette."

She said his name again. He cupped her cheek and touched his thumb to her lips. Her blue eyes were clear pools he could drown in. He would willingly drown in them—if Sir Roger's mission didn't condemn him to her.

The thought of losing her before he'd had a chance to hold her more than this once, to kiss her more than this once, exploded that racing missile. Giles returned for another kiss, a deeper kiss. He felt her hands clutching his shoulders, felt her melt against him. Her mouth opened to him, accepting, willing. God help him, he didn't want to stop. He wouldn't stop. He couldn't. But he had to stop, before he lost his wits completely.

He didn't have to release her.

He broke the kiss and lifted his head and forced air into his lungs.

Josette bowed her head against his chest.

Giles hugged her to him. "That went further than I intended."

She stiffened. He'd said the wrong thing, speaking honestly again. Lady Eaton had given no lessons on how to flatter a distrustful innocent he'd thoroughly kissed.

Her head lifted. The clear blue of her eyes looked like pools about to spill over. "Do you regret kissing me?"

He touched her lips. That earlier touch had lured him deeper than he'd planned. Her color heightened at the direction of his eyes, answering her question better than words.

She deserved the words. The words would stay with her long after other kisses had displaced the memory of this one. Giles rested his forehead against hers. "I regret nothing I do with you. I should, perhaps, not move so rapidly. I have just realized—you said you had no serious suitors. You've had no serious flirtations."

"Is that a bad thing?"

"It's a good thing, a very good thing." And he kissed her again.

Now she knew how he wanted her to tilt her head. Now she opened her mouth willingly for him. When she welcomed him to the kiss, his sanity smashed to bits, and honorable intentions shattered as well.

Only the sound of a door opening then shutting restored his sanity.

He lifted his head and looked at Josette. Color stained her cheeks and ripened her mouth. After a long second her beautiful eyes opened. He had destroyed the neat bun that held her pale blonde hair; it tumbled around her face and over his hand, covering the creamy softness of her shoulder. His thumb, pressed to the hollow of her neck, registered a heartbeat as rapid as his own.

"Giles?" she asked, using his name for only the third time.

A man with honorable intentions would remove his hands. He would step away from the temptation he'd just given into twice. Giles had his sanity back, but his honorable intentions were shot to pieces.

He managed to draw his arm from around her, but his hand wouldn't leave her slender form. It rested on the curve beneath the heavy fabric of her gown. God help him, she didn't wear rigid stays. "God," he prayed and managed to lift his hand off that touch of heaven and shift it to her arm. His other hand, still curved over her shoulders, still touching her heartbeat, that hand he couldn't lift away. He couldn't let her go, not yet.

Josette managed it for him. She stepped back, retreating to the safety of a chair. She sank into it as if her legs had failed her and clung to the arms.

Giles braced an arm on the mantel and prayed fervently for the good sense that had abandoned him. He wanted to shout. He wanted to laugh. Look at the pair of them, undone by a couple of kisses. He managed, after several seconds of staring at his clenched fist, to speak in a flat tone that totally belied his racing blood and tumultuous emotions. "Josette, you have a serious suitor now."

Her eyes lifted. They were brighter than the candles. "Yes, I do believe you are." She had tried to speak lightly, but her voice cracked. "That was—was not quite what I expected."

"Disappointed?" His hopes rode on the answer.

"No. Not at all." She glanced down then back up. "Am I allowed to say better than my expectations?"

He laughed. Trust Josette not to have the usual replies. "You shouldn't say so, unless you want me to kiss you again."

Her gaze dropped. "I would like to think on it first, before we ... ."

"Think away. I'll wait."

She laughed; finally she laughed. "Giles, I will need more than few minutes."

"Then I should leave. If I don't, I'll pull you out of that chair." He retrieved his cane.

Josette followed him to the door. He stopped, hand on the polished knob. He held his cane so tightly that his knuckles shone white.

"Will you accept callers tomorrow? Lady Eaton's soirée is that evening."

"Yes. Albert is returning by noon. Major Fellars comes also, to discuss his commission."

"Perhaps that would be a good time for my talk with your brother."

Her hands clenched. "Yes, it would be."

"What time should I call?"

"You do not have to, Giles, if you would rather not. Those times must be—must not be easy for you to speak of."

"But I will. Our own talk the other day, brief as it was, it clarified some things for me. I know my conversation with your brother will reap benefits for him and for me." He released the doorknob, quickly stepped close, and pressed a kiss to her lips. He stepped back before his senses scattered. "Until tomorrow, Josette."

"Tomorrow," she echoed. Her hand lifted to her mouth.

She stood like that, watching him with those pale blue eyes, until the footman opened the door and he walked out into the December chill.

Chapter 18 ~ Wednesday, December 4

For the rest of Tuesday, Giles had forgotten his mission. Kissing Josette had crowded spies from his mind. He woke the next morning burdened by it. He could not see a successful conclusion to his mission. The French spy arrested, yes; perhaps her master also gaoled. Celeste's fate would not affect Josette overly much. Yet if her brother Albert were involved—he could see that arrest destroying any hopes he had with her.

Nazenby would have to be convinced Josette was not involved. Once Sir Roger closed his net, anyone caught would have great difficulty proving her innocence.

Spies are masters of using the truth to tell lies. The words haunted him.

Reynolds admitted him. "Good afternoon, Lord Hargreaves. Miss Sourantine awaits you in the *petite salon*."

He followed Reynolds up the grand staircase. Only after he had left the house yesterday had he wondered who had opened the door and seen them. Celeste would have interrupted. Albert was traveling back to London. Giles had supposed the intruder was Reynolds, but the man gave no sign of having witnessed that kiss.

Josette served tea to a military man. Her brother had chosen to stand. The French spy was not present. He wondered where she was and if she had decided to attend the soirée. He wondered if anyone else would be shown in. LeBrun perhaps, or one of Celeste's court. He didn't expect Claude Thierry, not thrice in three days, not if the man were the French spymaster. Even the second visit had been a risk.

Major Fellars looked like the typical Hussar, a proud moustache dominating his face, his spine held upright by the ornamental braids that decorated his sharply cut military coat, his boots polished to a mirror-like sheen. He spoke like one, too; his brash voice booming as he described the regiment's preparations for battlefield maneuvers. On Giles' entrance he broke off and stroked his moustache, unimpressed by the courtesy title until Josette mentioned his rank.

"Ah, another military man. What regiment?"

"Lowly field soldiers, sir, nothing as dashing as cavalry."

He eyed Giles' cane. "Wounded?"

"At Albuera. Decommissioned now."

"Your service to your king does you credit. More of our fine men should be called to their duty for God and country. Were our recruits to double, we could roll over Napoleon and take Paris."

"I cannot argue with our needing the numbers to fight Napoleon's tyranny. When do you ship out?"

"Mid-January, my lord. I could hope for sooner. We'll take recruits until the first of that month. That's why it's crucial for Sourantine here to make up his mind."

Josette gave Giles a wide-eyed glance. "More tea, Major?"

"Thank you, Miss Sourantine. Another of those sandwiches would go down nicely."

Giles stepped over to her brother. "A word."

The young man led him to a window, the curtains open to the cloudy day. He glanced back at Fellars, who had shifted to the seat beside Josette. She offered him small teacakes. "My sister will try to convince him not to accept my commission."

"And he will try to convince her otherwise. But I believe it is your grandfather's acceptance that is necessary. Have you approached him yet?"

"I wanted Josette's support first. He listens to her."

"You think he will need convincing as well?"

"I don't know. Grandpapa supports our fight against Napoleon."

"So he is not a Bonapartist, as your sister-in-law is."

Albert snorted. "Celeste thinks Napoleon will bring peace to Europe. I tell her that's only if he controls it all. Look at how he crowned himself and his wife. He can't stand anyone having more power than he does. If he can't control his enemy, he'll crush it. But I can't talk to Celeste anymore about it, not in the house. Josette forbade it. She doesn't like our arguing."

"Josette forbade it? Does she then control Mdm. Sourantine?"

"I misspoke. Josette forbade *me*. If Celeste brings it up, I just leave the room while she tries to turn the conversation."

"What is your sister's feelings? France or England?" He held his breath as he awaited the answer.

"England, definitely. She was teaching Will and Antonia all about the Peninsular engagements and how tyrannical Napoleon is before we came down to London. Our father hated Napoleon, from his days as First Consul. Oh, he celebrated the formation of the Republic, but Robespierre disenchanted him. He used to say that France was demented with Robespierre and insane with Napoleon. He thought England had the only sane system of government. He and Grandpapa used to sit for hours, discussing politics. Josette said they could have been father and son, they were so alike."

Would the younger man say all this if he were a spy? Would he think it necessary to support his role? Would he go so far as to purchase a commission?

"Grandpapa," Albert continued, "thinks Wellington is our best chance."

"Your grandfather might not support one of his grandson's sacrificing himself in the cause. At least you do not have a doting mother also trying to dissuade you. What will you do if your grandfather refuses?"

"Sell up my stable and try for a line commission."

"You have definitely decided on this? Your sister's condition that you visit the wounded has not given you pause? A few months ago you would have seen me there." He gestured with the cane. "I am still not wholly recovered."

"She said you had been wounded, sir."

Giles could hear the immortal youth in the comment. "I survived several battles before Albuera. I was taken out of that battle early, trying to get my men into a better position. I trusted a scout—whom we later discovered was working for the French. You have that to consider as well, Sourantine: the dangers of battle, the dangers of betrayal."

"Is that why you left, sir? You didn't want to return."

"I was pushing pencils at the War Office and taking an officer's position that my regiment needed, and a close friend—a man whose opinion I valued—convinced me that other ways existed to serve England against Napoleon. I admit to you, however, that if I had recovered more quickly, I would be with Wellington now."

"Truly, sir?" The eyes he shared with his sister opened very wide. "I don't think Josette knows that you think that, my lord."

"No, I doubt she does. I am lucky, Sourantine. I have found a satisfying life here. After years in regimentals, I can confess to missing parts of that existence: the exhilaration, the rush from defeating danger. But I am also glad, very glad, that I do not face musket fire or cannonade in the morning. Soldiers, good soldiers, dread battle. Does your Major Fellars say that? Or has he never faced battle?"

"He admits that this would be his first time under fire, sir."

"He seems a man who gives stirring speeches about glory and honor, about the great rewards of victory, and that battle scars are the greatest medal a man can win. I've heard those speeches. Only the orator changes. I am certain the Hussars themselves seem brave and glorious. I believe it's the line regiments that win the war. Beyond that, Sourantine, I will not advise you on joining. That's a man's own decision, for it is his own life that's risked. Remember that."

"If you aren't to advise me, then why are we having this conversation?"

"I won't advise you. I will tell you what a good officer is. You are purchasing a lieutenant's commission. You should know that your commander won't last ten minutes in the first engagement. I've encountered officers of his ilk. If they didn't die in the first charge, we found them after, well behind the lines, shaking in their boots."

Giles outlined a few other points: learning to use terrain instead of books, listening to the sergeants, learning each individual man's strengths and weaknesses.

When he finished, Sourantine heaved a gusty breath. "A lot to remember, sir."

"It becomes easier with experience. After a few months, you'll know which soldier is your best shot or who has the canniest nose for the enemy up ahead. I learned much from Tony Farraday, grandson of Sir Henry Melton. He grew up in his regiment; his father was a staff sergeant before Tony himself enlisted at fifteen. He was my sergeant until his grandfather bought his commission. Are you willing to talk with him before you write for your grandfather's permission? You have time, Fellars said. Until January first."

"Where do I find him?"

He directed Sourantine to Melton Hall. "I'll write a letter of introduction for you. Don't be surprised if he's distracted. His marriage to Katherine Charteris is days away."

"Could you write the letter now, sir? I could leave tomorrow morning for Melton Hall."

"I would advise you to begin your journey this very day. You won't have Farraday's full attention after his wedding."

Albert agreed and rang the bell while Giles congratulated himself on removing him from the field of available spies. Sir Roger could not indict a man who had not been in London when the despatch was taken. As they waited for Reynolds to provide the requested paper and quill and ink, they rejoined Josette's labored conversation with Major Fellars.

"I have been telling the commander of the people I've met since coming to London."

"A wide range," Fellars said. "Most impressive, Miss Sourantine, to meet and remember so many people in such a short time."

"Her greatest coup," Giles said, giving her a teasing smile, "was to snare the son of a marquess as one of her many admirers."

She blushed. "My lord, I do not have many admirers."

"Myself. Lord Musgrove. Tobias Kennit. And who was the man dancing with you the other evening? Mr. Rampley."

"Hardly enough to count as many."

"We could even add Lord Wynstane to your admirers."

"He is my grandfather's age! And if you add him, then you must say that Edward Garland is among those who despise me."

"Only for trouncing him at whist. Before Monday he was definitely among your court. Fellars, you should be warned. Miss Sourantine is quite the Captain Sharp." Josette wrinkled her nose at him. He was relieved the name no longer insulted her. "Ah, Reynolds returns. Excuse me."

He walked to a side table. The butler drew up a chair. Behind him the conversation turned to card games.

A quarter-hour later Albert Sourantine left with Major Fellars. Giles joined Josette on the divan and leaned his shoulder against hers. *No hand-holding, no kissing*, he warned himself. He didn't trust the butler not to interrupt them. "What did you think of the major?"

"He is a fool. He understands nothing. He's never been in a battle, but he calls it the most glorious duty of man."

"I've served with bad officers and incompetent officers and drunk officers. Utter fools can take a position that the most seasoned veteran could not. Seasoned veterans can inspire men into a charge that saves the battle. I've seen failures and victories enough to realize that whoever succeeds in this campaign does it not by his own will but through the grace of God. All battle does is sort the wheat from the chaff."

"Is that what you said to Albert?"

"No. I told him we need good officers and that Fellars doesn't have it in him. If your brother has a head on his shoulders, he can become one of our best."

"If he survives that long."

"When he is destined to die, then he can do it in a riding accident or wheeling along in a fast phaeton or attacked by London thugs. You can't protect him, Josette. He's a man. He has to make his own decisions. Just as you must decide whether you support his decision."

"I know this, but he is my brother. I've looked out for him since Mama died. In Spain he will be so far away."

"That may be the attraction, standing on his own with no sister rushing to protect him."

"I have done that," she admitted. She scooted closer. "What letter did you give him?"

"Sister being worried? A letter of introduction to my friend Anthony Farraday. Your brother promised to visit him immediately."

"Tell me about this Anthony Farraday. Who is he besides your friend?"

"A former comrade-in-arms, wounded like me and cashed out. He can give better advice than I on how to be a good officer. He came up through the ranks. His grandfather bought him a lieutenant's commission. He rose to captain before he was wounded. You may have heard of his grandfather, Sir Henry Melton. I would trust him with my life, Josette."

The clock chimed. She jumped up. "Is that the time? You must leave. I have to dress for Lady Eaton's reception."

"It takes you hours?" He stood more slowly, reluctant to leave when he'd had so little time alone with her.

"Yes, hours and hours. And I shall dazzle you."

"A kiss first," he requested. She came willingly into his arms. Giles kept his embrace light. When he broke off the kiss, she looked bemused. He squeezed her then dropped his arms.

Josette followed him to the tiled reception area. "I should refuse you the house for claiming I have a court of admirers. I have no such thing, sir. Mr. Kennit likes my friend Melinda, and Lord Wynstane is a dear friend."

"I notice you say nothing of Gordon Musgrove or this Rampley man."

"Oh, off with you."

He flicked her cheek. "Shall I send my carriage for you?"

"I shan't be alone. Albert will be with me."

He didn't remind her that Albert had promised to leave immediately for Melton Hall. "No *belle-soeur*?" he asked, confirming it for Sir Roger.

"No *belle-soeur*. She maintains her refusal, even though a month ago she panted to attend one of Lady Eaton's parties."

He rolled away convinced that neither Josette nor her brother was spies. Where had Sir Roger said the despatch was today? Lord Westover's. And young Westover was Albert Sourantine's friend. Yet with Major Fellars in tow, the cub would have no opportunity to go to Westover's house. And if he followed Giles' plan and left immediately for Melton Hall, he could not be accused of treason.

Other friends of young Westover were part of Celeste's court. They would be disappointed that she did not attend the soirée. Who of them would leave the party to dance attendance on the French beauty? Who of them would use that as an excuse to pass the despatch over to her?

He had warned Sir Roger to put an extra man to watch the Sourantine house. And he now had more information to tell the spycatcher about the Sourantines, especially the father Henri. The older man might not take it as evidence, but the more weight of their innocence that Giles could lade onto the balance, the better.

He turned the horses toward Nazenby's house, where the old spycatcher planned his many snares and ordered his men about. White

Hall, Sir Roger said, was too public. Too many people had reason to stand about and observe those who came and went on government business. Too many doors could be opened by people who had no official capacity. Not even the lowliest servant was vetted to the spycatcher's satisfaction. Sir Roger's role in the government was known by few; he didn't want it advertised beyond that circle.

Chapter 19 ~ Wednesday, December 4

A knock sounded as Reilly penned the last pearl into Josette's hair. Albert stuck his head around the door. "We're late, sister mine."

She grinned at him. "We shall be fashionably late."

Her brother came into the room. "You did turn it up nicely."

"Flattery will not hurry me along, my brother."

He leaned against a bed post. "I like your Lord Hargreaves."

"He's not mine."

"He wants to be."

Josette smiled at her mirrored image. Today's brief kiss had piqued her longing for more of yesterday's splendid kisses. *Yes, he does seem to be mine.* "What do you like about him, Albert?"

"He says what he means. He doesn't speechify about duty and glory and honor."

"As your Major Fellars does?"

"As he does, indeed. I learned more in a quarter-hour with him than in a week with Fellars. Grandpapa will approve of him, if you can bring him up to snuff."

Celeste came through the open door. Pearls dangled in her hand. "I remembered that you wished to borrow this. *Non*, stay seated. I will show you how to wear them with style." She looped the strand then draped it over Josette's carefully arranged hair. One strand she tightened into a choker; the other fell over the pale blue of the plain gown. "*Tres jolie.* That color suits you, *ma belle-soeur*. I am happy that you chose it."

"If I had not, you would have."

Celeste's eyes narrowed. "*Oui*, we did compete for that, did we not?"

"And reached a compromise, that lovely deeper blue for you and this paler silk for me. You should wear that gown tonight—or that lovely yellow silk with the gold netting, the gown you said was *trop extraordinaire* for our simple salons."

"*Non*, I am at home tonight. And you, Josette, I command you to tell the names of everyone who missed me."

"We can wait while you change," she offered, and Albert groaned at the additional delay. "Your new green silk with the ruffles; no one has seen it yet. Madame Levoiseur did such wonderful work with that gown."

Celeste shook her head and remained adamant. "It is hoped that I shall have a dinner guest. A small party for two. Now, off with you. You shall break hearts, *ma belle-soeur*. And you, Albert, you look *tres beau*. You, too, shall break hearts."

She waved from the balcony as they descended.

The butler opened the door for them, but Albert veered toward the billiards room.

"Where are you going?"

"I've forgotten my cane."

For her ears alone, Reynolds said, "Another letter, Miss. Coleman took it an hour ago."

"The same mark for the address?"

"Yes, Miss. Not long after Coleman's return, Madame ordered the dinner for tonight."

"Her guest *must* be the recipient of those mysterious letters. Reynolds, I must know who this mysterious person is."

"Yes, Miss. Do you expect to see Lord Hargreaves this evening?"

Celeste called down from the upper stair. "Why have you not left? You shall be very, very late. *Allez-vous-en*, Josette. Go and enchant your paramours."

"I am waiting for Albert. Here he is. Were you shooting billiards with it, little brother?"

"Yes. Got it in, too. Knew I would. Malbury had to pay up."

They waved up at their *belle soeur*. Josette gave Reynolds a speaking look as she went into the cold night.

Albert hardly waited for Coleman to close the coach door. "Did you know she invited someone to dine?"

"I did not know until just now. Reynolds informed me."

"Does Reynolds know who her guest is? He doesn't?" He leaned back against the cushion and braced as Coleman rapidly took a corner. "Now, that is a surprise. Reynolds knows everything that goes on in the house."

"Including how late you sneak in? Or how early?"

He grinned, not at all abashed by her teasing, but he returned like a hound on the scent to his worry. "Celeste shouldn't entertain alone. Being a widow doesn't release her from propriety. Grandpapa would not approve."

"When you sail off to Spain, Albert, we will have no man to chaperon us."

"You'll be married before long. Hargreaves seems serious."

"He seems so." Josette still could not believe the rapidity of their relationship. She had to pinch herself—Giles Hargreaves, son of a marquess, interested in her! It seemed especially unbelievable when she recalled their first two conversations and those questions that crossed into rudeness. A mutual attraction had not seemed enough to stand for that discourtesy. Only Lady Eaton's advice and his confession to lagging conversational skills had kept her from rejecting him. And her reward was yesterday's extraordinary kisses.

He had teased her about being a Captain Sharp. That charge no longer worried him. Did he still think her a jade?

She'd never seen him fumble a conversation—.

"You've gone into a brown study, sister mine."

"Just thinking about tonight. Will you abandon me, Albert, as soon as we pass the door?"

"Not I," he swore valiantly. "I'll even stand up one dance with you."

Their carriage jolted to a halt, and Albert looked out. "Not late enough," he groaned. "Prepare to be overwhelmed, Jos."

Their carriage joined the long line that led up to Eaton House. Josette peered out the window as they waited. The palatial residence dwarfed their own home. Four stories and two accompanying wings formed a court. Torches and lanterns blazed, revealing liveried footmen with no task except standing sentinel at the base and top of the exterior staircase. The Eaton name was old, their status and wealth assured, and the London house proved their prominence.

When they finally gained entrance, they stepped into a reception hall that stretched the width of the first floor. Massive doors stood open to allow guests to rove freely. Celeste had chosen gilded and ormolu furnishings to enhance the richness of their own house, but her efforts seemed tawdry compared to the Eaton wealth on display.

Lady Eaton smiled at them, graciously remembered their names, even commented on Josette's pretty appearance. Then they threaded through the throng to the crush in the grand ballroom. Tall mirrors intensified the light of chandeliers and candelabra. The people and their reflections chattered, gestured, and shifted in overwhelming numbers.

Before Josette had found someone she knew, several of Albert's friends accosted them.

"You're late," Malbury accused.

Alex Westover bowed. "Miss Sourantine. Forgive that boor's rudeness. We must enlist your brother's services."

"Don't tell me," she laughed. "A horse. And blame his tardiness on me."

"The wait was worth it, dear Miss Sourantine," said a voice at her shoulder.

She turned to Costell. "Do not try to flatter me into a good humor, sir. Albert promised to dance with me. And now you all drag him off to see a horse."

"One dance only, sister mine."

"You must release him, Miss," entreated the dark young man who dwarfed Costell. She knew he was the younger Armitage, but she couldn't recall his name. His taller brother stood behind him. "Only he can resolve our quarrel."

"That does sound vital."

"Indeed it is." Malbury clapped Albert on the back. "I need his judgment on the prime horseflesh I bought this afternoon. These cretans haven't his eye."

"Is it the hunter you mentioned last week?"

"The very same. Had to snap him up. He was about to be sold to a Welshman. They don't have good hunting over there. He would be wasted."

Alex Westover shook his head. "You lost money on that deal, Malbury. A flashy goer with no stamina."

"I said he had a deep chest and would hold up over rough terrain. You see, Miss Sourantine, we must settle this dispute."

Her brother laughed. "I must break my vow to you, Josette."

"I am abandoned but not surprised. Tell Mr. Malbury he has bought a nag, my dear brother."

Malbury protested while the others laughed.

Clarence Wilton stepped forward. "Does Mdm. Sourantine not attend tonight?"

"No." The word was abrupt, but she would not prattle out a lie for Celeste. "Will I see you later in the card room, Lord Costell, or do you venture out with your friends to look at horses?"

"Later, Miss Sourantine. I have a tenner riding on your brother's judgment."

"Gambling on this, sir?" She shook her head, but Costell didn't hear, joining the circle around Albert as he was borne off.

The older Armitage brother had lingered. "You may not see him again this evening, *M'selle* Sourantine, especially as Malbury's determined to show off his purchase."

"Do you not wish to see this extraordinary horse, Mr. Armitage?"

"Not I." He offered his arm. "Not when I can dance with a lovely lady. Shall we join this set?"

A dance was guaranteed to bridge any awkward silence. She took up his offer and soon discovered that Armitage was a joy as a dance partner. Like Hargreaves, he topped her by several inches, and she enjoyed not dwarfing her partner. His sly comments about the other dancers had her laughing. When the set ended, he deposited her at Sir Roger Nazenby's side. Josette thought that curious. Was it planned?

Was Michael Armitage one of Sir Roger's men?

As the older man bowed in greeting, Armitage confirmed she was acquainted with Sir Roger. "At your salons, I believe? Sir Roger is fond, I know, of the occasional game of whist."

Josette smiled. "Good evening, Sir Roger."

Armitage talked with them briefly then excused himself. He shifted only a few steps to a turbaned matron guarding her lovely daughter. The girl's face lit up as he bowed, but he addressed himself to the older woman.

Sir Roger's eyes crinkled. "He did that very neatly."

She stopped fanning. "I beg your pardon?"

"Armitage." He nodded to indicate the young man leading the debutante to the next set while the matron watched with a protective eye.

"Did he achieve success the second time he asked, or the third?"

He tilted his head as he looked up at her. "The second time."

"Was I the third duty dance or the fourth?"

"Fourth. Do not judge him harshly, Miss Sourantine. Dancing with you could not be construed as a duty."

"Did Mr. Armitage start with age and work down? No," she smiled and resumed fanning, "you need not answer that. Whatever his strategy, he has won the fair maiden's hand. But I think her strict mama will allow him two dances, and I think that neither will be the supper dance. He shall have to be content with conversation for the third and that only after the supper."

"Ah, I believe you have foretold his evening correctly. Do you read people so easily? Is that why you are so successful a Captain Sharp?"

Giles had said that, and it had ceased to hurt her. Nazenby's use brought back the pain. Josette glanced around to see who was near enough to hear the slander. No one stood close, but she still lowered her voice. "I am successful at cards, Sir Roger, because my father began instructing me before I was out of the nursery. My nurse Mrs. Hodges was scandalized that he taught me my numbers from a deck of cards."

"I knew your father, my dear."

"He did remember you, sir. He called you the spycatcher."

In his turn Sir Roger quickly glanced to see who might have heard, but Josette knew no one had moved any closer. "Ahem. Some people have long memories. How did he know that of me?"

"You asked if I read people? He did, from their habits and their conversation. He said he could tell much about a man after a quarter-hour's talk. You questioned him once, most intently, over an evening's play of cards, about his fellow countryman Robert LeBrun."

"Ah, another name I have not heard for a long while. His widow died, and thus he returns to London ... where he becomes a favorite of your sister-in-law."

Josette didn't like the path that comment led to, so she asked a different question. "Do you still hunt spies, Sir Roger?"

"Behind every hedge and signpost. Do not spread that around, Miss Sourantine. That would ruin my reputation as a gentleman of leisure."

"You have had many years at this occupation."

"And hope to have many more. This is as vital to our efforts against Bonaparte as soldiers in the field."

"My sister-in-law would disagree."

"Is she a *Bonapartiste*?"

Josette evaded the question. "Celeste does not often concern herself with politics."

"Your father, did he support Boney's rise to power?"

Josette acknowledged wryly that she could not avoid all questions. "My father considered himself an Englishman with a heavy French accent."

"Surely he expressed his thoughts about the Revolution? He came over before the Terror, didn't he, in—?"

"In '85," Josette supplied, beginning to feel interrogated.

"A good eight years before the Terror. After the chaos under Robespierre, did he not consider Boney as the man to stabilize France?"

"My father—." She changed where that sentence was going. "My father likened Bonaparte to Julius Caesar, a man with an eye to advance and willing to grasp the first opportunity with both hands. Caesar heralded the dictatorial emperors. Has not Bonaparte become that?"

"Ah, a student of history."

"Yes." She fanned herself more languidly. She did not want the spycatcher to realize how tense she became under his questioning. "My father was no more than a simple card player, Sir Roger," she drawled.

"We all play many roles, Miss Sourantine. Nevertheless, I believe you yourself have speculated if he were a *chevalier d'epee* or a *chevalier d'industrie*. Have you decided?"

The words took her aback. She had heard them, spoken them. And very quickly she recalled where: in conversation with Giles Hargreaves—who had obviously shared that conversation with the older man.

Cold settled in her belly. Why would Giles repeat their conversations to Sir Roger? To Sir Roger the spycatcher? Was Giles, like Michael Armitage, one of Sir Roger's men? She had thought him merely occupying himself with work at the War Office. Had he shifted to Sir Roger's control when the military decommissioned him?

Josette drew on all her skills as a card player. Had Sir Roger expected her to retreat in disarray at the slight to her father? Or become so befuddled that she would answer anything? She managed a smile, though it was tight and felt as if it stretched too widely. "Now why would Lord Hargreaves repeat that conversation to you?"

The spycatcher's eyes widened, and he abruptly lifted his head to look at her more closely. She learned much of him when he threw the question back. "Should he not have repeated it? Was it shared in confidence?"

"Sir, it might ruin my reputation as a lady of leisure."

He acknowledged the hit with a little bow.

"Does Lord Hargreaves share all of our conversations? Or only particular ones? Ones that have to do with France?"

"I see why you are a formidable gamester, Miss Sourantine. You do not hesitate to throw the harder cards into play."

"You have conversations about that, too?"

He ignored her cutting tone. "You forget, I think, that I introduced Hargreaves to your salons, specifically to your card play."

A memory of that first evening, when Giles had joined her table, flashed suddenly and vividly. Together they had routed Kennit and Edward Garland. Behind him, watching every turn of card, had stood Sir Roger. When Giles had left, without looking back, Sir Roger had walked beside him. She could even remember the green brocade coat and waistcoat, closed with silver buttons that looked like coin pieces.

On the second evening, Sir Roger had watched as well. Had he not unnerved her, standing behind her to watch her select a card and play it? He had been ready to assume Giles' place at the table, when she decided to leave the game and Giles left it with her.

Just as suddenly and vividly, she understood Giles Hargreaves' attachment to her. He had dropped Celeste and pursued her. At Sir Roger's orders. He asked her countless questions about her family, about Celeste and her family, about their friends, about their sympathies for England and for France. At Sir Roger's orders.

Her gaze fastened on the older man, on the green brocade suit he wore, a suit with its many silver buttons. Thirty pieces of silver. To break her heart?

She couldn't accuse the man of that. Nor would she ask him why. She knew why. He thought they were spies. He obviously thought that. And he had set Giles Hargreaves the mission to find out.

Had they thought Celeste was a spy, with her Bonapartist sympathies and her salons that drew a wide spectrum of London society? *And now they think I am? Oh, dear Lord, why do they think that?*

Chapter 20 ~ Wednesday, December 4

Tobias Kennit saved her.

He entered and stood looking around, his height giving him the advantage of seeing over most of the crowd. Obviously he looked for Melinda, but he responded immediately to Josette's lifted eyebrow and tilted of her head. He threaded toward them with a skill born of many society crushes. No wonder he hated them.

Josette turned back to Sir Roger. She languidly waved her fan. "I remember that evening very well. Lord Hargreaves and I routed Sir Edward Garland. Mr. Kennit managed to recover his losses that evening. And I bought this delightful gown with my winnings," she lied.

"Delightful it is. Does your card play fund all your purchases?"

She ignored the offensive question. Kennit was nearly to them. "Do you know, Sir Roger, I do not believe that we two have ever played cards. We must do so. At this Friday's salon, yes? Perhaps Mr. Kennit and I against you and Lord Hargreaves. Now that would be a match. Neither side will be assured of victory."

"I look forward to it, Miss Sourantine, but—."

"And here is Mr. Kennit. Toby—." Not by a single flicker did he reveal that she'd never so familiarly addressed him. She fastened upon his arm as a rope thrown to someone drowning. "Toby, I have promised a game with Sir Roger on Friday. You and I against him and Lord Hargreaves. A splendid challenge, don't you think?"

"A titanic challenge," he agreed with an amiable smile. "One that I would willingly accept. Miss Sourantine, I demand a dance, and the next set is forming. Good evening, sir."

"Yes, good evening, Sir Roger. Our conversation has been most ... enlightening."

"Miss Sourantine." The older man bowed with the courtly grace of the last century. He smiled facilely. And with a bitter hate, Josette wondered how deep his pockets were. The money she would send to charity, as she had done with her recent winnings off Edward Garland. She had hated the vengeful self that had been revealed, but she contemplated trouncing Sir Roger Nazenby with great satisfaction.

And Giles Hargreaves, son of the marquess of Grasmere.

How Celeste would crow.

She missed several steps in the dance before the pattern steadied her mind.

When Kennit led her from the floor, he murmured, "Your color's better. You were so pale I thought you would faint."

"Thank you, Kennit. You saved me."

"My pleasure." He guided her into the hall and across to one of the smaller rooms. She didn't protest; his rescue merited an explanation. Several people stood about the room, a lesser parlor the size of the *grande salon* at home. Kennit found a corner with two chairs and angled them toward each other. "Now, sit down," he ordered. "How did Nazenby upset you?"

"Was it so obvious?"

"Only to someone who has watched you play cards since late August. Tell me."

"He thinks we are spies."

"He *is* the spycatcher. He suspects everyone. Behind every hedge and signpost."

Laughter verging on hysteria bubbled up. "He will not like that you know that."

Kennit shrugged. "Who does he suspect? You or the whole family?"

"All of us, I think. Perhaps only me. I don't know."

"Careful. Keep your voice down. What did he say?"

"Did you know that Lord Hargreaves has pursued an attachment to me only to discover if I am a spy? That explains his abandonment of Celeste for me."

"Hold on. Nazenby said that?" When she shook her head, he shifted his chair alongside hers and leaned on the arm. "Calm down, Jos," he said, using Melinda's name for her. "You have no confirmation of that. Anyone who confronted your *belle-soeur*'s egotism would run in another direction. I did. What do you think brought me to your salons? I came for the reputed beauty. Am I not the rake that wants to break women's hearts? When I discovered she has no heart, I found my way to the card room and a lovely young woman who plays cards beautifully."

"*You* never pretended an interest in me. You never flirted with me and swore affection for me and kissed me—."

"How far did this go?"

She looked down at her fan. Three of the splines had broken. The fan was ruined, the way her attraction for Giles Hargreaves was ruined. She cast it onto a table. "Not far," she whispered and tried not to think of his kisses.

"Still too far, I think. Break your heart?"

After a deep breath, she managed a smile to reassure him. "I refuse to let it be broken."

"That's my Jos. Now, tell me what Nazenby said."

"He asked about my father, if he supported Bonaparte. Papa didn't. He despised him, especially after he heard about Jaffa, when Napoleon poisoned his own men so his army could retreat. Then Sir Roger repeated something about my father that I have only ever said to Lord Hargreaves."

"And from that you deduce that Hargreaves works for Nazenby."

"Is that not enough?"

"They are friends. Sir Roger stands as godfather to Hargreaves."

She leaned away from Kennit. "Are you defending him?"

"No defense is necessary. I'm just pointing out some information. How you read it—."

"You think I have misread—."

"I didn't say that. Tell me about Hargreaves and you. How does he behave with you?"

"He pursued me. You saw. He flirted with me, but he also seemed—well, almost antagonistic." The memory of their second conversation hurt again. *A Captain Sharp. A jade.* Josette batted her lashes, trying to quell the burning tears. "The questions he asked, trying to discover what my relationship to you was. Lady Eaton said I had seriously overset his heart."

"Ah, Lady Eaton, the chiefest of Sir Roger's friends."

"Then she is also—. And the reason we received an invitation to this party—."

"Hush. Don't malign our hostess. Did Hargreaves stay antagonistic?"

"No. But he did continue to interrogate me about my family."

"And then he kissed you and set your world to spinning." His black eyes glittered. With his black hair falling over his brow, Kennit looked very much like the dashing hero. "Someone else needs to kiss you, Josette Sourantine. Give you something to compare it with."

"Not you," she denied quickly.

"Certainly not. That would offend Miss Ratcliffe. Would you consider Musgrove?"

Josette looked down at her twisting hands. "I don't want to encourage him."

"No, he doesn't need that encouragement. Costell? I don't suggest Garland. He'd take advantage."

"As you would have?"

"I don't take advantage of friends."

She pressed his hand, resting on the arm of her chair. "Thank you, Kennit."

He gave her the smile that had won countless hearts. "You called me Toby earlier."

"Toby," she amended. "Why did we not fall in love?"

"Too much alike."

"I am not at all like you. I am not wild."

"You are. Don't you like to queen it over the card room, where men vastly outnumber the ladies? Don't you like to play with rakes and fleece their pockets? And go off in corners and give secret kisses? Don't deny it, Jos."

"Then *you* must have a Puritan streak, for you have fallen for a vicar's daughter."

He grinned, unabashed, and she could not help responding to that good humor. "I have, haven't I? I'll have a job restoring my reputation."

"Oh, dear."

His gaze followed hers. "Ah, Hargreaves arrives. He'll come forewarned by Nazenby. You can't run from him, my friend. You have to confront him. Tell him what you suspect."

"Then I shall see only how well he lies. Thank you, but no."

"Will you both play a game then? Both of you pretending you know nothing while you examine every word, every look, every gesture for evidence? That's not how you outwit an opponent, Jos. Believe me. I've survived more fields of play than you have. Confront him."

"A mere hour ago I did not count him an opponent." She brightened her smile. "Lord Hargreaves, I had quite given you up. I am flattered that you found me in such a dark corner." She slanted a look at Kennit, as if to deepen the intimacy of their conversation. He had lounged back, crossing one long leg over the other as if he had no plans to abandon his seat.

Giles frowned at Kennit, but he turned to her with an answering smile and bowed over her hand. "Miss Sourantine, as promised, you dazzle me. Mr. Kennit. I did not expect to see you beyond the card room."

"I've broadened my horizons." He suddenly uncrossed his legs and stood up, his height matching Giles'. "Miss Sourantine, I enjoyed our dance. Perhaps another one, later? You must give me your promise."

"I so promise. But you need not hurry off, Mr. Kennit." She should not use him, she realized, not as a barrier for her heart. That battle she must fight within herself. No one else should be involved. So she spoke of Melinda and saw by the flash of his eyes that he understood the shifted ground on which she confronted Giles. "Miss Ratcliffe did not come this evening."

"I am dashed. The card room it is then. If you need an escort, Miss

Sourantine, you will find me there. I will always give up my game for a friend." He bowed and walked away.

Giles—*Hargreaves*, she scolded herself. *I must think of him only as Lord Hargreaves*—dropped into the vacated chair. As Kennit had, he leaned on her chair arm. "I did not expect to find you in such intimate conversation with Tobias Kennit."

"Hardly intimate," she drawled. "We are in a room full of people." Even in her ears, the words sounded cutting. She warmed her voice. "I have danced also with Michael Armitage and had a long conversation with Sir Roger Nazenby. Do you share many of our conversations with him?" There, it was asked, as Kennit had advised her. Pretending ignorance was not the answer.

He had not expected the question. "Not many, no."

"I understand he is your godfather." No, that was backing away from the issue. She faced an opponent; she must confront him. "Do you share only the conversations that would interest a spycatcher?"

"Sir Roger said you were upset."

"Upset?" Her voice was much calmer than she felt. Cool, even, while she boiled inside. How quickly the anger had returned. "Upset is not the word I would have chosen. Disappointed, yes. Troubled, even, or distressed. And righteously angry, yes. I am a daughter of England, sir; I would never undermine her. And I am saddened. Yes, saddened. By you."

"By me?"

"Yes." *Dear Lord, help me*. Those green eyes threatened to undermine her resolve. "You work for him, don't you? You are spying on us, on my family. You courted me only to gain information. You needed an entrée to my home, and my heart became your means. I do understand your motives, but not your method. You need not continue your charade, Lord Hargreaves."

He leaned closer. He closed a hand over hers. "It's not a charade, Josette. It began as one; I admit that. Very quickly it became something more. Why do you think I was so jealous of your friendship with Kennit? There were times with you, many times with you, that I forgot I had a mission to perform. On Tuesday, when I left you, I was ready to tell Sir Roger to find someone else to do his work. I didn't want to ruin what I discovered with you, what I hope to have with you."

Josette shook her head. She tried to free her hand, but he would not release her. "Do not tell me that you fear you have fallen for a French spy." Her voice sounded hard even in her ears.

"I won't tell you that. I have never thought that, not of you. You're no spy. An intelligent beauty, yes. The maddening woman I love, yes. But definitely not a spy. I've known that since the beginning."

The hardness around her heart began to crack. "Sir Roger said—."

"Sir Roger should keep his mouth shut. I didn't tell him my feelings for you. He would have considered my mission compromised. I am hunting a spy, Josette, but that spy isn't you. You were my means to gain entrance to your home. I never expected that you would gain entrance to my heart."

She wanted to catch his words in her hands, so precious they were, but she focused on what confirmed her doubts. "You needed entrance to my home? Then you have concentrated on my family. Who do you think is the spy? Not Albert. Not my brother. He is more rabidly anti-Bonaparte than anyone. Celeste? You think the spy is Celeste?"

"I know she is. We've known it since her last trip to the seashore. She takes war despatches there and sends them to France or takes them across herself. We have the smugglers she uses."

With those few words he explained Celeste's erratic trips. Celeste—a spy. That single word explained so much, including Celeste's mood swings. She must realize that she was suspected. "Why have you not arrested her?"

"We need her source. She copies war despatches intended for Wellington. That information has undermined several of his operations. We have to find the person who gives her access to these despatches."

All her protective instincts alerted. "And you think that person is Albert?"

"I know it isn't, but it *is* someone who can access the despatches while they are outside the War Office. I hoped to discover that person when he passed the despatch to your sister-in-law. That is why I needed constant entrée to your home."

Her mind had seized the puzzle and began trying to fit the pieces. Josette realized that her anger, her righteous anger, was dissipating. If she listened any longer, she might forgive his deceit. She might forgive his playing with her heart when he had only a coldly ruthless objective.

She retrieved her hand. "I understand your reason, my lord. I do not forgive it."

"Josette—."

"No, Lord Hargreaves. Please let me go. I must have time to consider this."

He released her hand. He let her stand and walk away. She didn't look back.

Had she wanted him to stop her? Josette had not decided when she entered the card room. She looked around until she saw Kennit. He had chosen a table near the door. He stacked the coins he had just won.

He glanced up to reply to a comment and saw her. She heard his words across the several feet that separated them. "Gentlemen, you must excuse me. A lovely lady awaits my attention."

"Thank you," she whispered when he joined her and proffered his arm

"No reconcilement?"

"No. Take me home, Toby?"

"My pleasure. I'll have my carriage brought round. What of yours?"

"I must leave it for Albert. Hurry, please." Now that she was away from Giles and away from the conflict, tears threatened. She dared not let them fall publicly. All London would then know she had quarreled with Lord Hargreaves. Let them gossip instead that she had left on the arm of a notorious rake.

Fifteen minutes later they rolled away from Eaton House. She had managed a careful farewell to her hostess. She had seen Giles talking to Sir Roger and quickly turned her back. She had nearly walked straight into Michael Armitage, but Kennit caught her arm and steered her out of the ballroom. She leaned back on the coach cushions and stared blindly out the window. The streets were as dark as her mood.

They crossed several streets before Kennit cleared his throat. "Want to talk about him?"

"No."

He filled the emptiness with a description of his visit to the Bradleys home in Eastcheap. Josette partly listened, but she understood Melinda's joy in seeing him. Mrs. Bradley had not been so joyful. "I had no time alone with her. The boys monopolized my time. They wanted me to play tin soldiers. Inspired, I think, when Hargreaves visited with you. I was mere clay compared to his bronze heroism."

She scowled at him for mentioning Giles, but the description of his Tuesday afternoon pleased her. "You have changed, Tobias Kennit. A month ago you would have ignored those schoolboys."

"I am a victim of love. I find myself seeking ways to reconcile a vicar to my reputation."

"Be yourself with the Rev. Ratcliffe. He may preside over a small rural parish, but he is a very learned man. He will see through any façade." Josette wished that she had had that gift.

The carriage ride soon ended. Kennit handed her down and escorted her to the door. He bowed over her hand as Reynolds dourly watched. "This evening will soon resolve itself, I promise you."

"It cannot resolve itself too soon for me, I assure you. Thank you, Toby."

"My pleasure." He touched the brim of his hat then strode back to his carriage.

The butler shut the door and took her cloak. "Did the evening go well, Miss?"

"Is my sister-in-law still up?"

"She retired some time ago, an hour after her dinner with Mr. Terry. Madame ordered that she was not to be disturbed."

Her interest in Celeste's mysterious dinner partner seemed eons ago. "Her dinner guest was Mr. Terry? Mr. Claude *Thierry*?"

"Yes, Miss, that is the man."

The puzzle pieces of Giles' spy game began to fit together. Claude Thierry. Another *émigré*. An émigré who had shed his Gallicism to enter London society. A man who avoided political conversations even as he seemed always on the edge of any debate. Sir Roger should investigate him.

Reynolds was continuing, she realized belatedly. "Your brother came with several friends before Madame retired. She visited briefly with them."

"Was that before *M'sieur* Thierry left?"

"After, Miss. Your brother wished that I inform you of his plans. He starts early for a Melton Hall. You should not expect his return until late Sunday. He packed a valise and left with his friends. I believe they are to stay the night outside the environs of London."

Albert could offer no help with her heart's dilemma over Giles Hargreaves. "You must send for Coleman. He remains at Lady Eaton's. I left the carriage for Albert, but he obviously will not need it."

"Very good, Miss."

Reilly undressed her too slowly. She snapped at the maid when she tugged her hair while braiding it for bed. Then she heard her sharp tone. "I apologize, Reilly. I have a headache." A heartache. "That is why I left the party early."

"Yes, Miss. Shall I prepare a tisane?"

"No. No, please. I just want to sleep. I am certain I will wake refreshed."

When the maid left, Josette remained at the dressing table, idly counting the pearls in her mother's necklace, the necklace Celeste had loaned her. She had had such hopes—.

Deliberately she turned her mind to Sir Roger's questions and Giles Hargreaves' admissions. *How could he ever believe I am a spy*? He claimed he had not believed. He claimed he had known Celeste—.

Josette bolted upright.

Giles' questions had returned consistently to Celeste. He might have begun with questions about Henri Sourantine and the family, yet always he had asked about her sister-in-law. Even so, he had not pursued her comment about Celeste's distress when she returned from the seashore. He had only acknowledged her own speculations for the mysterious trips.

He had known Celeste was spying. Just as he had claimed to have. He had known that Celeste traveled to the seashore to have secret contact with France.

Celeste had occasionally spoken of the roughness of the Channel waters, of the salty wind and sea spray that had ruined a gown and a velvet coat. Josette had ignored those complaints. Giles had not probed into those seaside visits because he knew the reason for them—to pass her information on to France. His concern was how Celeste received that information. *What kind of information*? Josette clenched the pearls as she reviewed that painful conversation. War despatches, he had said. Intended for Wellington.

Those mysterious notes, addressed only with a *fleur-de-lis*, the historical emblem of France—was the recipient also in this spying game?

Yet how had Celeste managed to acquire closely guarded information about Wellington's Peninsular campaign? Who did she know that would steal such information, information that betrayed England to the enemy?

The constant salons that cost so much—now she knew why Celeste had so adamantly refused to limit them. A broad range of London society attended, especially with town so thin of company. The Sourantines could be relied on for entertainment twice weekly. And Celeste had paid for such extravagance, for the food and wine and musicians and candles and all the other incidentals. She had known Grandpapa Newland would not approve. She passed on to him only some of the bills and the others she claimed to pay from another fund. Did the mysterious recipient of the *fleur-de-lis* messages also pay for the salons, expecting a return for his money in the information gleaned in the countless conversations as people danced and ate and drank and played cards mindlessly?

How had she acquired the information from the War Office? That would not come from casual conversation. Who had access to those documents? Giles had said he knew the accomplice was not Albert. Who? Who would even be able to get near such despatches?

Alex Westover.

The young man's name shot from the dark. His father had some capacity with the Horse Guards along White Hall. Josette had assumed the association was minor. Alex had always made light of his father's position. Had she wrongly taken his word? Celeste had not. She could clearly remember, when they came to London in August, that her sister-in-law had thrown Albert together with Westover and his friends.

Not Albert. He would not involve himself in Celeste's spying. He would not be so foolish as to look through the official documents in a governmental box. Not Albert. He was his father's son, trained by his father, educated by his father. He would immediately suspect any request to slip information from Lord Westover's private study and into Celeste's hands.

I believe Giles. Celeste is a spy. Too many of her own unanswered questions about her sister-in-law's activities were answered by that single fact. Her father had taught her Occam's razor. The simplest answer was the right one.

Albert could not be involved. Giles did not believe that he was.

Sir Roger Nazenby would not know that. He would suspect Albert. As he suspected her.

Josette pooled the pearls into a tidy circle. Yes, she now accepted Giles' explanation—even as she hated it. He looked for the contact who would slip information to Celeste, either at a salon or a morning call. A message sent by a servant, even a trusted one—as Celeste must trust their coachman—such a message that could be intercepted. It was too risky for passing on the stolen despatches. The contact would hand-deliver the information to Celeste.

Coleman's employment—now she also understood why Celeste put up with him. Albert had protested the Cockney's handling of the horses. Josette had disliked his rudeness. Reynolds, however, had explained that Coleman was in Mdm. Sourantine's personal employ. Not wanting the waste and expense of an additional coachman, carriage, and horses, Josette had bitten her tongue and told Albert to keep his complaints to himself unless the horses were in immediate harm.

Coleman was Celeste's servant. He delivered the mysterious notes. He drove her to the seashore and waited for her return from France. What else did he do for Celeste?

Josette rose from her dressing table and walked to the window. She pushed aside the curtain and looked into the darkness. She lived in a nest made by the French spy. She participated in salons hosted to glean information. She shared duties as a hostess and welcomed the wide variety of society, eager to see it, to be a part of it, to be known in it. She had willingly played the part Celeste assigned her. She cast friendly smiles on all who came, the *haut ton* and the impoverished gentry, the hide-bound patriots and the *émigrés* who walked the line between gratitude for their sheltering country and fealty to Mother France.

Could she tell their loyalties by a simple look, by a single conversation? She could not.

And it hurt to admit that she understood why the spycatcher had suspected her. She could not blame Giles and Sir Roger for playing with her heart. Measured against the realm they protected, her heart weighed as nothing.

Josette recalled how Giles had once flirted with Celeste only to switch his pursuit to her after her *belle-soeur*'s last visit to the coast. Gullible fool that she was, she accepted his courtship and gave him complete access to the house. She had walked into her broken heart. If she had applied the lessons she used when playing cards against a new opponent, she would not have been so easily gulled.

Unbidden came Giles' words tonight: 'You were my means to gain entrance to your home. I never expected that you would gain entrance to my heart.'

Could she believe those words? Should she believe him? He revealed his mission to her; he bared everything to her. Was that another ploy to use her?

Yet he claimed that she had gained entrance to his heart.

Josette dared not consider that. More than her heart was at stake. Albert's future was more important than any emotion. *I can live without Giles Hargreaves. Albert cannot live his life under a stain of treason.* And if Sir Roger were to push a charge of treason, Albert would hang. Giles claimed to believe her brother was innocent; that could merely be an attempt to lull her worries until they were ready to make their arrests. No, her broken heart would not take precedence over her brother's innocence.

Why hadn't Nazenby started his arrests? He knew Celeste was a French spy.

He needed her source.

And he might want the spymaster who funded her.

The source, first. Who was it?

She thought back to Alex Westover and his father's connections to White Hall. She could not believe he would spy for Celeste. Young and a little rash, he still would not steal important government documents, not for her *belle-soeur*. He was not one of her eager swains. He also admired his father too much to risk his wrath. No, Alex was not the traitor. But the source had to be a familiar in the Westover household. He had to have such acquaintance with Celeste that their meetings raised no suspicions. And his motive? Did he hope to win Celeste's affections? Or did she pay him?

The enamored James Costell? Or Richard Malbury, always a little in debt? Clarence Wilton? No, Wilton wasn't devious enough.

Costell or Malbury?

Malbury. She would bet money on it. Like Albert, she would only put money on a sure thing, but she would bet Malbury was Celeste's source. How could she prove it? For prove it she must do, to protect Albert. She must prove it to Nazenby's satisfaction.

And then can I reconcile with Giles? a little voice wept.

No. She silenced that voice. She had to wake from that dream. He had deceived her. He did not care for her. No man who cared for a woman would so deceive her.

Chapter 21 ~ Wednesday, December 4

"You should have found a way around Miss Sourantine's questions," Giles snapped.

His anger had mounted from the moment Sir Roger Nazenby had shared his interview with Josette. While the spycatcher appeared complacently resolved, Giles had little doubt about Josette's emotional state. Repressed energy tightening every muscle, he had refused the chair Sir Roger offered. Wondering how he could recover the damage Sir Roger had inflicted, he stood at the mantel, bracing a fist against the marble.

Sir Roger templed his fingers. Giles' looming presence did not affect him. "Miss Sourantine did not ask that many. And I did want to answer them. We need her. We need her eyes in that house. As close as you are, Hargreaves, you're still not close enough. Closing this chain down becomes more and more of vital importance to Wellington's plans."

"Then you're trusting that Josette Sourantine is as honest as we need her to be."

"Twice tonight I misread her," Nazenby said. "You tell me: have I misplaced my trust?"

"You haven't misplaced it." A bitter vice closed around his heart, for the pain Josette now suffered. "She's angry at you. At me. With reason. I've hurt her." He remembered the quick and deep revenge for Lord Wynstane that she had taken on Edward Garland. "She may not be amenable to helping us."

"Miss Sourantine's emotions were not a consideration when you began this. Capturing these spies was your sole goal. Has M'selle Sourantine captured your heart instead?"

Had she captured his heart? She had certainly intrigued him and attracted him from the beginning. He enjoyed being with her, even this evening when she was so angry. He had also sensed that he was winning his battle against her anger. He had told her that she had found his way into his heart. Was that true? He did want to protect her, not just from any arrest by Nazenby but against any of the other evils that crowded the world. And he desired her, a desire that didn't stop when he walked away from her kisses. Was that love?

Giles stared at his clenched fist and considered the vise around his heart.

Sir Roger reached for his brandy snifter. "Before tomorrow noon, we shall know if our elusive source snapped up the bait."

He looked down at the spycatcher. Here was one thing, at least, that Josette could thank him for. "Albert Sourantine will not be in your net, sir. I sent him away this very afternoon, to Tony Farraday at Melton Hall. He could have nothing to do with stealing the despatch from Westover's house."

"Then the boy has not yet learned to follow orders. I saw him at Sally Eaton's tonight. With Westover's cub and his other friends. Lucas Armitage was with them. That young man is proving quite valuable as our eyes and ears."

A knock, then the door opened to admit Nazenby's ancient butler. Wordlessly he presented a letter on a silver tray then retreated. Sir Roger broke the seal and quickly scanned the page. "Ah, from Parker. We've had another stroke of luck. He has evidence for me, in Celeste Sourantine's own hand."

"Who is Parker?"

"One of my agents. We managed to insert him into Claude Thierry's household on Monday. We tried at the Sourantines, but their servants have been with them for years."

If Sir Roger had managed to plant someone at their house, then Josette's heartache might have been spared. He should never have let her leave with Kennit. He should have talked her out of her anger. He nearly had. He should have convinced her that he did care for her. Why had he hesitated?

Because he doubted she was as purely innocent of the spying as he wanted her to be?

No, not that. Yet he had hesitated, when he should have told her that the spying didn't matter, that they would weather any scandal together.

Feeling the weight of Nazenby's stare, Giles bestirred himself. "What is this evidence?"

"Part of a sealed note that Thierry received this afternoon. Addressed with only a single flower and delivered by a coachman who received a spoken reply. I think we can safely assume that Thierry is the recipient of Mdm. Sourantine's mysterious letters. He threw it in the fire, but Parker managed to retrieve the bottom portion before it burned."

"Careless. Thierry should have stayed until the note burned completely."

"I shall continue to pray that our French enemies remain so careless. It's these everyday slip-ups that give us our best clues."

"What did the letter say?"

"It's in French, naturally, but that's no bar to Parker. He's fluent in five languages. The words remaining are *cannot go. You must find someone else*. And she signed it. Foolish woman. That evidence will condemn her."

"He must want her to make another crossing to France."

"Obviously." The spycatcher looked smugly satisfied. He refolded the letter. "The rumors of the despatch have circulated for nearly ten days, and already they plan to get it to France. They have only to steal it, and we can close our trap. I did not expect to snare Thierry. This is great news."

"You still do not know who passes the despatch to her."

"We may discover that. Your *M'selle* Sourantine may tell us in order to protect her brother. And if that fails, Madame the spy will tell us under interrogation."

"And if the source is Westover's son? To arrest a peer with connections to White Hall, you will need better proof than a confession signed under torture."

"We don't torture our prisoners, Hargreaves. And I am certain the source isn't Westover. One of his friends. One of the Sourantine court or her brother-in-law."

"Not Albert Sourantine."

Sir Roger shrugged. "We shall know soon enough. Our French beauty may have received the despatch tonight while we amused ourselves at Sally's. We will know as soon as Armitage retrieves the box. Why do you think she says that she cannot go? We have held off arresting her smuggler friends until we can arrest them all."

"Her crossing to France is still possible. What if she slips your net?"

"As soon as she heads for the seacoast, we shall arrest her, with despatch in hand. No spy would dare trust this information to a mere messenger."

"So that's the reason you refused to act on Tony Farraday's word. You thought she would send that first forged despatch by messenger."

"It's not popular, what we do," Sir Roger said obliquely. "Our evidence must be clear. The despatch in her possession is clear evidence. And with that in her possession, a confession will be easy to wrest from her. Madame the spy can name her source and her spymaster to save her pretty neck."

"Do you want to save her neck?"

"Twelve men may not want to see a beautiful woman swing, Hargreaves. She may be flighty and concerned only with fashion and flirtation, but I credit her with that much intelligence."

"I think you underestimate her, Sir Roger. You've never spent an hour in her company. She could have been a great actress. All Drury Lane would bow to her skills. I think none of us have ever met the Celeste Sourantine behind the social mask."

"We shall meet her soon enough. I expect to close my trap before Sunday."

Giles walked over to the chair he had earlier refused and retrieved his cane. "Then I should leave. You will have much to set in motion tomorrow." While he had his standing with Josette to retrieve.

.~.~.~.

Thursday, December 5

He woke with a feeling of dread so strong that he was up, staring out at the early morning light, when his valet came in.

He managed to control the feeling as he settled into his morning routine. A ride in the park blew away the cobwebs from the previous evening. He resolved to be among the first callers on the Sourantines. And he would send flowers. With a personal note for Josette. The butler would ensure that both reached her without interference from her sister-in-law. He seemed to have spent much of his time retrieving his standing with her—from the rumors about the Peverell sisters to Celeste's interference and his own suspicions. Only in the past few days had his courtship gone smoothly—and then Sir Roger stuck his oar in. Yes, he would see her as early as society's rules would allow.

Giles ventured to his club to while away the few hours. He was deep in his newspaper when a tall figure loomed over him.

"What do they call a man who breaks a lady's heart? Hero?"

He looked up. Tobias Kennit lowered himself into the club chair nearest his. Giles folded the newspaper. "Kennit. I was not aware that you are a member here."

"I'm not." He nodded to indicate the other side of the room. "Musgrove brought me in."

Giles saw the peer conversing easily with Lord Cavanaugh and Derwent Wilton. Musgrove, however, was looking across at them. He nodded an acknowledgement when his gaze crossed Giles'.

He laid aside the newspaper and picked up his coffee. After a bracing swallow, he asked, "Did you flip a coin or cut a deck of cards?"

"We cut the deck. I cheated. I wasn't certain Musgrove would say everything he needed to. He'd like to cut you out with Miss Sourantine."

"While you are more objective?"

"I can be. I've my own strait and narrow road for the woman I've chosen. I don't expect it to be easy. It's never easy."

Giles shifted in his chair. "Are you presuming to give me advice? I don't take advice from a rake."

"Then don't. But don't think it's a problem you can fix with flowers." He gave a short laugh. "Takes much more than flowers, Hargreaves. There's a reason Sally Eaton has never accepted Nazenby's countless offers for her hand. He's a cold, ruthless bastard."

"And you know him so well," Giles countered sardonically.

"I do. He used me, one too many times. Same as he's using you. I can do more than play cards. I speak French like a native. I can *be* French, and I was when he needed me to be."

"That doesn't fit with what I've heard of you."

"Oh, yes. I was *born a rake*. Is that what you've heard? And you don't take advice from a rake; I heard you. Let me spin you a little tale, Hargreaves, of a gullible young fool, fresh from university, desperate to stop Napoleon."

Kennit's blue eyes glittered. Giles saw the repressed anger in his tense face and the clenched hand resting on his chair arm. Despite himself, the rake intrigued him.

"Say Nazenby learns of your desire to perform a great patriotic duty. Say he knows you have a certain fluency in French. He gives you a simple instruction: court the daughter of this *émigré* and keep your eyes peeled. Say you follow such instructions three or four times. You get a reputation, my friend. And when you return from a greater mission, a necessary and desperate mission, and you're wrecked inside, you might decide you deserved that reputation. You might polish it up because you no longer cared who would be hurt."

"You're saying this happened to you?"

"I'm saying Nazenby doesn't care who is hurt."

"He can't care," Giles defended him. "He's protecting the realm. That comes first."

"No matter how many lives he destroys? Nazenby won't care whom he arrests along with the spies he's after. He doesn't care who dies, Hargreaves. I knew a woman who died because of Nazenby's mission to protect the realm. Make certain that your woman doesn't."

"There's no reason for anyone to die when he starts his arrests."

"Can you guarantee that? Desperate people do desperate things. That I know," he added deliberately.

"Nazenby won't arrest her. He knows she is not part of the spying."

"Are you certain? Even if she stays free, her reputation will be forever tainted by the arrests. Unless you stand with her when it all shakes out."

Giles drank more coffee while he considered. Kennit urged him to a public commitment, a commitment that would only stop the gossip if it were marriage. Did he want to marry Josette? She had no rank and an adventurer's name. Three months hosting the salons had given her the reputation he had once confronted her with. The words *jade* and *Captain Sharp* had turned into a joke between them, but his parents wouldn't understand that joke. The coldly logical side of his brain cautioned that he would disappoint them.

But the heart of him, the soul of him countered with his strong attraction to her, an attraction he knew she shared. He had claimed that she had gained entrance to his heart. Only afterwards had he reckoned how true that claim was.

Yet still he hesitated. Why? Did his instinct still question her innocence? But how could she not be innocent? Was he manufacturing an excuse to avoid a public admission of his feelings for her? Or because he himself was afraid to admit his feelings? Because a commitment to her meant changing his life drastically yet again this year.

He put down his cup. A waiter stepped forward to fill it. He waited until the man moved away to serve someone else before he looked back at Kennit. "What do you advise?"

Some of the tension left the rake's face. He settled back in his chair. "Josette knows the truth about the spying, about your use of her to watch the house. And she's intelligent enough to work out that the next move is yours. You fumbled that, didn't you? Surprised me, card player that you are. Maybe you got in deeper than you planned. I don't blame you: I did the same. But she shouldn't have tumbled to your game until Nazenby started his arrests."

"He told her, not I."

"Yes, Josette told me. But other things you had said, things you had asked, they had already raised her suspicions. Only her attraction to you kept her quiet. Until Nazenby opened his mouth."

He shifted, a little annoyed at Kennit's lecture, a little angry that the rake used her name so familiarly. "What are my choices, as you and Musgrove see it?" he asked with a snide edge in his hardened voice.

"If this has been nothing but a game, don't go near her again. She won't betray you; that's not your worry. But if it became more than a game—and I will bet it did—get over there and see her. Today. Now."

"She could refuse me the house."

"Are you hesitating, then? Do you suspect her?"

"No—."

"Damn right, it's no. Celeste is your spy, not Josette. You should have kept your attention on her rather than decide to play with hearts. Or was that Nazenby's decision? I thought he gave that up after the fiasco in '04."

While Giles' curiosity was piqued about Kennit's experiences, he wasn't distracted from his own mission. "You knew Celeste Sourantine was spying?"

"Guessed it, didn't know. She's too friendly with Robert LeBrun, and he's always sold what he could find out to the highest bidder. He kept his dirty paws to blackmail until four years ago. And the French would be paying pretty highly for anything about Wellington."

"You know this?"

"Heard it."

"Where?"

"I told you, I can be taken for a Frenchman. I didn't come to talk Nazenby's game with you. He knows more than I can ever find out, and he shares only a little of it with his own men. I came for a friend. Don't go near her if you're not sincere. She's not a fool."

"Is that a threat?"

"A warning."

"Pistols at dawn?"

"And ruin her reputation? No. Josette will do her own fighting. She'll read you, now that she knows Nazenby's game. Knowing how her mind works, I'd say she figured out the whole scheme last night, down to the last tittle and jot. If you want her—and I've thought a couple of times you were that serious—if you want her, then tell her the truth."

"I told her the truth last night. I intend to repeat it today. A 'warning' was not needed, Kennit, from you or Musgrove," he added harshly.

"No? Well, I don't like to interfere. I wouldn't have if it weren't Josette."

"A rake with a heart?"

"She's a friend. She'll need friends aplenty when the rumors fly after Nazenby's finished with his arrests. She'll need a strong shoulder to lean on then."

"An office you would obligingly perform?"

"Musgrove would. I've got a woman of my own to stand by. She'll be shocked and hurt, not as much as Josette. I'll be there for her, not Josette. That's your office, isn't it? If you did tell her the truth, stand by her through the worst of it. And after. She's worthy of you, of your *great* name, if that's why you're hesitating."

"That's not why."

"Worried she's not an innocent?"

"No," he snapped.

"No, indeed. Knew it when you kissed her, didn't you? Stepped over the line with that, Hargreaves." He gave Giles a hard stare until he got the nod he wanted. Then he was up and walking away without a backward look.

Giles leaned back, a little amazed by the revelations of this quarter-hour. He tried to imagine Kennit working for Nazenby. In fifteen short minutes, his view of the man had shifted from profligate libertine to disillusioned spy for the realm. His friend Tony Farraday had also become disillusioned with Sir Roger's methods. Farraday's experience gave validity to Kennit's story. The spycatcher apparently had never cared who was hurt in the pursuit of his goal.

Kennit had obviously been left twisting in the wind by the spycatcher. As Tony Farraday had been. *As I will be?* As Josette certainly would be when the arrests started. What was it Kennit had said? *There's a reason Sally Eaton has never accepted Nazenby's countless offers for her hand. He's a cold, ruthless bastard.*

This morning Giles had awakened with a strong dread riding his bones. Now it assailed him again. Why did he hesitate to commit to Josette? Last night he had wondered if what he felt for her added up to love. He still didn't have that answer. He knew only that he had to see her, he had to protect her, he had to have her with him. Letting her endure alone the shock when Sir Roger arrested her sister-in-law—especially if the spycatcher also hauled in her brother—that was not an option. He really had no choice. That decision occurred days ago. When he kissed her or before? Giles didn't know and didn't care.

The newspaper slid to the floor as he abruptly abandoned his chair. He would be early to the Sourantines, but social conventions could go to the devil.

Chapter 22 ~ Thursday, December 5

Her hand on the doorknob to the library, Josette heard a woman speaking stridently in rapid French. Celeste. Who was she now ringing a peal over?

She hesitated. She didn't want to interrupt the scene, but she needed her writing things. Melinda's mother had written Monday a week ago; she should not delay her answer another day. And she wanted to mention Tobias Kennit as a kind gentleman before the other gossip reached Mrs. Ratcliffe. If she could smooth Kennit's entrance into the Ratcliffe family, that would be a small thanks for his rescue last evening, not once but twice.

Another spate of rapid French. Celeste could not be berating one of the servants, not in French. Why had she chosen the library at the back of the house? She usually received visitors in the *petite salon* while Josette preferred the library with its view of the garden. Even stripped for winter, it reminded her of Little Houghton. Yet now Celeste had taken it.

And that tantrum meant that this was no social call. Who could have drawn Celeste's wrath down upon himself?

A man spoke, a long series of sentences. Josette could hear only the rise and fall of his voice through the door. He sounded calm, a vain attempt to soothe Celeste. From experience Josette knew nothing could control her sister-in-law's outburst.

Her letter could wait. She did not want to be caught eavesdropping. Yet even as she turned to leave, Celeste spoke again. Her voice sound more frightened than anger. The higher-pitched voice carried through the oak panels, and Josette's quick ears performed the translation.

"You *must* find someone else to take it to France."

To France! Giles' revelations had haunted her all night, and now Celeste's demand seemed an admission that she was a spy. Josette had to hear more. She stepped closer, almost pressing her ear to the door to hear the man's reply.

"No one else can go," he replied, also in French. "Not for another week at least. You must deliver it, you yourself, my little beauty. I remind you that your reward will be great."

"I cannot take it. I cannot! They suspect me already. They will be assured of my guilt as soon as I arrive at the inn. I will not be able to return without being arrested," only she said it as "*Je ne reviens pas sans arret pour moi.*"

The man's response was too low for Josette to hear.

Celeste's agitation shrilled her voice higher. "Palmer is dead! Killed by one of Nazenby's spies! I know it, me. His men sent me that news after I returned to London."

"You have lost your transport to France?" Josette knew that voice, but she could not place it. "If you have no means to convey information across the Channel, then we no longer have a use for you."

"Of course I can still send information to France. The smugglers wish to continue our arrangement. But *I* cannot go. If I do, they will *know* I am a spy! They will arrest me! If we do manage to get away, I can never return."

"You have only to finish this last little transport to complete your bargain with us. Your reward awaits in France. And if this despatch contains the information you say it does, you may expect an even greater reward. If it gives the very details we need—."

"It does. I you assure, it does. Napoleon can win the war with this information, and England will no longer threaten on the continent."

Angus the footman came through the servants' door. Startled, Josette retreated from the library and fled to the entrance hall. There, she stood irresolute, her eyes blank, turning over what she had heard. Celeste was to carry a despatch to France, a despatch that must contain information about Wellington's Spring campaign. For this information she would receive a substantial reward. She was indeed a spy, as Giles had said.

Should I send Giles word? If the despatch guaranteed Napoleon's victory over England, then it must not leave these shores. *But how can I prevent it? Unless I turn Celeste in for arrest. Can I do that?*

She had a very selfish reason for hesitating, God help her. She could not imagine the son of a marquess involving himself with a woman related to a spy. A spy would be arrested and convicted and— Josette swallowed—and hanged. Here was the greater deterrent to reporting her sister-in-law, Edmund's wife, to the authorities. Celeste would be convicted of treason and hanged. She pressed her hands to her eyes. She dared not think of that end.

The third thought that came was no easier—Giles had known from the beginning.

That's what he had said last evening. He began his relationship with deceit. His voice echoed clearly: *Then it became something more, something much more.*

What should she do? She was English. She could not let France receive a despatch that would harm England. Yet if she intervened, Celeste would die.

She was still standing, vacillating between those hard choices, when Reynolds spoke beside her. He startled her so much that she jerked and cried out.

"Miss Josette? Shall I have Mrs. Bridgerton prepare a tisane?"

"A tisane?"

"Yes, Miss. Angus said you seemed—out of sorts. Are you not well?"

"I am perfectly well." She pressed her fingers to her brow, trying to smooth away the frown as she tried to calm her racing heart. "Reynolds, who has come to visit Celeste?"

"Mr. Terry and Mr. LeBrun."

Ah, Thierry. He owned that suave voice that tried to persuade Celeste to risk herself. Josette strove for calmness, but her voice quavered. "Celeste is down early, especially for a visit from her admirers. How did they manage to rouse her before noon?"

"They did not come for a visit, Miss. Madame sent for them, last night."

"Last night? When was this? You did not speak of it when I returned."

"She sent the notes after you retired. Coleman delivered the notes after he returned from Eaton House. One of the notes was addressed as the others had been, with a flower. The other was to Mr. LeBrun. Since Mr. Terry arrived this morning, expecting entrance, I must assume that he has been the recipient of Madame's secretive messages."

"And Coleman delivered these notes as well?" Of all the servants in the house, Coleman was the only one that her sister-in-law had personally hired. The other servants had been with the Sourantines for years, hired by her father or even further back, by her grandfather when he purchased the house, as Reynolds and Mrs. Bridgerton were. Angus had grown up from coal boy to page and now footman. Even Jane the kitchenmaid preceded Celeste's entry into the family.

The Cockney coachman considered his only service to the Sourantines to be the coach. He tended it and the two teams of horses himself. Any other requests that Josette or Albert had made, Coleman met with disdain, explaining clearly that he was only a coachman. Yet for Celeste he had lowered himself to run errands. And Coleman, as coachman, was the only one to accompany Celeste to the seashore. Her fashionable sister-in-law had not even taken Reilly.

Smugglers transported Celeste to France and back. Smugglers worked on the seashore.

All this merely enlarged the puzzle she had solved last evening. Realizing that the butler waited for her to emerge from that brown study, Josette turned to the patient man. "Have the gentlemen been here long?"

"They arrived by the back lane after you went into breakfast, Miss. Madame chose the library to receive them. They have been here not quite a quarter-hour."

"A matter of some urgency, I suppose."

"Madame did not confide in me."

She had to think. She could not think through what she had to decide while Reynolds waited beside her. "I'll—I'll just go upstairs. I have—I have some things to put away."

"Shall I send Reilly to you, Miss?"

"No. It's—It's papers, some letters. Please inform me when the gentlemen leave." She didn't have a plan. She only knew that she didn't want to confront Celeste.

Josette had no more direction when she reached her bedchamber. Hands twisted together, she glanced around as if some object would give her direction. The second floor seemed very quiet. Reilly and Patty the chambermaid had already gone downstairs. If Celeste had followed habit, then Reilly would return in an hour to help her mistress dress for the day. The personal maid would need another hour to deal with the maelstrom Celeste had created. But her *belle-soeur* had broken her usual pattern—because Claude Thierry wanted her to go to France.

The early December chill had seeped into the room. Josette went to the fireplace and poked the coals, winning a little more warmth. Two thoughts kept spiraling through her mind: Celeste was a spy and Giles had lied to her from the first. Both thoughts filled her with a despairing confusion. What could she do? What would she do? She had to tell someone about Celeste and this despatch she must have stolen. Yet in doing so, she signed her sister-in-law's death warrant. And Giles—.

Giles had deceived her. Which man was the real one? The Giles who pursued her to capture a spy, or the one who claimed she had gained an entrance to his heart?

She drifted to her dressing table and stared at the brushes and little powder pots on the embroidered mat, stared at their reflection in the oval mirror. He had lied at the beginning; did he lie now? She wanted to believe him, but should she? Yet why not? Now that she knew his mission, would he need to continue the basic lie of a courtship? He would not. So he must be telling the truth when he said something more than a ruse bound them together? Or was that another lie?

And that was the crux, she realized. Until she knew that truth, she could not go on with him. She had to know. Only then would she be able to grasp happiness or begin to cope with the dark loneliness.

Josette touched the strand of pearls still coiled on her dressing table. Her mother's pearls. Edmund had given them to his new bride on their wedding day. Celeste had been kind enough to let her wear them last evening, and they had shown to an advantage on the pale blue silk. On the drive to Eaton House Josette had touched the pearls and felt a burst of pride in wearing something of her mother's. She wanted nothing to do with them now. It was a spy who had loaned those pearls. They were forever tainted by their association with last night.

She needed to return them. While her sister-in-law was occupied with her fellow spies, she could slip them back into Celeste's jewelry box. Reynolds would send word when her sister-in-law was free. With the pearls back in place, Josette could find an excuse to leave the house, perhaps to visit Melinda. That would give her a few hours to work out her dilemma, a few hours to cool her loathing for her spying *belle-soeur*.

She slipped down the hall to Celeste's bedchamber. The tooled green jewelry box had pride of place on the dressing table. It was locked, which Josette had expected. She found the key in the first place she looked, under a tangle of ribbons in a tiny drawer. The lock turned easily. Pleased with her success so far, she opened the lid to drop in the pearls. Folded papers sprang open. Rammed into the jewelry box, they had partially unfolded when she lifted the lid. The broken wax seal, large and red, looked official. The papers were folded off their original crease so they would fit into the box.

Celeste's panic echoed: "You must find someone else to take it to France."

Giles had said, "She copies war despatches intended for Wellington. She sends them to France or takes them across herself."

And Claude Thierry's glib voice offered a greater reward if the despatch contained the information that France needed to defeat England.

Josette dropped in the pearls and removed the papers. Once out of the casket they unfolded completely. A single glance confirmed the War Office seal. A longer glance revealed attack plans, troop movements, supply routes, outlined in detail over several sheets of parchment.

These papers were the proof that her *belle-soeur* spied. When had Celeste decided to betray the England that had sheltered her family from the Reign of Terror? When had she decided to serve Napoleon? Patriotism did not motivate her. She had goaded Albert about Napoleon only after he had boasted of Wellington's deeds. She played the *Bonapartiste* only because it fit her role as a French beauty in London society. Never once had she claimed a desire to return to France.

Unbidden came a long-ago memory, Edmund talking after a visit to Celeste's parents in Cambridge. He had described the Nemours' former manor, the village that had been their home, the family possessions—ages old—that had to be abandoned. The Nemours dreamed, he had said, of the restoration of their property and monies. They had lost so much. Why could it not be restored? What had they ever done against France, against their fellow countrymen? Why were they still *persona non grata* in their homeland?

Had Celeste dreamed of fulfilling her parents' dearest wish? Her father's lectures at the university had embarrassed her, he who had blue blood working to support his family. Celeste had spoken many times of the friends her mother wished to visit often asking why her *maman* was not allowed to return and chat with her friends and visit the Paris shops? Instead, and this Celeste had added in a sour voice, her *maman* must smuggle letters to her friends to have any word at all of her family, her home. *This exile is breaking Maman's heart*, she had declared.

That was how Celeste had known the smugglers. They had carried her mother's letters to and from France. Another little step, and they could carry information about the war.

Josette folded the despatch along its original creases. Giles should have this. Sir Roger should have it. This information, in French hands, would destroy Wellington's entire army. Her earlier scruple about turning in one of her own family vanished. If she let Celeste take this despatch, then Josette herself would be guilty of each soldier's death.

Pressing the paper to her breast, Josette returned to her chamber. She would take the despatch to Giles. No, she could not face him, not yet. Not until she were calmer. She closed the door and leaned against it, her heart trying to jump out of her breast.

She would take the despatch to Sir Roger. He would know what to do.

She could not delay this errand.

Josette changed her morning dress for a heavier walking dress. She would not risk Coleman's allegiance to Celeste by calling for the coach. And that would be an additional delay. She would pretend that she wanted a walk and then hire a hackney once she was well away from the house. She donned a hooded cloak and gloves against the morning's cold. Then she refolded the despatch and stuffed it into a reticule. She hurried down the upper stairs—only to stop before she reached the last step.

Celeste stood in the hall. Arms folded, as if she waited for Josette.

"There you are," she said, confirming that blinding guess.

"I have an errand I must attend to. Will you tell Reynolds? I should be back before noon." She came off the last step, using all her card playing skills to maintain a serene countenance.

"Come speak to *Messieurs* LeBrun and Thierry before you leave."

"I am in some haste, Celeste."

Her *belle-soeur* took her arm. "A simple hello does not take long."

Josette considered ripping away from Celeste's taloned grip. Yet how quickly would they seize her, if they knew that she knew their game? She must pretend to innocence. That was her only protection. "Celeste," she tried another protest. "I really must complete my errand."

"Nonsense. Nothing can be that pressing. Unless it is a matter of national importance?" Her tittering laugh made light of the question that had frozen Josette to the bones.

"No, it is not that serious," she said, just as lightly, and let herself be tugged into the library. Celeste gave her a little push deeper into the room then shut the door firmly and leaned against it.

When the two Frenchmen saw her, they stood. Her dear sister-in-law's first words, still spoken lightly, worried her. "Here she is, claiming a foolish errand. I told her that she need not try to escape."

Her reticule, stuffed with the folded War Office papers, hung heavily from her wrist. With Celeste's apt words crept in an icy suspicion that they knew what she held. Josette's knees grew weak. But she lifted her head and smiled brilliantly. "Good morning, gentlemen."

LeBrun bowed. Thierry fingered the cane he affected. "You have a pressing engagement? Where must you go so early? It is not yet noon."

"A visit to the apothecary and then on to my friend."

"And you were going to walk?" LeBrun circled behind her.

She swiveled her head to watch as he came around, but he stopped a little behind her. She turned toward him. "I thought Celeste planned to use the carriage. I can hire a hack."

"This that you need from the apothecary, it is important? And your visit to your friend, it cannot wait until calling hours?" Usually hidden, Thierry's accent seemed more pronounced.

"My friend Melinda Ratcliffe. I believe you met her at Monday's salon. She told me last evening, at Lady Eaton's, that her uncle complained of gout. Her aunt Mrs. Bradley has no good remedy for that painful condition. I remembered a receipt my grandfather Newland used. I thought to take it to them." It was a good lie. Would they spot it?

"You do not send the receipt? You must take it yourself?"

She sighed as if trying to be patient. "Our apothecary is familiar with this particular receipt. I thought I would have it made up and take it myself. By doing so, I can explain the other little things that Grandpapa does when he takes this medicine."

"You go to much trouble for a friend."

"I would not want anyone to suffer pain if I know a remedy. Besides, Melinda is a close friend. I have known her all my life. Celeste knows her, don't you, Celeste?"

But Celeste didn't reply. Josette suddenly realized how closely the men stood. LeBrun blocked her way to the door.

"Give it to us," Thierry said.

"I beg your pardon?"

"Give us the papers you have."

"You want Grandpapa's receipt for gout?" Icy fear gripped her, and the words came out cracked. They knew. Somehow they knew. They had known before Celeste confronted her in the hall. Had Celeste gone upstairs to retrieve the despatch so they could read it? And she had found the despatch missing and the pearls restored. She would know immediately that Josette had discovered it and taken it. *What can I do?* Her gaze skittered sideways as she clawed for a plan.

"Where were you going to take it?" Celeste demanded.

The fire burned cheerily. If she could slip past Thierry—. Her reticule would have to be opened, the folded papers pulled out—. No, better to burn the reticule with the despatch. "I told you," she answered, holding fast to her lie. "I was taking the receipt to our apothecary."

A flurry of movement behind her, and her reticule was snatched away. She cried out, more at the shock of LeBrun's move than from actual pain, but she played that lie. The first one was now useless. "What are you doing? You hurt me."

LeBrun jerked open the velvet purse and shoved in his hand. With difficulty he removed the despatch. "Yes, this is it. She did take it, as you suspected, Celeste." He dropped the blue velvet reticule onto a chair.

"Your errand certainly could not wait," Thierry said dryly.

"She has worked against me," Celeste claimed, "against us, since her arrival in London. I knew. *Moi*, I knew." She rounded on her sister-in-law and shoved her. Josette staggered into a chair and gripped it for support. "You hate me, this I know. I hate you back. I have always hated you. Trumped up Provincials who live so grandly—when my papa must slave for the food he eats and the roof over his head. He is a *chevalier d'honneur*! He deserves the grand house, the twenty servants, the horses and coaches. Do you know what I found when last I visited him and *Maman*? They were eating on chipped plates. Chipped plates! *Ma père et ma mère!*"

"Celeste, you know Grandpapa Newland offered—."

"Grandpapa Newland! I spit upon him! The so-rich M. Newland with his house in York and his country manor. People bow to him, Robert, as if he had the blue blood. I laugh at them! He is no more than a peasant who still works with his hands, and these stupid English bow to him. And they swarm over his grandchildren, all to feed off the money that dribbles through their fingers. Pah! The so-wonderful Sourantine children. I spit upon them, too! I hate them!"

Her venom appalled Josette. "But Celeste, we welcomed you into our family. We loved you because Edmund loved you. You are *ma belle-soeur*. Edmund doted on you."

"Edmund! That imbecile! He strutted around like a *seigneur*. He had no thought but horses. I hated him! I could not stand for him to touch me! He wanted me—me!—to hide myself in the country and breed babies, all to please his peasant of a *grandpère*. Me! I was to be no more than a breeding mare. When he would not let me return to London, I took care of *Seigneur* Edmund and his plans."

"Took care of Edmund? What do you mean? What are you saying?"

"Let us not bring up past indiscretions," Thierry interjected in that silken voice Josette was beginning to hate. "Our concern is with the despatch."

"You have been spying on me!" Celeste exclaimed. "Since I returned from the seashore, since before then, yes? I knew, just as I knew Sir Roger Nazenby was watching me. Then *Mon Seigneur* Hargreaves began to court you, and you could think of nothing but him. Fool! You are easily gulled. He wanted a flirtation, nothing more, and when I would not give him my attention, he turned to you. Little fool, you forgot to watch me. I fooled you all!"

"She remembered her mission well enough this morning," LeBrun reminded. He turned on Josette and demanded, "Where were you going to take the despatch? To Nazenby?"

Josette didn't answer. Too many deceits crowded her mind: Giles and his pretended courtship; he had spied on Celeste, not she. Celeste and her spying. Celeste's hatred for her in-laws, a hatred that extended to her late husband. Had those words meant murder? Josette couldn't shift the pieces into place. Hearing Celeste, believing her, changed all those years when she thought everyone had been happy.

She continued to massage her wrist and hand, as if LeBrun's snatch at her reticule had indeed hurt her. Remembering the fingernails that Celeste had dug into her arm, Josette chose to stay behind the chair.

"That matters not," Thierry said. "We have the despatch now. You, Celeste, must take it to France immediately."

She looked appalled. "But I cannot. I *told* you—. I thought we had agreed—."

Claude Thierry looked amused. "Oh, my little beauty, you must think. With this little scene your continued presence in England is now impossible. You have become useless to me, even a danger to me. They know you are a spy. They do not know your master, not yet. That must not be discovered."

"But the moment I fly, they will pursue me. They will arrest me!"

"Which is the reason you must leave immediately, just as Saultsein and I planned. You cannot stay, not with this despatch gone, not with what your *belle-soeur* has just learned. Nor can she stay. She will tell them. See, it is in her so-pale eyes. She knows that I am a spy, that we are all spies. As soon as she is able, she will go to Sir Roger Nazenby."

"Then we will have to make her not able," LeBrun said, so casually that he surely did not mean murder.

"What do you mean?" Celeste asked.

"She must go with you to France, my little beauty."

"I won't go," Josette said flatly. "You can't force me."

"This can," LeBrun said. From his pocket he drew a gleaming pistol, a pretty silver thing but still lethal. Josette felt the cold of the grave mantling her. *Dear Lord, he does mean murder.*

"*Imbecile*, put that up," Thierry snapped. "There are better methods, aren't there, Miss Sourantine? There are easier methods. We need not use force or even threaten to harm her. We need to make only one little point. Should Sir Roger arrest Celeste, she has only to say that your brother Albert stole the despatch for her—."

"That's a lie!"

"A convenient one." His closed smile looked as smooth as a snake hiding its fangs. "Sir Roger will accept it as truth. His long attempt to find the spy and her source will be over. The Sourantine name will be tainted forever with the blackness of treason. And your *frère* Albert will swing at the end of a hangman's noose. Or you can be silent and go with Celeste to France. One day very soon you can return. After the invasion, of course. By then your Lord Hargreaves will have found another wife, but your brother will be alive. And as relatives of one of Napoleon's most valuable spies, your family will be rewarded."

"Because Napoleon will control England," she snapped.

He bowed.

"I cannot do this. I cannot allow you to betray my country. I cannot allow soldiers to walk blindly into ambushes. It would be as if my own hand loaded the weapons used against them. I cannot."

"It is a simple choice: your country or your brother."

Josette inhaled sharply. *Dear Lord, it is a simple choice.* "I hate you," she spat.

He laughed. "But you will go with Celeste, yes?"

"Yes."

A knock broke Thierry's concentration on her. He signed to

LeBrun to hide the pistol. Celeste arranged herself on the daybed as the door opened and the servant came in. Her back to the door, Josette did not know who had entered until Reynolds spoke in his blandest voice. "The coach is ready, Madame."

"*Bon!*" Celeste sprang up. "I must run upstairs a moment. Josette, wait you a little longer, and we shall drive you to the apothecary for that receipt. Tell Coleman we shall be down in a very few minutes."

But Reynolds didn't leave upon that obvious dismissal. "You have need of the apothecary, Miss Josette? You need not go out if you are unwell."

She turned to the man who had solved the problems of this house for so many years. Before she could speak, Celeste interjected her own lie. "It is a receipt for her friend, *n'est ce pas*, Josette? We save her a walk in the cold. *Allez-vous-en*, Reynolds."

His gaze remained on Josette. She feared if she spoke or signed to him, Albert would be doomed. His hesitation seemed hours long, but he bowed at last. "Very good, Madame."

The butler opened the door for Celeste. She hurried out; he lingered, still watching Josette. They heard Celeste dashing up the stairs.

"I put Lord Hargreaves' flowers in your room, Miss. If anyone should inquire to send after you, as he does when he visits, what must I say?"

He forced her to answer. Her glance shifted to Thierry. His snake's eyes were narrowed on her. LeBrun's hand rested on the pocket which held that deadly little pistol. Would they shoot Reynolds? Who, then, would tell the constables what had happened in this house? Who would point the finger of blame toward Thierry and LeBrun? Reynolds had to stay alive. He could explain everything to Giles. After it was too late.

"I am going to my friend Miss Ratcliffe. I am taking to her uncle Mr. Bradley a receipt that my grandfather uses for his gout. Their home, the Bradley home, is in Eastcheap, if you remember."

"Shall I tell this to Lord Hargreaves, Miss? When do you expect to return? He is always most specific in his questions concerning you."

"I do not know when I shall return." That was definitely the truth. Did she dare a message? "Tell Lord Hargreaves that it is Mr. Bradley's complaint, the one they spoke of on Sunday. Mr. Bradley talked a good hour of that complaint."

"Very well, Miss." He turned to leave.

"And Reynolds, my brother—." She added nothing more. LeBrun's hand had dived into this pocket. Josette forced a smile for the butler. "No, I shall tell him myself."

The old man's gaze flickered to the Frenchmen, then he bowed himself out. As he opened the door, they heard Celeste clattering down the stairs in the heels she refused to give up for the more fashionable slippers.

Her sister-in-law hurried in, dressed in a mink-lined cloak, her pretty face framed by white fur. She carried the tooled jewelry box and a bandbox. The latter she gave to Josette. "We go, yes? But I have no ready cash, Claude. I gave it all to Mal—to him last evening."

"A moment only, and I will write for you a note that will pay for everything you need."

As Thierry set to work, LeBrun gave his pistol to Celeste. "In case your *belle-soeur* is not so amenable when we are gone from you, *ma petite*."

"You do not come to France with us, Robert?"

"Thierry still has a use for me."

Josette tried not to watch LeBrun explain the workings of his pistol to Celeste. She tried not to watch Thierry seated at her writing desk, penning the note that gave Celeste her reward. Her gaze fastened upon her reticule, still in the bergere chair where LeBrun had dropped it. Would they notice it and have her take it with her? As a sign that she had left unwillingly, it was a poor one. How long before a servant noticed it, Angus coming to refuel the fire or Mrs. Bridgerton to see if the room needed straightening?

When Thierry stood, she jerked her gaze away from the blue velvet pouch with its brown drawstrings. To her it seemed huge, dropped on the creamy yellow fabric of the chair, an obvious thing they must see. Would the French spymaster notice it? Celeste and LeBrun did not have an angle to see it. Would her misfortune continue, and they would take the two additional steps to see it? She looked away and stared bitterly at her sister-in-law, *belle-soeur* no longer. And Thierry walked past the chair.

He handed the folded letter to Celeste. "Give this to your contact in Calais. He will see you generously bestowed. Once in Paris, the proper authorities will release your reward to you. Near Chartres, *n'est ce pas?*"

She stuffed the letter into her own purse. "I begin to be excited, Claude."

But he didn't listen to her bubbling words. He turned to Josette. "Too bad this is not a card game, M'selle Sourantine. You might have had a chance of winning. Ah, but I hold Albert as my trump. That was a master play," he congratulated himself.

"They will hang you, *M'sieur* Thierry."

"They do not even know who I am," he said confidently.

Chapter 23 ~ Thursday, December 5

LeBrun seized her arm. "You will not alert the servants, Josette. You will be *complaisant*, yes?" He didn't wait for agreement but hauled her by main force to the door that Celeste obligingly opened.

Once they started past the grand staircase, his grip became bruising. She had only one revolt, as Angus opened the exterior door. She added together LeBrun's pistol and his careful instructions with Celeste's hatred and a crossing with smugglers, and they totaled her doom. She would not walk willingly to her own death. She struggled against his grip.

LeBrun tightened his fingers and hissed in her ear, "Remember your brother, Josette. You will not see him hang, but he will, most assuredly, if you do not cooperate. I do guarantee it. I will give the evidence myself."

She stopped struggling, but she could not propel her feet. He dragged her a stumbling two steps then shook her roughly. She found her feet.

Angus bowed as they passed him and entered the cold rain. When had it started raining? She looked up and let the rain sting her face.

Celeste's carriage waited for them. The yellow wheels seemed to glow through the stinging rain. Coleman opened the carriage door. As LeBrun propelled her forward, Coleman gave her a crooked smile, and she hated the swarthy man. Thierry climbed in, then Celeste. LeBrun shoved her in. He came so closely behind her that he sat down as she did, bracing an arm across her as the carriage started. He didn't remove his arm. They rolled quickly along the empty street. The carriage did not stop until it reached an inn on the outskirts of London.

LeBrun removed his arm. "Keep the pistol at ready, *ma petite*."

"I shall," Celeste breathed. "*Au revoir*, Robert, Claude."

The spymaster kissed her sister-in-law's hand. "*Adieu*, my little beauty. You will enjoy being the toast of all Paris, I promise. And you," he scowled at Josette. She lifted her frustrated face and met his gaze, trying desperately to hide the multitude of escapes she was contemplating. "Do not think to escape, *M'selle*. If Celeste should miss with her little pistol, you must still contend with Coleman. He has two pistols and is an excellent shot. If you wish to live, you will go quite happily to Paris."

"Do you think I am fool enough to believe that I will reach

France?" she retorted. "She will have those smugglers drop me into the Channel."

"Celeste will not do that. We are not murderers, *M'selle*, only patriots of Mother France. Your *belle-soeur* must keep you safe. Her reward requires your presence. Yes, my little beauty," he added at Celeste's squeak, "I wrote this in the letter. *M'selle* Sourantine is your safe passage to the coast and across the Channel. Once in France, we can ransom her from her so-doting grandpapa. You did not consider that, did you, my beauty?"

"No, I did not." Her murmur revealed that she had planned just as Josette suspected.

"Keep her safe, and you will have a greater reward. *Adieu*, Josette."

Thierry had the audacity to seize her hand. She recoiled. He squeezed it punishingly then kissed it. Then he laughed, sprang down, and slammed the door. A shout to Coleman, and the carriage jerked forward, picking up speed on the hard frozen ground.

Celeste snatched out Thierry's note and read it, her brow puckering more and more. She did not deny Thierry's words, and Josette did not want to challenge her when she frowned so. The little pistol was still her in sister-in-law's lap. As she read, she rested one hand on it.

Josette glanced at the door latch and thought about springing from the rolling carriage. She might be hurt, but there were people on the road. Surely Coleman and Celeste could not seize her before she had screamed for help. But the few times that she had worked the latch from the inside it had stuck. Celeste would have time to seize her pistol. She could shoot and kill as Coleman continued to drive, and Josette would be dead, very dead. *Not yet*, she warned herself. *There will be a time. God willing, there will be a time.* She braced against the cushions and looked out the window.

Her sister-in-law read the note several more times. With one hand she folded it and stuffed it into her reticule. Then she settled back and aligned LeBrun's pistol on Josette.

She didn't turn her head from looking out the window. "Please, Celeste, do not point that thing at me. It could go off. Then you will not have your safe passage or your ransom."

"It will not go off. My finger is not on the little trigger, see? *You* have lost your son of a marquis, *ma belle soeur*, after you stole him from me."

"So I have," she managed with surprising composure. "Who stole the despatches for you, Celeste?"

"Albert."

"No more games, *ma belle-soeur*. Why would Albert steal war documents for you? He would guess they would go to France, and he hates Napoleon. Who—?" She stopped, remembering her sister-in-law's slip of the tongue. "Malbury. Richard Malbury. And you would lie and blame Albert, who is innocent."

"I do not say it is he. And Albert is not so innocent. Nor are you. If I am arrested, then you two will die with me."

"Celeste—."

"*Non.* I will not listen! I have the pistol of Robert. I would rather he had come and shot you. Somewhere on the road. Then we would all be safe."

She inhaled harshly. Her dear *belle-soeur* would do it; she would like to have Josette killed. And she would leave her body on the side of the road, unburied, her family never knowing what happened to her. "Thierry said I am your safe passage," she reminded.

"Bah! You are a safe passage only if we are stopped on the road."

"And across the Channel," she reminded her shakily. Death shadowed her. "If the revenue cutters stop us in the Channel—."

"I should still do it. Perhaps I will. Coleman can do it for me. *Oui,* Coleman will do it."

"He will commit murder for you?"

"He has done so before," she said calmly, practicably, as if the red deed were no more than opening a door.

Josette looked out the window at the rushing countryside. The rain had stopped, but in her heart it poured, a deluge of fear. She dared not risk Celeste's volatile temper. The longer she lived, the greater the possibility that Celeste would continue to follow Thierry's plan. She shut her eyes, turned all her concentration inward, and prayed.

. ~ . ~ . ~ .

The red-haired footman who opened the door to Giles must have taken lessons from Reynolds. "Both the ladies are gone from the house this morning, my lord," he said in answer to Giles' query.

"Gone? This early?" His dread intensified. "When did they leave?"

"Not more than a quarter-hour ago, my lord, perhaps a little more."

"Were they escorted?" If it were two Frenchmen, he would know Josette was in danger.

"Mr. Terry and Mr. LeBrun."

"To where?"

"They were to go to the apothecary and then to Eastcheap, Lord Hargreaves."

A visit to the apothecary and Eastcheap did not sound dangerous.

He heard a conversation behind the door. It opened wider to reveal Reynolds. "My lord, will you come in?"

Giles hesitated. The butler had never favored him. If his answers were of no help, he only wasted time here. Hoping to discover if Josette needed him, he stepped in.

Gathered at the base of the grand staircase were a dozen servants, from the butler and the housekeeper in her starched cap down to the lowly kitchen maid and the scrubby groom barely tall enough to hold his horse. Reynolds signed to the boy, and he clattered across the tiled floor and out, to do his duty.

The butler took station in the midst of the servants. "We were going to send for you, sir."

"Now, Reynolds, we hadn't decided yet," the older woman countered.

"Who is better, Mrs. Bridgerton?" the man retorted, his expression animated for the first time in Giles' acquaintance with him. "Master Albert is gone, to return we know not when. Lord Hargreaves has seen military service, and we know he cares for Miss Josette."

Those few words proved the danger, but they also gave Giles hope. "I gather the departure of the ladies Sourantine was not under pleasant circumstances."

"Under the worst circumstances, my lord. We think Mdm. Sourantine and her guests took Miss Josette against her will."

The footman stepped forward. "We know they did, my lord. She were struggling, my lord. That Mr. LeBrun had her by the arm."

"And she left her purse, sir." Mrs. Bridgerton proffered a blue velvet reticule, cupped in her hands like an offering. "Miss Josette would not willingly leave the house without a little money in her possession. It is Mr. Newland's first rule to his grandchildren."

"Perhaps you should begin at the beginning."

"The events of today did not rightly begin this morning, sir. Last evening, Madame sent two letters out, one to Mr. LeBrun and the other addressed with a flower, a *fleur-de-lis*."

"Yes, Miss Sourantine informed me of those mysterious notes. I assume that the recipient came this morning with LeBrun."

"Quite right, my lord. Claude Terry. Early this morning both gentlemen came to the house through the garden. Before they shut themselves into the library, they were asking Madame to leave immediately on a trip. She was refusing their request."

'You're taking too long in the telling," the housekeeper said, exercising her authority. "Angus, tell your part."

"Well, my lord, I were coming down the servant's passage, my lord, and I saw Miss Josette listening at the door to the library. When she saw me, my lord, she fair ran to the entrance hall. I told Mr. Reynolds what I seen."

The butler took up the tale. "I went to see Miss Josette. She seemed distracted, sir, as if she could not reach a decision, and Miss Josette has always known her own mind, as you know."

"What did she tell you?"

"She would tell me nothing and retired to her room. And then, my lord, I am afraid that I took it upon myself to commit a transgression: I listened at the door."

"And nearly got caught," Angus rushed to say, "when Madame came out the door."

"If you heard their conversation, it must have been in French."

"It was, my lord. I speak French. As Miss Josette knows. Mr. Newland stipulated that requirement when he was hiring a butler to serve his daughter and her new husband. All the servants are learning French, my lord, at Miss Josette's direction."

"Does Mdm. Sourantine know you speak her language?"

"Madame never bothered to learn this. A fact for which I am very grateful today, given what I have heard about secret trips to France and stolen war despatches."

Ah, the confirmation he needed, finally. "How did Miss Sourantine come to be taken from the house against her will?"

"A bare minute after Madame went upstairs, she came down again. Apparently, between her informing the two gentlemen of the war despatch she had received and the retrieval of it for them, it had gone missing. Madame demanded to know if anyone had entered her chamber. I knew of only Reilly her maid."

"I am not a thief, my lord." A spinster maid, her pinched face reddened and puffy, spoke up. "I took nothing."

"I told you not to worry, Reilly," the butler reassured her. "I believe Miss Josette took the despatch. That is what Madame believed. She accosted Miss Josette when she came downstairs dressed for an outing. Madame required her attendance upon them in the library. Angus and I listened at the door."

"It weren't quite shut, my lord. We heard them most clearly, my lord."

"They surmised that Miss Josette did not speak truthfully about her errand to the apothecary. Mr. Terry became most insistent that she travel with Madame to the seacoast."

Insistent. Required. Accosted. Demanded. Words that portended much more than Reynolds' dry account conveyed. "Thank you. I needed to know all of this."

"We did try to intervene, but they did threaten Master Albert would be arrested for complicity in spying. I think Miss Josette feared that more than her own life, sir, for she refused to look at me when I entered the library. Nor did she look at Angus when Mr. LeBrun forced her from the house. We were discussing what to do when you came."

Giles jerked on his gloves. "I'm no more than a quarter-hour behind them?"

Reynolds glanced at the ormolu clock on a console table. "A little more than that now, sir. Since you are ahorse, you should overtake them easily. You will wish to take the Ipswich Road."

His mind raced ahead, trying to plan what he needed once he caught up to the carriage. "Do the two gentlemen travel with them to the coast?"

"No, my lord. They are to stay in London."

"I am in your debt, Reynolds, in the debt of you all."

The servants beamed. The butler merely bowed. Mrs. Bridgerton exclaimed, "Bring her back to us, sir."

"I will. Send Angus or go yourself, Reynolds, to Sir Roger Nazenby." He gave the direction. "Sir Roger must be apprised of these events. And expect me to steal you away from Mr. Newland's employ. Josette will want a familiar face when we marry."

The butler stiffened. "I am Mr. Newland's butler, sir." Yet he unbent enough, when he opened the exterior door, to say, "Go with God, my lord."

First he had to find her. On the Ipswich Road. That made sense: Celeste would be using her smugglers for the Channel crossing. Once he stopped the carriage, he had to coerce Josette's freedom from the spy. And the coachman would be armed. Tony Farraday had described in detail how the man had enjoyed threatening him with two long-barreled pistols. Giles only had one pistol with him. He needed more. He needed help, please God.

As he swung into his saddle, someone hailed him. He wheeled around to see the Armitage brothers trotting toward his way. Albert Sourantine rode with them.

Michael Armitage was laughing as he drew his horse up. "Morning, Hargreaves. We would have been well on our way to Melton Hall if not for this young cub. He forgot the letter of introduction that you wrote for him."

Young Lucas Armitage swatted Albert Sourantine on the arm. "He'd forget his head if it weren't nailed on."

"Forget that," Giles snapped. "You three are an answer to prayer. Our spy has flown and taken Josette with her as hostage. They're on their way to the coast."

Michael came alert. "When?"

"Not a quarter-hour ago."

"If we ride fast," Lucas said, "we can overtake them just beyond London."

"Do you know which road?"

"Ipswich." Giles could see young Sourantine struggling to understand. "Once on the coast, she'll ship with the smugglers to France. But I dare not wait till they reach the coast."

"We'll catch them, man," Michael said firmly, reassuringly. "If they have taken that yellow-wheeled phaeton, they'll be easy to spot."

"Wait," Albert protested. "That's Celeste's coach."

"That's right."

"Celeste wouldn't take Josette hostage."

"Your *belle-soeur*," Giles said sturdily, harshly, "is a French spy. We've been tracking her movements for months. We would have arrested her on Saturday. We only needed her source for the information she passed on to Napoleon's men."

"Not Celeste. Not my sister-in-law!"

"How else does she have funds for all these salons? Think, man. She's taking pay from the French government."

"But—why would she take Josette hostage?"

"Because Josette has the evidence to prove she's a spy," he explained with more composure than he felt. His horse caught his anxiety and kicked out, fighting the bit. Giles tightened the reins and brought him under control. He patted the gelding, trying to settle his own nerves.

"We should tell Sir Roger," Michael said.

"Sir Roger Nazenby?" Albert was rapidly catching up. "Is he your commander?"

"He hunts spies. Here, Lucas, you take Albert to Sir Roger. He has men on his personal staff for just such an emergency." He gave the order curtly, wanting to get on the road. Josette was in that coach. In his mind he saw yellow coach wheels rolling over the rain-softened road, kicking up clods of dirt, swaying from side to side. A wheel might drop into a hole, the pistol might go off—. He dared think no further. "

"I should go with you. It's my sister in danger. From my sister-in-law. Ye gods!"

"Sourantine, you are suspected of being a spy. The best way you can prove your innocence is to muster out the very men who will arrest the spy and her fellows."

"That's the best way to prove whom you support," Lucas chimed in. "Old King George or Boney the tyrant."

"I would never support Bonaparte."

"So you say, but you could be the source. You could be the one who steals the documents from Lord Westover's. As a despatch was stolen last evening."

"He didn't take it," Lucas defended. "I watched him all the evening. Had to be Wilton or Malbury."

"That evidence will help him with Nazenby," Giles said rapidly. He *had* to get on the road! "Take him there, Lucas. Get him to send his men to meet us on the Ipswich Road. And tell him to arrest Claude Thierry and Robert LeBrun. They're as deep into this as Celeste Sourantine is. Armitage, do you have your pistols?"

"I do. Lucas, give Hargreaves your weapons."

Sourantine watched wide-eyed as two pistols were handed over and shoved into Giles' pockets. "You are serious. This is dangerous."

"Go."

With a blanched face, Sourantine wheeled his horse and followed Lucas Armitage.

Michael fell in beside Giles as he urged his horse to a canter, the fastest pace they could manage in a city filled with coaches and wagons, carts and pedestrians. "You think it will come to weapons, sir?"

Dawn's oppressive dread no longer had a stranglehold, but he still worried. Too much remained beyond his control. "Expect blood, Armitage. For days Josette has been telling me that Celeste is desperate. The butler even said she was upset, and butlers do not remark upon their masters' emotions. And her coachman will be ready to shoot. I told you about him. He would have killed Tony Farraday."

They often had to drop the horses to a walk, but they reached the outskirts in half the time it would take a coach. The road, frozen hard for days, had a slick top surface from the morning's rain. Mud flew up as they kicked the horses to a gallop. They passed few people and none going their direction.

They came on the yellow-wheeled carriage much more quickly than Giles had anticipated, another answer to prayer. It rolled quickly, skimming over the soft inch of mud, with nothing ahead of it but oncoming wagons and carriages heading for the capitol. The coachman displayed his skill, passing the approaching traffic without slowing.

They gained steadily but gradually slowed to match the carriage's speed. Giles didn't want to approach until the road cleared of civilians. They followed a half-hour, an hour. The horses cantered easily. They passed an estate's entrance, another, then open pasture and fields. And the last cart passed them.

With the road ahead clear, the coachman whipped his horses to greater speed. The carriage rocked. Josette and Celeste would be having a bumpy ride. The road curved. Tall hedges hid the neat little farm they had passed.

"Give him a warning shot," Giles shouted.

Armitage drew his pistol. He took a quick confirming look that no one came behind them, then he carefully aimed and shot.

The coachman looked over his shoulder. The carriage veered. He straightened it then snapped the reins and shouted to the horses. Their speed increased. The wheels bumped over the frozen ruts.

A woman peered out the coach window. The wind ripped her red hair loose from the ermine hood. Their French spy. Was Josette still inside? Would Celeste be risking a look if she held Josette hostage? The woman stuck out her arm and waved a bright object at them, then a coach wheel jolted over a rut. She withdrew into the carriage.

They passed a large pasture, the workers spreading hay for the cows. They passed the farmhouse, the dairy barn and outbuildings, another pasture also dotted with cattle, the browned grasses already spread with hay.

"He can't keep this pace," Armitage shouted. "He'll blow the horses."

But the yellow-wheeled carriage didn't slow.

. ~ . ~ . ~ .

At the gunshot, Celeste jerked. "*Qu'est-ce que c'est? Qui?*"

Giles, Josette exulted. The answer to her prayer.

Coleman shouted. The carriage increased speed.

Celeste lifted the curtain and looked out. "The spycatcher! He will arrest me!" She thrust the pistol out.

Josette sprang for the opposite door and jerked at its stubborn latch. A jolt nearly slid her onto the floor.

Her sister-in-law heard her efforts, somehow saw her, and came back into the coach. "*Non!* Back to your seat, *ma belle-soeur.*" She waved the little pistol, thinking nothing of its danger on this bumpy road. "You will not escape me. I need you for the crossing. They will not shoot at me and endanger you."

The carriage rolled on. To keep their seat they had to cling to the straps by the doors. The passing countryside was little more than a blur. Josette saw farm buildings then trees stripped of their leaves.

"Coleman can't keep this speed," she told Celeste. "The horses will give out. Then what will you do? You will have no transport to your smugglers."

"Silence!"

The carriage joggled them, swung sharply to follow the road's curve, then it jolted hard, spilling Josette from her seat. In going down, she fell onto Celeste's legs. The little pistol jumped out of Celeste's hand. With a cry she dove after it. Both of them scrabbled for the little pistol, but the carriage's continued sway kept it skittering away from their groping hands.

The gun slid toward Josette. She clutched at it, missed, then Celeste shoved her away. She kicked, the coach shook badly, and the gun slithered away from both of them. Celeste lunged for it. Josette lunged for the door.

The coach swayed sharply around another curve. Josette hung grimly onto the door. When the road straightened, she jerked at the latch.

The door swung open. She nearly fell out. For one awful second the ground rushed past her, the yellow wheels flung mud into her face, then she got her hands under her and shoved herself away from danger.

Celeste cried out in triumph as the pistol came to her.

Josette braced her feet under her and jumped. The pistol cracked.

She fell hard and rolled. For a horrible moment she couldn't get her breath. Then the pain hit.

Horses pounded past. She heard a shout, but the pain obscured the words. She wanted to roll into a ball, but it hurt too much to move.

"Miss Sourantine! Miss Sourantine, are you shot?"

Hands touched her, lifted her. She cried out and tried to wrench away, but the pain doubled.

"No blood. Where are you hurt? Come, Miss Sourantine, move your arms, move—."

A great noise, not far distant. Screaming. Her pain eased a little. "What—? Who—?" It hurt to breathe.

"It's Michael Armitage, Miss Sourantine. I came with Hargreaves. Where do you hurt?"

She concentrated, trying to control the pain enough to listen to him. "What happened?"

"You jumped—."

"Not me. What—the noise? Horses?"

"I think the carriage crashed. I can't see from here."

"Giles—."

On his name came a shot, followed quickly by a second.

"Listen to me, Miss Sourantine. Can you move your arms, your legs?" As he asked, he felt over her limbs, having cast aside propriety for necessity.

"It hurts to breathe," she whispered.

"Ribs, maybe." She cried out when he touched her lower leg. "You may have hurt an ankle. You fell pretty hard. Rolling helped, or it might have been worse."

"I learned—a long time ago—how to take a fall—from a horse. I thought—a carriage would be about the same—. Oh, it hurts."

A third shot. The silence afterwards lengthened ominously.

Armitage looked back at her. "Here." He held something cold to her lips. "Drink this."

The whiskey burned its way down. She sputtered, and when she caught her breath, he poured in another mouthful. She turned her head away to prevent a third. "Wait—. Giles—."

"He rode ahead."

"Is he—?"

"I don't know," Michael Armitage admitted. "Will you stand up? I'll support you."

. ~ . ~ . ~ .

The carriage door swung open. A woman half fell out. Her pale hair glowed against the black coach door. Josette!

"Josette!" Giles shouted.

She didn't look toward him. Her hands flailed then found a purchase beneath her. She thrust herself back inside the coach, and he heaved his relief.

Only to lose his breath when she again appeared in the doorway, this time crouched on her feet. A small gun cracked from inside the carriage. Josette jumped. The coachman whipped the horses to greater speed. She landed hard and rolled with her momentum. Then she cried out.

Giles checked his horse, Armitage a half-second behind him.

He couldn't let the spy escape, not even with a faked despatch. They still didn't know her source, and they had no evidence to convict her spymaster. They needed Celeste for her testimony. "See to her," he shouted to Armitage and spurred his horse back to speed.

The carriage rocked dangerously as it rounded the curve. He tried to cast out his worry over Josette, but the image of her leap from the coach and her hard landing on the frozen ground kept intruding on his attempt to recall the road ahead. He had traveled it twice to meet Tony Farraday when he claimed to have found the spy's transport to France, not from Kent as expected but off the coast of Essex. If he remembered the road aright, two more curves came soon, then a bridge, then a flat straightaway. Surely the carriage horses wouldn't last that far.

They didn't last past the second curve. He heard the crash before he rounded the grove.

One of the horses thrashed on the ground, squealing its pain. The other lay silent. The carriage was on its side, the uppermost wheels still spinning.

Flung away from the carriage, the coachman was struggling to his feet. He lurched toward the wreck. His wits worked slowly, for the man didn't spot Giles until he had dismounted. Then his hand shoved into his pocket, came out empty. He reached into the other pocket, and Giles knew he was going for a pistol. He jerked his own out. "Don't!"

His face a grimace of pain, the man ignored the warning. He brought up the pistol. He had to brace his arm, but he leveled it straight at him. Giles dodged. The two pistols cracked, one after the other. When the smoke from the gun powder cleared, the coachman lay on the frozen road.

Giles reached into his other pocket and drew out Lucas Armitage's pistol. The man hadn't moved. Leaving the horse, he went to him, rolled him over. His open eyes stared emptily. Giles didn't need to check for his heartbeat to know he was dead. He closed the empty eyes, murmured a swift prayer, then turned his attention to the injured horse. The silence after that third pistol shot seemed absolute.

He reloaded both pistols before he ventured to the coach. He had heard no sound from inside. He didn't expect to hear one, not looking at that crash.

He pocketed the pistols then hauled himself up. In the crash the carriage door had banged shut. He wrenched it open and peered in.

Celeste Sourantine lay sprawled against the other side. She had fallen from her seat when the carriage rolled over. Her deep blue eyes stared up. Her beautiful face seemed to smile. In her upflung hand was a little silver pistol. Only from her complete stillness and the awkward angle of her head did he know she was dead.

Behind him was a thunder of hooves. He glanced around and watched five men riding toward him. One of them stopped to help with Josette, now on her feet, supported by Michael Armitage's arm. The other four came on. Sir Roger's men, come much too late.

Epilogue ~ Thursday, December 12

Josette sat propped on a settee in the *petite salon*. Her bandaged ankle rested on a soft pillow. Her wrapped ribs kept her from moving easily. Reynolds hovered, ready to spring forward with any assistance she might need. Giles had drawn a chair close. He occasionally reached over to cover her hand with his or to touch her arm or her hair.

The world at large had accepted the story of Josette's fall down the staircase when she had tried to stop Celeste from leaving. She had not heard everything that Giles and Sir Roger Nazenby told the world about the carriage accident. She had not wanted to ask. Her injuries had prevented her attendance at the funeral. In the ten days since, Giles had virtually moved into the house. He had limited her visitors to her closest friends.

This morning, however, came a new visitor, Sir Roger Nazenby, dressed in shades of brown and sporting a yellow silk cravat. Giles was finally willing for his superior to interview her. She did not smile at the man. She did not lift a hand in greeting. She merely gave him the level gaze that served her well at the card table.

Her emotions toward Nazenby had hardened. She understood the necessity of what he did, but she didn't like how he turned his work into a game. He bet not with coin but with lives. Her sister-in-law had been wrong to spy. Her death had spared her the traitor's trial and execution, even as it spared the Nemours and the Sourantines that dual ordeal. But Josette still wished Nazenby had found another way to capture his spies.

"I have been expecting you, Sir Roger."

The older man shot a glance at Giles as he took a seat. "You are well enough to speak with me, Miss Sourantine?"

"I did not injure my head, sir, and I am much improved, I promise you."

His gaze flicked to the hovering butler and back to Giles. "I see you are well cared for."

Josette smiled at Giles, who tightened his clasp on her hand. "Very well cared for. Ask your questions, sir. I daresay my butler knows as much as I do of your spies."

Nazenby cleared his throat. "I regret you were injured, Miss Sourantine. I did not expect you to become embroiled so deeply."

"Did you not?" she asked wryly. "Why else would Giles tell me

Celeste was a spy, if not to alert me and prod me to watch for the missing despatch?"

"We certainly did not expect that you would be placed in such danger."

"You surprise me, Sir Roger. I did not think you cared one jot or tittle about my safety."

He chose not to take offense. "Perhaps only a jot."

"And my sister-in-law's death, that is only an inconvenience to your investigation?"

"Josette," Giles started warningly.

"No, Hargreaves," the older man intervened, "Miss Sourantine is entitled to her anger. She is wise to play all her cards now. I am certain she blames me for the unfortunate outcome of our investigation."

The admission mollified her. Remembering Celeste's last tirade and her own suspicion that she would be dead if not for Thierry's promise that she could be ransomed, Josette bit back any further defense of her sister-in-law.

"It's not the outcome we wanted," the spycatcher continued, "but better than a public trial, don't you agree, Miss Sourantine?"

"In that, sir, we do agree. Ask your questions. I will tell you what I know."

"Shall we start with your discovery of the dispatch? Hargreaves tells me you found it when you returned some jewelry to her room. When Mdm. Sourantine discovered it was missing, she suspected you immediately. Why was that?"

"I was foolish. I had borrowed my mother's pearls for Lady Eaton's reception. When I returned them to Celeste's jewelry box, I found the despatch. I realized its importance and took it. I intended to give it to Giles or to you. As soon as she noticed the memorandum was missing and the pearls were returned, she had only two people to blame, her maid or myself. I believe Reynolds told her that Reilly had gone downstairs some time before, which left only myself."

"That is correct, sir," the butler confirmed, his voice expressionless.

"And you were going to deliver it to Hargreaves or myself?" He made work of pulling a paper from a pocket inside his waistcoat and consulting it. "I thought you had said you were going to the apothecary's."

"The trip to the apothecary was a lie, sir. I had to have a reason to leave that would not seem suspicious, and that errand would explain my need for haste. Neither M. Thierry nor M. LeBrun believed me. Once they found the despatch in my reticule, they determined not to let me go. I am not certain they would have let me leave anyway. Their behavior to me was too rough, too suspicious."

"Which is why they forced you to travel with Mdm. Sourantine?"

"I was to be her safe passage. Once in France, Celeste was to ransom me to my grandfather. Without that part of their plan, I think she would have killed me and left my body on the Ipswich Road, sir." Giles' indrawn breath and tightened clasp were evidence of his shock. She had not shared that apprehension with him. To him she added, "I have Claude Thierry to thank for my life. He suggested the ransom and wrote it into that letter to his contact in France."

"He knew her very well then," he said harshly. "He knew she was motivated by money."

She did not add her own speculations, that Celeste had entered spying to help her family recover their estate and stayed in it for the money that funded the salons.

Nazenby cleared his throat, drawing her back to the information he wanted. "When you were with her in the coach, did she tell you anything about her contacts?"

"In the coach, no. Here, while we were still in the house, yes. M. Thierry ordered her to go to France. He did this in front of me. When she resisted and warned him that she might be arrested, he suggested that she take me as her safe passage. He also told her, in my hearing, that he no longer had a use for her. Is that the information you wanted?"

"It is indeed. So, Thierry is her spymaster. We only suspected that, Hargreaves and myself, when we discovered that he was a French émigré. We have you to thank for that, Miss Sourantine. He had successfully hidden that information from my operatives. When Michael Armitage picked him up, he tried to protest his innocence. That lasted until he discovered you were still well and in England, Miss."

"Will Josette have to testify against him and LeBrun?"

"That may be necessary." Sir Roger crossed one booted foot over the other. "I am trying to convince Thierry it is in his best interest to name his operatives. In exchange we can offer him exile. The Frogs can decide what to do with him. As yet, he remains unconvinced. I have my hopes, though. He is not a man who would go to the gallows for his country. I would like our next meeting to include Mdm. Sourantine's source. It should be rewarding to set them against each other. Desperation and fear are powerful motivators, more powerful than money."

"Money motivated Celeste," Josette said bleakly. The promise of the ransom had earned Josette the time needed for Giles and Michael Armitage to reach her.

"It also motivated her source," Sir Roger disclosed. "Thierry said that the man had earned several large sums. The last information that went to France, however, was discovered to be false."

"That would be our first faked despatch," Giles inserted.

"Yes. Thierry had begun to think we had turned Mdm. Sourantine's source. He has not guessed that we still do not know the man's identity. He told Mdm. Sourantine only that her last information was useless and that the next must prove more valuable or he would find a more reliable agent."

"So," Josette mused, "that was the reason for her great apprehension. I did wonder."

"Yes, Miss Sourantine. She desperately needed the funds he provided. She would, of course; the salons were an enormous expense."

"Is that how you discovered she was a spy?"

"No, it merely was one way we confirmed it. She had too much money, much more than what my banker source told me your grandfather provided to her. I actually never expected a woman," Sir Roger admitted. "Or that the spy would use smugglers far from Kent. Your sister-in-law had me quite fooled with her game of flirtation. Hargreaves' friend Anthony Farraday discovered the truth."

"Actually, his fiancée Miss Charteris discovered it," Giles corrected. "They will be coming to meet you, Josette, after their marriage this weekend."

"Mr. Farraday is the man that Albert went to visit?"

He nodded. Sir Roger uncrossed his legs and leaned forward. "I do have one more question, Miss Sourantine."

"Celeste's source?"

"Yes. We have no clues at all, and without your sister-in-law, we have no evidence. I need to know what information France received. The source will know what he took. Thierry claims to know nothing about the man, as does LeBrun."

"You arrested Robert LeBrun?"

"We did. The next day. He was trying to use Mdm. Sourantine's smugglers to leave the country. We arrested the whole lot of them together, LeBrun, a man named Jem Webb, his young mate Tom, and a Mrs.Gilson, who apparently ran the smuggling operation from her inn. All rolled up in a neat package. But I was asking about Mdm. Sourantine's source. I believe it to be a friend of young Westover. I suspected your brother for a while, but Hargreaves would have none of that."

"It is certainly *not* my brother, Sir Roger."

"Yes, I am convinced. His desperation to save you convinced me. But her source?"

"She never said, not in so many words. Even when I said his name, she refused to admit it. She did let slip part of his name, here in this room, before she caught herself. I do not want to influence you with my guess. I will only say what she did, the first part of his name: *Mal*—."

"Ah, Malbury, Richard Malbury. I landed on him a few days ago, partly because your brother is no longer a suspect, partly because he is flush with cash after being broke for the past month. Well." He clapped his hands on his knees and stood. "I thank you, Miss Sourantine."

Giles stood as well. "When do you arrest Malbury?"

"Half a name is not evidence, and without evidence we have no case. I shall have to delay his meeting with Thierry—although that name dropped into an interrogation of LeBrun might reap more than a few benefits, especially if he thinks Malbury has information about him. Between LeBrun and Thierry, Malbury may fall. This could become very interesting."

"But no arrest?" Giles persisted.

"Without strong evidence, I cannot arrest a peer of the realm. You yourself reminded me of that, didn't you? Had Mdm. Sourantine been able to testify—ah, well, that is a tragedy. We shall keep a watch on him. He shall go down in our records as a traitor. We may even be able to set up a situation in which he can convict himself. My focus for now is Claude Thierry." Nazenby bowed formally to Josette. "My thanks to you, Miss Sourantine, and my wishes for your rapid return to health."

She looked up, willing to concede the spycatcher had done one kindness. "I think I must thank you as well, Sir Roger, for I hear nothing of spying in relation to Celeste's death, merely that she died in a carriage accident."

He stood looking down at her, a little frown between his brows. "A bit more may come to light, but she will not be known as a traitor. That information I have kept quiet."

"Will you continue to keep it quiet, even when Claude Thierry and Robert LeBrun come to trial?"

"Their trials will be closed. A matter of security to the realm, Miss Sourantine. Celeste Sourantine's name will not be mentioned by us in those cases."

"I appreciate this, Sir Roger, for both my family and the Nemours. I believe her death has devastated her mother."

"I do not do it for you or your family or hers," he said bluntly. "To release that information would be to alert Malbury and any of her other contacts. If we are to trace the full extent of her web, then we must have secrecy to work in." He bowed again. "Good day, Miss Sourantine. May you continue to heal. You may receive a letter from the Prince Regent, thanking you for your service to the Crown. I trust you will keep that letter secret until long after we have finished with Bonaparte?"

Giles escorted the spycatcher out. She heard their voices echoing off the cream-and-black tiles, then Sir Roger's footsteps as he descended and Giles' as he returned. She held up a hand to him, and he crossed quickly to her. Reynolds faded from the room.

"I am glad that meeting is over," she told him. "I was dreading it."

"I think he was, as well. He is not usually so careful with his questions."

Josette fell silent. She looked at the fire. He sat quietly beside her, holding her hand. Beyond the physical pain with every deep breath and the sharp pangs with every movement of her ankle was deeper pain, emotional pain. Celeste, for all her ills, had been her sister-in-law, a part of her life for many years. She could not be happy for her death or for Coleman's death.

She sighed. "I wish—I wish that I hadn't taken that despatch." She admitted what had haunted her for days. To him she could say what she had to hide from everyone else, even Albert. "It's the reason Celeste died."

"No." He squeezed her hand. "No regrets, my love. You had no control over that carriage crash. We were on to her. Sir Roger had already made plans to arrest her. We can't know what would have happened then. Don't wish to remake the past. Would you remake our first meeting? Those few hours set in motion all the events leading to her death."

"I did not want her to die. Or Coleman. Even when I was so frightened, that was never my wish, Giles."

"It seems cruel to say, but perhaps it was better for her to die then, so quickly, painlessly. She would have hanged as a traitor." He lifted her hand to his lips. "I would not have you dwell on her death. You won't forget it, I know that, but brighter memories will crowd out the dark ones, this I promise."

She believed him. She knew that happiness eventually came after dear ones died. Whether their deaths were a lingering anticipation or a quick tragedy, the dark emptiness was filled with light. "Brighter memories sound wonderful."

"They do indeed," and he kissed her to prove it. Then he leaned back. "And tomorrow I meet your grandfather. Now that meeting truly worries me."

"He is only one person. I must brave your parents."

"You are forgetting that he is bringing your younger brother and sister. Three to two. I think I have the greater hurdle to jump. And you have already won my mother. I wrote her about your needlework. I expect to find you two closeted together, all tangled up in skeins of wool, and me completely forgotten."

She laughed, as he had intended. In a few short weeks, from mid-November to now, her whole world had changed. He had changed it. And except for Celeste's death, she would not go back to her life as it was before.

"You've gone quiet again," he said, smoothing her hair back from her face.

"Thinking."

"No regrets?"

For answer, Josette lifted her face for another kiss. Not knowing all the cards, she had played a game of chance, and with God's grace she had won. Giles kissed her with more intent, and she smiled and opened herself to the brighter memories they were making together.

Thank you for reading *The Game of Spies*.

In a dark time of my life the first book in the **Hearts in Hazard** series kindled a glimmer of hope that helped me survive those depressing days. I worried, occasionally, what creative outlet that I would have when I finished *A Game of Secrets*. Before I close the last chapters of that book, the ideas for *A Game of Spies* poured out. This book almost wrote itself.

I hope you enjoyed this excursion into spies and whist in Regency England as much as I delighted in writing it for you.

French spies in Regency England was never an idea I toyed with as a writer until *A Game of Spies* launched itself at me. I fell in love with Giles Hargreaves almost as quickly as Josette Sourantine did, as he evolved into a man worthy of such a woman.

To see how the conflict against French spies begins, with Tony Farraday and Kate Charteris, read *A Game of Secrets*. The third in the **Hearts in Hazard** series has a slightly different focus; that book is *A Game of Hearts*.

Toby Kennit has his own story in *The Dangers for Spies*. Lord Musgrove discovers that he's not as cold as he thought in *The Dangers of Secrets*. And other books in the series offer more conflicts against French spies ... as well as plain murder, bloody and foul.

. ~ . ~ . ~ .

Read on for more information about the **Hearts in Hazard** series.

For any questions, comments, and speculations, please contact winkbooks@aol.com. You can find my books on my Amazon author page or my website ~~ www.writersinkbooks.com

To receive monthly information about all of my books, please join my monthly newsletter list. Contact me at winkbooks@aol.com and receive a free peak of the book I am currently writing. I won't pester you with affiliate links or pass your email to any other person or institution.

Indie writers thrive on reviews. With *any* book that you enjoy, please share with other readers looking for escape from the stresses of life.

Dream it. Believe it. Do it.
~~ M.A. Lee

Hearts in Hazard by M.A. Lee

Mysteries with a dash of romance, set during the Regency Era of England

1 ~ *A Game of Secrets* ~ Smugglers, secrets and spies: Kate tries to hide in plain sight; Tony tries to catch a spy. First they fall in love, then they fall into trouble with smugglers. Will they survive?

2 ~ *A Game of Spies* ~ Salons and soirées, flirtation and dancing, gambling and spies: Josette and Giles fall in love over a deck of cards—and try not to die.
Spymaster Giles Hargreaves was introduced in *A Game of Secrets*.

3 ~ *A Game of Hearts* ~ **Two couples** :: One titled widow, one wealthy businessman: two hearts shadowed by their past. One bright young flirt, one hard-edged young man: two hearts crossed by circumstance. Mix in a courtesan and two rakes, all out for mischief, and murder bloody and foul.

4 ~ *The Danger of Secrets* ~ Deep in the wintry countryside, a house warmed by relatives and friends: secrets of family, secrets of hearts, secrets of blood and pain. Match a daughter to an unknown father; match a spinster to an earl; match a serial killer to his next victim.
Gordon Musgrove was introduced in *A Game of Spies*.

5 ~ *The Danger for Spies* ~ Impossibilities? Rakes don't lose their hearts. Spies don't give up the game. No one hides in plain sight. Codes are unbreakable. A man can't hold onto revenge for years and years. Impossibilities are designed to be shattered.
Toby Kennitt was introduced in *A Game of Spies*.

6 ~ *The Danger to Hearts* ~ A country manor in early Spring: older woman and younger man. Horses, cats, needlework, roses and afternoon teas ~ What could possibly go wrong in an idyll? Trouble in the past, trouble now, and murder.
The character Jess Carter was introduced in *A Game of Secrets*.

7 ~ *The Key to Secrets* ~ Debutantes should snare fiancés, not murder them. Constable Hector Evans must solve three murders. Is his former love guilty, of is she a convenient scapegoat?
Constable Hector Evans was introduced in *The Danger to Hearts*.

8 ~ *The Key for Spies* ~ Spies and traitors. Lies and treachery.

Unexpected love where bullets fly. One traitor destroys loyalty. What will two traitors destroy?

9 ~ *The Key for Hearts* ~ A convenient marriage inconveniently causes murder.

10 ~ *The Hazard of Secrets*. Two hearts with dangerous pasts—Can they keep their secrets, or will murder force them to reveal all?

11 ~ *The Hazard for Spies* ~ Disguised to spy. Will murder destroy their chance for love?

12 ~ *The Hazard for Hearts* ~ Two wives haunt the castle. Will she be the third to die?

M.A. Lee also writes the **Into Death** Series, set after World War I.

Digging into Death ~ A governess seeking refuge, a handsome young man, an archaeological dig: romance is inevitable; murder is not. Suspicions escalate, artifacts are stolen, and then a second murder. Has the love of her life beguiled her straight into death? Available in paperback and e-book

Christmas with Death ~ Christmas is for miracles, merriment, and murder. Set in 1919 at an English country manor for a party throughout Christmastide. Available in paperback and e-book.

Portrait with Death, publishing soon ~ the conclusion of the Isabella Newcombe series

Nonfiction by M.A. Lee

Think like a Pro Writer series

Old Geeky Greeks: Write Stories with Ancient Techniques ~ Storytelling has its roots in the strong foundations of classical antiquity. Avoid the re-packaged "exclusive insights" and "wham-pow webinars" and return to the source, organized as a seminar in book form.

Think like a Pro: New Advent for Writers ~ Seven lessons to guide your growth from newbie writer to "thinking like a pro writer". Now available in paperback and e-book.

Think / Pro: A Planner for Writers ~ An undated planner with daily word counts, progress meters, project planning, and goals analysis. Paperback only. How else will you record your goals and progress?

Discovering Your Novel ~ a 52-week course for new writers, offering guidance from original idea to publication and marketing.

Discovering Characters ~ Delving deeply into your primary characters entails more than just templates and character interviews. You also need to know your secondary characters. Focus on more than appearance, more than intellect, and explore your characters hearts and souls. Discover them!

Discovering Your Plot ~ What writers need and want for plot structures and genre expectations. Control pacing, tension, and suspense with a stronger comprehension of the major sections of a novel.

Discovering your Author Brand ~ The greatest secret to catch the attention of fly-by readers? Branding. Writers need to brand their books, their series, and themselves as the author. Packed with examples and explanations from past successful marketing efforts.

Discovering Sentence Craft ~ Zeug-what? Chiasmus? Auxesis? Are those spelled correctly? Well, yes. These are literary devices used for centuries by the best writers to make their works memorable. Writers are artists, seeking ideas from the creative muse. We're also crafters, looking for the best ways to present those creative ideas. DiscS~Craft presents techniques for using figurative & interpretive concepts as well as the structures of inversions, repetitions, oppositions, and sequencings.

Just Start Writing :: Inspiration 4 Writers, book 1 ~Writing can be a dizzy whirl of a carousel, all colors and mirrors with unicorns and griffins and dragons to ride. How do you get your ticket, climb on the carousel, and join the writing ride? If you want to pursue your writing dream, *Just Start Writing* will help you start.

*2 * 0 * 4 Lifestyle series*

2 * 0 * 4 Lifestyle: Transform Your Whole Self (coming soon)

2 * 0 * 4 Lifestyle: A Planner for Living ~ *Intermittent fasting. Bible Journaling. Keto Diet. 7-Minute Workout. Five minutes with God.* If the newest fads to follow are leaving you cold and edgy, time to re-think your daily plan. Return to Luke 10:27 to involve the whole self—heart, soul, mind & body. 2 * 0 * 4 offers an undated planner to help you muse and move, feast and fast, and live and love. Paperback only. How else will you write in it? Available in the Meadow and the Mountain River editions.

Pen Names of M.A. Lee

Remi Black ~ Fae Mark'd
The Fae Mark'd Wizard
Weave a Wizardry Web
Dream a Deadly Dream
Sing a Graveyard Song
Kindle a Fae's Wrath (coming soon)
Quench a Dragon's Fire (in the sketching stage)
Dance to Bone-Edged Music (in the sketching stage)
Fae Mark'd World
To Wield the Wind :: Spells of Air 1
To Charm the Air: Spells of Air 2 (coming soon)
To Curse the Wyre: Spells of Air 3 (sketching stage)

Edie Roones ~ Seasons in Sansward
Summer Sieges
Autumn Spells
Winter Sorcery
Spring Magicks (in the sketching stage)

All books from Writers' Ink are available at Amazon.

. ~ . ~ . ~ .

For any comments, questions, and speculations, contact
winkbooks@aol.com. Use the subject line to direct your email to a
specific book or series.

www.ingramcontent.com/pod-product-compliance
Lightning Source LLC
Chambersburg PA
CBHW030300200626
46816CB00002BA/713